That night he began to have The Dream, always the same—driving along a highway and coming upon a car accident. Ambulance lights flashed as curious motorists pulled over. The sight filled him with dread, but he stopped anyway to look down into the cockpit of a crumpled sports car where the broken body of a young man was stretched across the seat. The boy's neck hung over the door at a terrible angle, blood obscuring his face.

"Who is it?" he would ask.

A tall bald man with glasses would turn and say, "James Dean is dead."

WHO KILLED JAMES DEAN?

WARREN NEWTON BEATH

TOR

A TOM DOHERTY ASSOCIATES BOOK
NEW YORK

This is a work of fiction. All the characters and events portrayed in this book are fictitious, and any resemblance to real people or incidents is purely coincidental.

WHO KILLED JAMES DEAN?

Cover art by Eric Peterson

A Tor Book
Published by Tom Doherty Associates, Inc.
175 Fifth Avenue
New York, NY 10010

Tor® is a registered trademark of Tom Doherty Associates, Inc.

ISBN: 0-812-53873-0

First edition: September 1995

Printed in the United States of America

0 9 8 7 6 5 4 3 2 1

A NOTE TO THE READER

This is a work of fiction. Although inspired from real life, the characters and events portrayed in this novel are either products of the author's imagination or are used fictitiously.

GIRL FAN OF JAMES DEAN DIES
BY SMASHING CAR INTO TREE

SAN JOSE—AP—The police listed as a suicide the death of Lisa Neeley, a pretty 17 year old high school honor student who catapulted her car into a pepper tree on the Los Gatos Road south of San Jose. Authorities are puzzled as to what motivated the girl, a daughter of a wealthy Santa Clara contractor. They conceded it could have resulted from Los Gatos teenage discussions of the death of actor James Dean in 1955 in an automobile crash.

Friends said the girl was a member of a group which considered Dean's death as "glamorous." Her father, M.L. Neeley, reported she had seemed disturbed lately but he refused to accept the suicide theory.

She drove her car at an estimated 80 miles an hour against the tree—the same tree struck by an automobile in which her classmate, Jerrel W. Morris, 16, was killed in May of last year. His death was listed as accidental. . . .

San Jose *Mercury*, January 14, 1958

... And then there was this time when we were playing a little community theater in the San Fernando Valley. It was a production of *Oedipus at Colonnus*. This was in 1950—before any of us amounted to anything. There was this young kid in the cast named Jimmy Dean. He couldn't have been more than twenty years old, and he had the role of the Cumaean Sybil and would have to hang over the set in this big jar all during the play.

He was an uncouth and mangy sort of kid, and some of the other members of the cast used to make fun of him, rag him. He played an oracle in the show, so they'd sort of tease him and say things like, "Sybil! Sybil! What is it you really want?"

Jimmy would just look down at them with that sweet smile of his and I'll never forget what he answered.

"I want to die."

The Memoirs of Rex Bench:
It's All Right, Ma, I'm Only Acting!, 1967

Ghouls won't let JAMES DEAN stay dead!

Want a photograph of Jimmy lying bleeding in his death car? Fifty dollars or no dealing. Minutes after the collision, Dean's own photographer arrived, and while Dean was lying slumped and dying in the wreck of his new sports car, the journalist went to work with his camera. And those last pictures of Dean are apparently really something.

They're strictly for the morbid of his idolaters. And they can be bought—Fifty dollars or no dealing.

And of such grisly facts is the Dean Legend made. . . .

Fury—The Magazine for Men, June 1956 35 cents

James Dean was never killed! Informed sources, whose names we cannot disclose, say that Jimmy was horribly mangled by that "fatal" accident last year. He is said to be afraid for the world to see his now-marred face. So to you, Jimmy, we write this open letter:

Come out of hiding. Your fans love you—will always love you, no matter what you look like! ...

Modern Screen, September 1957

... *The story the driver told me was as weird as any I've heard.... It seems that on the night of December 30, 1955—which was three months to the day after Dean's death—he was driving south on Route 41, headed for Paso Robles when ... he thought he heard a car coming from the direction of Bakersfield.... The noise got louder and louder.*

Then suddenly a blurred white streak whizzed by. A second later there was a screech of brakes, followed by the sickening crash of metal ripping metal and glass shattering into a million pieces. The sound was loud, the truck driver said, trying carefully to be precise, yet in a way it wasn't loud either. It was almost "like the echo of a sound."

Then silence.

The crash brought him back to his senses. He hurried to the intersection, feeling sure that he would see a truly sickening sight. He saw nothing. No tire marks. No wreckage. No shattered glass....

In Paso Robles we stopped at a one-arm diner for coffee.... When he finished his story, don't you think one of the other truck drivers in the diner didn't cross himself too. "It's very bad!" this other one said. "That was Señor Dean in that car. He drives that road every night between sundown and sunrise. It's as though he is looking for something or someone."

Or as if he is a lost spirit, looking for a place to rest.

"James Dean—
The Ghost Driver of Polonio Pass"
Whisper magazine, June 1957

PROLOGUE

September 30, 1955
Highways 41 and 466, California

Jimmy Dean was at the wheel of the brand-new competition model Porsche 550 Spyder which he named "Little Bastard." It was an impudently low-slung air-cooled horizontal-opposed four-cylinder engine dual twin-barreled downdraft carb silver bullet zipping through heat mirages on a stretch of desert highway straight as a ruler. LITTLE BASTARD was affectionately stenciled in sassy red script across the rear.

Desolate landscape pinkened beneath hills to the west as Dean headed west into the sinking sun. The photosphere flared for an instant off the macadam and blinded him with tracers of green actinic light.

Warner Brothers was protective of their investment and had forbidden his racing during the production of *Giant*, but as the film neared completion he had entered a competition to be held on Saturday in Salinas three hundred miles to the north. It would be the racing debut of a car he had owned only two weeks. In the seat next to him was mechanic Rolf Weutheric, an employee of the Porsche dealership where he had traded in his Speedster on the faster, larger Spyder.

Up ahead at a distance evaporating in fractions of seconds was a crossroads. Beyond it a black-and-white 1950 Ford approached from the opposite direction.

At the last moment and without a signal of intention, the Ford cut in front of the sports car. The collision was nearly head-on. Debris hurtled through the air as what remained of the Porsche skittered toward a roadside ditch with Jimmy Dean trapped in the seat. Feet entangled in the clutch and brake, he was murderously crushed, flailed, and impaled all at the same time.

A Ford wagon had been following the Porsche. It pulled in behind the wrecks. Two men jumped out. Bill Hickman ran to Jimmy. The other man was Sanford Roth, and he carried a 35mm camera. Roth began snapping pictures from a vantage on the highway.

Hickman cradled Dean's head and called out in a rage, "YOU SONOFABITCH! HELP ME! QUIT TAKIN' PICTURES AND COME HERE AND HELP ME!"

Jimmy Dean heard none of this. He was in darkness. Then he came to with a convulsive breath.

The taped voice of Elvis Presley took up the story in an intimate Mississippi drawl.

"His head's all groggy and wrapped in bandages that itch. He can't move. The room looks strange. No television. He's got this impression that time's passed. It's some kinda amnesia. He can't recall how he got there but remembers his childhood clear as crystal. Sees hisself nine years old comin' home from school to find his momma crying 'cause she been diagnosed with uterus cancer. Big C did its dirty work, jus' like it did my momma. He gets chills when she puts her bony hand on his cheek. No one tol' him not to be ashamed, 'cause he never confessed it to anyone."

The hiss of a match as Elvis lit a cheroot.

"This was in Santa Monica. They decided to bury her in their home state of Indiana, but his father claimed he was too broke to go. Too broke, hm? It was little Jimmy and ol' Granny who took his mom's body on the train. He ran back to the baggage car all the time to make sure she was still there.

"His father never did come to fetch him back. That's the real story how Jimmy got farmed out to an uncle who called him 'Li'l Bastard' even though his parents had been married five whole months before he was born. He slep' with a lock of his momma's hair 'neath the pillow. His father hardly wrote, barely even sent little checks."

A pause.

"Back to that sickroom. It sure ain't no hospital. The blinds are drawn and there's incense goin'. Jimmy starts to 'member a crazy mansion like this in the Hollywood Hills. It had a white gravel drive, tennis courts, and a big ol' Greek swimmin' pool out front. But he's so pilled-up he dozes in this never-never land of green light, goin' in and out."

The listener pictured an obese Elvis behind sunglasses in a dark motel room, reclining on plumped pillows as he rumbled into the recorder.

"When he gets the strength to explore his body, he finds horrible black Y-shaped stitches running from his peter to his chest. It's frightening, like a smile. Like his two halves are comin' apart. Then somebody pulls the covers back up to his chin.

"This tall woman's standin' over him like a vampire in a kimono of black Chinese silk tied at her belly so her bosoms hang out. She asks him, 'Do you remember the crash?'

"But he don't. It's too painful, see? Though he's had a coupla nightmares about a big ol' black car comin' to kill him.

" 'You are James Byron Dean,' she says—his momma give 'im that middle name. 'You are a movie actor.' Well, he asks for a mirror but she won't let him. Plus, his head's all wrapped up. 'Do you know where you are?' she asks. It hurts his neck to nod 'Yes,' plus it makes this grinding noise 'cause it's been broke. 'Do you remember the last time you were in this house?' But it's all dim and cloudy. 'I brung you some things to read,' she says, and leaves."

Elvis took a breath. "He fumbles for the magazines. *Death Drive, the True Account of the Death of James Dean.* He's thinks, 'I ain't dead.' He flips to the cover: *Modern Screen*, June 1957.

"Well, that riles his emotions all up. Just then the tall woman comes and takes the magazine back. 'Don't struggle,' she says. 'There's plenty time.' He makes a grab at her wrist 'cause he can't talk. But he remembers two more things. She hosted horror movies on TV, and he was afraid of her. Now, he's her prisoner.

"Why? Maybe for ransom. Maybe there's negotiations goin' on out there somewhere for his return.

"Her eyes soften and she says, 'Once I promised I would light a candle to guide your soul.' She unfastens his fingers and smooths his eyes closed so he can't open 'em.

"He knows he's gotta escape. So he slowly musters his strength, makin' note of her comings and goings.

One night he sneaks out of bed in the dark, tryin' not to tear them stitches.

"He steps outside the door, all dizzy. He hears spooky voices downstairs like a choir of ghosts. He hunkers down and takes a peek. It's some kinda weird ceremony. There's candles and a big black and white blowed-up photograph of a highway with his own face super'posed over it. A voice says, 'James Dean is dead.'

"He feels a gut-wrench. A lot of memory is returning, too much.

"The voice chants, 'Where is the Blood?' It's totally freaky. He sees a mask of his own face on a table staring up with empty eyes. Other voices are chantin', 'There was no blood in the body. He bled to death and his neck was broken.' "

Elvis's voice was husky with cigar smoke, and there was the squeak of mattress springs.

"More candles are lighted at four corners of a black altar, where there's somethin', or somebody, tied up. It makes this mewin' noise like a baby dreamin'.

" 'Jesus Christ,' Jimmy thinks. He needs to find a way out, so he runs to a door on the upper floor and ducks inside. It's dark. In the center of the floor is a shiny bronze casket. A scare runs down his backbone like it was piano keys. The coffin's closed, but covered with white lilies 'round his own studio picture.

"He runs right back out, his heartbeat rushin' in his ears—if the sound ain't the swellin' up of them voices through the floor. He stumbles through a dark hall lined with his movie posters, staggerin' down a winding stairs to a garage.

"There's a wrecked car on the concrete, tires all mangled and the steering wheel all twisted. He can barely make out the number on the hood. '130.' It was the number of his car, and memory comes back on him all at once. He 'members the crash. He sees that Ford turnin' into him and hears the crunch and breakin' glass. Feels the breakin' bones.

"Then he notices a mechanic workin' under the hood. The guy pulls himself out to smile friendly, and Jimmy recognizes Rolf. But there's a pumpin' black heart in his hand. Pumpin' oil, jus' like a gusher.

"Jimmy's not even sure how he gets outside, gulpin' night air like a drowning man. He fumbles with the bandages figurin', 'If I'm dead, wouldn't I know?' He starts to run. Fresh air feels like skin bracer on his face. But instead of the lights of Hollywood, there's a strange flatness to the land. It's like bein' on a painting and running toward the edge. And behind him, he don't see the house he expected. Instead it's that mansion from *Giant*, just a movie set in the middle of nowhere.

"That scares him so he keeps runnin'. Ahead, a distant highway unrolls like a strip of film. He finds himself at this rural intersection, wavin' his arms at the first car to come along. It slows down and stops. A black and white 1950 Ford Crestliner with fender skirts, jus' like the car that hit him. But right now, he could care less.

"He leans breathless into the rolled-down window, tryin' to find a rusty voice to speak to the stranger who's gonna save him. There's a man in the car, and his face is familiar. It's a guy Jimmy raced against once. A guy who died in that race. Guy named Jack Drummond.

"Then blue flame comes like a tongue from Jack's mouth and rages around the upholstery with a suckin' sound. Then, a noise like thunder. Suddenly it's rainin', but only inside the Ford, trickling down onto the man's face with hissing drops that wash steamin' gouts of flesh in black sluices.

"The car lurches off swervin' and spittin' gravel, a scream fading. It leaves Jimmy standin' there shocked.

"He's breathin' hard and tryin' to get hold of hisself. Dead grass rustles at his ankles. His heart's goin' like ninety. Somethin' tells him he's not alone. He turns and sees the tall woman again, that horror movie lady."

There was a shiver in the voice.

"She's holdin' this rack of black candles, on either side of her a boy, and a girl. Natalie Wood and Sal Mineo. Natalie's hair is drippin' wet and her dress is all soggy. Sal's got them brown puppy eyes, but his shirt is drenched in fresh blood. They look at Jimmy real strangely.

"The woman from the house says, 'Welcome to Hell, Jimmy.'

"He reaches up to check his face, but his tremblin' fingers find only bone and mold. When he finds his voice, the night's filled with *his* scream.

" *'James Dean is dead!'*

"Natalie and Sal gently take his arms to escort him back to the house, the woman with candles leadin' the way. . . ."

The sentence ended in dark laughter.

Larry Schmallhorst took the plug from his ear and punched off the cassette player. It certainly sounded like "E," this bootlegged tape purporting to be the King in exile after faking his death. "E," like "M" or Ur-Mark, the unknown source of the synoptic gospels. The recordings had been circulating in the Hollywood underground for six months, rumored to be the still-living but secluded Presley's working notes for his autobiography.

A hoax? Probably, but Elvis had been deeply into Jimmy Dean. Not only had he memorized all the dialogue of *Rebel Without a Cause*—which he replayed ceaselessly in his private theater—but to get the real skinny he had made it a point to date both Liv Ermaine and Natalie Wood in the late fifties.

And there was the insistent story that it was Elvis, with his vast resources and Memphis Mafia, who had stolen the Dean death car off a freight truck in 1960 to add to his personal collection of Deanabilia in the catacombs beneath Graceland.

Another nice bit of color, Larry thought.

Like the Ghostly Hitchhiker story. A driver would roll down his window at Dean's death site, and the young hitchhiker with bruised limbs and torn clothing would lean into the car. Through a bloody smile he would say, "I'm sorry to bother you. But, there's been a traffic accident—"

And the ghoulish figure would vanish.

Good stuff, Larry Schmallhorst knew, as a breeze crawled down the back of his shirt. He had to remind himself it was not September 30, 1955, but September 28, 1994. He thought of an alternative subhead for the article he would pitch to the editor of *Eastern Way* airline magazine: "Do you believe in ghosts? Many fans of the late James Dean do . . ."

For his cult of followers . . .

"For his cult of followers, James Dean still rides this highway, a vampire forever young on the blood of his faithful. This intersection is a sacred site to these pilgrims, and many describe intensely religious experiences. The more candid will say to you in all seriousness—

" 'Jesus didn't work for me. James Dean did.' "

Thirty-three-year-old Schmallhorst stood at the isolated intersection of highways 41 and 46, a haunted site prone to strange assaults. There was seismic activity from the San Andreas fault, and inexplicable showers of stones from cloudless sky. The junction was in the bottom of a vast bowl of arid pastureland. Brisk wind blew from the west. Movie idol James Dean had died at this very spot almost four decades earlier.

Larry had left his car at the chromium monument a quarter mile away, a landmark erected at a cost of 15,000 1977 dollars by a Japanese millionaire obsessed with Dean. Above Dean's name was a symbol of infinity, while the chromium reflected cars passing en route to the fatal intersection, images elongated and strange. It was not undefiled: someone had blasted the letters JAMES DEAN with a shotgun.

Jimmy Dean, whose death commenced the Dean curse and its chain of unnatural deaths. A Beverly Hills surgeon who installed salvaged parts from Dean's wrecked racer was killed in his next competition. The death car had gone on a grotesque tour across the country, continuing to rack up a body count. Not only did it slip from a display to break both legs of a bystander, but a truck driver hauling it was crushed beneath it when his rig crashed. A Fresno garage where the hulk was being warehoused burned down. The carcass was restored, only to disappear off a freight car in 1960.

Can a sports car have a soul? Larry wondered as he stood at the fated spot with inklings of fear.

The sun was beginning to eclipse behind the humps of the Cholame Hills. He did not like the fact that he was the only living thing at this desolate spot with no cars visible in either direction. It was an eerie place and, to millions throughout the world, hallowed. In two days dozens of fans would gather here reverently to commemorate the thirty-ninth anniversary of Dean's death. Perhaps it was a religious longing. Some ideas are more powerful dead than alive.

Old and anonymous graffiti was scrawled on the back of a highway sign—

> *It's been fourteen years since I been back here*
> *James Dean*
> *It ain't changed much, it's still the same bad scene*
> *Fate played its hand it spelled Death*
> *For James Dean—*

The seat of Larry's pants was creased between his buttocks from the long drive in his Mitsubishi. He rocked nervously on the heels of his Nikes and tried to visualize the ghost of that crash which put this nondescript point on the map on a long-ago day as balmy and beautiful as this one.

Larry drifted back, imagining flung metal and muffled concussions as Little Bastard spun into that barbed-wire fence. Four decades later a fine mist of oil and gasoline still lingered on the air. He looked to the gully where Jimmy's car had wound up seventy-five feet away from point of impact. Passenger Rolf Weutheric was thrown free, and survived to sell his story and sue Jimmy's estate.

Larry looked to the west from where the Ford had come. A small town inquest tied up loose ends: accidental death. And a pop legend was born.

Until James Dean, Larry had been a lifelong stranger to obsession. His quest had started as research for a modest magazine article on the occult angle, but expanded until he envisioned a book entitled *Who Killed James Dean?*

Because he now believed that James Dean's collision

was not an accident but an ambush, and the murder weapon a 2,000-pound Ford.

Originally prepared to exploit the public's posthumous obsession with Dean, Larry now felt evangelical zeal about this particular highway fatality. Larry had come to the crime scene on this day for a rendezvous with an individual who promised him specifics. He took from his pocket the invitation which would also identify him: it was simply a card, the Tarot trump called the Hanged Man.

Larry was still not a Dean fan. No, Jimmy had been a real asshole, and Dean fans were crazy. It was fine with Larry if he never met another.

There was more than one victim of the accident thirty-nine years ago. Hundreds, maybe thousands, if you counted the rabid souls who spent their lives in a James Dean haze, bankrupt and barren existences devoted to contemplation of a fallen star. All in love with Jimmy and living through him, their rooms turned into shrines.

These bright-eyed worshipers gave Larry the creeps. Like he was feeling now as his beeping Rolex informed him it was 5:45—the time of day when Dean's crash occurred. Larry had set the alarm for his own curiosity—or so he told himself.

The wind died at the same moment. West up the highway the setting sun washed the gritty surface of the macadam in sparkles. Larry was momentarily blinded by the sun's photosphere. A tumbleweed crackled against his leg.

Out here the overactive imagination could do strange things. On a far knoll to the east the ghostly image of a small sports car appeared shimmering in the corrugated ripples of a heat mirage.

And she vanished—he meant "it."

His breath relaxed.

But like a lizard which had for a moment assumed the protective coloration of landscape, the car reappeared a quarter mile away moving toward where he stood in the roadway. He thought he could even make out the license plate: 2Z77767. *Dean's number.*

Fear started at his ankles and surged up as he heard the faint whine of engine across the empty flats. It turned into a buzz that stung the air, the racer straddling the white line as Larry took a cautious step toward the shoulder.

But the Porsche suddenly veered and left the road, the hood emblem a gun sight locked on him like a smart missile.

Many things he had seen and people he had known zipped through Larry's mind. Even a joke: *What's the last thing that goes through a gnat's mind when it hits a windshield? His asshole.*

There was a terrible impact. For a moment he was peacefully afloat.

Until his mangled body ricocheted into the barbed wire like a rag doll.

The highway was quiet.

Through waves of pain, Larry was vaguely aware that the sports car had stopped with engine idling. Upside down he saw the driver dismount. Gloved fingers raised Larry's face to look into the eyes, black and white fingers that looked like bones. Larry heard the basal grind of his own neck, sure sign of a fracture. He tried to speak but gurgles came.

The driver's eyes smoldered with sensuality. Larry was looking into James Dean's inverted face. Then Dean's lips brushed his own and parted to cover Larry's mouth. Schmallhorst wriggled and squirmed on the barbs, felt things tearing loose inside as his internal organs were drawn downward into throat and mouth.

Viewed from the single cumulus cloud overhead the highways appeared like the Nazca lines inscribed on the plain to form a sixty-degree angle. Larry Schmallhorst was oblivious. He was dead.

One of his Nike tennis shoes remained in the westbound lane, still laced.

1

Wednesday, August 24, 1995
Over Oklahoma City

The victim's corpse was discovered nearly a year ago upside down on a barbed-wire fence on a desolate stretch of California highway, legs crossed so the right created a right angle with the left. The sole clue was a headlight ring from a Porsche.

Twenty-five-year-old Lou Ehlers scanned a complimentary copy of *Eastern Way* magazine. The hit-and-run was one of "Twenty-five Unsolved Mysteries of James Dean's Death," sidebar to an article entitled "Jesus didn't work for me. James Dean did."

There was an Annie Leibowitz-type photo of a man with a black leather jacket over his shoulder, posed on the center lane of a rural road. ". . . Cleveland Carroll Devereux, Dean biographer and high priest of Dean worshipers, strolls Highway 46 near the California crash site."

The article said Devereux was a high school teacher, and went on to describe an annual gathering of James Dean fanatics at the California intersection where the actor had wrecked in 1955. Rabid devotees gathered around a chromium monument, Devereux their spokesman. " 'You get the feeling you're approaching some revelation. It's all right here in this spot. . . .' "

Lou took the flavorless spearmint gum from his mouth and meticulously wrapped it in foil, his ears having already popped over Arkansas. As Eastern Flight 406—a Tristar L-1011 wide-body jumbo Whisperliner, "the quietest, cleanest plane in the skies"—skimmed a flat bank of cumulus, he adjusted his seat over the starboard wing and reclined in search of comfort as the other passengers watched a Kurt Russell comedy.

The story about the hit-and-run victim set him thinking about accident and fate. The jet was accelerating into the wind stream at higher altitude, and Lou was pressed back into his seat, drifting.

. . . In the hammer throw, a competitor makes three full, quick turns of the body before flinging the weight. The ball is solid iron. The handle is spring steel wire and one end is fastened to the ball by a ball-bearing swivel. The other is attached to a rigid, two-hand grip by a loop.

It had been five years ago, a sunny blue-skied Friday afternoon at the track of Ohio University, which was hosting the NCAA Division II track and field championships. The throwers had been bouncing hammers off the track during warmups. The reporter was standing about 180 feet away in an auxiliary field outside the

throwing sector. It was about 2:15 P.M. when Lou
stepped into the ring for his turn. Witnesses watched
him stagger and release the hammer in an off-balance
throw. He simply over-rotated a little bit.

The reporter's name was Ernie Hockman, from Xe-
nia. Lou expected him to back up, but Hockman wasn't
looking. The crowd yelled "Heads up!" Hockman
turned and started to run with the clipboard over his
balding dome, but the 16-pound hammer struck him in
the back of the skull with a crack heard all over the sta-
dium. He went down face first into a fence, fluttering
notes exploding from smashed clipboard. He had actually run to intersect the ball that should have missed
him by 35 feet.

Lou started toward him, but was stopped by coach
and teammates.

Hockman was partially conscious, and someone told
him, "Relax, don't make any movement." Someone else
ran to the first aid area for towels to stem the bleeding.
A doctor emerged from the stands, told Hockman to
blink if he understood. Hockman blinked, but couldn't
speak. "Work on your breathing," the doctor told
him.

He did for two or three minutes, before his eyes
rolled up. The doctor worked on him for an additional
15 before an ambulance arrived; it took five more minutes to be sped to County Trauma.

Lou didn't know the extent of Hockman's injury, and
remained in competition thinking that throwing would
clear his mind. It didn't. He fouled on his last attempt
and failed to make the preliminaries. The discus was
next, and he fought for composure. But his mind wan-
dered. Mentally, he was lost. Afterward, his coach
broke it that the reporter had died.

Lou hadn't slept that night, everything going through his mind—did Hockman have a family? Help came from everywhere; even Hockman's family called to offer support. But Lou, shielded by his parents, never talked to them. He had no idea what to say. For five years he had thought of getting their address and phone number, but that was all.

Opening his eyes, they fell on the pages. ". . . Dean embodied the angst of adolescents who had disgust for the generation that caused World War II. He gave this crisis of meaning an icon and was the catalyst for the whole counterculture revolt that peaked in the '60s."

Psychobabble, but maybe he could use it. His major at UCLA was comparative religions, and he was fishing for possible thesis topics. He placed the magazine in the travel bag at his feet. What about movie star cults? From the religious angle, rather than the psychological?

The obsession of some fans certainly approached religious intensity. There had been the case of John Lennon, stalked and killed by a worshiper. John Hinckley's obsession with Jodie Foster had nearly resulted in the death of a President. Theresa Saldana stabbed, and Rebecca Shaeffer murdered, by a fixated maniac. Celebrities hired bodyguards; there were obvious sociological implications. Deadheads. Trekkies. *The Rocky Horror Picture Show*. What about a thesis that developed the religious parallels? Weren't the Eleusinian and medieval mystery religious star cults, of sorts?

What if he could make this sort of a case?——Dean's death had transformed him into a sort of contemporary god: the passage of the magical threshold was a transit into a sphere of rebirth. Since the beginning of time, the

god-to-be was swallowed into the unknown and only
appeared to have died. Osiris or Christ or Odin—what's
the difference? The same hero went through time with
a thousand faces, always representing redemption
through suffering, the descent of the light into darkness
in order to redeem it.

Something to think about.

Which was the problem: he had been thinking about
a thesis rather than working on one the past two years.
Preoccupation for five years—like a low fever—with
the over-rotation which had sent his hammer off the
track to kill a man. More recently like a high fever, with
the death two months ago of his parents in a private
plane crash outside Anchorage, Alaska.

Lou had buried them in Columbus, where they had
lived and where he'd grown up. Now, in the Eastern
Tristar, he was en route back to Los Angeles from Ohio
and a meeting with the estate attorney. He thought how
his distance—not only geographical, but emotional—
must have concerned his parents in their last years. Being their only child made more intense the guilt over his
emotional drift.

"Lou," the attorney had said, "they worried about
you. I never saw your mom and dad the last three years
but that they didn't tell me, 'I just want him to be able
to get on with his life, finish his degree.' " That was
how he introduced the kicker: "That's why they stipu-
lated in the wills that you can't come into your inheri-
tance until you finish a degree. There'll be a little
allowance from a trust fund which should hold you for
six months if you're frugal. If it means getting a job, so
be it. Under all circumstances, they wanted you to get
out in the world and become part of life again."

Maybe he stayed in a holding pattern because it delayed other decisions. A degree in Comparative Religions? What to do with that? Enter an education program and teach high school, or junior college? He had no answers, only questions. That was what had attracted him to Comparative Religions in the first place. But he just couldn't imagine a year of immersion in the arid plains of "Ethical Dualism" or "Jainism: A Study in Asceticism."

An hour later he was unlocking the door to his Westwood apartment, Jim Thorpe running to rub against his ankles. Lou had named the Siamese before ascertaining her sex. He'd found her one morning as a kitten curled asleep in his Speedster, covered with lice, with runny-blue eyes huge in a starved face. Large and glossy now, she mewed plaintively.

He enjoyed the cat's arousal at the whir of the electric can opener. "Didn't Donna feed you?"

Thorpe fed and litter dumped, he checked the answering machine. There was a message from his thesis advisor, Bluestein—a lanky Texan who smoked marijuana and wore cowboy boots—which Lou ignored. Bluestein felt his shit-kicker pose gave him a certain musky cachet in scamming on coeds. Lou had picked him, an unlikely choice for anyone's advisor, as the academic line of least resistance.

He went into the bathroom to examine his flight- and grief-ravaged face. He had been unable to see it—really see it—for five years. Tonight he would have one Heineken, maybe another, and try it again. Then disembodied features might begin to appear—blue-hazel eyes below thick blond-brown hair—before he lost it again. He went into the front room and watched the Sports Channel on the wide-screen.

Tomorrow, he would jog two hours, then put on

greasy overalls and lose himself under the vintage Speedster, which was his only release and escape. He'd change the oil whether it needed it or not. If it was hot, Donna from downstairs would come out with a beer or ice tea, in her cutoff jeans and a bikini top that barely covered the very large breasts which had rotated counter-clockwise the one time they'd made desultory love. Lou told himself he'd never had a strong drive that way, or perhaps he sublimated it in strenuous workouts. Perhaps pleasure was what he traded Ernie Hockman for his life.

She would try to start conversation, he would mumble distracted responses from underneath the car. In a while she would get discouraged and return to her own apartment. When it was safe, he would go back up his own stairs to wash up and decide how to spend the rest of the day.

Washing up, he would look in the mirror and be unable to see his face.

Later in that next, letdown week, the Columbus probate attorney forwarded documents of a personal nature he'd run across sorting out the decedents' affairs. Lou received via UPS a fat manila envelope containing several yellowed clippings, accounts of the accident at the UCLA track meet when his errant throw had killed the sports reporter. There was also a scrap of paper on which was written the phone number of Hockman's aged parents.

Ernie had been a middle-aged bachelor whose whole life apparently was athletics. Lou was cravenly grateful there had been no wife or children; but Hockman was also an only son.

More than once that week, Lou sat on the couch with the number before him and dialed several digits—

sometimes three, other times as many as six—before replacing the receiver.

He was sitting on the sofa in that blank state with le-
gal papers spread before him, when there was a knock
on the door.

"Hi," the girl in hot-pink aerobics spandex said
brightly.

He thought of her as Donna Downstairs, because that
was where she lived. She was saying she had baked too
much casserole, so brought him up some to microwave.
Donna was into sexual yoga, and today wore a black
harness over all that pink. He invited her in when she
showed no signs of leaving.

"What's this?" she asked when she saw the airline
magazine opened on the settee. Donna was snoopy.

"Nothing," he said.

"James Dean," she said wistfully. "First time I saw
you, I thought you looked like him. *Rebel Without a
Cause*—I have it on tape. It's my favorite picture.
Wanna watch it, sometime?"

She brought it over that night, dragging the mahogany coffee table away from the sofa so they could sit on
the floor. The legs of the table left ugly furrows in the
woof of a carpet that Lou kept vacuumed as meticulously as a Zen sand garden. Donna made microwave
popcorn, dimmed the lights, and ignited sandalwood incense.

He could not recall ever having seen the film with its
oddly cosmic theme—his very first day of high school
Dean's entire class goes on a field trip to Griffith Planetarium to watch the end of the universe.

"What does he know about man *alone*?" the effemi-
nate and love-struck Sal Mineo asked during their
narrated tour of the apocalypse.

Lou began to feel uncomfortable as soon as the cred-
its, as Dean curled fetally on a public street with a toy
monkey. He was especially uneasy when Dean cried.
There was a peculiar nakedness to Dean's face, expres-
siveness even to the balletic movement of his body. Lou
wished he was watching the film alone.

"Maybe there's some information here for you,"
Donna said, noting his reactions.

He was noncommittal and annoyed, but the business
of movie star cults had possibilities. Take Donna.
Something powerful was happening to her as the soft-
ness of Dean's lips heated her up. It can't be me, he
thought as she snuggled and breathed deeply.

He thought of pleading tiredness, but that was not
honest. "Donna," he said gently as she rubbed against
him, "we've done this and it doesn't seem to go anywhere. You're a very attractive woman, but the lovemaking's just been a pro forma thing, hasn't it?"

She was not sure what pro forma meant, but her
blushing cheeks told him she understood enough.

Lou returned to the image of Dean, who had a
strange and hypnotic magnetism that cut across sexual
lines and drew interest into himself like a psychic black
hole. Dean, who died violently on a lonely California
highway.

He had an idea for the thesis. Religious myths of the
ancient Near East followed an ancient pattern. Their
legends related how a god was killed, often by a wild
boar, and the corpse was deposited in a river. Through
his death the vitality of Nature was lost. But with the
finding of his corpse, the god returned to life and became identified with an annual ritual for the recovery of
the vegetation after the heat of summer.

On a personal level, Lou could not explain to Donna

that he was feeling a startling current of identification. Not with Dean, but the twenty-three-year-old college student whose car turned in front of a Porsche and killed a star.

We are both members of an elite and unhappy club, thought Lou, scratching Thorpe's ears.

2

Friday, September 2, 1995
Westwood, 6:02 P.M.

"Movie Star Death Cults," George Bluestein enthused as he eased his 6'3" frame in a lounger by the pool of Lou's apartment, scratching a match against the sole of his rattlesnake-skin boots. He lighted a cigarette. "This is good, Lou. Really sexy stuff. I wish I'd thought of it."

"You probably will," Lou said. George had an unsavory reputation for appropriating ideas.

Bluestein threw his head back in a guffaw. The lanky professor had stopped by out of concern when his calls had not been returned, to find the student he considered his protégé out by the pool.

Lou felt more like his banker, having loaned Bluestein over a thousand dollars in the last two months.

George read aloud from *Eastern Way*. " 'In the center of the drought-ridden San Joaquin Valley—72 inches in the hole as far as needed rainfall—is situated a site sacred as Delphi to the cultists: the intersection of two state highways where a movie star died . . .' "

He looked at Lou. "I was out there once. It's called Cholame. You park near that monument, and you ask yourself, 'If these mountains behind me were to tumble, and a thousand years from now archaeologists were to dig through the rubble and unearth this marker . . . what do you think the answer'd be to the question, Who was the god of these people?' " He raised his brows. "I'll tell you. It'd be 'James Dean.' "

He was up pacing in button-fly Levi's as he read, " 'Water tables are sinking and the hollow, gray people are clustered on the spot where the divine blood spilled on 9–30–55. For these shadow people, the junction of 41 and 46 is the world navel, the crack in the cosmic egg—' "

He looked up again. "Shit, it's *fucking Lourdes*. It's the place of magical transformation and assumption. And the fortieth anniversary of Dean's death is the end of this month. What other modern cultural figure has more to-do made about his *death* than his birth?"

George was in his early fifties, still boyish if slightly blurred by dissipation.

"Jimmy Dean," he said with crinkled blue eyes glazing. "God, I remember the day he died. I was twelve years old in Texarkana, Texas. Jesus. He was my youth. Hell, he *invented* the teenager. I'm serious. Before him, you jumped right from twelve to twenty-one. It was weird. People are obsessed with Dean. The mysterious death of the god is a prerequisite to a cult. And you might look for the fucking. Intercourse is a popular way to achieve symbolic union with a god."

But everything was sexual to George. Bluestein's expression was supplanted by awe. "My Gawd," he said. "What's that?"

Lou turned to see Donna coming, hot pink racing stripes running up black spandex bicycling tights of snakeskin sheen.

"Donna," Lou said with misgiving, "this is George Bluestein. He's going to be my thesis advisor."

"Donna?" George said. "Oh, Donna."

She smiled. "Lou, the paper says there's some kind of James Dean convention at the Hyatt next week. I left it on your door."

"Donna," George said, "have you ever had a past lives regression? I'm askin', because there's something familiar about your eyes."

Amazingly, Donna seemed to be responding to the hoary line. Lou gathered up magazine and sun lotion as he excused himself.

"Hey," George called as an afterthought. "Jimmy Dean's been on everybody's mind this week. I want you to come with me downtown. You should see this. I have a friend who has a gallery opening today. I bet we can catch it before it closes."

That was George, the camp counselor hustling everybody into cars.

"Donna," George added in what Lou knew was no afterthought, "you come, too. I don't know you, but I feel like you're a free spirit."

"If Lou's going . . ." she said uncertainly.

"What's it about, George?" Lou asked.

"My friend's a painter, does lots of movie stars. A great old guy and a real character, you'd have to meet him if that was the only reason. But he's doing the next big Dean statue that's gonna be installed out at Griffith Observatory. It's even bigger than the Kendall statue already there. Prepare yourself for the experience of Lysander Pollack."

"A gallery opening?" Donna said. "I'll change."

It bothered Lou when Donna acted ditzy, as if she wasn't thirty units into an Architectural Art degree; she was at a point in her romantic career where she was afraid brains intimidated men.

"No you don't," Bluestein scowled. "You're fine. Look at me. And wait till you see Pollack. He makes me look like a cover for *GQ*."

"I want to at least put on a sweater," she said. "Give me a sec'."

Bluestein smiled at her retreating figure.

"George—" Lou began. But it was hopeless. Bluestein was already off on another tangent.

"Little brother, I actually stopped by to turn you on to something."

"Another 'investment opportunity'?"

"I wouldn't be talking to you if I wasn't strapped for liquid cash. It's going to sound hare-brained but give a listen. What if Elvis Presley doesn't die, but goes into hiding? He gets a room in a motel in southern California and takes to his bed and starts to binge eat, waited on by a loyal cadre of Indonesian refugees who don't speak English. His intent is to make tapes to be shaped into his autobiography, but one of his body guards runs off with the cassettes. Meanwhile, Presley dies of a heart attack and is secretly buried at night in an unmarked grave."

"You're not serious, are you?"

Bluestein's eyes were fevered. "Except that I heard a sample, and by God it sounds like him."

"Everybody does Presley. He's probably the most imitated person in the history of the world."

"Call it a gut feeling, I know it'd have to be sub-
jected to a voice analysis, and so does the dude who's
selling them. He just let me hear a taste, it was 'E' talking about his mother. You know he kept a picture of her
on a black easel at the foot of his bed for years? He
claimed she spoke to him from the beyond, and there
were all sorts of psychics and clairvoyants in and out of
Graceland."

"Is the dude the same guy you score pot from?"

"And he's never burned me yet! Lou, if these tapes
are for real it could be big. This guy'll unload all for
just six hundred dollars, hours and hours of the King
going over his life. It's hot. Even if he's faking me out,
what's to stop us from faking somebody else out, and
for a lot more than six hundred dollars?"

"You're cuckoo," Lou said simply. He decided
against telling George the sweet ride was over, that he
would be on a strict budget at least for as long as it took
him to complete a thesis. He did not want to involve
him in his life any more than he already was.

Donna insisted on riding with Lou in the Speedster
while George followed in his white 1967 Cadillac convertible, their destination a tony gallery on Canon
Drive. Lou wished he had not left the apartment as they
cruised down Hollywood Boulevard and the World of
the Fan. Memorabilia shops catered and attested to
thousands—no, millions—of private shrines throughout
the world. The buff "collected" a star. Donna explained
all about it, confessing a little guiltily to collecting
"Disneyana."

"You know, Mickey and all that."

She told him how there were people into Monroe and
Madonna, and there were people into Lassie; there were

those whose inner worlds were devoted to Laird Cregar, and others to King Kong; Lucille Ball or Frankenstein, no film personality so obscure there was not someone, somewhere, who lighted candles and made of them their temple. It all depended on the emotional need of the fan, which celluloid star was adopted.

There were lobby cards and original posters to be had. For the impoverished, there were inexpensive black and white movie stills at Larry Edmund's Book Store, while the wealthy collector could easily drop $2,000 for a rare autograph at Book City Collectibles or The Scriptorium in Beverly Hills. There were tours of the graves of the stars, just like religious tours of the Holy City of Jerusalem. Valentino's crypt would be pointed out, and the Silver Lake stairs up and down which Laurel and Hardy had silently wrestled a piano in the Golden Age of Film.

Once you became aware of something, you encountered it everywhere. Synchronicity. James Dean had permeated popular culture since his death, but Lou's mental discriminator had always filtered him out. In fact, he was all over.

Lou stared out at the windows of the poster and cinema memorabilia shops. In all the tourist traps, Dean was represented by calendars and assorted knickknacks. Driving through the Boulevard traced with pink and blue neon, Lou saw his likeness gazing soulfully from a large mural at the corner of Wilcox.

On Canon Drive, Lou knew they had arrived when he saw through the large windows glittering figures dodging canapé trays. He hated it already.

Once inside, Donna acted gaga as Bluestein in his western shirt dragged them through the wine-cooler and finger-sandwich crowd, straight to a squat but striking figure in a black poncho holding court for an admiring circle.

"How do you know somebody stole Sal Mineo's knife wound?" someone asked skeptically.

"I have a friend on the force," Pollack replied. "Connections are everything in this town! He told me that after Sal's death, the knife wound was cut out and preserved as evidence in a forensic warehouse. That's where it's been until now, pending the Supreme Court appeal of his killer. A simple matter to abscond with a jar, no?"

Lou pictured something ugly and gray swimming in formaldehyde.

"Why would anyone take it?" a girl asked.

"As a relic," Pollack replied sagely. "Religious resonance! Sal was an emblem of the Age of Dean. I don't doubt it's in someone's collection, right now."

There was appreciative, if uncomfortable, laughter.

The painter appeared to be in his late sixties with a florid and full-bearded face scowling beneath a soiled black beret that dripped oily curls of hair. An old scar the color of a fish's belly ran down the forehead and jumped across the cheek, perhaps a souvenir of collegiate fencing class. There were dribbles and stains on the front of Pollack's silky black shirt with French cuffs.

"Now, take the Spyder in which he died. It was not just *any* car. Our story begins in Sarajevo, Yugoslavia, over eighty years ago. There was a six-passenger Graf and Sift complete with African mahogany woodwork and Aubusson carpets. Twenty-eight feet long, Venetian crystal bud vases—the works. It was specially designed for the Archduke Franz Ferdinand. In 1914, he goes for a drive and is shot by an assassin—and so started World War I."

He paused dazedly until a rapt listener objected, "What's it got to do with Jimmy Dean?"

"Hm? This car passes to nine more owners, and each dies in it, the last crash in 1923 when six members of a wedding party are killed on the way to church. The car is restored and winds up in the Vienna Museum of Industrial Development, where it's destroyed a decade later by Allied bombs." His voice was portentous. "In 1968 the wreck is traced to a dump site outside of Stuttgart. Now that site, according to archives of the Porsche Motor Company, is where Dr. Porsche came just after the war to buy consignments of recyclable steel to build their new line of racers. The Spyders! See what I mean?"

George abruptly introduced Lou and Donna. Pollack looked startled, his unenthusiastic hand a boneless fish in Lou's own. Suspicious black eyes appraised, but they weren't for Donna; it was as if she wasn't there.

"Lou here's doing a master's thesis on Dean fans," Bluestein was saying. "Lysander met Jimmy Dean. Didn't you, Ly?"

Pollack acknowledged Bluestein with a smile that managed to be gracious and contemptuous. "Yes, so I've become rather known as one of the 'Dean artists.' "

Lou, extricating himself, could see why. The paintings were mostly of James Dean in attitudes ranging from the familiar to the bizarre. An emaciated Dean menacingly holding a knife in his hand against a backdrop of existential black, while a large canvas, vaguely reminiscent of Picasso's circus figures, depicted him as a bullfighter, checkered racing flag substituted for the traditional cape.

The attendees were thinning out, the gallery owner shaking hands at the door as Pollack wobbled from several hours' champagne imbibing. Donna was no longer at Lou's side. He saw her cornered by Bluestein. Starting toward them, he found himself pressed against the likeness of Dean as a seductive Arab boy in a poster for *The Immoralist*.

The intimate voice at his shoulder was saying, "His first play. He won the coveted Antoinette Perry Award for that—Lou?"

Pollack was an intimidating figure, even standing unsteadily. "I'm sorry we didn't have more of a chance to converse. Perhaps you would be so kind as to give me a lift home? It would give us an opportunity to talk."

The gallery owner's whisper was entreating. "It would be an immense relief."

Me designated driver? Lou thought, begging off.

Pollack was stupefied.

Bluestein pulled Lou aside. "I've got to talk to you, Little Brother," he said tensely. "Me and Donna are hitting it off like a house afire. I'm getting strong signals off her. We're kindred spirits—it happens this way sometimes. It doesn't seem to me there's anything between you two. Not on your part, anyway—"

"George, you don't have to ask me. She's a big girl."

Bluestein seemed relieved. "Big, hell. She's . . . *buxom*. I mean, how often can you really use that archaism? It's like 'portly.' You don't mind her leaving with me?"

"The only thing I mind is taking this guy home. He's not getting the message, and that gallery owner's encouraging him."

George's face was compassionate. "You're so right. Lou: these are all *queers*. It'll work out perfect. I'll tell Donna you're taking Ly home because you need to talk to him, and she's riding with me."

Pollack lumbered obtrusively between them. When

Lou checked Donna's eyes, she gave no signal that she needed to be rescued.

He shrugged, annoyed.

"Here we are, because of Jimmy," Pollack was saying over the Porsche's wind stream as he held on to his beret so it wouldn't fly off like a bat. "In a Speedster, yet. Jimmy had one before trading it in on the Spyder. You know, he came to my studio in Santa Monica and wanted me to 'do' him like I had Monty Clift? But I didn't know who he was, so I blew the upstart off!" He laughed. "I soon learned Jimmy was the new thing in town. I aspired to be one of his retinue, get in on the ground floor. You haven't arrived until you have leeches and star-fuckers."

Pollack smiled. "Me? I felt that my own ambitions in Hollywood were modest, even self-effacing: I wanted to hitch my wagon to a rising star. I was unashamed, but it wasn't to be. I started work on his 'head' the very night he was killed, working from my morgue."

"Morgue?"

"My collection of photos."

Lou started to feel sorry for the old man, especially as they pulled up to the West Hollywood address, a small grey stucco house squat between high rise apartments, with a rusting sculpture perched next to the porch.

"I work all night, and I'm not tired at all," Pollack said. "Won't you come inside? Just for a moment, I insist."

He did actually insist, and Lou found himself waiting uneasily by a molting bird of paradise while Pollack unlocked the door. Inside were fumes of paint and linseed oil. "Something to drink?" Pollack offered. "Coffee?"

"Decaf?" Lou said with misgivings as he spied a blackened pot simmering dangerously on an encrusted hot plate.

The artist activated indirect lights, and Lou was overwhelmed by the reflections and refractions of James Deans, dozens of canvases in varying states of completion, like a funhouse of myriad trick mirrors with the dead idol's eyes on you at each turn. "Wow," Lou said inadequately, sipping the strange-tasting brew from a paint-smirched mug.

"How old are you, Lou?" Pollack asked.

"Twenty-five."

"Hm. This project should be a very interesting experience for you. For some people, the fascination with Jimmy takes shape as an intense inner-directed emotional journey. You will be one of these. It's in your face."

"My face?"

"A lot like Jimmy's, you both have this depth of sadness. I've often wondered what happened to Jimmy's *Ka*—his undying divine spirit."

Instead of being flattered, the artist's Gothic voice gave Lou shivers. "As far as incarnating, I'm sure he could do better."

"Oh? Placements are according to a higher karmic law. Perhaps he had lessons to learn on a different arc! Who's to say? Jimmy believed in personal immortality. And I don't claim to know the circumstances of your life—though I hope I may." He toasted Lou and grinned. "Irish coffee."

Which explained the adrenalized relaxation Lou was beginning to feel. "Interesting ring," he said lightheartedly.

"You like?" the artist said, displaying the leering

horned face on his middle finger, but Lou wasn't sure that was what he had meant at all. "Baphomet, an old god. Hey, he winked at you!" Pollack winked.

Lou turned uncomfortably away. "There's something different about these paintings, the way they reach out. Even more than . . ."

"My opuses at the gallery? That's discriminating; those are for the unwashed. These all have something extra in them which puts them in the category not for the uninitiated."

The painted flesh looked unhealthily white. Lou thought one of the Deans winked at him, too, this particular Jimmy waving from his racer with a skeleton's hand.

"Follow me," Pollack said impulsively. "I want to show you something I'm proud of, though it's gotten mixed reviews from the 'fans.' " He led the way to a musty room, snapping on a harsh light suspended from the ceiling.

Lou was dragged around an easel to confront a massive work-in-progress which depicted Dean with his little-boy-lost face as a robed Christ at table with Apostles.

"I call it *The Last Supper*," Pollack said. "There in the background I'll have the silver Spyder with a white light descendant from heaven. Do you recognize any apostles? It's all an in-joke sort of thing."

The canvas was eerily three-dimensional except for unfinished sections with penciled guidelines and perspectives. The first two figures starting at the left were men with their arms over each other's shoulders. They wore lipstick and rouge.

"Who are those—" Lou began.

"Prom queens?" Pollack finished. "Rogers Brackett and James DeWeerd. Jimmy always had guardian angels, or mentors. When the student is ready, the teacher always appears."

"'Was Dean . . .?'"

"Gay?" Pollack said with glee at Lou's discomfiture. "There's the matter of his 'love child' to contradict that. Oh yes—he sired a young Dean. I guess the expression now is 'bisexual.'"

Pollack loved to pique, but Lou decided not to play.

The artist continued, "This fellow with the eye patch is Raymond Kienzle, otherwise known as Nick Ray. He directed *Rebel*. That big blond hunk is Frank Saunders, a salesman at Racer's Edge, where Jimmy bought the death car. See what Judas is doing? Dangling gold car keys with the Stuttgart crest—the Porsche racing insignia—before Jimmy's plaintive eyes."

"Judas is . . .?"

"A scowling Rolf Weutheric. He was Jimmy's mechanic, in the seat next to him when they crashed. I modeled his distinctive hair after a Brillo pad. Why a Judas? After the accident, he portrayed himself as Jimmy's good friend in some ghostwritten fan magazine articles at the same time he was suing Jimmy's estate for damages. But he left the country before the litigation was resolved."

"This woman looks like a witch, or vampire."

"Right on both counts. The only female figure—Liv Ermaine, celebrated in the tabloids as 'Jimmy's Witch Woman.' She was a television horror film actress in the fifties, precursor to 'Elvira, Mistress of the Dark.' Next is Cleveland Devereux, high-priest of Dean-dumb—when he's not teaching Chaucer to pimply pubescent brats at some high school up north. He and Liv hate each other, so I put them together. And that kid in the Cal Poly shirt is Donald Turnupseed."

"Turn up speed?"

"Apt, but 'seed.' As in, 'That which thou sowest is not quickened, except it die.' He's the one who actually took Jimmy out."

The hapless college student whose Ford hit Dean, Lou thought. Poor bastard.

Pollack scratched an errant mosquito corpse from where it had mired in black foreground paint. "It's the Ford which could be more accurately called the 'death car,' rather than the Spyder, don't you think? What'd you say?"

"Nothing, just ... inches and seconds. Accidents." Like Ernie Hockman's death.

"Jimmy might disagree," Pollack said. "He said he didn't believe in accidents, and that death was always a choice. And in his final months he believed someone was out to murder him. That that's the case has been a more-or-less open secret among Hollywood cognescenti for four decades."

"Right," Lou said. "I saw Elvis at the minimart this morning."

Pollack put his bulbous nose close. "You tell me: Jimmy gave away his beloved cat the night before he left."

"I've got a beloved cat I'd give away sometimes for two cents."

"You want a scenario? A heavy black and white Ford lies in wait on a frontage road adjacent to a highway. Perhaps there's checkpoints or aerial reconnaissance. Perhaps radios or walkie-talkie. At a prearranged signal the Ford glides out onto the highway from its lair perhaps a quarter-mile away. It spots the Spyder and lurches into it. The racer's occupants are vulnerable in their low-slung aluminum eggshell, while the Ford's pilot is armored in a heavy customized tudor."

"Why would a college kid want to kill Dean?"

The artist withdrew suddenly from Lou's space. "Ah, dangerous territory now. Remember, Howard Carter ignored the writing over Tut's tomb!"

"Did he know him?"

"Perhaps when we know one another better. Getting a little beyond the purview of your thesis, aren't we? Three of the faces on the canvas are blank. Aren't you curious?"

Lou was more annoyed. "You haven't made up your mind."

"Astute. How about that rich executive who built the monument out there at the death site. Or Schmallhorst? The hit-and-run victim?"

"You knew him?"

"Stood right where you are now. I would've paid more attention if I thought I was going to paint him one day. But the most practical idea is Jonathan Cottlee, this French millionaire who's into Jimmy. If I inserted him, he might buy this masterpiece. Would that be too venal? I await inspiration."

Lou's vision swirled a bit and fell on the rows of paint tins lining the walls along the floor. All contained silver paint of muddy consistency. There were only subtle differences in the shades, some nearly gray and others so light as to be nearly the color of egg whites. One was almost electric blue.

"For my Spyders," Pollack explained glumly. "For forty years I've been trying to achieve just the right shade. Someday, perhaps I'll get it right."

If you don't, it won't be for lack of trying, Lou thought.

Pollack brightened and snapped off the light, guiding Lou back to the other room. "Have you read Cleveland's book?"

Lou's face was oddly warm. "About Dean? I've never read a book about him."

Pollack pulled a volume from a shelf. "I'll loan you my copy."

A clipped review fluttered out, which Lou retrieved. *... James Dean is his personal quest for the Holy Grail. Devereux's obsession with Dean's death had placed strains on his marriage. Why would someone risk home and happiness to root out obscure details from a long-forgotten accident?*

"The business of your thesis," Pollack said. "The cult aspect. The things that took place in Hollywood in those days were incredible! I've seen aging doyens of the cinema bathe in goat's blood to restore their complexions. We've lost that sense of magic. That's why I hate this town." He took a drink from another convenient wine bottle.

Lou was feeling woozily hypnotized by one painting on the mantel depicting Dean in the death car, its custom wheels spinning like mandalas. "I gotta get out of here," he said.

Pollack took the canvas up, saying emotionally, "You like? I want you to have this. Here. It's yours."

Lou was embarrassed. "I don't think so. We've been drinking, and you'll be sorry tomorrow."

"I *insist*—" Pollack said belligerently.

"I'm sure it's worth a lot," Lou stammered. "It wouldn't be right."

Pollack smiled, inspired. "Then *pay* me."

Lou wrote him out a check for $450 right there, wondering how much he really would pay to get out of the studio.

Outside, Pollack shoved the painting into the passenger seat of the Speedster and smiled. "Enjoy. Use it as a meditative tool, and a reminder—James Dean died for your sins."

His drunken laugh echoed as Lou pulled away. In the rear mirror the old man capered barefoot in a lonely dance on the wet street, screaming imprecations at the apartment buildings. Lou was already kicking himself in the ass for wasting money he could ill afford.

He pulled up at the apartment to find not only George's white Cadillac in his own parking stall, but lights off in Donna's apartment. He parked in the alley and lugged the painting upstairs. Half-drunk and exhausted, but the other half wired on caffeine, he settled into bed with Devereux's book. The frontispiece was a foldout diagram to scale of Dean's accident, apparently based on the Highway Patrol investigation. It showed the Ford leaving two sets of skids commencing in his own lane thirty yards before impact—despite the fact that the car's driver claimed he never saw the other car. Dean apparently did not even have a chance to apply his brakes, though he had dodged to the shoulder. Lou recognized the reflex of a race driver.

Macabre illustrations included Dean in a casket, in cemeteries, with assorted firearms, and with a noose around his neck.

Lou hoped drowsiness would overtake him, but no such luck. He was three-quarters through the thin book before he finally removed his watch and put it under his pillow where it couldn't taunt him.

It was all about the force of an idea. Devereux wrote that American culture had never experienced a hysterical convulsion of young people like that which followed the death of James Dean on a California highway. *Life* magazine called it *Delirium over a dead star*.

A year after his death, Jimmy Dean was receiving

5,000 letters a week—more than any living star. There was a James Dean Memory Club, a James Dean Foundation, and an Indiana grave visited by 500 fans a day, many of whom chipped souvenirs from the stone. Dean masks of artificial flesh you could fondle were in production, and rings purportedly made from the aluminum skin of the death car—which was itself on tour of bowling alleys and county fairs across the country. One-shot magazines, commemorative medallions, documentaries, tribute record albums—

Talk about obsession.

Devereux had actually written two books in one, the first an excruciatingly detailed reconstruction of Dean's last day and his accident, but the second a thinly disguised memoir of the author's own compulsions, picking up his story at age sixteen and following it through adolescence to—adulthood?

Like the blurb on the cover said: *From an early age, Cleveland Carroll Devereux seemed unable to shake the ghost of James Dean. Growing up, he seemed to have been an emotional drifter who haunted the intersection where Dean was killed. Only one thing excited his imagination and that was a single image: a lonely stretch of highway across which blew dry tumbleweeds, and a beautiful, long-dead boy who had been killed there. . . .*

As a teenager he began to collect Dean—the expression used by fans—spending outrageous sums on original movie stills and lobby cards, and consecrating one room of his house into a shrine dedicated to Jimmy. Starting from almost nothing, he gradually amassed one of the most complete collections of Dean memorabilia—or "Deanabilia" as the fans called it—in the nation. Slowly his interest began to take a different direction, focusing on the central mystery of Dean's life: his death. Devereux had become driven to recon-struct the crash in minute detail.

Death. Death. *Death*. Devereux had written: . . . *Death Drive, a potential of acceleration, an ultra gear or overspeed torqued to intolerable tensions which can be released only once because the explosion of energy will vaporize its own mechanism.*

Lou looked at his new painting at the foot of his bed through eyes unfocusing and figured he could count on having a dream; it was that kind of a night.

A weird dream it was. He came to in a wrecked car, a 1950 Ford with the front bashed in. The steering wheel was pressed against his chest by the engine block.

He squeezed his way out to find himself standing on a desolate stretch of highway as dusk fell, the sun be-ginning to dip behind brown hills to the west. The high-way sign did not read 46 but 466—just like in the fifties, according to the book. It was the intersection forty years ago.

He was looking upon a strange marquee dedicated to James Dean, and it brought a chill. On the shoulder of the road were flowers and gilded crosses, at his feet fan notes written to the fallen star. Picking some up, he felt he was eavesdropping on another world of loss and loneliness, and was oppressed by a terrible guilt. It was all his fault.

Squinting up the road to the east, he saw a small fig-ure walking toward him. He glanced away, then realized the figure was nearer. As long as he watched it seemed not to move, but if he did a double-take it came start-lingly closer. It was a smiling middle-aged man in a windbreaker. He wore glasses and his hand was ex-tended in greeting.

But Lou realized the glasses were askew on his face, lenses shattered. Thick red blood dribbled down the bald head from a big crack in the skull. Lou recognized Ernie Hockman and woke up gasping. In his confused state the dark seemed to be alive with fluttering pages from a smashed clipboard, rising around him like pigeons.

3

February was cruel to the Midwest, and Grant
County was a cold gray. Jimmy Dean's last revisit to his
Indiana roots had been Christmas of 1953 between re-
hearsals of *The Immoralist*. This time was different. The
national opening of *East of Eden* was still seven weeks
away, but everyone knew stardom was imminent. Warner's had extended his contract and in early January announced his casting in *Rebel Without a Cause*. Most
impressive to little Fairmount in Hoosier heartland, *Life*
magazine had assigned a young photographer to produce a photo profile in the setting of his hometown. In-
dications of impending power were the stipulations
Jimmy tried to impose, including insistence on a cover
guarantee and the hiring of a personal friend to write
the story.

When the young photographer declined to pass the
demands on to the editors, Jimmy pouted for days. He

came around only as they visited his old high school drama class.

The journalist stifled a sarcastic yawn as The Star obliged the young students with impromptu Stanislavsky horseshit. The journalist savored a secret: he knew this trip to Indiana was also a panic flight for the actor, the second time during preproduction for *Rebel* he had left the director and producer in limbo. In December Nick Ray had had to fly to New York to fetch Dean.

Jimmy protested too much his contempt for Hollywood, but felt slighted if he wasn't treated with deference. He obviously didn't know what he wanted. The photographer wondered whether Jimmy recognized his own ambivalence about his hometown with its fifteen churches.

It was mutual antipathy. The journalist had heard the stage whispers in a little café where he had taken a breather from Dean's ego. The locals considered him a draft dodger who bragged about evading service, "I kissed the doctor."

Jimmy's folksy encounters on the streets of Fairmount were stilted and it was coming out in the photos. Jimmy's fear of seeming provincial extended to the aunt and uncle who raised him. His response was parody as he performed little pieces of comic theater, the boy who'd never liked farm work posing with sows and cows for the diligent camera. The only natural shots showed him interacting with his eleven-year-old cousin Markie, whom he obviously loved.

In his one candid moment Dean expressed self-contempt for trying to come off like Jean Cocteau, but he could not stop himself any more than he could sleep. Hemorrhoids and diarrhea had flared during the week, but what apparently terrified Jimmy was the fever blister. He could not stop playing with it, spending an hour each morning before the bathroom mirror with his lower lip turned inside out. Jimmy said he always knew knew the bathroom better than any other room in a house.

He also confessed how his obsession with his own features had started as a teenager, the morbid absorption with any imperfection. His slight facial asymmetry made him crazy, and he tried to compensate in photos by always resting his cheek on one hand. He stretched and pulled at his eyes as if he could reshape himself. He became lost in his pores, and when he squeezed his nose the constellation of oily worms that emerged horrified and fascinated him. When he saw the painting *My Last Dutchess* it brought up primal fear.

He was very eccentric. There had been an awkward moment when the photographer had gone down to the dusty basement in search of Jimmy, and startled his subject ferreting desperately through junk. Jimmy recovered quickly, digging out an old Victrola to play some ancient 78s. But that look of guilt lingered, and the distinct feeling Dean had been looking for something secret.

Even in his hometown, Jimmy always insisted on taking circuitous routes as if to shake pursuers. He also left his bedroom at night, and not by the stairs but the window.

Most bizarre, one morning Jimmy had taken him inside empty Back Creek Church and knelt before the altar. If Jimmy was actually praying, the photographer had an idea what for: Dean had spent a large part of the visit closeted with the telephone, making secretive calls to agents Dick Clayton in Hollywood and Jane Deacy in New York.

George Stevens had been in preproduction on Edna

Ferber's sprawling *Giant* since 1953 and the most eagerly contested role was that of Jett Rink. Every actor in Hollywood was vying for what was easily the most colorful part in the film. Jimmy hung out in Stevens's offices flirting with secretaries and charming the director. And now in Back Creek Church, which he had attended as a boy, Jimmy began to recite a strange prayer.

"Adonai our reasonable God, King of the disinherited. You are the son who is to overthrow the Father. I call upon you to grant your followers glory, riches, and power. Enemy of the impostor and breaker of promises, who was to redeem mankind and has not, who was to appear in glory and has not. Who was to intercede for man with the Father and has not. Adonai, force this donothing King and coward God to descend into the host to be punished—"

Then he stopped. There was only Dean's sly smile, and the flirtatious giggle which announced a mood swing.

Back at the farmhouse Dean raged through the house to his aunt's slack-jawed bewilderment before disappearing wordlessly into the old barn. The photographer followed and saw Dean searching the floor boards for one that was loose, this time oblivious to his audience.

It went on for an hour, Jimmy finally heaving the heavy hay bales aside to get at the wood underneath. He was filthy, exhausted, and almost defeated when an upturned edge of pine caught his eye. He pulled at it until the wood cracked, and took from the hiding place something so dusty it must have been deposited there in his boyhood. Jimmy held a dirty pouch in his hand, wrinkled as a scrotum and made of what he claimed was human foreskin. His fingers trembled as he loosed the leather cinch.

What tumbled out into his ashen palm were two

small kernels which Jimmy claimed were his own yellowed baby teeth. He returned into the house with them as if it was some signal victory.

Jimmy had come home for three reasons. Since the first of the year he'd had an uncanny feeling of being followed around Hollywood, the paranoia becoming common knowledge—like his insistence on entering his favorite restaurant, the Villa Capri, through the kitchen and sitting in the farthest booth facing the door.

The other two reasons involved Liv. She said it was required. Liv had local celebrity as Hollywood's televised *Draculina*, her carefully cultivated oddball public persona. Married to a producer, she was a practicing occultist who advised Jimmy that to recover himself, he would first have to find himself, or at least those parts of himself hidden around the Indiana farm and countryside. As long as those items were in the control of someone else, he would also be in their control. That was magic.

She alone not only claimed to believe him about Pontifex, but said it had all started in his hometown. She didn't think he was crazy, did she?

He had explained how Pontifex claimed to be a European investor group representing all walks of industry and arts, bound together by a common interest in what they termed "high-risk projects of cultural significance." Jimmy said it was represented to him as a sort of penance by successful men on both continents who had created an entity outside of their normal spheres of involvement for the sole purpose of developing experimental ideas that would make significant contributions to popular culture.

Jimmy believed that he had all his life been their project. When they killed him, it would be complete.

Liv said that to be free of them he would have to die to himself. Not literally, but symbolically. A grave or casket was needed for the rite.

Jimmy knew where to find the latter. No one had to know the importance of the private ritual. There was an awkward moment in Wilbur Hunt's general store—funeral home as he became mercurial and spooky, as if impulsively drawn to a display casket. He told the photographer he wanted his picture taken in it, but first had to calm the other's queasiness.

"An actor has to be willing to accept all experiences," he said as he climbed into the box. "In his short span he's got to experience everything."

"Bullshit," Wilbur Hunt grumped in the background.

Jimmy closed the lid and his breath relaxed, finally. He told himself that the fearful and paranoid Jimmy was dead, and it would be a new creature who emerged. Squeezing his eyes shut, he tried to divest himself of his ego like layers of garments.

But then he was ten years old again and hearing Dr. Weird's voice next to his ear in the hermetic darkness. "My God, it jumps out at you! Three major planets in the House of Death! Mars is powerful because the House of Death corresponds to Scorpio, which Mars rules. There is interest in sexual magic, psychic power, and afterlife. Unfortunately, there's also likelihood of sudden, violent death. But it augurs well for career. Many actors have their Mars here."

No slouch at manipulation himself, Jimmy had to admire DeWeerd's skill in making them co-conspirators in a belief in his manifest destiny.

Suddenly he couldn't breathe and threw open the lid, shaken as he flashed an uneasy victory sign for the camera. He said only, "It squashes your nose." He couldn't get out fast enough.

* * *

"Death's the one thing I respect above all else," he told the photographer as they drove up the two blocks of rain-glistening Main Street in the Winslows' '49 Ford, "the only thing left to respect. It's the one inevitable, undeniable truth. Everything else can be questioned. But death is truth. In it lies the only nobility for man, and beyond it, the only hope. Have you read *The Tibetan Book of the Dead*?"

Jimmy explained the process of dying. "First, you feel heavy as the earth inside you dissolves to water. When the water dissolves into fire, your circulation ceases. Fire dissolves into air, and warmth begins to dissolve. When air dissolves into space, you get the last feeling of losing contact with the physical world. Space and consciousness dissolve into an inner glow. You've become luminous. An image of light, like on film. You know the movie I'd really like to make? The story of Sydney Franklin, the American bullfighter. Or *Faust*. Except in my version, he would be an actor who sells his soul for sixteen glorious months of success in Hollywood. I tend to be very interested in death, spend a lot of time thinking about it. Carefully crafted and successfully sturdier defenses cover this . . . abandoned mine shaft to emptiness . . . which I confuse with lack of conscience."

The photographer yawned.

Jimmy pretended not to notice but clicked off the large and awkward Telefunken tape recorder he'd positioned between them on the seat. It was annoying to the photographer, like that morning at breakfast when Jimmy used a little hidden microphone to surreptitiously interrogate his grandpa about his roots.

Jimmy looked out the car window and tried to see the sensitive and easily moved boy he believed he'd been just six years ago. But he put nothing past himself. In New York they'd said he would fuck a snake to get ahead. The image fascinated him and became a recurrent theme of the napkin-cartoons he drew and left in lieu of a tip at restaurants.

He casually turned on the recorder again. "Studying cows, pigs, and chickens can help an actor develop his character. There are a lot of things I learned from animals. Acting's the loneliest thing in the world, you know that? The actor must be superhuman in his efforts to store away in the core of his subconscious everything that he might be called on to use in the expression—"

He fell silent as they drove past a house which during his boyhood had been like no other in Fairmount. Not only was the table always set with white linen and gleaming silver, but there were colored light bulbs and a life-size oil of Rudolph Valentino between tuberoses over the mantel. Next to it was a poster of the Tree of Life, that ancient glyph of Cabalistic symbols which depicted the unfoldment of the universe through divine emanations represented by ten spheres.

It was the home of James DeWeerd, prissy pastor of a Wesleyan Church who lived with his senile mother. DeWeerd's war record as infantry chaplain made him an idol to the boys around Marion, Fairmount, and Gas City. He'd returned from Monte Cassino with the Silver Star, the Purple Heart, and a chest full of fragments. The shrapnel crater in his stomach was a source of fascination. Some locals called him "Dr. Weird" because he was into strange things like yogurt and yoga, read books in foreign language editions, and did breathing exercises on a wicker mat while reciting mantras. A selected youth was often his dinner guest in that house, watching home movies of Mexican bullfights or listening to Tchaikovsky on the phonograph. DeWeerd's service decorations dampened local criticism about an eccentric bachelor who liked to take boys to the YMCA gym in Anderson and invite them to swim nude.

Jimmy had been only fourteen when the Reverend first started taking him for rides in a Ford Tudor convertible. In the upholstered seat he'd had his first sexual experience. By the time he was sixteen just the sight of DeWeerd's car was arousing and disturbing. He might imitate the older man's odd mannerisms and mincing walk for the hilarity of friends, but it was to counterweight shame.

DeWeerd said of God, "Only a projection of human wishes which lives only as long as humans maintain its image among themselves."

It'd given Jimmy a delicious shock to think that the god his family and neighbors worshiped at Back Creek Church did not exist. The Reverend had the gift of making things magical, as when he described coming upon Jimmy's high school drama teacher Adeline Nall riding naked on a broom through moonlit Park Cemetery with breasts flapping.

"Keep going," Jimmy said reflectively to the photographer as they neared the Winslow farmhouse on Jonesboro Pike. "I wanna show you where I was born. And also where mom's buried."

DeWeerd, too, had always driven past the Winslow homestead when dropping Jimmy off, a consequence of his mutual distrust for Aunt Ortense. When someone said, "The Reverend's teaching Jimmy Greek," she'd replied. "That's what I'm afraid of—" She wasn't as dumb as she looked.

DeWeerd's high school graduation gift to his protégé James "Rack" Dean had been a trip to the Indianapolis 500 to see the great Iron Man Kretz sweep to victory.

That was June 1949, and Jimmy was soon to leave for California and a reunion with his father. From the time Jimmy told him about the loss of his mother, DeWeerd counseled him about death. To learn to die was to learn how to live. After an exciting afternoon of spinouts and crashes, talk in the Ford returning them to Fairmount turned naturally again to dying.

"Death is to be respected, not feared," DeWeerd repeated. They discussed the draft, DeWeerd having counseled Jimmy on evasion by registering as a homosexual at the National Guard Armory in Marion. Then Betty McPherson, a young physical education teacher who was also an art student, popped up like a devil in the conversation. When Jimmy visited the older woman as she worked at the church, the door was always locked.

"Are you having relations with her?" DeWeerd asked.

Jimmy was amused by the euphemism. "You're the one, who said, 'Why live with one hand behind your back?'" The love-struck DeWeerd was simmering with jealousy, hurting because Jimmy was leaving for Santa Monica and, hopefully, drama classes at City College. When they did not stop at the Winslow house but drove past, Jimmy knew what it meant.

There was an oily sheen of perspiration on DeWeerd's upper lip as he turned onto a dirt road to park under a secluded tree, the same tree as that first time on the long-ago day he had told the boy how he got the wound in his stomach. Asking Jimmy if he wanted to feel it, he'd lifted his shirt to expose the gaping hole. "Do you want to put your hand in?" the Reverend asked breathlessly.

Jimmy's whole fist practically fit. The intimacy frightened and excited him, and he had poured out his belief he must be evil or his mother would not have died and father not left him. He was afraid people would suspect how he really was inside.

DeWeerd listened raptly but offered strange comfort. "You're depraved and vile. You have to seek salvation." He sensed Jimmy felt secret evil inside himself and proposed magical cures which consisted of secreting what he called "medicine bags" around the farm and the countryside. They contained little things associated with Jimmy, like hair clippings, and even a gallstone. DeWeerd said the items had Jimmy's resonance and would stand in for him as offering to the Powers.

More personal intimacies followed on subsequent drives, and on that day after the Indy 500, an eighteen-year-old Jimmy had dissociated to gaze indifferently across soybean fields as the Reverend went down on him for what both knew would be the last time. He looked directly into the setting sun in the west, letting it sear his eyes and distract him from the slurping noises. Pain had its uses.

"You'll have friends in California," a red-faced DeWeerd said contritely when he was through, and wiping his purple lips with a handkerchief. "Don't worry. They'll find you and help you carry on what we've started."

Jimmy believed the pastor was just trying to assuage his guilt. "Who? What've we started?"

Dr. Weird frowned. Over the last year Jimmy had become grumpy, "ornery" as his Aunt Ortense said. The Reverend forced that uncomfortable smile, flirtatious and repulsive. It was also at these moments that Jimmy felt exultation of power over a lonely aging eccentric who tried to cover his own aching nakedness with a fabric of illusion about secret powerful friends, affiliations with mysterious networks.

"Your preparation. I want to give you this." It was a well-thumbed and underlined copy of *The Tibetan Book of the Dead*. A Tarot card was inserted as marker, depicting a shaggy-breasted ram with spiral horns and a third eye in its forehead, a naked man and woman enchained at its feet.

"The Goat," DeWeerd said. "Satan the deceiver. People tricked by appearances make a demon out of their folly. They divide the nature of existence and create two gods. The devil exists only because men are subject to the illusion of duality. Isaiah says, 'I create both the evil and the good.' Each beam of the Sun casts a shadow. Everything's light and darkness mixed. It's the Arcana of *Ayin*. That's a Hebrew word for 'Eye.' The letter also has a secret numerical value of 130. 13 is the number signifying unity, and 10 is the number of the last circle on the mystical Tree of Life. The meaning of the card is—Do you remember?"

"Bondage," Jimmy said easily. The Reverend had taught him some of that, too.

"There's another meaning, 'Seeing things clearly.' Do you know why?"

"No," Jimmy lied. But he knew. Good and Evil were both illusions. DeWeerd was full of shit, an aging queer who did not want to be forgotten.

The pastor's hands trembled as he felt power waning. "I have my pack with me, take another."

Jimmy picked a card, and DeWeerd nodded sagely. "The Magician. He's you. It's the Magician who controls earth's major forces and draws the fire down from heaven. That's the symbol of infinity over his head. He wields the magical weapons with which he'll conquer."

Darkness had fallen by the time the older man dropped him off at Park Cemetery that night. "Don't

forget your head," DeWeerd said tremulously as Jimmy
reached into the backseat for the paper-mâché Frankenstein head he had made for the senior spoof, "Goon
With the Wind."

The Ford sped off, Jimmy's arms prickling with
gooseflesh as cornstalks shivered beyond the road.

Any magic from that point on would have to be of
his own making, his own demonic ability to create himself. He had put his glasses in his pocket and donned
the Frankenstein head. He recalled an H. P. Lovecraft
story called "The Outsider" about a boy who lived
alone in a castle without mirrors, but after many years
got courage to scale the ladder of bones to the outside
world. Only, he discovered everybody was afraid of him
because he was a monster. The story had made Jimmy
cry. . . .

The spool of magnetic tape ran out, making a flapping noise that roused Jimmy from the reverie as he
rode with the photojournalist.

DeWeerd had moved to nearby Marion in the inter-
vening years, but Jimmy did not look him up. DeWeerd
would not tell him what he wanted to know. Some of
the medicine bags had been hidden by them both in
places Jimmy himself had forgotten because it wasn't
important at the time. Jimmy had not known they could
be used against him, that he was handing over parts of
himself for future use. But the precious teakwood box,
DeWeerd had hidden alone.

Jimmy directed the photographer to park at the curb
by the Seven Gables apartments where he'd been born
to a mother with frustrated dreams of artistic accom-
plishment, and a dental technician father who worked at
the VA Hospital. But suddenly he didn't want to see it.
He forced himself to get out and look around in the rub-

ble at the base of the fireplace bricks. He felt the journalist's amused gaze but didn't care. It seemed hopeless, the box could be anywhere.

On the way back to Fairmount he bought roses at a Marion florist's and placed them on his mother's grave with a card. It was Valentine's Day and that night was the Sweethearts' Ball.

Jimmy brought his bongo drums to the high school dance and played with the band. The photographer snapped as seniors requested his autograph.

Afterwards they were driving back to the Winslow farmhouse where Jimmy knew he would head upstairs and make a call to Dick Clayton, put his dental bridge in a glass of water, and curl up with Kazantzakis's *The Last Temptation of Christ*. And rack his memory of DeWeerd's psychology.

Just then they came upon Park Cemetery, its gravestones like bleached whale bones in the headlights. It took Jimmy back to another long-ago night.

He had been just fourteen when DeWeerd asked compassionately, "Don't you wish you could see your mother just once more?"

Jimmy had bristled with self-contempt for ever confiding his yearning. DeWeerd's insistent hands turned Jimmy to face him.

"There was a time long ago when people were closer to the natural order of things. This was before the kind of Christianity which keeps your aunt and uncle on their arthritic knees before the altar of a bearded ghost at Back Creek Church." DeWeerd chuckled seeing the hint of a smile play across Jimmy's lips. He described what was needed. "What's more important to you than anything in the world?"

It had dawned on Jimmy what DeWeerd was talking about.

"Do you still have it?"

Jimmy had nodded gravely, frightened and titillated. But loath to part with it.

He finally brought the relic to DeWeerd and watched him place it in a small teakwood box, the size of a jewelry box. Jimmy received instructions only after swearing an oath to secrecy.

That night he'd pretended sleep upstairs in the Winslow farmhouse then crept out the window. The cold of the cemetery had been sharp, just like now. Cypress spires whipped the sky, trees DeWeerd said were sacred to the dead because their roots restrained souls from returning.

Numb from chill, he waited by the waters of Back Creek trying not to be afraid of the dead, standing where he had been told to stand at the exact time he had been told to wait. Nothing, until—

He detected a perfume in the darkness. Then the forgotten smell of his mother's breasts and hair. He felt cool fingers in his cowlick and face, opening a void. His mother had appeared to him.

The next day DeWeerd had said it was only an astral zombie that he had created out of Jimmy's own belief. And he refused to return the teakwood box, which Jimmy now saw as very powerful. DeWeerd said it had dissolved, its magic used up.

But Jimmy had learned enough about magic to know it wasn't true. Because of what it meant to him its power would never be exhausted. It existed to be used against him, and that was why Liv said he had to find it.

That was what the cemetery brought back to Jimmy.

Now, in the headlights, one of the gravestones stood out.

"Pull over," Jimmy said, suddenly intent.

"Huh?" the photographer said. But obeyed.

Jimmy got out and walked in the light to the great granite marker inscribed CAL DEAN. The name of his great-grandfather now seemed a portentous amalgam of his own name and the character he'd played in *Eden*. Of course. It was pure DeWeerd.

He fell to his knees and began to dig around the base with his fingers. Concrete was cracked at the base, and Jimmy took the switchblade from his pocket and began to pry. One of the chunks was loose, and when it came away he realized it had been removed before, and replaced.

His groping fingers found it, covered with concrete dust. He blew the gray powder from the teakwood before opening the lid, hardly daring to breathe.

The contents were intact.

And he had to destroy it, Liv said. "As long as it exists, your life is not your own."

But now that he held it again, he knew he couldn't.

The journalist was impatiently flashing the brights to get his attention. Jimmy bundled the box in his jacket, wiping his fingers on his pant legs as he stood. He had no idea what the other man would think, and did not care. What was one more eccentricity?

But as he approached the car he saw the journalist's expression. A rotten melon of fear split in Jimmy's stomach. Maybe it wasn't the magazine who had sent this man at all, this man who seemed to be looking at Jimmy with DeWeerd's eyes.

"Pontifex" meant "bridge-builder." Jimmy had been promised bridges, and they had been delivered. Bridges from Indiana to New York, from New York to Hollywood. From little parts to big parts. From bikes to sports cars. From an angry and empty little boy to a movie star. He had sold his soul for sixteen glorious months of dreams come true. But now the devil wanted his due. The time to pay was near.

The journalist's sardonic smile gave Jimmy a chill.

4

The desert's a rich and ambivalent symbol,"
Bluestein said as he foraged coffee in the cupboards of
Ehlers's kitchen. "All you got's instant? The desert's
the opposite of the Garden of Eden on the one hand, but
it's a place to find God, on the other. It's a symbol of
spiritual sterility. The absence of God *and* the demonic."

George found some tea, which at least contained caffeine, and began a pot of water. Lou was sick to his
stomach and couldn't watch.

"It's also the domain of light," George continued,
"the pure and blinding light of truth. And Hockman had
his hand out to you, so he didn't seem to mean any
harm. It's a good dream. Maybe he was telling you everything's all right, quit beatin' yourself over the head."

A poor choice of words, Lou thought, wondering
what the hell George was doing in his apartment wak-

ing him up at 8:30 in the morning. If he was waiting for Lou to ask how it'd gone with Donna, he'd be disappointed.

George sat abruptly. "Let me tell you about a dream I had about heaven—it really was the Great American Dream. There was this beautiful celestial city with these freeways and autobahns. It was the afterlife, and everyone was segregated according to his karma, but this hierarchy was all about cars. If you'd learned the lessons of life well, you got a really good car. If you were so-so, you had a sort of midrange economy thing. And the fuck-ups—they were limping around in these old Corvairs and Pintos that were all primered and had bald tires. . . ."

Lou yawned.

"I don't mean to talk so much. I'm just feeling great this morning," Bluestein said enthusiastically.

Lou let it pass, stroked Thorpe's arching back as George shambled nervously to inspect the painting leaned facedown against the wall.

"You got one of Ly's pieces, huh? I'm not into it, but if I had to fuck a guy it'd be Jimmy Dean. I mean he's more beautiful than most woman, isn't he? You pay for it? Ly's gonna love you forever. The homosexual thing's never bothered me. I don't get those kind of vibes from him. Did you?"

Lou didn't respond, and Bluestein loped toward the bathroom, leaving the door wide as he urinated. "Donna's a real nice woman, Lou. She's got a good heart, and she sure thinks a lot of you. I don't think she's experienced much sensitivity from men in her life."

"Don't hurt her," Lou said quietly.

"Huh?" George looked very hurt himself as he zipped up, then flushed. "Lou, you'd probably have been very surprised if you'd been a fly on the wall last night."

Here it comes, Lou thought.

"We talked about you, and I began to absorb all this psychic pain from her. By the time she was through crying, I felt more like a big brother to her. I know very well that she's a special person."

"I'd just hate to see her hurt, that's all. Your water's boiling."

Once George was gone, Lou considered going back to bed but opted for a shower. He'd barely started the water when there was another knock; he wrapped a blue terry-cloth towel around his waist.

"Hi," Donna smiled bravely. "Can I come in?"

His face was confused. "I was just getting in the shower."

"Fine," she said, "I'll wait. Can I turn on the tube?"

He nodded and walked sullenly back to the bathroom. What the hell now?

He took a long one and did not come out until he was entirely dressed. All his life people had wanted to bend his ear with their problems—that was, before he cut himself off. She seemed more together when he returned, until she began to cry.

"Donna. What is it?"

"I'm okay," she said, trying to smile as she dabbed lapis lazuli eyes with Kleenex. "Your friend George is quite a guy, huh?"

Lou said uncomfortably. "Yeah. He's a nice guy."

The tears started again.

"Donna, what happened?"

She smiled bitterly, crimsoning. "Nothing happened. That's just it. He couldn't get it up, but he kept trying. Then he'd cry for a while. It was a nightmare."

Lou felt his back tighten; he didn't want to be hearing this.

"Why, Lou?" she sobbed. "I give and give and give, and always wind up with guys who have some kind of problem. If they've got anything really going for them, they're like you, they're not interested."

He hated it worse when she tried to smile, as if her life was a comedy of errors.

"Why is this, Lou?"

"I don't know, Donna."

"I don't feel like being alone today. Do you mind if I go with you?"

"Where am I going?"

"I don't know. Just, anywhere."

Lou started to berate himself about the $450 he had paid Pollack for the painting, money he could ill afford in his new situation. It gave new urgency to the thesis, and he experimented with ideas as they drove.

Symbols like James Dean enacted upon their own bodies the great symbolic act of scattering their flesh, like the body of Osiris, for the salvation of the world; his passing and returning demonstrate there's really nothing to fear.

Donna said she wanted to treat herself to some Mickey stuff, directing him to Larry Edmunds, the most venerable bookshop on Hollywood Boulevard. Lou browsed as collectors made the rounds.

A Japanese fellow at the counter was inquiring about Marilyn Monroe; a file was brought out crammed with stills, which he handled reverently by the corners. That girl with the ironed hair and acne? She was into Frances Farmer. The pudgy kid with Coke-bottle lenses? "Do you have any new Lon Chaney?"

W.C. Fields, Charlie Chaplin, Judy Garland, Monty

Clift; other names Lou didn't recognize: Theda Bara, Lupe Velez, Carol Borland, Dwight Frye.

Then he heard, "Any new Dean?"

Lou saw a gawky young fellow, mashed pimple leaking through the back of his T-shirt, eagerly confronting the bearded troll behind the counter. "Any new Dean?"

The clerk brought out a large display book. "I heard you the first time. These lobby cards," he said, unenthusiastically sizing up the kid. "Original issue. 1955."

"Lobby cards?" the kid said.

"They were issued in sets of eight, with the picture."

An 11×14 card showed James Dean about to kiss Natalie Wood in the old mansion.

"How much?" the kid asked.

"One hundred fifty," the gnome replied, a bit sadistically.

The kid sucked crestfallen breath. "A little out of my league."

The man closed the book with finality, and satisfaction. "Here. Some stills. Two-fifty, black-and-white. Five bucks, color—"

"Lou," Donna was saying brightly, and not alone; she never met a stranger. "This is Terry, and Sheena. Terry's making a documentary on James Dean, so I told him what you're doing. He wants to talk to you!"

"Terry Marc Childes," effervesced a young man shorter than Lou, with wiry hair and white teeth.

Lou found himself categorizing the kinetic bundle. Hollywood was full of dynamic young hustlers desperately wanting to be somebody. Childes's Asian girlfriend was more interesting, her smile breezy and her palm cool.

"Terry's interested in your thesis," Donna catalyzed. Her helpfulness irritated him.

"You've got an academic background," Childes en-

thused. "We gotta get together. I really want your input
on this project. You got an intellectual approach, and
that's what this thing needs. It's gonna be big—Lou.
My brother was at a party last night and guess who was
there? Erik *Estrada*. And get this—he's a big Dean fan.
Just think if he could narrate the film I'm doing."

They talked long enough for Lou to learn Terry was
a would-be actor and former disc jockey whose antics
and drug abuse estranged him from a father who put
him in rehab. Now clean almost a year, dad was giving
him a new start by offering a $25,000 reward for the
missing James Dean Porsche.

"It's a gimmick," Terry said. "The reward'll be pub-
licized this year on a segment of the syndicated series
Where Is It Now?"

"Do you really think you'll find it?" Lou asked.

Terry made a frightened face. "I hope to hell not—
but look at the publicity! That's great coverage, huh?
Would you like to meet some people from the fan club?
The rendezvous is close by—I just gotta stop by my
place and check messages."

"Sounds like fun," Donna said. "Why not?"

"Let me pay for this book," Lou said.

Donna was disappointed. "You're only getting one
Dean book?"

"For starters. Let me take care of myself, okay?"

As they pulled into traffic behind Childes's Toyota,
Donna bubbled, "Exciting, huh? A filmmaker?"

"Everybody in Hollywood has a project 'in development,' " Lou said patiently. "This guy works as a gofer
in a production company—that's a glorified secretary."

Terry pulled into a little house off Melrose, and Lou
realized the actual breadwinner was Sheena, a dress designer with clientele including a few celebrities.

A beautiful boy walked in from a bedroom off the hall.

"Sleepy head," Sheena said affectionately.

The newcomer stretched luxuriously, and Lou realized it was not a boy at all, but a girl in an androgynous cable knit sweater. Blond hair chopped short offset the striking blueness of pale eyes.

"Cherie Lowe," Childes said. "She's a Dean fan, too."

Her shy smile went through him. Lou had the impression she was uncomfortable with beauty and tried to ugly herself up in old jeans—unsuccessfully. When she toughened her face it only made her enigmatic. Throwing herself onto the couch, she leafed through a movie magazine.

"You look like Jimmy," she said as if it was a challenge. "I bet people tell you that."

"I do,' Donna said.

Cherie looked rather like James Dean herself, and Lou wondered whether it was conscious.

"What's your film about?" he asked Terry.

"All the mystery stuff. Especially the car."

"Weird story," Sheena said with a shiver, the pacing Childes barely acknowledging the drink she placed in his hand.

"After the crash," Childes was saying, "the 'Little Bastard' is bought by a Burbank plastic surgeon named Eschrich—he's got his own 'special' to race, wants the undamaged engine, trans axle and other salvageable parts. His doctor pal Troy McHenry gets the Spyder's trailing arms and installs them in his race car—then he's killed racing at Pomona."

"Do you believe in the curse?" Donna asked.

Childes's hands animated his words. "You betcha. The engineless shell is first exhibited locally by Budd

Kunstler, the Hollywood car guy. Then it goes on national tour—'This accident could have been avoided'—that kind of crap. But the Spyder disappears from a sealed truck en route to California from Florida, and that's where I come in." His smile expected approval.

"Go ahead," Lou prompted.

"Dean's car was one of seventy delivered to the U.S. by the Porsche company. I figured, Dean's chassis number would be high—maybe in the 0060 range—but I needed to know the actual number. The number on the pink slip was P90059. I did what nobody ever did before: I got hold of the head of Porsche's Customer Racing Department, and they searched the production records."

He leaned closer. "I found out Dean's Spyder was delivered from their doors on July 15, 1955, with an engine number of 90059 and a chassis number of 550–0055. I got the serials on other internal components. For the first time, we're able to positively identify any parts that come off the Porsche."

"So?" Lou asked.

"So?" Childes frowned. "With these numbers, I can identify any part of the car! If it was even just to *know*, that's something. Imagine holding one of those pieces in your hand, and knowing where it came from. That's gotta be a head-rush!"

Mystique, Lou thought, like Cherie's studied insouciance.

Donna said, "Terry told me in the bookstore about a major motion picture on Dean coming out."

Childes was distracted by the ringing of his phone. "Sheena—will you grab that? Yeah. A one-point-five million production, *The Last Days of Jimmy Dean*. They're gonna re-create the accident. Two helicopters and five ground-based cameras, right on the exact place

Jimmy bit the weeny. High-speed collision, eighty-five miles an hour—"

"It's Jonathan," Sheena said.

Terry ran to the phone; apparently Jonathan was the reason Terry wanted to check his messages. Donna followed Sheena to the drafting table in the kitchen, very interested in her designs. Which left Lou and the girl.

"Must be an important call," he said.

She looked at him curiously. "Terry's got a rich friend who's into Dean. The guy's crazy to find Jimmy's death car. But I think Terry's trying to scrounge up backing for his film."

"You live here?"

"Just for the weekend. I'm from Fresno, have you heard of it?" She lifted her arms to peel off the heavy sweater, startling him with the glimpse of navel. She smoothed the shirt underneath, a shirt covered by the face of James Dean.

"Sure," he smiled. "It's in the United States. How did you get interested?" He indicated her shirt.

"Really want to know?" She lay back on an elbow, lighting deftly with one hand a cigarette which looked large in her small fingers.

"He saved my life. I was fifteen and really bummed-out because my first boyfriend dumped me. I was thinking about suicide, and *Rebel Without a Cause* happened to be on at that exact moment. There I was, thinking about killing myself when his voice came on the TV with this line from the movie—'Life *can* be beautiful.' And he *was* beautiful. It turned my whole head around. Jimmy's the only actor that's ever moved me to tears— and I'm not emotional . . . I'm such a zombie, it was so terrific to be able to *feel*."

She flickered a smile, but it was the sort of vulnerability that asked you to hurt her.

"I see the craziness, but I also see the good wonderful things. I learned to not be afraid to communicate, I learned that we're all pretty equal. There really are no stars, but there are special attractions between certain people—attractions that can be fatal, but make life seem to become *large* and *intense*."

"Jonathan can't make it," Terry interrupted as he returned, obviously disappointed. "Let's go."

"Where—?" Lou began.

"The cemetery," Donna answered with a smile. "Terry has some fans waiting for him."

Lou followed Sheena's car onto Wilshire, thinking of the force of the idea that had set their little caravan in motion. The collective unconscious was a graveyard of rust-encrusted scrap iron and corroding images, but sometimes a pure archetypal idea floated up from the gloom, attracting sliverlike small fish who followed it hungrily in its climb to light at the surface.

He mentally defended a thesis to an imaginary committee. "*First, there's the broad mythological context. In the nineteen fifties, Eisenhower is stricken by a heart attack and becomes the wounded Fisher King. It's the Age of Paranoia and Anxious Conformity. The nuclear cloud creates an emotional wasteland of fear, and neuroses. At the same time, affluence has spawned this creature called the Teenager. The time is ripe.*"

Ripe for—?

"*A savior, of course. Enter James Dean. He's their image, and his death in the desert revitalizes the parched land. It renders him the ageless counterculture hero, crystallized and perfected by absence. Symbol and instant icon . . . a Christ for the Clearasil set with his movies as gospels and manifestos.*"

Cherie's feelings obviously weren't morbid to her,

any more than a Christian's contemplating the Cross. She probably found it spiritually nurturing and consciousness-expanding.

"For the Dean fan, it's about encounter with mystery, and the supranormal. It's not about death, but resurrection and life—"

The term "mystery religions" was usually reserved for cults such as Eleusis, Dionysus, Orpheus, Isis and Osiris, and Attis—though several cults in the Middle Ages fulfilled the three requisite conditions: they were restricted in membership, required the performance of initiatic and other ceremonies under conditions of secrecy, and promised spiritual privileges to members.

"You need mystery. You need a hero who has passed through the heroic cycle. Most important, there must be an early sacrificial death which assumes him into mystery. There must be the scattering of his flesh to feed his followers, the spilling of the blood to refresh the wasteland.

"You need holy places and holy relics. You would need pilgrimages and devotions. You need a hierarchy of followers. You need anointed spiritual guides to interpret meanings, and preserve the eternal flame. And there must be resurrection, a translation into light. That was Dean's image on film—

"And you need—

"Weirdos," he said aloud.

"What?" Donna responded.

"Nothing," he mumbled as he followed Childes in a sharp turn around a bank on Glenwood to enter through wrought-iron gates. Suddenly they were within a high-walled island of mortuary quiet in the center of downtown Westwood.

"Westwood Memorial Park," Terry said when they dismounted. "The most exclusive real estate in Califor-

nia. Armand Hammer's buried in that crypt. Marilyn
Monroe's that way—there's always Japanese men
bringing her red roses. But there are our friends—at
Natalie's grave."

Natalie? He recalled a sick joke: What's the only
wood that doesn't float? *Natalie Wood.*

Cemeteries weren't his favorite places, nor did he
like the feeling of interrupting a séance. Four women
stood on grass in identical sweaters, scrapbooks clasped
to their breasts.

Childes was getting Sheena loaded up with camera
equipment. "They meet here every few months and
have brunch over her grave. That's *Patsy Polmquist*,
president of one of the larger Jimmy fan clubs."

Lou knew her from Devereux's book. A nun to the
cult of Dean from way back, Jimmy was her spiritual
companion, although technically married to an insurance salesman. Tall, with red hair, Patsy published a little newsletter and corresponded with fans all over the
world—a sort of James Dean clearing house.

Cherie was assuming the lotus position on the grass,
putting on earphones and lighting a cigarette as she
watched behind Polaroid sunglasses.

Patsy introduced Diane, Maureen, and Becka. Diane
was the youngest, tall and wan with long blonde ironed
hair. Becka, from San Diego, sported a panoply of
James Dean buttons. Maureen was so unremarkable Lou
forgot her face between blinks.

"Jim Backus is over there," Diane said eerily, indicating a corner of the lawn. "He was Jimmy's dad in
Rebel. Weird, isn't it?"

That was the word. Lou felt the eyes of the female
quartet upon him, arms folded like albino bats. Maureen
whispered something to Patsy, who smiled. "She says
you look like Jimmy. She's right."

"Well—" Lou began.

Terry cut him off. "Where's Ly?"

"Pollack?" Lou asked.

Terry was suddenly grouchy with Sheena as she helped him string the microphone cord along his arm, arranging the camera on his shoulder. Lou was the only one careful not to step on graves. Patsy sensed his discomfort and patted his hand. "It's okay. This is very 'Jimmy.' "

"Patsy—" Terry called. "Let me get a little of you kids on Natalie's grave."

Polmquist smiled obligingly. Childes asked her about Jimmy—and death. She complied blithely.

"Jimmy was always drawing sketches of himself with candles around his corpse. It was his *mortido*—his will to death—which led back to the loss of his mother. He liked to cruise Sunset in a hearse. . . ."

There was a rumble, and the clatter of a loose muffler as a crumpled station wagon rolled past the mortuary with Pollack at the wheel.

"Shit," Terry said disgustedly. "Ly, you ruined the shot!"

"You can cut it later," Sheena soothed. Terry resumed with Polmquist, ignoring Pollack sidling up to Lou.

"So," Pollack said. "Kismet. You've been meeting some of the fans?"

Lou quietly indicated Cherie with a nod where she sat playing with a dandelion. "Know her?"

Pollack pursed his lips. "A little butch? Isn't she one of Devereux's crowd?"

Childes glanced at them reprovingly, pressed on with Patsy. "What about Dean 'pilgrimages'? Are there yearly festivals?"

"My goodness, yes," Polmquist said, momentarily confused whether to look into Childes' eye or the lens.

"In fact, next week there's a DeanCon—Dean Convention—at the Hyatt. There'll be all sorts of fans there."

Diane chimed, "And another—the international Dean-Con—later this month. The occasion is the fortieth anniversary of Jimmy's accident. It's going to fall on a Friday—just like in 1955, the day Jimmy died."

"Let me ask you about Cleveland Devereux—" Childes began.

Polmquist bristled. "We don't discuss *that* book."

"*That* got a rise," Donna murmured.

"That's why he saved it for last," Pollack whispered with malicious glee. "What you're going to realize is that there is a major schism in the ranks of Dean devotees. There is the James Dean Fan Club, with its nucleus here in L.A., and its further points held together by the newsletter and the conventions. And there's the heretical Devereux sect—their apostasy is a fixation on Jimmy's death."

"You talk like they're Cathars, or Bogomils," Lou said.

"Thought you'd like that. The members of the L.A. fan club shun Devereux's annual 'Death Route Run' as too morbid. Instead, they will travel to Fairmount, Indiana, Dean's hometown, on the anniversary of his death. They sink their MasterCards and Visas to the hilt to make the trek. They'll go to the service at the Friends Church, and then march in a cortege out to the cemetery and Jimmy's grave."

"I'm glad you're not superstitious," Polmquist was saying to Terry.

"Why's that?" Terry prodded.

"The last person Lysander brought to interview us is dead. Larry Schmallhorst was his name."

"An upbeat ending," Pollack applauded after Patsy recounted the story for Terry's camera.

Afterward, there was a rearrangement of Pollack and the four women on the grave.

"Ly," Terry said, "let me get you on the death thing. The Second Coming angle? Stand right on Natalie's plaque. Pretend her name is your mark."

Lysander obliged, adjusted his beret and modulated his voice for Childes's camera. "I wouldn't go out to the actual intersection at the end of this month, not on a dare."

Terry smiled impishly. "Why not?"

Pollack's timbre was dramatic, like a Transylvanian peasant warning someone away from Castle Dracula. "Because some believe that this year's anniversary will be different. Because this year, Jimmy's coming back."

"What? From the dead?"

Pollack beetled his brows. "One of the prerequisites for the return of a god to earth is a ritual restaging of his final Passion. Farfetched? And it's been confirmed that an independent film company is going to make a new picture. *The Last Days of Jimmy Dean. . . .*"

"Who believes he's coming back?"

"Liv Ermaine," Pollack said brightly.

Terry was thrown, realized Ly had stepped out of character to indicate a gray hearse pulling up the drive. Childes lowered his camera to gape as a woman in black alighted, her bust massive beneath the roomy caftan, swept-back hair held in place with a distinctive comb of shiny bone.

Lou recalled Jimmy Dean's ghoul-friend from the Devereux book, an unflattering portrait. Her moment in the sun had been her television persona as *Draculina*—a sort of Charles Addams knock-off for horror films. Her career never recovered after Dean's death, ending in cheap horror films.

She stepped up to the grave, transfixed by Lou, then smiled at Pollack in approval.

"You're right, Ly. He *does* look very like Jimmy. Looking out here from the car my heart almost stopped. I thought it was Jimmy, come to say—

" *'When are you ghouls going to eat?'* "

She threw her head back and cackled, jiggling the onyx beads ornamenting her firm bosom and revealing two missing front teeth. She exuded sexual vitality even in her seventies. And full of surprises. She produced a Tarot pack from the folds of the caftan. "I want to find your card," she said huskily to Lou. "Pick one."

Donna nodded encouragingly, until Lou reluctantly chose a card.

Ermaine flipped it. "Eight of Pentacles," she said sagely. "A young man with a hammer, an artist at work in stone. Does this card have special significance for you?"

A young man with a hammer. "No," he said hoarsely.

Liv's unbelieving eyes were superior as Terry took her arm, positioning her so he could get the hearse in the shot. The weird sisters moved aside in coordination, watching Ermaine raptly.

Lou felt a strange anxiety when he realized the spot of grass where Cherie had been sitting was vacant. Then he saw her by some crypts in the sun, tracing the gold names with her fingers.

Donna startled him by gasping, "Jesus!" He thought ants had covered her feet as she jumped aside, but she had noticed the plaque beneath her toes. "Dorothy Stratten."

"Were you into the occult?" Terry asked Liv when he was rolling. "You and James Dean?"

Ermaine's smile was flirtatious, but cautious because of the missing teeth. "Jimmy and the occult? You know, that's the second most-often asked question. The first is, 'Was he gay?' "

"What's your answer?" Terry asked.

"About the cock-sucking, or the occult?"

Terry was delighted. "The occult."

"Some bullshit. But I'll tell you the truth. With Jimmy and me, the occult was just a little game we played. I used to phone him at all hours, and wake him up in this groaning hellish voice, reading this shit to him. I still remember it, and let's see. Something something—" She paused dramatically, finally spoke at majestic volume.

" *'By the virtue of the Holy Resurrection and the agonies of the damned! I conjure and command thee, spirit of James Dean deceased, to answer my demands and obey these sacred ceremonies! This on pain of everlasting torment! Berald! Beroald! Balbin! Gab! Gabor—*

" *'Arise! Arise, I charge and command thee . . .!'* "

Patsy and her crew were awed, eyes popping. The former *Draculina* was satisfied.

"I take it the answer's 'no,' " Terry said.

Liv smiled mysteriously, the setting sun over the cemetery wall framing her head in a bloody corona.

There followed a ceremony proper, for the occasion. The fan club women certainly looked very grave. It was Pollack who had been asked to deliver the . . . whatever it was.

"It was forty years ago this month," Lysander said, "that Jimmy attended a sneak preview of *Rebel Without a Cause*. A strange film. A haunted film. The three young stars died untimely deaths: Jimmy in his car, Natalie in the frigid waters off Catalina, Sal stabbed to death in his parking lot. And yet they have left us their luminous images . . ."

Lou felt like a fool, standing there with hands folded the way Sheena had arranged them all as backdrop.

Cake followed; Diane had baked it. Sheena circulated with waivers for the interviewees to sign so Childes could use them in his film. Terry was getting Lou's address and number from Donna, but Lou was looking for Cherie.

He approached her softly, not to startle. "Who is she?" he said of the female in the crypt.

She turned, embarrassed. "Heather O'Rourke. The little *Poltergeist* girl."

Lou read the dates and said sadly. "She was only twelve when she—"

"Look—" Cherie interrupted, intense. "I make little speeches sometimes, so excuse me. When I was in high school and I cut my wrists, I was just wanting to communicate. I think there was a part of me that wanted to get a thrill out of it like, 'If somebody sees this, they're gonna like me.' Of course, they didn't like me better, and I hated myself. . . . Now, I've got too much respect for people I like to play games with them. If you're really into Jimmy, I feel like I already know you. It tells me things about a person."

"What things?"

"It tells me about, looking for something. About searching. Sensitivity, and creativity. Good things. What do you think about death?"

Lou stammered. "I guess . . . it's part of an ongoing process, for the world to continue to exist. It's through the death of all sorts of organisms that human life is supported. Maybe through James Dean, people participate in his death and explore it at a safe remove. Maybe it relieves some of their fear to—"

"The trick's to feel," she said disappointed, sadly acknowledging he didn't know how.

Lou was stunned. Wrong answer. He had failed a test.

"They're heeere," a high voice whispered, and Lou jumped at the hand on his arm.

It was only Donna. "The guys are here to lock the gates. They're running us off."

He looked at her with annoyance, Cherie smiling with something like amusement. Tolerance? He replayed that smile as Donna dragged him to the car.

"What's the matter with you?" he demanded.

He noticed Patsy and her girls crumbling pieces of cake in their fingers and sprinkling them on Natalie's grave, and Cherie's languid arm in the window of Terry's car.

"What characters," Donna was saying as they drove onto Wilshire. "That strange little man who was Liv's chauffeur? Patsy said he used to room with Jimmy. Jimmy wanted him to be 'Plato' in *Rebel*, but the part went to Sal instead. Jimmy got him rhinoplasty—"

"What?"

"A nose job."

" 'Blow-job'?"

She laughed. "What's wrong with you? Plastic surgery. By the same doctor who's got the engine to Jimmy's car. Weird, huh?"

He let Donna precede him into his apartment, where he fixed her cocoa. She began stretching on the floor, placing her hands on her knees and extending her tongue until she could stare cross-eyed at its tip. She made a fierce grimace and tensed her shoulders so she resembled a lion. Lou didn't understand, but didn't doubt it was something to do with chakras and kundalini force.

"I feel better," she said, rolling her tongue back in her mouth, patting Thorpe's fur. "Thanks for today. You were there for me."

"I want to borrow your VCR tomorrow," he said uneasily. "So I can make my own copies of these Dean tapes."

"Does this mean you're going to get started on your thesis?"

"I'm actually getting started to think about getting started. I think." Neither did he mention to her about the element of duress imposed by his dead parents.

They watched the late show, and she fell asleep against his shoulder as he leafed through the book he'd bought, a big picture book with half the text in Japanese. He realized Jimmy was a great exponent of his own posthumous myth, so intent on leaving a narcissistic photographic record of himself.

Donna stirred, eyes opening slightly then closing again. "She's not your type," she muttered.

"What?"

But she didn't answer, just began to snore. It was singularly unattractive, and he recalled how when Siddartha wanted to leave home and become the Buddha, his father had sent courtesans to entertain him. When they fell asleep he saw the open mouths, and the dresses fallen apart to reveal their nakedness, and found them loathsome.

Embarrassed for her, Lou turned back to the book.

5

September 4–8, 1995
Hollywood, California

Watching female beach volleyball championships on
TV, Lou had often in his loneliness fallen quickly and
poignantly in love with a lithe fawn in a bikini, her
shoulders sagging in defeat as she returned to the line
after a missed spike—-and then would come a commer-
cial and she'd be gone. It was harmless, he'd feel sad
for a half hour and snap out of it. He was having the
same response to Cherie, only there would be no com-
mercial reprieve. Television was definitely superior to
life.

All that week he thought of her. He was feeling a
new interest in things, sparked by Dean. He even took
the initiative to interview several fans with help of a
recommendation from Patsy Polmquist. What was fascinating was that the Deanphiles not only sounded identical, but seemed to live in identical apartments.

Always the same pattern: the disciple would meet him at the door and he would be ushered inside by someone, not very physically attractive, who glowed at the prospect of showing off a personal shrine. There was fur or hair on the sofa. Existence was near poverty level due to the acquisition of sacred relics displayed in compulsive order. The devotee was frequently reduced to eating Saltines with Cheeze Whiz after an annual pilgrimage to Fairmount, returning with nothing to show for it but 400 pictures of themselves with Dean's tombstone.

Then—until Lou began to take more control—the scrapbook was trotted out with its pictures of Dean's long-dead mother smiling toothily, or the late Aunt Ortense in her shriveled and mummified nineties. All the while, a little terrier humped his leg.

The biggest surprise was the hierarchical structure to Dean worship, a rabid one-upmanship based on the rarity of the collectibles you owned, or scored on your nearness to someone who had known Jimmy Dean.

If you had an autograph preserved on special acid-free matting, you were a real collector. If you had only postcards and calendars, you were nowhere. If you had met Liv Ermaine, that was good. But Jimmy's Aunt Ortense was worth two Liv Ermaines, because she was dead. If you had sent a registered letter to the poor fellow who had been driving the other car in Jimmy's accident, and obtained his signature, that was very cool.

Odd and colorful characters, but a community of eccentricity does not a cult make. But the Devereux thing—that had possibilities. His book and personal following apparently centered more on Dean's death than his life.

But that was far as Lou got. *Ernie Hockman is dead,* he remembered. *You're forgetting. What right do you have to go on and think and plan, when the least thing you do on this day will be something Ernie will never do again?*

Dean fans at least had each other.

Lou knew the heart of their obsession was still evading him. He wasn't grasping the essential mystery.

Then one night, as he stared at the wall in defeat with defenses lowered by five Heinekens, he found himself slipping *Rebel* into the VCR to just *watch*. Stuporous and maudlin he might have been, but could not deny that for a little while he *saw* and *connected*.

It was a powerful experience. In a WarnerColor palette of eerie blues and smoldering reds, James Dean painted a boy's passage into manhood in one day and one night. With incisive sketches and quirky details, he pulled tremendous life and truth from himself to create a performance charming and magnetic. The intensity and reality of his observations drew Lou wholly into yearning participation in the juvenile fantasy of triumph against the mysteries of love and death and sexual ambiguity. It was a lot of mythic baggage for any twenty-four-year-old to bear.

Jimmy's image was absorbing, enchanting, and seductive. It cut through time with a painful incision and radiance that hit Lou like a punch. The awareness *this boy is dead* provided poignant counterpoint, cosmic motifs like ghosts on the screen. Dean not only acted in the movie, he *haunted* it. The weirdly moving theme music perfectly underscored Dean's moods and the sense of a cool and magical night of infinite possibilities.

But, just like when he fell in love with a female volleyball player on the Sports Channel, the images ended and Lou was left on the sofa with a hole in his gut.

How to keep it alive? That was what drove the fan. He made the note to himself before staggering to bed and passing out.

6

Saturday, September 10, 1995
Hyatt Wilshire, 12:46 P.M.

The many faces of James Dean were numinous as they stared down from dozens of blow-ups on the walls of the Hyatt Wilshire. The annual DeanCon was the biggest and best ever, so said the program. The theme was "A World of Dean," and fans had come from all over the country and the globe. Lou was overwhelmed and adrift among James Dean T-shirts on the convention floor. If Helen's face had launched a thousand ships, James Dean's had set in motion a cultural juggernaut in mid–twentieth century.

"It's very bad!" the Mexican said. "That Señor Dean in his silver car. He drives that road every night between sundown and sunrise. It's as though he is looking for something or someone."

Or as if he is a lost spirit, looking for a place to rest.

The article was in *Whisper* 1957 June 35 cents; Lou replaced the magazine in its plastic sleeve and returned it to the woman with the James Dean wristwatch who hovered closely as he handled the precious item. She wanted $35. He self-consciously picked up another sleeve.

JAMES DEAN RETURNS!
Read His Own Words From the Beyond.
The crash itself was nothing. I felt no shock. No hurt. I could see myself lying there, looking down on that other person who was Jimmy Dean and yet wasn't. . . . I watched with amazement and wonder, and the realization gradually sank over me—this was what we called "Death." . . . The other body that lay down there was only a shell. I, the real I who had inhabited it, was still alive. . . .

All stories were: True. STRANGE. Incredible. Weird and Factual. *JIMMY DEAN SPEAKS FROM THE GRAVE!!!*

Jimmy Dean's Alive!
Never in the history of movies has there been such a mass uproar as since the "death" of James Dean. Jimmy has served as an inspiration to millions of teenagers. Here, for the first time is THE TRUE STORY OF JIMMY DEAN.

$50,000 REWARD
Offered to find Jimmy Dean!

Dean had dictated several full-length autobiographies including *I, James Dean*, which boasted: *Here Is the*

Real Story of My Life—By James Dean as I Might Have Told It to Joe Archer.

Another magazine caught Lou's eye, a salacious story boasting a photo of Dean allegedly from a gay porno film he had made during the lean years. But the still was murky and he could make out only a nude boy in a tree with his hand on a hard-on. *"It is difficult to say who is attached to that mammoth, erect cock, but it sure looks like Dean, a giant in more ways than one . . . !"*

In banquet rooms collectors erected tables to display wares for sale, trade or exhibition. Dean dolls and buttons and neckties and tribute records, a zillion stills, press books, sheet music, rare books, posters, there was—entirely too much.

A red-bearded man set up a shellacked board displaying the highway patrol diagram of Dean's accident, replete with little toy cars, and began demonstrating the tragedy in miniature for all comers as if it was a shell game. Other fans enthusiastically swapped inquests for photos of the skid marks.

Lou found himself searching for a particular girl, trying to deal with what couldn't be anything more than the sort of juvenile crush normal people outgrew after high school. People don't fall in love at first sight, except in the movies. But he'd been in emotional suspension since the accident in Ohio. It was loneliness that drove his fantasy, and self-contempt—

"Ah! My patron!"

He turned to see Pollack parting the waves of shoulders on his way toward him, trademark beret unmistakable in the glazed and milling humanity. Today he wore a cape, clutching in one large hand a cane with a silver head of Anubis, the dog-headed god and guide of souls.

"Hello, Lysander." Lou recoiled slightly from alcohol fumes.

"I've been looking for you high and low," Pollack said. "Isn't this phenomenal? You'll find all these people friendly and eager to share their enthusiasm for 'Jimmy.' The problem is to get them to shut up." He leaned closer. "Want a good way to disentangle yourself from their effusions? Just ask whether their high priest Cleveland Carroll Devereux is in attendance, and if so, will they point him out? The Deanfan's face will cloud, and he will condense into a dew before your eyes."

"It works?"

Pollack looked kindly. "It's the depiction in his book of Deanfans, and the sagging udders of the fan club's sacred cows. You've got to love Cleveland—he went back to Dean's hometown and actually pissed on Jimmy's grave."

Lou was shocked. "You're kidding."

Pollack raised woolly brows. "Really, a perversely Deanlike gesture. Cleveland likes to think of these sheep kneeling in his urine. Plus, it's with pee the Eskimo inscribes his magic circle about his personal fishing hole. Beware the yellow ice, Lou! I do see a couple of highly-evolved types over there—" Pollack was leading him to a crowd that had gathered around a silver Porsche Spyder.

Not a real Spyder, but a kit built by a specialty outfit capitalizing on the Dean mystique; it was fiberglass rather than aluminum, but its owner had installed an authentic Porsche engine rather than the stock Volkswagen. There were oohs and aahs.

Terry Childes had his video camera on his shoulder. "I bet we're doing the same thing."

"Talking to fans," Sheena clarified.

"Whose car?" Lou asked.

"You haven't met Jonathan?" Terry introduced Lou

to a tall, tanned, young Frenchman inexplicably named Cottlee.

"They wanted one on display at the convention," Cottlee said modestly. "I thought I'd help them out."

Not just any young man, Terry explained. Jonathan Cottlee was founder and president of a French perfume company which he'd recently sold for 50 million dollars, remaining as president and guiding spirit. He was also interested in Dean—hence, the car.

"Nice," Lou said, admiring the craftsmanship.

"He's gonna let me use it in my documentary—" Terry began. Sheena whispered in his ear. Childes was inspired. "Hey, Lou. Do me a favor and get behind the wheel? I want to get a little tape on you, just some convention color. Sheena, do something with his hair."

She began to muss it into a Deanlike wave. Lou objected, but Cottlee was already offering his scuffed leather flight jacket. Lou was annoyed, self-conscious of the stares they were drawing. Pollack opened the racer's door and pressed him behind the wheel, saying judiciously, "He needs sunglasses."

"And a cigarette," someone from the gathering crowd added.

Lou felt he was being lowered into a casket. Sheena donated a smoke and stuck it in his lips while Terry lined up his shot.

"Look surly and angry," Terry directed. No problem.

"That'll do it," Childes finally said with satisfaction. Sheena was proffering paper and a pen as Lou stripped off his costume. "A waiver," she said. "Please sign, here."

Lou declined the opportunity to see the tape in the viewfinder. "Have you seen Cherie around?" he asked Sheena casually as she arranged waivers on a clipboard.

"Probably with Devereux," she said.

"Devereux's here?"

"Ah," eavesdropped Pollack. "Cleveland Devereux is here, but is not here. That's to say, his presence pervades this convocation of worms, but you won't find him among them. He is persona non grata here on the floor—but I believe we will find him holding court in the coffee shop. You'd like to meet?"

"Yeah."

"Catch you later," Terry said. Cottlee nodded and shook hands.

"Damn," Pollack said, leading Lou out the foyer and around to the hotel restaurant. "I've got to get that fucking Frenchman to my studio! He's got a Rolls in his garage next to a Silver Ghost Harley-Davidson. He lives in this palace in the Hills, and hangs out with his favorite rock bands. One sucker like that, and you're set for life—"

The booths were loaded with fans identifiable by their buttons and convention badges. At a far table, Lou saw her. Cherie was stunning and sexy in a black sequined blouse and black slacks which somehow weren't really her. He recognized Devereux from the book jacket, a handsome man in his early forties, long hair combed back to curl in tight ringlets over the collar.

Lou was already tongue-tied, and jealous.

Pollack interrupted their intense conversation. "Cleveland, I'd like you to meet—"

"You're Lou," the author said as he removed his dark glasses.

Lou was getting used to it.

"Cherie told me about you," Devereux said.

Lou avoided her eyes, concentrating on the others whom Pollack was introducing, first indicating three females.

"Ah, the Dean Widows! These three virgins are Amy and Sharon and . . . Vonda?"

Sharon, with her angry face and a ring through her lower lip, did not look like a virgin, but otherwise they were the same genus as Polmquist's group. Amy wore coveralls to hide her plumpness, and Vonda was a wallflower with thick glasses. Sharon was contemptuous of Pollack, but the other two were delighted by his attentions as he singled out a startled man with dark skin.

"And this pockmarked cadaver is Ruiz. He's from Texas—a bachelor coming up on fifty. He goes into debt every year over his Dean purchases, and fare for pilgrimages to California and Indiana. Let me guess—" Pollack peered over Ruiz's shoulder. "You recently bought a Dean autograph, and have brought photos because you're anxious about its provenance. You want to discuss its authenticity with Cleveland for his imprimatur—?"

"Ly, give us a break," Devereux said.

"Don't stand, we were leaving," Amy said cheerfully. Ruiz gathered his photos and got up obediently, the Dean Widows rustling out reluctantly behind him, fascinated with Lou.

"Sit," Devereux said unenthusiastically. "Are you enjoying DeanCon? Or does this all seem morbid?"

It was eerie stuff Lou had seen in the floor. There was a recorded message, *At Last the Voice of Jimmy,* on flexidisk. An afterlife of crime was described in *Suspicious Cops Nab Ghost* and *James Dean Killed Sal Mineo.* Other magazine stories rumored Dean not dead, but hideously disfigured and in hiding.

"It's a whole culture. I'm continually surprised."

"Lysander mentioned your thesis. It's interesting—your background as you approach this. Comparative religions."

"Lou would like to talk to you about your involvement with Dean," Pollack said.

Devereux ignored the artist. "I'd like to see some of the work you've done."

"I haven't exactly started yet—" Lou began.

Devereux nodded. "I see. It's 'in development.' Doesn't sound like there's any rush. But Cherie and I need to catch a little sack time right now. We've been up all night, do you mind?"

Perfunctory handshakes, and they left. Cherie had not once raised her eyes.

Pollack shrugged philosophically. "I should have prepared you. Cleve's territorial about his own Dean research. But there was no need to be rude."

"He's probably just wary," Lou said. "Maybe he's been burned before. What's Cherie to him?"

"Who knows?" Pollack said disinterestedly. "I'm sure he fucks 'em all."

Lou felt masochistic satisfaction as his face drained. His crush was crazy and stupid, and pain served him right. As they walked back to the convention floor with its massed memorabilia, he wanted to believe he'd recovered a part of himself. But all afternoon he felt like one more lost soul in an emotional fog. He wished he could peel Pollack off long enough to sort his feelings, but instead found them both going to dinner at a nearby bar—on Lou. Two shrimp plates.

Lou ordered beer, Pollack wine.

Pollack leaned over. "Did you notice how many of the faces we saw today seemed to be sort of . . . misshapen?"

Lou had noticed a strange disjointed effect; even Cherie had a little of it.

"Human oddities . . . especially Cleveland's disciples; I wish you'd seen more of them. Publication of his

book was like dragging a magnet through iron filings—
he's gathered all sorts of weirdos to whom he's John the
Baptist."

"You said he's still doing research. On what?"

"The inquest, for instance. He believes there was a
fix in at that little rural backwater with its alcoholic dis-
trict attorney and corrupt constabulary. Despite a pat-
ently illegal left-hand turn, the verdict was accidental
death. A biased proceeding in which poor Jimmy was
actually put on trial for getting a traffic ticket two hours
earlier, and driving a car which was the wrong color.
The DA several times suggested to the jury that Jimmy
wasn't wearing his prescription glasses, and the testi-
mony of the highway patrolmen was totally discounted.
Cleveland is making a case that the site of the crash
was carefully chosen—just over a county line, in fact,
to put the death in a certain jurisdiction."

"He's into the murder theory? It sounds like the
plot's expanding. It's not just the college kid now."

"The multiplicity of scenarios is in itself ominous.
Did you know all sorts of thefts followed Jimmy's
death? His body was even rolled en route to the hospital. His house was burgled, and burned down within a
year. His headstone's been stolen twice."

"His headstone? Why?" Lou raised a finger, ordering
another bottle.

"Probably for magical value, religious resonance.
Think like a magician! Hollywood is the symbol capital
of the world, and a hotbed of occultism since the twen-
ties. Maleficarum was the oldest practicing witch coven
in southern California, and Jimmy attended some
meetings."

"I read about it."

"I think Liv applied, but couldn't pass the physical. It
was an all-male group."

"You haven't asked her?"

Pollack laughed indulgently. "There are things you'll understand when you're my age—if you spend your life in this town. We're all like dinosaurs, species soon to be extinct. People like Liv and Tony and me. We share the past and we share memories, even fondness. But relationships become contingent on a tacit mutual agreement to deceive one another, and foster each other's illusions about the gilded past—Liv has built a sort of cottage industry around her cachet as 'Jimmy's friend.' "

"Who's Tony?"

Pollack sighed. "A police lieutenant, still obsessed with Jimmy's death. But his investigation is hopelessly biased—he has a personal ax to grind, I'm afraid. But he has his uses, keeps me posted about things like the theft of Sal's knife wound."

"You know a lot about occultism." The empty shrimp shells on Lou's plate were nauseating him.

"I'm trying to cut down. These days I merely invoke the occasional astral zombie."

"Zombie? Like voodoo?"

"How do you think I do my paintings? Why they're so lifelike?"

"Jimmy poses for you? Get out of town."

Pollack shrugged. "His etheric husk, anyway. They're hard to control, and dangerous." Then his face brightened. "Did you hear what you said? 'Jimmy,' you said! It's the first time. You're becoming an actual fan, Lou! Despite yourself." He clapped the younger man's shoulder.

Lou smiled, but looked pointedly at his watch. "It's late, and I probably should have stopped a few beers ago—"

"You know what you're missing, Lou? You really

ought to go to Fairmount, Jimmy's hometown. Sentimental journey—you've got money and you've got time. It would give you a feel."

"I'm kind of a stay-at-home," Lou said, "speaking of which, I better be going while I can still drive."

"It's the shank of the evening!" Pollack said incredulously. "You really don't have much of a life, do you? You need a small revolution against yourself. We'll wait in the bar a while, then hit the convention motel room circuit. It's de rigueur!"

Eleven o'clock found Lou weaving as he followed Pollack up and down the balcony stairs of the Hyatt. Lysander was having no luck finding anyone in his room; many fans were apparently still on the convention floor, but others glanced out their windows and declined to answer his knock—putting the artist in a foul mood. Lou was becoming more uncomfortable. "Eez very bad, Señor," he said.

"What?" Pollack asked.

"Let's drop it and head back."

Pollack swayed belligerently. "We'll fall in on Devereux's group and see what they're up to."

"I don't know," Lou said. "He wasn't too friendly."

"All the better," Pollack said. "He owes me big. I helped him on his book."

The painter pounded aggressively on a door on the ground floor.

When it opened, Cherie stood like a deer startled in headlights. "Lou," she said softly.

He liked hearing his name on her lips and went a little woozy, the four hours of nonstop drinking taking his stomach on a little dip. "You look better out of the sequins," he said. "They're not you."

Behind her, a macabre scene.

People were arranged on the floor around a cassette player. Lou recognized Terry and Sheena, and the red-bearded man with his portable accident. There was Ruiz, and the Dean Widows augmented by other females from the convention. A thin young man in a white shirt was sunk into the couch rolling a cigarette, tennis shoes on the coffee table; he had bad acne and stringy blond hair tied in a ponytail. The smell was marijuana.

Devereux sat in a chair smoking a long cigarette, not marijuana. All were listening to a tape which seemed to be a collection of weird noises and high-pitched shrieks.

Devereux glanced up, and Pollack dodged past Cherie. "Hello again, Cleveland. We thought we'd drop in while we were in the neighborhood. Anything to drink?" He headed for the makeshift bar. "Lou, have you met Bill Bario?"

The kid on a sofa strewn with Dean memorabilia nodded, drooping cigarette in clenched teeth.

Pollack indicated the man with the toy cars. "Otto Green, with his movable tragedy . . . he has an annual Zen car rally retracing Jimmy's final drive."

Green smiled.

"Make yourself at home," Devereux said ironically, turning off the tape.

"That tape," Pollack said over his shoulder as he mixed his drink. "Cleve, why don't you tell Lou the story?"

"Let's not."

"I insist," Pollack said.

"All right," Devereux said patiently. "Once I drove alone out to Park Cemetery, where Jimmy's buried."

Pollack chimed in, "I told Lou he's got to go to Fairmount. Lou's rich. Not as rich as Cottlee, but rich enough."

Sharon passed a joint to Cherie, who accepted it.

"I found the little road to the grave, and killed the lights," Devereux continued. "It was freezing cold. Even the stars were sharp as razors. I got out and stood for a while on the grave. On an impulse, I placed my little Sony on the stone and waited for something to happen."

"What was going through your mind?" Pollack prompted.

Devereux shrugged ingenuously. "I thought of how he had transformed my life. Those few seconds at that intersection in far-off California—if they hadn't happened, there wouldn't have been a book."

"Or a Cleveland Devereux?" Pollack asked. "So you pissed on his grave."

Eez very bad, Lou thought to himself.

Devereux smiled. "It was a personal sort of communion. It immediately established me in a unique complex relationship to Jimmy."

"Cleveland has an irreverent streak," Pollack said to Lou. "He thinks that's what separates him from other fans. Makes him superior."

"I am superior," Devereux said.

Cherie proffered the joint to Lou; he hadn't had the stuff in years and was in no shape for it now, but didn't feel capable of prissy disapproval. *You need a small revolution against yourself.*

"Would you like something to drink?" she asked hesitantly, noting his condition.

"A beer? If it wouldn't be much trouble," he answered, following.

"Jesus, not beer," Bario said without looking up. "Why not milk?"

"I'm sorry," Cherie said self-consciously. "There isn't any."

"Live a little," Pollack said. "Give him a Scotch. No—what did we used to call that drink?"

"A 'Highway 466,' " Bario said. "Because one drink, and you're smashed."

Pollack slapped his thigh and launched into a monologue about the liver.

Cherie placed the drink in his hand. "I put a lot of water in it," she said apologetically.

Lou was feeling emboldened, even a little of Pollack's belligerence. He wasn't exactly himself, and it felt good. "So. How did you and Cleveland get together?"

"I read his book," she said, "and I wrote him. I'd never done anything like that before. He answered me, and then I came up and visited."

"He's pretty nice, huh?" There was a trace of sarcasm.

"Lou—" Pollack interrupted. "You wanna buy some Reata plaster from Ruiz? Yeah—Ruiz here's from Texas. He goes down and fills bags with plaster from the Reata—the crumbling set of *Giant*. Comes here and tries to sell it to reimburse his airfare."

There was laughter, Ruiz's pocked face flushing darkly; Pollack was aleady off on a tangent.

Lou looked back to Cherie. "Are Terry and Sheena part of your 'group'?"

She was tense. "Terry? Sheena? They kinda glommed onto us at a convention last year."

Pollack was loudly needling Terry, who apparently didn't know he was being teased. "What's so important about finding the fucking car?"

Childes's face was slack, then annoyed. "What's so important about the fucking Shroud of fucking Turin? This is the most famous car in history! This is *the* most important car. Think of the fucking Holy Grail. I mean, you look at a trans axle, or pinion arm, and to most people it could have come out of a washing machine. But a recognizable car with steering wheel and tires and bloodstains on the seat . . . and *an engine* . . . You know what I mean. The mystique. It's heavy."

Lou leaned closer to Cherie. "So. Do you work? Go to college?"

"I'm on disability," she said, embarrassed. "I had some problems on my last job."

Lou saw the unmade hotel bed covered with posters and souvenirs. "You told me at the cemetery that Jimmy was about searching. Sensitivity, and creativity. Good things. Is Cleveland all those things?"

She hesitated. "He's hard to get to know. He doesn't trust a lot of people."

"I can tell. Do you mind if I sit down?" There was an uprush of shrimp from his assaulted stomach, and his slide to the floor was like the descent of an elevator.

She joined him.

He said, "Do you ever wonder whether you've found a sort of father figure in him? I mean, he's a lot older than us. I mean, you."

"Yeah," she said slowly. "Then I feel guilty, like I'm using him. Why would somebody like him need me?"

"Well, for one thing you're really very beautiful. You're young. Sometimes when a man reaches a certain age he has a crisis about getting older."

She was defensive. "He's a friend to me. He tells me stuff like, 'You talk about yourself a lot, other people aren't gonna take to that so easy.' I can talk to him about things other people would just blow off—he worries about me." Then, "Look. If you're not into Jimmy— If you're here just for . . ." She stammered.

"Academic purposes?"

"Sure. Well, people are going to want to know where

you're coming from. To somebody not into it, this could all be pretty laughable. Nobody wants to get ridiculed. That's why he was unfriendly."

He saw himself taking a cigarette from the pack in her hand, probably the second one he'd smoked in his life. He put it in his lips backwards, and she turned the filter around. He nodded thanks.

"You know, I thought about what you said at the cemetery, about feeling. Maybe it's the word 'fan' I don't like. But I watched *Rebel Without a Cause* again, and I think I experienced it."

"What do you mean?"

He wondered how manipulative he was being. "Well, I tried to turn my mind off, and he sort of got through to me."

"What way?" she said suspiciously.

"Well, it was all about loneliness. Isolation. I felt like he was inside me, and when it was over I felt like I lost a friend. Somebody who understood. Do you know what I mean?" She nodded, and he felt himself homing in. "Cherie—"

"Ly says you're rich," Devereux interrupted from across the room. Lou realized everyone was looking at him, and the best he could do was smile stupidly.

"He bought a painting," Pollack said proudly. "But he won't go to Fairmount. He needs a little revolution against himself."

The words were coming slowly across the room, and Lou wondered where the joint between his fingers had come from this time.

"Why won't you go to Fairmount?" Bario said with annoyance.

Lou bristled, besieged and defensive. "How did that end?" he heard himself slurring to Devereux. "Your story. That night at Dean's grave?"

"Did I see a ghost?" Devereux laughed, but it was not unfriendly. "No. But the tape really sounds weird."

"Sugar," Pollack said to Cherie, "get Lou a fresh one, drinkwise. I feel his approaching rite of passage."

Devereux was fiddling earnestly with the tape player; the atmosphere in the room had relaxed too much.

"Let's shut off the lights," Terry said; Sheena rose obediently.

The tape started and there was that howling sound with a sharp whistle at its edges. Lou shivered, wondering if the next drink would warm him. He had forgot what he and Cherie had been talking about. "This is good shit," was all he could say.

Her face looked worried. There was vague laughter from the Dean Widows, but it sounded drowned. He decided to close his eyes a little.

7

Sunday, September 11, 1995
Over St. Louis, Missouri

It was a terribly confused dream, Ernie Hockman hammering the dents out of Dean's wrecked Spyder as Cherie looked on, Sal Mineo's knife wound on a silver chain around her neck. Lou must have shouted in horror—

And woke everyone on the red-eye flight. Passengers stared as the blanket slipped off his lap. Blanket? His mouth was full of sour shrimp, and he swallowed it down, twisting to look out the window, where he saw only night and a sloped wing. Jetliner? He was speechless and blinking, disoriented.

The stewardess startled him solicitously. "Are you all right? We're over Missouri, we'll be setting down in Indianapolis shortly. Your friends wanted me to assure you the doctor will be waiting."

"The doctor?" His head swam and pounded. He was in the first-class section.

"The transplant is a 'go,'" she continued happily, "and there'll be a wheelchair at the airport."

"Why? How'd I get here?" he asked.

"Your father and your friends brought you on a wheelchair. Don't be afraid, they warned me you might be confused when your medication wore off. There's a note pinned to your shirt."

The envelope was fastened with a Dean convention button, the enclosed note in Pollack's distinctive calligraphy.

Lou—
Welcome to Indiana. I'm going to have a rental car waiting. I've got your Visa. A small revolution against yourself

—Ly

P.S. I told the stew you were going to see an eminent cardiologist. Friendly skies!

He could hear Pollack laughing. And Devereux. Cherie?

"Would you like a beverage? I'd offer you dinner, but your father said you aren't supposed to eat anything the next twenty-four hours because of the surgery."

Lou was nauseated. "Nothing, thanks. Maybe water."

He closed his eyes and was overwhelmed by hangover, picturing himself being wheeled comatose up the ramp. *Cherie—did she try to stop them?* He couldn't believe what was happening.

Deplaning at Indianapolis, he made his angry way to a coffee shop to sit miserably in a booth watching jets take off. He found a return ticket inside his shirt—but it was for tomorrow afternoon. Maybe the artist actually thought he was doing him a favor. Maybe Pollack was just drunk.

A hand on his shoulder roused him, his head snapping.

Cherie stood there disheveled and guilty. She said softly, "I want you to know, I didn't have anything to do with that deal last night, putting you on that plane. I tried to. I tried to—"

"How did you get here?" he asked wonderingly.

"I was mad, I made them let me go. But you were in first class, and then I thought I lost you when we landed and I couldn't find—" Her sleepless eyes filled with tears.

"Sit down." He patted the seat next to him and took a deep breath before saying hoarsely, "I'm trying to get my bearings."

"You're not mad at me? They used your card to buy my ticket."

He shook his head. "It's not your fault."

She looked terrible, hands trembling as they lighted a cigarette.

He said, "I don't think anybody ever played a joke on me before."

"You sound flattered."

He knew he was going to act angry, but maybe Pollack had been doing for him what he could not do for himself. He had to admit that during the previous week he had fantasized about being alone with her. "Look," he said. "You may not believe it, but I do remember some of the things I said last night. Early this morning, whatever. And I was out of line. It was just the combination of—"

" 'Eez very bad,' " she smiled.

"What?"

"That's what you kept mumbling." She stopped him. "Don't apologize. You were sweet, I'm glad you talked to me. The question is, what are we gonna do now?"

He rubbed his aching temples. "Order some coffee? You don't look like you got any sleep on the plane."

"I was too worried about what you'd do when you woke up."

"I was passed out. I've checked my wallet, I don't have money for a room. Where you could sleep, I mean. We can see if we can get the return flight moved up." But he realized he really didn't want to do that.

She was looking at the road map on the wall.

"It's about sixty miles away," he said.

She nodded. "I've been there, but not for two years."

He fumbled in his pockets for the note. "According to Ly, I've got a rental car around here, somewhere." They walked to the Hertz booth on legs a little steadier for the caffeine.

"Are we going?" she asked. "This is wild."

"Maybe it's my time to be a wild guy. Maybe Pollack was right."

It was drizzling across the parking lot as they found the red Dodge Colt. Her enthusiasm subsided, and he wondered if it was more remorse. She couldn't know that despite the time change exacerbating the hangover, he was almost ebullient as they got on the highway north. The whole adventure was surreal.

Lowering gray clouds made the fields of corn shiver. "So this is where Dean grew up," he said to break the silence.

She nodded. "From the time he was nine, until he was eighteen. Then he went to his father in California. He hadn't been around his dad for years. His dad tried to make up for it by taking him bowling."

"It didn't work out?"

"They lived in this little apartment by the VA Hospital, and his dad had remarried. The stepmom was a bitch. Jimmy wanted to join the theater arts program at

UCLA, but his dad bribed him with a '39 Chevy to take prelaw at Santa Monica City. Jimmy even pledged a fraternity but it didn't last. The frats thought he was weird."

"How weird?"

"Like, he'd make these Salvador Dalí sketches of bloodshot eyeballs floating in the air. Or matadors with huge dicks."

Something was bothering her. Lou asked, "Was Cleveland mad you got on the plane?"

She flinched. "It was a rough conversation. It bothers me sometimes, he gets so cosmic about Jimmy. It's sort of impersonal, like he loses sight of the tragedy and the human being."

Lou had to ask. "Do you have a relationship with him? I mean, romantically."

"Jimmy?"

"Cleveland."

"He's protective of me," she said, slumping tiredly. "The love-child thing."

"What 'love-child thing'?"

She pressed the dash lighter curiously and said, "I used to see a therapist, but then Cleveland started to put this auric shield around me, to help me out. It's like a barrier to lower vibrations. See, I'm adopted. My step-parents never told me about where I came from, but Cleveland got involved in all that. Like, why was I so drawn to Jimmy? Why did I feel like I knew him, and that he knew me, the first time I saw him in a film? Something drawing me karmically to all this."

"And?"

"He regressed me. Hypnotically. Sure, he's studied that. To remember before I was born. See, Cleve believes Jimmy had a daughter by Pier Angeli. It was a big secret. He thinks Pier had a kid and gave her up."

He looked at her in shock. Dean's was an androgynous sort of beauty, and Cherie could certainly be considered a waiflike version. "When were you born?"

"Nineteen seventy-two. But it wasn't me." She laughed.

"I was going to say, you don't look forty."

"My real mom was a druggie, and Cleveland thinks there's a good chance she was Jimmy's daughter."

Bizarre, yet a tumbler falling into place. But more likely her years of obsession and unconscious imitation had subtly transformed and remolded her features in the icon's image. "And what do you believe?"

She laughed with self-deprecation, the cigarette jaunty. "I guess I wanna believe it. Sure, I'd like to think that Jimmy's inside me. You know, I even had a chopped Harley for a while? Imagine me, a biker? It would sure explain a lot of things. Why I relate to him. Why I feel like he fills in a part of me that's missing."

Lou said cautiously, "I'm sure a lot of fans know that feeling."

She gazed. "It's like a dream. But Cleveland's accessing documents all the time, and pulling it together. He probably didn't want me to tell you. He's protective, like I said. He thinks I might not be safe."

"From whom?"

"Just . . . people who might want to use me. Or hurt me."

"Is everybody unsafe except him?"

When she didn't answer, he thought he'd gone too far. "What are these stepparents of yours like?"

"Generic Christians," she said, closing her eyes and stretching. "I just wish I knew them. I've just met you and I feel like I know you, and I spent sixteen years with them and I don't know anything. I guess I put them through hell, I've done some flaky things."

Like cutting your wrists, Lou thought but didn't say. "Have you ever tried therapy? For the bad feelings?"

"Cleve despises doctors."

That was a conversation-stopper. "You've been to Fairmount before?" he asked more brightly.

"Once, at Museum Days. Fans come from all over and there's a parade. At night there's little ceremonies at the grave, séances, incense, and stuff—it drives the hicks nuts. Morrissey shot a music video here after he left the Smiths. Bob Dylan came by after a concert at about three in the morning and got all the Winslows out of bed so they could go to the cemetery."

Not only was there a cynical edge to her voice, but she was afraid of something.

"Look," she said to evade him, "I think I've got to close my eyes for a little bit. I'm so wasted I can't see straight."

"Yeah," he said. "Get some sleep, we're both drained."

She turned away and closed her eyes, and was almost immediately asleep, as if she had been unplugged.

He turned off onto a country lane through undulating farmland. When he saw the sign he thought of waking her, but let her rest.

Fairmount, Indiana—Home of James Dean

The sun was lowering as he drove up Main Street of a bucolic little town, trees brilliant fall colors. He recognized landmarks of Dean's boyhood from photos in the biographies. At the end of Main he ran into the museum, really just a converted residential house. It looked closed, but it wouldn't hurt to ask the man hoeing out front.

He got out quietly so as not to wake the sleeping girl,

wishing he had a sweater. The old guy in overalls chopped industriously around flowers, his eyes clear and alert. He was energetic for a heavy man.

"Museum closed?" Lou asked.

The oldster paused thoughtfully, Lou wondering why it was such a hard question. Arm resting atop the implement handle, the man finally replied crisply, "You from out of town?"

"Out of state," Lou said, suddenly not caring if he saw the museum, figuring California was anathema to locals. He was in Quaker country.

But the man cocked his head. "Guess it wouldn't hurt to open 'er up for you," he said reluctantly. "Come on, then. You probably wanna see the Dean Room."

"Not if I'm inconveniencing you."

"Fine," the man said testily. "I'll take you inside. Fairmount Museum. You a Deaner?"

"A what?"

"We call 'em 'Deaners.' Jimmy Dean."

Lou said defensively, "I've heard about the Dean Room, but don't let me put you out—"

"She's already open," the man said stepping aside.

In the weak moribund light was a clutter of antique bottles, and blue telephone insulators the shade of a fly's stomach. There were dusty sepia photos, and ancient farm implements, and harness. There was also the James Dean Room.

Lou did not want to appear too eager, slighting all the rest of the history of a town obviously proud of its past. He respectfully worked his way to the only room the out-of-towners really came to see.

Not a local favorite, Lou recalled from Devereaux's book, the room devoted to Dean was a grudging concession from townsfolk who had lopped the bronze head off their only monument to their most famous son back in '57.

He chilled inexplicably on the threshold, and crossed his arms. The Dean Room alone was unheated, the temp about ten degrees lower. But it had allure. He resisted an impulse to go out and wake Cherie.

He stepped in, suddenly sad at all the haunted bits of memorabilia from a childhood and adolescence. It hit him for the first time: more than a symbol had died on that dusky California highway forty years ago. A boy was killed.

There were Jimmy's bongos and boots, racing trophies and high school letterman sweaters. Lou saw a matador's cape amidst homely bric-a-brac from all over the world. Most pathetic was Jimmy's eighth-grade biology science project, a murky soil sample. Eeriness spread like frost over him, hundreds of pictures sucking him backward to a faded photo of a gawky hayseed and his slatternly wife holding a smiling baby on the shoulder of some rural road.

"That's his mom," a gruff voice said.

Lou whirled to see the man with the hoe leaning in the door. "You scared me," he said as he caught his breath.

"I knowed Jimmy," the man nodded as he approached. "He was purty defensive where she was concerned. His mom. He said, 'She wasn't a slut. I am pissed at her for dying, and pissed at him for leaving me here. She woulda have taken care of me. She woulda protected me.' "

"Protected him? From who?"

The man shrugged as he checked dust on a display case. "Maybe DeWeerd. Maybe his dad. Some say Jimmy Dean made a deal with the Devil. But you know what I think? I think it was Ol' Winton—that was Jimmy's dad—made the deal. Think about it."

"What do you mean 'a deal with the Devil'?"

"Some say he wasn' none too happy havin' to marry little Mildred, who he got in the family way. Some'd say he traded off his firstborn male child, sent him back here to DeWeerd as soon's Mildred's out of the way."

"I'm not following you."

"Just as well, but there's some bad feelings around the family for a while. 'Cause the insurance—Jimmy's dad come into a lot of money from Jimmy's policy. But it was Marcus and Ortense that raised the boy. Maybe Winton's conscience come to bother him, 'cause those last few years he made a deal with Curtis Company to license Jimmy up, and he split that money up pretty square with the rest."

Lou had read that Curtis had licensed Dean's image, slapping injunctions on unauthorized products.

"Clothes, calendars. All sorts of crap. Warner Brothers tried to sue to stop 'em, but the family won out. Ol' Winton died a few years back and we got some of the stuff he had all those years. Alzheimer's, he had."

Lou saw pictures of a funeral with the members of Jimmy's old high school basketball team hefting a polished casket down the steps of Friends Church in a drizzle. There were framed newspapers headlining the death of a local boy in California.

"I'll let you go," Lou said suddenly. "I appreciate you opening up. It was interesting, and you have a nice little town."

"We think so," the man said briskly, bustling along after Lou as he stepped out into chill air to find the sun had set, and Cherie still asleep.

"You goin' to the cemetery?" the man asked as he resumed hoeing. "That's usually the next question—

'Where's the cemetery? I wanna see Jimmy Dean.'
Well, it's right on up this road about three-quarters mile.
You don't look like you're into that funny stuff."

"What 'stuff'?"

"Killin' chickens and such at the grave. Sacrificin'."

"Sacrificing chickens?" Lou said with an uncomfortable laugh.

The man pushed his hat up and mopped his face with
a red kerchief. "Sure. Killin' a human being is the most
powerful medicine, but killin' an animal's purty strong,
too. S'what they say."

Loud did not ask what the hell the old guy was talking about, but knew his own exhausted mind was not
functioning at its optimum. He chalked it up to jet lag,
but was uneasy as he quietly opened the car door.
"You've been a help. I appreciate it."

"Traster," the man said. "Bing Traster. Don't mention
it. You're on the ol' Jonesboro Pike, you just keep going till you see cem'tery on your left."

Lou started the engine, then found himself heading
up the road as much not to offend the old man as anything else.

There was the cemetery, white stones in a gray mist
that carried drizzle to the Colt's windshield as it turned
up the gravel drive. He thought of Devereux's visit to
this same spot.

"Hm?" Cherie said in alarm as she startled awake,
raising her tousled head. She saw over the dashboard
and her eyes went wide. "Where are we?"

"I stopped at the museum," Lou said as they drove
slowly over ruts. "I didn't want to—"

"We're at the cemetery," she said, face going white.

He stopped the car. "I thought you'd like the surprise,
I was sure you'd want to visit—"

She shook her head. "I don't like going to his grave. It's too sad for me."

He put on the emergency brake and turned in the seat. "I had no idea. Do I need to take you back?"

She looked around at darkness and headstones. "But you want to see it."

"I think I do. I mean, I've come all this way."

She seemed to calm, but fumbled in her purse for a pill. "Then you should. I understand. But I'll wait in the car."

"You've got a headache?"

"It's Prozac. We're already here. But don't be too long, okay? It's up there, the one with a lots of flowers."

"How do you know?"

"Pictures."

In the wash of his headlights he saw the rose-colored stone immediately atop a small hill, covered with tributes.

"Okay, I'll just be a minute." He stepped out and took a breath in the dark. He walked to the homely marker.

JAMES B. DEAN
1931–1955

He stood there with eyes aching from cold, his breath white before his face. He could not help but be moved. Here lay the boy he had watched on TV a few nights ago. This was what even genius came to. Because even Jimmy's detractors grudgingly admitted that was what he was.

Lou walked around the other side. The skin of his face tightened as he realized this grave was open.

The sound of rushing surf in his ears was more than

wind. The hole was blasphemous, an obscene desecration among the prim tombstones and well-tended plots. There was something almost beatific about Lou's shock as a Bible verse crossed his mind. *"He is not here but is risen."*

Sudden movement from behind the cypresses made him start. From the corner of his eye he saw flitting shadows in the hedges. He knew instinctively he was the object of their interest, and made no move. Maybe it was shock that froze him.

He thought of the girl in the car. Then he heard a noise in dead leaves. A dark shape hit him in a body-block and he felt his foot give at the lip of the hole. He was tumbling into the grave, fingers clutching black soil as clods rained down.

He hit the bottom of the concrete vault with a dull thud, the impact softened by a bed of collapsed earth. It was a moment of pure terror and fear of being buried alive. His groping fingers felt only tendrils of dank roots overhead. He heard himself yelling, aware of scraping footsteps around the hole. Flashlights blinded him; whoever had violated the grave was after him. All he could think was that he'd stumbled on their grisly work.

Someone said gruffly, "Give me your hand!"

The grave-fear was worse than the faceless form overhead. Lou seized the extended hand, his arm nearly wrenched from the socket by steel fingers. No sooner was he above ground and panting than a knee to his legs crumpled him facedown in the gravel. He felt another knee in his back, and brusque voices as handcuffs were snapped expertly around his pinioned wrists.

Not until he was flopped onto his back did he see law enforcement uniforms, black leather holsters and trooper hats.

"What are you doing?" a voice demanded.

Lou had the anger of fear. "What are you—"

"Shut up," an imperious growl cut him off; there was the squawking of police radio, and the transmitting of the Dodge's license number as flashlights played on the ground.

Lou panted white frightened breaths.

"What are you doing here?" a kneeling man in plainsclothes demanded; Lou couldn't see the face.

"Nothing. I found it this way." He felt strange hands extracting the billfold from his pocket.

"You're from California? Do you know anyone here?"

"The old man gave me directions," Lou rasped. "He told me it would be all right. If you'll let me explain."

"What old man?"

"In town," Lou said, a sudden grateful recollection. "Traster. He had a funny first name. Movie star name."

"Bing Traster?" an older officer asked overhead, laughed. Lou nodded desperately, losing circulation in his arms, the breaths above him ghostly huffs.

"Bing Traster's only been dead around thirty years," the officer said contemptuously. He flashed his light on a nearby headstone, and Lou saw the name.

Traster.

He didn't argue after that.

8

Thursday, April 8, 1955
Hollywood, 10:42 A.M.

The Warner Brothers cast and crew at Griffith Observatory saw the red flash over the Sierra Nevada Mountains just before dawn. It was apocalyptic: the detonation of an atomic bomb at a Nevada test range hundreds of miles away. The mood on the set was strangely subdued as technicians adjusted tracking dollies before the bronze planetarium doors, enlivened only by Jim Backus doing Mr. Magoo. Natalie Wood, in a canvas chair, listened raptly to Nicholas Ray. A dialogue director scampered after pages of script fluttering across the lawn.

From the roof of the planetarium James Dean gazed like a prince upon Hollywood spread at his feet beneath pollutant haze. Not only was his agent negotiating a new contract which would include nine films over six years for $900,000, but George Stevens had granted him the coveted role of Jett Rink.

Jimmy saw the palm trees of Hollywood Cemetery on distant Santa Monica Boulevard, and his hand closed over the mezuzah without which he never appeared before a camera. It made him think of Syd Kirkland.

They had met five years ago when Syd was living in the Sunset Plaza apartment of Rogers Brackett, an influential radio director fifteen years their senior. It was Brackett who had renamed Maurice Fleischmann "Syd Kirkland." By any name, Brackett's protégé was a gifted young sculptor who knew Brahms from Berlioz, Sartre from Camus. He actually read the books which were always under his arm, and underscored them in pencil—or blood obtained by switchblade if no pencil was handy.

Kirkland had the intense fragile face of a decadent poet, and wore leather even on the casting calls he roared up to astride his motorcycle. He obediently went to auditions at Rogers's insistence even though acting wasn't his thing.

Rogers had come serendipitously into Jimmy's own life right after Jimmy was ejected from the college Greek house due to a fistfight. Seeing Jimmy's hunger and ambition, Rogers got him a job ushering at CBS. Evenings Brackett introduced "Rack" Dean of Indiana to fine arts. Jimmy suddenly found himself a Hollywood insider with entrée into the movie-money milieu of pool parties, screenings, and dinners at the Mocambo. To broaden Dean's horizons they also attended some meetings of the exclusive witch coven called Maleficarum, which met on a rotational basis at various mansions in Bel Air and the Hollywood Hills. Many "names" were always present. The cadaverous Brackett was well-connected in the closet network of Hollywood.

The sabbats, or black masses, seemed mostly an excuse for oily, naked males to dance among flickering candles. Brackett's nude body was once painted silver from the waist up and black below. His upthrust excitement was evident as he lifted a chalice and intoned, "I am the Chariot. I bear the Holy Grail, in the center of which is radiant blood, symbolizing the presence of Light in Darkness."

Jimmy didn't like the sacrifice part—a cock slaughtered at the height of the ceremony to increase the supply of force in the magic circle. "A living creature's a storehouse of energy," talent agent Henry Willson explained avidly, "and when it's killed the energy's liberated. The animal should be young so that its supply of force has been dissipated as little as possible."

It was kicks, giggles. And Jimmy was making important contacts at mere cost of the odd blow-job.

Syd and Jimmy insulated themselves from self-contempt by forming a coalition of ridicule against Brackett and friends, calling them "the vampires." They were two boys whistling in the haunted house which was the fairy demimonde of Hollywood. It pissed Rogers off when he came across his two protégés laughing uncontrollably.

Dean enjoyed walking a tightrope of feigned disinterest to maintain the older man's growing fixation. An ugly triangle could have shaped up at Sunset Plaza as Brackett's attentions turned from the Semitic Kirkland to blond Jimmy. Fortunately, Syd was becoming bored with it all, drinking a lot and talking about moving out.

Syd and Jimmy became lovers one night when they were parked high in the Hills drinking wine. Kirkland asked in his thick Brooklynese, which Rogers's elocution coaches had failed to correct, "Have you ever made love with a man? I don't mean kiss, I don't mean let somebody blow you. I mean, really made love?"

It hurt like hell. Jimmy was ashamed and humiliated. Syd confessed a sadistic streak, and admitted it hadn't needed to be as rough as he'd made it. Syd told him he hadn't enjoyed inflicting the pain but knew Jimmy craved it. He quoted Lawrence of Arabia's *Seven Pillars of Wisdom* with its sensual description of his beating by Circassian riding whip at Deraa. "The blows hurt more horribly than I had *dreamed of....*"

Syd's last word about sex was, "Now that's over, we can move on." A coffee-logged night followed as they bared souls, comparing absent mothers and unapproachable fathers. Syd had analyzed his own personality clear back to the Hasidic rabbi—a friend of the family—who'd initiated him into sodomy at fourteen.

And they talked for hours about death.

Alcohol contributed to the subsequent waning of Syd's physical passion, but Jimmy's own fascination was only beginning. Jimmy began to look more like his friend. They spent almost all their time together as Kirkland tried to help him with his dyslexic reading, and even teach him a few simple tunes on the piano. They read Kafka's *Metamorphosis*, Mann's *Death in Venice*, and tackled Proust until Jimmy's attention deficit capsized the effort. After Syd introduced him to Charlie Parker and Béla Bartók, they ceremonially burned Jimmy's own record collection.

But it was a passion for bullfighting that really drew them together. They stuck toothpicks in French rolls for horns and practiced imaginary kills. The boy from the Bronx had extorted Mexico bullfight lessons from Rogers early in the relationship. "Studied *under* some of the greatest," Brackett would say lasciviously, "and came back with the *butterflies of love*," his expression for crabs.

Syd gave Jimmy an authentic bloodied matador's cape—his most prized possession. He watched bemused as Jimmy adopted his own expressions such as "*mano a mano*." When Syd tore from a library book a Picasso etching of a girl threatened by the Minotaur, Jimmy had to find the same book at another library and tear out his own.

"The bull represents the uncontrollable forces," Syd explained, "and the bullfight is man's struggle with his own animality." Jimmy was fascinated as Syd told him about ancient Mithraic and Dionysian bull sacrifices, and began to retell the same stories at cocktail parties.

One night following a black mass at the mansion of Willson, a powerful man numbering many secret homosexuals among his clientele, Jimmy and Syd sneaked off to a bedroom in search of hilarious and exotic erotica like they'd found in Clifton Webb's sadomasochistic boudoir.

Outside the French windows, young boys whom Jimmy doubted were even fourteen splashed in the Olympic-size pool. Many were Hispanic, recruited from East L.A. with promise of a party, alcohol, or even food. The more hip insisted on cash.

Syd said, "I just remembered something." He handed Jimmy a newspaper folded to fit in the pocket of his Levi's, its headline screaming: MOVIE IDOL JAMES DEAN KILLED IN BULLFIGHT.

Jimmy laughed, but was moved. "I like it. A lot."

"I thought you would." Kirkland smiled, taking a drink from the bottle in his scuffed flight jacket; it was a point of pride that he always brought his own liquor. "I got it in Tijuana."

Jimmy resumed ferreting through Willson's record collection in search of jazz, but noticed Kirkland studying a painting of Valentino in a bullfighter's suit of lights above the mantle. Syd was transfixed by Rudy's flared nostrils and eyes seductive with mascara.

"He's in costume for *Blood and Sand*," Kirkland said. Beneath the portrait was a glass ball. Syd shook the reliquary and black lint drifted around. "Pubic hairs," he said darkly.

"You're kidding?" Jimmy said.

Kirkland indicated the portrait with his bottle. "Pubic hairs from Valentino, the first star. When he died they lined up all around the block to see him. It was stupid, he croaked in a hospital bed. Peritonitis . . . not very glamorous. Now he's a joke."

"Not to these old fairies," Jimmy said.

Syd's intense eyes were not laughing. "He died all wrong. It was bad timing. Miscalculation."

Jimmy looked at him quizzically, but another voice intruded.

"I was wondering where you fellows were." Brackett materialized in the doorway where he had been eavesdropping, began unbuttoning his plaid vest after placing his cigarette in an ashtray near the bed. "I'm going to take a dip."

Kirkland said, "We were just looking for the coffins where they all sleep."

"What?" Brackett asked.

Kirkland continued, "I was just saying, they didn't know how to handle talent in Valentino's day. Did they?"

Brackett stripped, Jimmy glimpsing bony malarial legs and looking away.

"You have to use a different touch with genius," Rogers replied amiably. "It was hardly fair to Rudy. He could have been brought along more gradually."

"I'm talking about the way he died," Syd said, taking another drink.

"So was I," Bracket answered with sardonic eyes.

"Well," Kirkland said, "I'm sure we've profited from those mistakes."

Brackett's smile was tolerant. "Sydney, you've really got to slow down on the booze. Jimmy, can't you talk some sense to him? His complexion's turning gray, and there's bloat around his tummy."

Kirkland stalked out. Jimmy quickly apologized before catching up with him in the hall. "What was that about?" Jimmy asked as they entered the sunken den filled with hungry faces of other young actors.

It was usually at the shoes that poverty showed. Young men posed and lounged, tried to scintillate smiles and assume photogenic postures. The Latin types were most popular this year, the blond angelic waif second in demand. Jimmy recognized movie stars in Willson's stable, but was good at concealing Hoosier awe. Hadn't Ty Power held his chin to say, "You know, you really are a beautiful boy"?

"It's no accident we're here," Kirkland said fiercely, indicating the boys floating like fish in an aquarium. "Or them. It's not just a bunch of aging fairies surrounding themselves with fresh meat."

Jimmy moved aside for Rock Hudson's passage to the wet bar.

"And we're just like them," Syd hissed as he finished the bottle.

"I know," Jimmy said with sophistication.

Syd became angrier. "No, you don't know."

For months they had reinforced one another's pretense that they were themselves the predators and not the preyed upon, but it was wearing thin for Kirkland.

He shook his head at the 'names' circulating among the boys, diners selecting their lobster from a writhing tank. Outside the window Brackett was poised on the diving board, all sunken shoulders and knobby knees.

"Let's blow this pop-stand," Kirkland said, dropping his bottle on the floor.

"Rogers'll be pissed," Jimmy cautioned.

"Fuck him," Kirkland said, leading the way out through the lanai to the Harley parked at the curb.

Jimmy's hands were casual around the other boy's hips as they roared off toward Santa Monica. When Jimmy asked why they were taking such a weird route, Syd replied that it was to lose anyone who might be following them.

They parked on the strand and rode the carousel until they had to lie on the sand from nausea. Jimmy obediently took the linty amphetamines Syd offered.

"You know me better than anybody," Jimmy said later as they walked on the moon-glistening beach. "Did you know that?"

Syd nodded. "I don't want the responsibility. Come on. I wanna go to my studio."

Brackett had leased a little studio apartment for Kirkland to work on his sculpting, because Rogers couldn't stand the smell of wet clay. Upon arrival, Jimmy put a Billie Holiday record on the hi-fi but scratched it. Syd blew up and snatched the disk off the turntable, holding it carefully by the edges. His anger was all out of proportion.

Jimmy said cautiously, "You know there's something to what Rogers said. Like, you're drinking so much. Since you two got back from New York."

"I've seen and heard too much," Syd said. "I saw too much at the Apple."

"New York?"

"At Alec Wilder's." Wilder was a close theater friend of Brackett's; Rogers stayed with Alec when he went to the east coast.

Jimmy had no idea what he was talking about. "What'd you see and hear?"

Syd didn't respond, and Jimmy began playing mumblety-peg with a switchblade on the hardwood floor.

Kirkland's black eyes were feverish. He stood and ripped the shroud off a large sculpture he was working on.

Jimmy recognized Brackett's head, but Syd had done evil things to the face.

Syd was manic across the room. "I got a warning from Rudy in that creepy portrait. It was like he was looking right into my third eye."

Kirkland's cigarette dangled as he spoke. "Those boys tonight? If you talked to any one of them, and they were honest, they'd tell you the same story whether they were from Nebraska, or Bumfuck, Iowa."

"What story's that?"

"They're all picked from small towns in the Midwest. Certain criteria. They have little or no relationship with their fathers, their mothers are dead. They're artsy kids, precocious in speech and drama. They all came to Hollywood where they're taken under wing by a sponsor who's in Maleficarum. But the coven's only the bottom level of a larger structure. An international corporate structure called 'Pontifex.' "

It was the elaboration of Syd's fantasy which gave Jimmy chills. "International?"

Syd blew up. "Overseas! Europe's been full secret of societies and heresies, from the Cathars to the Knights

Templar to Rosicrucians. Alchemists? What about the Golden Dawn, or an offshoot? Pontifex maintains the magical tradition and combines it with twentieth-century psychology."

Jimmy was afraid for Syd, and when he felt that way he always said or did the wrong thing. He giggled.

"You think this is a joke?" Kirkland threw himself on the bed, curling up in pain around a toy monkey. His eyes turned malicious. "Let me show you something." He strode quickly to the wall and whipped a spattered sheet from the clutter of the floor.

Fumes of linseed oil and turpentine hit Jimmy in the face. All he saw were dozens of label-less cans of paint in various shades of silver and gray. Some were almost mercury, others close to a cobalt blue. There was a chaos of mixing tins and powders and squeezed tubes of titaniums and albumin white.

"What's all this?" Jimmy asked.

Syd's laugh was harsh. "It's a commission for Rogers. I'm trying to find a particular color, a shade. I don't know what it's for, only that it's all about you."

"What?"

"It's not just colors I'm blending. He wants you mixed into it. Here, I'll show you." He cleared a workbench with his arm and emptied a folded envelope onto the surface.

Jimmy saw only tiny yellow slivers, and pale fuzz.

"It's parings from your nails," Syd said. "And bristles from your razor. It's pieces of you to go into it, Rogers collected and saved them. I can see him poking around with tweezers in the trap of the sink in his pad."

Jimmy flushed. "You're making this up."

Kirkland snapped the envelope onto the floor. "Hell

he didn't. It's like all those little medicine bags when we were growing up, whatever you want to call them. 'Items of resonance,' things connected to you."

"Why would he do anything like that?"

"That's the question, isn't it?" Syd flopped back onto the bed.

Jimmy said wonderingly, "Maybe it's Maleficarum shit. Maybe he thinks I'm gonna leave, and it's a goofy love spell thing."

Kirkland snickered, eyes shiny. "Not fucking likely. Your leaving him, that is."

Jimmy rested his knee on the mattress and touched Syd's shoulder. "I'm trying to understand. What's the right thing to say?"

For a moment there was no response. Then Syd whirled off the bed, saying, "Follow me."

Jimmy obeyed, following him down to the parking lot where they mounted the bike and roared up Santa Monica to eerie old Hollywood Cemetery.

Syd knew a hole in the wall on the Gower side, which surprised Jimmy, who was doubting he really knew Syd at all. They skulked to the mausoleum, where Kirkland picked up a spike he had secreted along with a sizable rock in an urn by the entrance. "For the vampires," Syd joked. Jimmy couldn't laugh.

Then Syd jimmied the door with the spike. Dean followed him inside musty darkness illuminated only by the flickering of Kirkland's cigarette lighter, up an aisle lined with marble statuary.

Syd turned into a niche of crypts and held the flame by a name-plate. "Valentino," he whispered reverently as if it would speak. "Rudy."

Jimmy shivered. "Let's split."

"Rudy knew," Kirkland said with awe, "because he

was the first, a prototype. One of the failed experiments before Pontifex perfected their art. They learned the subject's death had to be a little more romantic, dramatic. More visual." Syd's voice had a dead sound in all the marble. "Think about those boys again. Think about us. Preselected. We've all been picked, and not just for our looks."

"Picked for what?"

Kirkland turned to him and whispered, "For stardom, baby. To be the Big One. Many are groomed, but only one will be chosen. Maybe it'll be you." He laughed.

Jimmy's own voice echoed nervously. "Or you."

"Not me," Syd shook his head. "Ultimately, I'm too Jewish. And I stammer during the tests. I'm a disappointment. After all the lessons, all the grooming. But they allowed for that. That's why there's so many of us. Many are called but one will be chosen. But you know what? I don't give a shit."

Before Jimmy could object, Syd turned to the nameplate on the crypt and inserted the spike underneath. He began to hammer it with the rock. Amazingly, the plate fell out with a resounding crash in the silence. Jimmy realized it had already been loosened.

There was the shadowy form of the ornate casket, but Syd was reaching around it to extract something, all the time looking at Jimmy significantly.

Syd's fingers found it. He held a small teakwood box.

Jimmy's breath caught. But it was not the box he had himself given to DeWeerd at age fourteen, though similar.

"I see it on your face," Syd hissed. "You had one just like it. I recovered mine when I was in New York. Nobody's gonna get it from me again."

Kirkland's face was ashen as he opened it with trembling fingers.

The box was empty.

Kirkland winced, then his own breath was sucked into his chest as his face dissolved in a stunned expression. Jimmy watched as Syd slumped to the marble floor laughing, letting the box drop with a clattering sound. The lighter went out at the same time, and they were in darkness with the dead.

Syd started to cry. "This time next year, I'll be dead."

"Stop it," Jimmy said. "You won't."

Kirkland looked up with eyes that welled. "I know it. I've got a third eye right in the middle of my forehead. Wanna feel it?"

Jimmy touched the other boy's forehead, finger tingling.

Kirkland said, "It tells me something else. Before this year's out, Jimmy Dean will move in with Rogers." He began to sob again.

"You won't be dead," Jimmy whispered in the mausoleum, cradling the boy's head.

Jimmy Dean recalled this as he looked down at the cemetery from the Griffith observatory roof. On the lawn, Mushy Callahan helped Corey Allen into a protective vest for the switchblade fight scene. Gaffers checked boom microphones.

He had been in New York with Rogers in 1952 when they got word of Syd's death, and he was using Brackett's Sunset Plaza address on the west coast. "That damned bike," Rogers had said, shaking his head. "Booze and a bike, on Mulholland. There's a lesson, Jimmy."

But what was it? Jimmy asked himself. Now he

jumped onto the guard wall, balancing easily over the concrete. There were gasps sixty feet below.

Jimmy smiled, walking the ledge with arms extended. He pretended to stumble so he could hear the silence of hearts stopping, before correcting with a pirouette. Then he did the scissors dance. The queer dance.

Nick Ray was pale as he ran up the steps to talk Jimmy off the ledge. "Come down here a minute," he said. "Talk to me."

"What about?" Jimmy said distractedly.

"The future," Nick said casually. "Did you see the blast? The Atomic Age. Your age, Jimmy. Come down so we can talk."

Jimmy had gambled with Nick on *Rebel* and liked what was happening. The way Ray worked with him and accepted his ideas. He reluctantly obeyed, felt Nick's relieved arm around his shoulder.

The future was one of the things Nick always brought Jimmy around to when his star was depressed. Like the heroes in his eccentric pictures, Ray was an outsider, a Hollywood maverick. He wanted to develop another screenplay for Jimmy, about a rising young Hollywood actor who gets involved with the California sports car racing circuit. The hook Nick was carefully fashioning was that it would be a gritty and authentic depiction of racing. Jimmy would do his own driving, and help work out the camera angles to catch all the action.

"Do you want to direct some day?" Nick said. "Form our own production company? It'll happen, we'll make it happen. Don't worry about financing, I've got an angel. Know what that means? No studio Jew breathing down our necks."

"Necks?" Jimmy said, making to bite Ray's neck.

The director parried playfully. "I'm serious. He wants

to be anonymous while it's in the talking stages. Now can we get back to work?"

Jimmy had an idea for the knife fight scene that afternoon involving the insertion of a bullfight theme, with Buzz shouting 'Toro!' and making like a picador. Nick agreed.

9

September 12–18, 1995
Westwood

Pollack met Lou contritely at LAX in his battered station wagon with a half-dozen roses hastily bought at the gift shop. Lou had sent Cherie home on the scheduled flight, a departure expedited by state troopers sick of "Deaners," while he languished eight sleepless hours in the Marion jail. Between interrogations he burned up telephone lines to Pollack in Los Angeles obtaining verification of the explanation of his presence in Indiana.

"You look like shit, Lou," Ly said heartily. "I'm just glad it was straightened out! I accept full responsibility. I'm not sure what I was thinking—my own memory is rather selective, but I think it was a nostalgic hearkening back to the grand practical jokes of the Golden Age of Hollywood."

Lou was sullen. "It was hardly that."

The painter was obviously relieved Lou had spoken.

"Who could know you'd be arrested and interrogated for the theft of James Dean's body?" He stroked his beard. "Ah—the *ultimate* collectible. The ultimate for the *Dean collector*. My friend Tony has some Indiana law-enforcement connections, and he says they're trying to keep it out of the papers, the family awaiting ransom demand. Not that there'll be one. Other than that, how was your trip?"

"I was given a tour of the Fairmount Museum by a man who'd been dead thirty years."

"I seem to recall that from your phone call. Your ghost's name was—?"

"Bing Traster, and I don't consider him 'my' ghost. What happened with Cherie?"

"Cleveland was waiting to whisk her off to points north. They had quite a row. It's all very interesting," the artist mused as he negotiated traffic.

Lou's voice was stinging. "What do you mean— 'interesting'?"

The artist was cowed and conciliatory. "Someone from the other side is obviously trying to reach out to you. No doubt—it's Jimmy."

"I meant Cherie and Cleveland."

Pollack was oblivious. "All this anniversary activity's probably agitating his eternal restlessness, poor dear. The media keeps stirred up the psychic energy in the collective unconscious. When did you start smoking?"

"In jail," Lou said, replacing the red-and-white flip-top box in his pocket.

The artist said, "Isn't this exciting? Look how your world's enlarging! You left a supernatural skeptic, and now you've met your first ghost."

Lou did not tell him he had already put his mind at rest on that score: it was an example of Hoosier wit at the expense of a "Deaner." The old guy at the museum had given a phony name and sent him off to the cemetery to be confronted and questioned by the troopers. It was just a local joke.

Lou rifled the clutter of the glove box. "Let me guess, you don't have any aspirin—"

"Aspirin," Pollack said, "is bad for your stomach. Do you know cold cucumber slices over your eyes will fix up those bags? Jimmy Dean can't contact you directly, but it sounds like he's trying to get your attention. That means he wants help."

"What kind of 'help'?"

"To identify his murderer." He pulled across traffic without signaling. "What if his soul's held captive in limbo until the truth comes known?"

Silence ensued until they pulled up to the Westwood apartment, Pollack saying, "I'll stop by and see you once you've got some beauty sleep, and I'll have a surprise. Hm?" He winked.

"Don't count on it," Lou said.

"Don't forget your roses," Pollack called bleakly.

The cat had missed Lou.

That week he avoided Donna and George, both of whom wanted to bend his ear, Donna confused by the professor's demented attentions, Bluestein wounded because she refused to see him. Lou was thinking about Cherie. He knew he could locate her through Terry, but a telephone call meant he'd have to talk to Devereux. The picture of Pollack and Devereux pushing him through at LAX in a wheelchair—he was sure Cleveland was still laughing.

But as he looked at Dean's face in Lysander's portrait, he felt a strange new warmth that was almost intimate. He recognized the warning signs of mere

interest turning to fascination. What could account for
the change? He had an idea.

The descent into the underworld, often represented by
a symbolic burial, was a potent initiative experience.
One arose identified with the god. It was immersion, a
baptism. Those moments in the grave did more than ter-
rorize him. He had come out of that hole different in
some still unidentified way. Maybe there was something
to what Pollack had once said, that for some the fascination with Jimmy took the form of an inner-directed
journey.

Maybe that was why he finally consented to see
Lysander late Sunday afternoon when the tipsy painter
showed up unannounced bearing gifts, a bottle of Blue
Nun in each hand. As further peace offering he extended a Jimmy Dean ashtray, the idol's ceramic likeness poised to rise from the ashes.

Lou accepted the pathetic *objet*. "Come on in," he
said.

Pollack flared his poncho as he ensconced himself on
the sofa, tossing a videocassette onto the coffee table.

"What's that?" Lou asked.

"The James Dean Story," Pollack said as worked the
cork out of one of the bottles, "a crummy little 1957
documentary. The first directoral effort of Robert
Altman—who later went on to better things. Put it in
your TV. Hm?"

The film was black and white. "Fast forward—" Pollack directed as Lou knelt at the VCR. "Keep going . . .
right about—*there*."

It was the grainy image of a man in overalls garden-
ing, pausing to submit to an interview for the talking-
head film.

"It's him," Lou said in a dead voice. "What's he
saying—?"

"Some folksy Hoosier bullshit," Pollack said as he lurched up to turn off the television. "I'll leave the tape. The important thing is what he said to you, which you so kindly recounted during your repetitious phone calls from jail. Traster came to you from the astral plane—obviously. He's dead. Do you know cigarettes are bad for your complexion?"

"Unlike alcohol?"

"Very 'Jimmy,' " the painter said, framing Lou in his fingers. "It's so difficult to give a crash course on the occult, but you're a student and you're young. Why do you think Jimmy's corpse was stolen?"

"The same kind of mentality that would steal his wrecked car. I don't know—"

Pollack made a face as he took a pinch of snuff from a gold box. "Like Sal's wound, for its cere-monial power." Pollack's eyes were gimlets. "Think of what Traster said. It's entirely true—at the heart of every cult is animal sacrifice. Sacrifice! Its persis-tence in thought can be seen as a haunting memory of a past reality. Jimmy scattered clues all through *Rebel*."

"He did?"

"Recall the planetarium scene, when Taurus appears? Jimmy moos. And the gang calls him 'Moo.' And they dedicate the song 'Milk Cow Boogie' to him. What if Jimmy's saying, 'Look, I'm the sacred Apis bull'? The ritual sacrifice?"

"Bull-shit," Lou laughed.

"I've had more thoughts about the crash. There's the little matter of the ambulance's unscheduled stop fol-lowing a 'minor collision' en route to the hospital. What if the ambulance drivers were on the take and stopped so someone could look Dean over and give him a fatal injection, in case he had happened to survive the wreck? There's no autopsy—only the cryptic notation that no blood is left in the body. Where has it gone? Why no autopsy? What might one reveal? Poison? Drugs? —Why do I feel you aren't taking me seriously?"

"I can't believe you take yourself seriously."

Pollack punched his shoulder playfully. "You're a shit, Lou, goddamn me for being so fond of you. But I'm colorful. That's my safety—I'm Laurel and Hardy. Harmless. But the accumulation of all these materials is ominous. An astral zombie, you might be able to invoke with a small relic. But the resurrection of a god is a major undertaking. That's where the corpse would come in."

"The deal you mentioned at Natalie's grave? The Second Coming of James Dean conjured by cultists?"

"The astral zombie is invoked for a limited time, for a specific purpose. It runs on magical double-A's, whereas a god must be harnessed to the powerful battery of the collective unconscious. Have you ever seen an aerial photo of the intersection where Jimmy died?"

"No. Why?"

"Were a geocentric tropical zodiac wheel superimposed on the intersection, the vector lines would form the configuration of aspects which astrologers call the Finger of God, in which two planets each are in quincunx to a third planet. The apex of the triangle denotes a specific karmic opportunity and evolutionary purpose for the personality; it's a pointer to the next step on the 'way.' It's a powerful killing ground, the forces rampant. And the natural place for an undertaking like the invocation of a god-form."

"Like on the anniversary this month?"

"The stars are coming into alignment! Plus the ground is already rich with blood. Schmallhorst's, for one. The coroner's report was released six weeks later. My friend Tony showed it to me. Schmallhorst's insides—his guts—were also torn loose. In fact, they were jammed up into his chest cavity."

"Force of impact," Lou said adamantly.

"It's the signature of an astral form."

"In a zombie car, I suppose?"

"The car was real. Recall the headlight ring? From a *Porsche*. More exactly. . . .a Porsche *Spyder*. A better question is, 'Who do we know who owns a Spyder?' "

"Jonathan Cottlee?"

"Right! The guy who's supposedly crazy to find Dean's car? What if that's just a ruse? What if he already *has* it?"

"Cottlee has a replica, it's not a real—"

"What the fuck's the difference to Schmallhorst?" Pollack spluttered. "We're talking about two different things!"

Lou was enjoying the other man's discomfort. "There must be dozens of those replicars in southern California," he needled. "Did you notice the headlight ring on his car at the convention? Was it missing?"

Pollack waved his hand in dismissal. "It could have easily been replaced. It's not like he couldn't afford it. A black magician could have programmed the zombie to drive the car. And he has enough money to have procured the body without getting his own hands dirty. Hell, it may be at his mansion right now."

"Lysander, are you pissed because he won't buy your paintings?"

"Of course I am—but that's irrelevant. Christ, Lou,

you're the one who's seen a ghost." Pollack looked sly.
"Tell me: didn't your little trip to Indiana result in a
calling forth from deep inside you?"

"A re-calling? The reincarnation business?" Lou
smiled.

"We've all got a karmic script with the goal of being
reborn in some scenario in which personal evolution of
the soul will be best served."

"What would Dean have to learn in mine?"

"Well—" Pollack said carefully, "consider. Jimmy
was once in a car race where a kid named Jack Drummond was killed, and some said it was Jimmy's fault,
that he took too many chances on the track. Maybe, in
your incarnation, he's got to come to terms with it
because . . ."

"Because I killed someone?" Bluestein, Lou thought.
How many people had George told?

"I didn't mean to hurt you," Lysander said. "But let
it germinate."

Lou was dazed after Pollack was gone, but strangely
enlivened. His life had been on hold too long, or like a
record skipping. He had even come up with his own explanation of the ghost at the museum. The old guy who
had given him the tour had been a cousin, perhaps even
a son of the late Bing Traster, and used his familial resemblance to play jokes on city slickers.

Lou thought this as he checked his reflection in the
mirror, Deanish with the cigarette dangling in his lips.
There was an element of flattery to thinking he might
have a karmic connection to James Dean. He already
felt a tad one up on the Deanfans. How many could say
they had been in James Dean's grave?

On restless impulse, he got in the Speedster and returned to Larry Edmunds' Bookstore, definitely feeling

superior to the lost souls browsing the aisles. He scanned the Dean biographies, choosing several books, then all.

As always, there was a "Dean line" at the counter. Its occupant this evening was a young man who smacked of the tourist—wife with two small children in tow, Instamatic around her neck; a very angry woman. One child was crying, and she slapped the hand of the other toddler when it pinched her for attention.

Her husband was examining lobby cards from *Rebel*. Lou knew the look; the reverential way he regarded the item, thinking how it would look on his wall in Nebraska or wherever.

"Out of your league," said the smirking beard of the contemptuous clerk.

"Gee," the hick was saying regretfully. "That much?"

Now, the beard was looking at Lou. "Help you?"

"All right," Lou heard himself saying. "Let's see them again."

The display book sliding across the counter, towards him. Lou wondered what he was doing; there was a definite itch.

"Mint," the man behind the counter said.

The colors were nice, Lou thought; it really was an art form and sure to appreciate in value.

"They don't stick around long," the clerk said with a practiced eye for buyer's indecision. "Lots of demand."

Lou was reaching for his American Express card. The guy from Nebraska was looking at him with envy, and it was pleasurable. Which made him nervous. A little like losing your virginity, joining the ranks of the collector.

When he walked out of the shop, he found himself trying to conceal the package, as if everyone on the street knew he had just depleted his allowance fund by a much-needed 573 dollars. *For what?* An armload of books and three lobby cards. He could explain they were for his thesis, if confronted.

Maybe they could even be written off on taxes.

10

Monday, September 19, 1995
West Hollywood, 11:52 P.M.

Lysander Pollack unlocked his studio and returned to the station wagon to wrestle out the unwieldy wire pens with two chickens, which fluttered and squawked in protest. He had picked them up on Oliveras Street, needing them for the summoning prerequisite to the evening's creative work. The amount of energy let loose by even a small sacrifice was great, out of all proportion to the victim's size.

He'd neglected to mention to Lou that bulls weren't the only animals in the *Rebel* bestiary. Jimmy was also called a "crumb-chicken," and participated in a "chickie-run." And the gang hung a chicken over the door of the Stark house. In fact, *chicken* was the detonator word in the film, the one that always set Jimmy off.

A Tarot card was on the door—Liv had surely dropped it by per his request. He intended working the

motif into *The Last Supper* by having Jimmy use the
Hanged Man as a coaster. It was his pleasure to massage arcane and cryptic messages into his canvases,
which generations would chase their tails interpreting.
He'd already worked into the border of the table an inscription in phonetic Greek:

θεσυσ Διδντ Ωορκ Φορ Με. θαμεσ Δεαν Διδ.
Jesus Didn't Work For Me. James Dean Did.

Inside the studio he navigated tumbling clutter to the
light switch. The bulb was out, or the utility company
had cut off his power for nonpayment. In darkness, he
clutched the cane and tapped his way along like a blind
man toward the desk piled with correspondence and
fanciful little unicorns of excess acrylic. His hand rested
on something, the mug from which Lou had drunk.

He had preserved it unwashed, drunkenly clearing off
a corner of work table with an extravagant sweep of his
arm so he could chalk in Lou's face on its surface. Then
he'd framed the portrait in a charcoal pentagram, and
placed the mug on Lou's face, black tallow candles on
either side. Cutting a piece of nylon clothesline, he had
made two love knots. *Couldn't hurt. What the hell?
Once the looks go—*

Emotion came in his throat. He had made the young
man the last figure at table in *The Last Supper*, hoping
he'd accept it as a tribute. Ly half-despised himself for
his love, reaching for the flask under his poncho and
taking a long swallow right where he stood.

Wiping lips and beard with a greasy forearm, he
stumbled into the hall, feeling his way to the back room
with its cot and Jimmy's pale life masks on the walls.
He lit a candle and sat down heavily, breathing hard
with the pain of barking a shin en route.

His eyes fell on the three-dimensional mobile of the Tree of Life. To the mystic it was an object of meditation, and each of the 22 paths connecting its ten spheres corresponded to a card in the Tarot major arcana. To the magician it had more practical applications of the forces to which it allowed access.

The sixth and center sphere was Tiphareth, its symbols the Cross and the cube. Six was the number of balance and harmony. Tiphareth was gateway of death to life, the point of change from the planes of force above it to those of form below. It was where the god was sacrificed—sacrifice meaning the transmutation of force from one form to another. Pollack saw a line of continuity from Tammuz, Adonis, and Attis—all the dying and reviving gods who populated the consciousness of their times. Helios, Osiris, Christ—all the sun gods had their abode at Tiphareth.

And since 1955—James Byron Dean.

What were gods except thought-forms ensouled and activated by the force of the human imagination? In practical occultism these forms were built up with great care and the most elaborate attention to symbolism, because they could be used thereafter to evoke the force they were intended to represent.

Take James Dean. Millions of heartsick grieving in unison and creating a thought form on the Astral Plane, their focused mental energy imbuing it with life until it was nothing less then an artificial elemental—something like an angel. Or consider it as a cosmic force whose apparent vehicle of manifestation to psychic consciousness was a form built up by the human imagination—

"What if we never died?" the Goat had asked Ly forty years ago.

Pollack waxed nostalgic, thinking how he had been a

mere slip of a lad then. The Goat had looked at him with those big blue eyes and kissed him lightly, rising onto his pillow to light an unfiltered cigarette. Outside the window Pollack could see the Greek colonnades surrounding the swimming pool beyond a drive of white gravel.

"Would you like to live forever?" the Goat had asked as he stroked Pollack's hair. On his longest finger was a ring with the face of Baphomet, the only outward sign of the Goat's status as an adept.

"Think of the crow's-feet, dear," Ly had quipped.

"I would like to think of you being who you are—right now—forever."

"I think I would settle for your ring. It's marvelous."

"You've said that before. Let's try it on your finger." The Goat had exhaled a stream of smoke, infatuated blue eyes teasing; on the table beneath the French window were two tallow candles and an inscribed pentagram encircling the handsome young Pollack's own likeness. Across it, a cord tied in two love-knots.

Pollack pined for the wild Hollywood of the nineteen fifties. *Them wuz the days. Ah, we wuz beautiful. . . .*

"And what do I have to do to deserve this bauble, not to mention sipping from the fount of youth?"

The answer was, simply mix some paint. To specification, achieving a particular shade of silver and including several esoteric ingredients—including ground baby teeth, nail parings, and hair clippings—in a consistency which would adhere to an aluminum surface.

And I did it, God help my soul. One batch which I never saw again. And which shade I've ever since been trying to reproduce for my paintings.

His guilty reflection in the wall mirror reminded him he had become one more aged predator, the very thing the Goat had been when Pollack himself had been his—

artist in residence? No, a kept boy, a pleasant diversion from the rough trade.

"You can do better than that, Ly," Tony Bulova had told him. *"Better than him. You could do better with me. You're destroying your talent."*

Ly's smile had been cynical and no doubt slightly inebriated. *"Oh? Are you applying for Knight in Shining Armor? Make an honest woman out of me?"* He had stroked Tony's hair, and spoken softly. *"Do you want to install me in your little apartment on Franklin? Do you think you could keep me in the manner to which I've become accustomed? It's too late for us, Tony."*

In those day he always sounded like Bette Davis in some B soaper. My God.

Pollack heaved himself up, peeling back the Indian prayer rug to reveal the magic circle he'd inset in the floor with small ceramic tiles. He made sure the heavy drape was secure over the window, and lighted two more candles.

Now, where was that fleck of aluminum from Jimmy's Porsche? It was the relic of the subject necessary to manifest the astral form of James Dean. That was the secret of the paintings.

The form would not talk, it had no soul. And when its eyes met his, there was nothing behind them. But it would pose uncomplainingly for hours on end, assume the familiar expressions. It was the ideal model because it was itself a reflection of the archetypal idea. It exhibited no irritation at being plucked from the other plane, an empty thing summoned from the vast imaginative energy of millions of Dean fanatics over forty years. The practical magician in Pollack knew they would never miss the bit of life force he siphoned off for his purposes; it was like illegally hooking up a cable to the collective unconscious.

But the reflections had been getting weaker the last year; he knew that the concentration essential to his psychism was being eroded by alcohol. It wouldn't be long until it faded altogether.

His memory was also going, apparently: he could not find the aluminum fleck, safely preserved in a glass vial.

Turning, he saw something shimmering near the wall.

It was a rippling image struggling to come into form, which was very odd because he had not even started, the chickens still squawking and unbloodied in the other room. Yet it was happening: the image was assuming a tenuous visibility, and it wore the robe from that first Broadway play when Jimmy played a seductive Arab boy.

The familiar face smiled at the artist teasingly, began a seductive dance before his stupefied eyes. Quite beautiful and hypnotic.

"Jimmy?" he said hoarsely, an amazed smile on his face. "Is that you?"

Pollack let himself flop back on the cot. It passed in front of him with eerie arabesques, and a shadow crossed Ly's heart. That it should come unbidden like this, was perhaps a bad sign; that he could see suddenly and effortlessly into the spirit world might mean his own time was running out.

Then the figure was before him, wistful face close to his own.

Icy fingers rested on his eyelids and closed them. "No!" Pollack grumped as he opened them, trying to dispel it.

Jimmy's expression was poignant, hurt. It made a pass with its fingers through Lysander's forehead, and Pollack felt it as a knifelike pain, as if a blade kept in a freezer to chill had been plunged into his skull. Icy pain, of something sharp and cold penetrating deep into his brain, blinding—

And just as quickly it was removed. Pollack gasped.

Dean's face was curious as it examined its own fingers in wonder.

Pollack watched from where he had fallen backward to clutch his temples. *This is a psychic attack,* he thought to himself through pulses of agony. Someone was raising the zombie against him. Didn't they know he was no threat?

I'm a clown, harmless. You don't kill a buffoon. Why? No—

The form of the dead actor paused in front of him, reaching out with a delicate hand.

Pollack watched the hand reached effortless through his own shirt, and inside his chest. He caught his breath as cold fingers closed around his heart.

Jimmy's face was angelic.

Then the fingers began to squeeze like pincers on Pollack's arteries. The tingling up the artist's arm was frosty, the vice across his ribs excruciating.

Stop. You're killing me.

The fingers crushed his heart so that his knees were drawn up to his chest, and then Pollack was on the floor. He could not breathe; the pressure was explosive. His final thought was more a single word as his fingers clawed the floor, the spectral form riding his back like a horse, its arm still inside him.

Lou—

Jim Thorpe shrieked.

"What's wrong?" Lou gasped at the cat, which had been curled on his sleeping chest, startled as she sped off into the kitchen. "Be that way," he mumbled, working at stilling his galloping heart.

Then he remembered the dream. He'd been on a vast plain where two highways met. It was a crossroads, like his life. There was the fear of a question, and fear of an answer, but he could remember neither. The wind rose from the west and cooled his face. That way was death, westward, and the wind seemed to be whispering that death was not all that bad; it rattled the dry heads of the wild barley around his legs like so many tiny skulls.

He looked up the highway to the east, and that way was life and resurrection.

The detour which had brought him here was no accident; he had been searching, though he did not know for what. He'd been running away from emptiness, and it had brought him to this lonely spot.

He drew his collar up around his neck and realized he was wearing a red jacket—but it was not strange because it was his. The rocks and the highway spoke to him, telling him that he had arrived. *I'm home. This is mine. Part of me has always been here and this place has always had a part of me.* The only pain was the thought of leaving.

Peering up the highway, he saw the old road where it broke off from the new section, and with it came understanding. That road was narrower and less traveled, which was why it was in disrepair; to follow that abandoned road was to come closer to source, and truth.

He saw the body of the young hit-and-run victim upside down in the barbed wire fence on the shoulder. Blood dripped down from his hair and the dust lapped it up. There was nothing to fear; Schmallhorst's eyes were open and the expression on his face enlightened. One broken arm was outstretched, a bloody finger pointing east up the road.

I understand, Lou thought. He began to walk with a light heart.

Once he looked back and saw people clustered at the intersection, the fans from DeanCon. They were not moving, merely watching. They seemed lost—like prostheses looking for missing limbs. He understood that it was given for some to go only so far, and they stood their ground because they could not cross a line in the dust.

But something was wrong. Up ahead, three highway flares sizzled hotly across his path, and a crewman in a red Cal Trans uniform was setting up a zebra-striped sawhorse. Lou felt anger, and his steps were determined as wind at his back prodded him.

Beyond the Cal Trans worker was a stark figure like a crow. He recognized Pollack from the poncho and the distinctive cane.

The Cal Trans worker paused, held up a gloved hand of caution.

Lou realized who the Cal Trans guy was. Threads of blood ran down from under the helmet, and into cracks in the forehead. The glasses were askew on the face, lens cracked. Only the smile and eyes seemed intact.

"Lou," Ernie Hockman said, "don't come any closer."

That was when the cat had cried out.

Now, Lou sat up in the dark bedroom. "Damn you," he said aloud just to hear a voice. "Damn you, Lysander Pollack."

11

Jimmy was running late. The session with his Beverly Hills psychoanalyst, Greenspacht, had run overtime. Liv Ermaine was his second appointment tonight, and he had known from her telephone voice that the rendezvous piqued her interest—the abandoned Getty mansion where they had shot some *Rebel* interiors. Thinking he was possibly being followed, he took a circuitous route to meet the eccentric horror movie hostess.

The Porsche Speedster he drove was his new gift to himself. He had already competed in his first race at Palm Springs, winning the prelim and qualifying for the finals, where he received a second after the winner was disqualified on a technicality.

The spire of St. Timothy's reminded him of Pier Angeli, the tall and shy Sicilian whom he'd met in June on the set of *Eden*. She was under contract to Warners too, and they'd quickly fallen in love, spending stolen time together in a secret cottage on the beach talking about themselves and their problems, about life and life after death.

He even told her about the coven meetings he had attended with Rogers. It shocked her Catholic sensibilities, but she accepted it. It was his confession about the relationship with Syd which had dissolved her into tears.

He had known it would hurt, so why had he done it? He'd just started seeing Greenspacht at the studio's insistence, and the analyst said it was to disturb her. He called it "approach-avoidance."

"Does it bother you making love to both men and women?" Greenspacht had asked.

"Why live with one hand behind your back?" Jimmy replied.

Greenspacht said, "But this girl has changed your life."

"I can almost feel, now," Jimmy said cautiously. "I don't know. I feel sick."

"I think you've found someone you care about, and it scares hell out of you."

Jimmy bit his lip. "Yeah, it does, 'cause I'd given up so long ago. Now, I feel good as a result of someone real I actually talk to, and I haven't felt this way since I can remember . . . not more than three or four times in my life. I just don't want to fuck this all up, you know? I want to change and grow. I don't want to wreck this chance. Now I just feel numb and weary."

Greenspacht seemed happy. "This could be a big turning point."

"Yeah, I want it to be. If only I could feel relaxed in my head."

"Just remember, you can't come out of a shell all at

once. It's going to be gradual, but you have to start somewhere."

"I feel thrilled, or shaky. I can't tell."

"We'll have to work at discerning exactly what you feel. You can't distinguish pain and pleasure, so it's all a blur. These incidental relationships with the older producer, and that other ... What was his name? DeWeerd? Do you think they filled voids of estrangement from your own father?"

"Sure. Maybe."

"If I understand, Brackett took you to New York, where his financial sponsorship sustained you, and his acumen guided you. He helped you land some television work, and carefully selected a vehicle for your emergence on Broadway."

"*The Immoralist.* I was living with him on West Thirty-eighth. You see, before that I was starving. I mean, not eating. I figured, 'If you're gonna sell your ass to strangers, why not—' "

"Don't be defensive, nobody's judging you. As a result, you won a major dramatic award and found a high-powered agent. Kazan tapped you for *East of Eden*. You didn't need Rogers anymore, or the connections of the Hollywood underground. The breakup was acrimonious?"

"It was at this drunken party in New York, at Alec Wilder's. Rogers *commands* me, 'Do the scissors dance for Alec.' It was this seductive scene from the play. I blew up, stormed out. Never talked to him again."

Greenspacht leaned back and laced his fingers. "It sounds as if these mentor figures have fortunately appeared at crucial points in your life when you were ready. Rogers was just DeWeerd, on a higher arc. Perhaps this guilt's for abandoning them when their usefulness was expended. Perhaps it's not too late to change a life pattern by acknowledging your debt. You may use these resentments to generate emotional memories you call up in your acting, but after a point it's self-destructive. The death thing? Maybe you'd better run again over that business about the coven . . . in the Hills?"

"Maleficarum," Jimmy said fidgeting. "Or in New York, at Alec Wilder's. It started as a kick, a gas. It was getting in touch with your natural currents, exploring the bizarre. It was ritual, and modern life is impoverished of ritual."

Greenspacht was unimpressed.

Jimmy's discomfort became acute. "Like the Aztecs. I've always been fascinated with them. They were very fatalistic people, and I sometimes share that feeling. They had such a weird sense of doom that when the Spaniards arrived, they just gave up to an event they believed couldn't be avoid—"

"Colorful," Greenspacht said, "but that's the past. You have a new life, new relationships. You broke away from all that. Or have you? What of this 'Liv' person?"

Jimmy played people off against each other, and he had done this with Liv and Greenspacht.

The psychiatrist had counseled against the trip to Indiana, given Jimmy's psychological state, saying, "You're making these fantasies real by succumbing to them." Upon Jimmy's return, Greenspacht was very disappointed in the whole business about the teakwood box. "You're avoiding something," he said in subsequent sessions. "I haven't forgotten, and I'm not about to let you off the hook. Did you bring it?"

Jimmy had blanched. "Is it really necessary?"

Greenspacht nodded gravely. "I think you're at the moment of truth, if you seriously want to break out of the belief structure imprisoning you. And it's not like it's forever. Just until you can see it for what it is."

But Jimmy had not brought it, and would not for two months. In fact, he had not brought it to his therapist until this very night of his appointment with Liv.

His hands had trembled as he placed it on the psychiatrist's oak desktop. Greenspacht opened it tentatively, face impassive. "You've taken a big step, Jim. How do you feel?"

"All right," he answered with deflating breath, somehow proud the shrink had called him "Jim." "I think I feel all right."

"And you trust me completely?"

"It's hard. Real hard."

"But you've made a real beginning. We both look to the day when I give this back to you, and you cherish it for what it represents, and not what it is."

Jimmy had nodded, but did not feel the relief he had expected. The psychiatrist said that would come later.

Jimmy tried to stay in the moment as he headed in the Speedster toward the old mansion on Wilshire, glancing furtively in the mirror for pursuers. He had first met Liv through their mutual friend 'the Hawk,' a twenty-year-old boy whom Jimmy had wanted cast as Plato in the film, and on whose behalf he'd actively campaigned with Nick. But it was no dice. "Too pink," Nick said. But the Hawk had remained a fixture on the set, to fetch Jimmy a sandwich or coffee, and run interference against people he didn't want to see. Jimmy got him a nose job for consolation.

Now the Hawk was waiting outside the mansion's door. "Watch my wheels," Jimmy said quietly.

He stepped into the shattered doorway to see a woman fully a head taller than himself waiting in the shadows. She dropped her coat, revealing a black kimono. Her greeting was to slap her thigh with the Circassian whip Jimmy had specially ordered through a catalog of exotica.

He was afraid, and both knew he liked that.

"And what's Greenspacht's hourly rate?" she asked with amusement.

Liv was a teacher with her body; she said her black nipples were the points in the circle corresponding to the human soul, the areola corresponding to "O," Or the "no-thing." Her oily spheroidal breasts symbolized the primogenitive world egg. Below the loosely knotted cord was the inverted triangle of pubis she had shaved exquisitely to replicate the angles of the Great Pyramid at Giza, though it pointed downward to indicate the phenomenal world.

Jimmy stripped off his shirt with few preliminaries. He liked to get right to it. He braced his arms against the balustrade of the old stairs, but not before she saw the burn marks on his stomach.

"Naughty," she said reprovingly.

She flagellated his back until her arms were tired, and he curled on the floor, gasping in pain. It was the only thing to make the Dream go away.

"My turn," she said as she slipped easily out of her sheath, kneeling beside him to loosen his pants and set to work with her mouth.

She taught how in primitive languages the words for "copulate" and "eat" were the same. Women's genitals had a spirit which drew men to devour them. They were gateways to immortality, and also executioners of men.

When excited, she hissed like a vampire from the red gash of her mouth, insisting Jimmy call her by the Syrian name of Astarte—that goddess who could swallow up man or god, root and branch, as the sea swallowed the lightning bolt to never let it out again. Shortly, she was astride his inert body and working it furiously.

But Jimmy found himself thinking of Pier, and the events of last summer that had led to their breakup.

"That's just it," he had whirled on Pier during one of their frequent arguments in July. They were at the beach house. He paced the sun deck and rubbed his temples against a headache.

"It's a charmed life, in the last twelve months I've pulled rank stunts which would've landed anyone on suspension. I brag I've had my cock sucked by some of the biggest names in Hollywood. I'm twenty-three years old and tell studio vice presidents 'Fuck you!' and they take it. I can't do anything wrong, even when I try."

"Why do you try?" she asked with sloe eyes. "You told me, 'You've got to treat these people like shit, it's the only thing they understand.' "

"Because, I have to know if it's really me who's accomplished all this. You can't understand."

"I'm trying," she said as she pulled her robe tighter against the Pacific chill.

"Okay," he said slowly, almost accusingly. "I'm afraid I've lost my soul." He laughed self-consciously.

"What?" She looked frightened.

He continued to push the buttons of her Catholicism. "The Maleficarum coven. They called forces and powers down, and you could ask them for things."

"Jimmy, you're scaring me. What kind of 'things'?"

"Anything," he mumbled, shrugged. "Maybe a part, maybe someone you wanted to notice you. Men, women. Something you wanted to happen. Big things, little things."

"Wait a minute," she said carefully. "I'm trying to

picture this. You asked for something? What did you expect?"

He was nervous. "I don't wanna talk about this anymore."

She made him meet her eyes. "I do understand. You don't believe in yourself, or that you deserve any of this. It's like what you wrote in that book—"

She took his copy of *Death in the Afternoon* from atop the bongos and opened to the fly leaf. She read aloud, " 'God gave James Dean so many gifts to share with the world, has he the right to throw them away in the bullring?' You even have it color-coded. What's this? 'Death'? 'Disability?' 'Disfigurement,' 'Degrada—' "

"Give me that!" he said fiercely.

She was relentless. "They've got you believing your talent doesn't come from you. You feel like you made a deal with the Devil? Have you told Greenspacht about this?"

"Leave me alone," he said.

"Don't you see that's how they wanted you to feel? Rogers and DeWeerd are behind you, you've got new friends like Nick, and Jeff. It's just Jimmy that's haunting Jimmy, the same self-doubt you've always felt. You can't believe you're worthy of what's happening to you, like you can't believe anyone would love you for—"

That was the first time he hit her, but not the last. He apologized. He cried.

Pier wanted to marry him, but her mother had prevailed in her objections. It wasn't the religious issue, but his worsening drinking resulting in her daughter's bruises and blackened eyes. At the same time, Pier wanted him to stand up to her mother. When it didn't happen that way, she tried to force his hand.

The next month, late August, Jeff Hackett had appeared at Jimmy's bungalow on the Warners lot. Everyone was talking about Jimmy's increasingly eccentric and bizarre behavior, like stashing his undeposited cash salary in a bureau along with a loaded gun. *Eden* was wrapped, but Jimmy refused to move out. The studio was threatening forcible eviction in increasingly harsher terms, but Jimmy seemed frightened to relinquish his connection to Cal Trask.

Few besides Jeff knew Pier had announced to Jimmy she'd missed two periods. Hackett was one of Jimmy's new friends outside the industry.

"You gotta know I don't want to be in the middle of this," Jeff said as he surveyed the rat's nest even grips were calling "a wastebasket with walls." "Pier took roach poison, they actually gave her last rites."

"Where is she?" Jimmy asked numbly.

Jeff wondered whether it was her plight, or the proximity of death, which piqued Jimmy's interest. "At the Chateau, on account of she's not speaking to her mother. I feel sorry for her. Do you love her, or what?"

"They drop her from the picture?"

"She never had a chance, but she's convinced it's because she started to show. But she hasn't. She's cuckoo, like you."

Jimmy had gone to the Chateau to find the cottage dark as he crept inside. Pier's liquid eyes peeked remorsefully from over a sheet pulled to her chin. They were disjointed as they searched his.

"Don't blame Jeff," she said weakly. "I made myself a royal pain in the ass. Don't be hard on him. You know," she said affectionately, "I don't understand what's happening. Or why I act the way I do sometimes."

"Like killing yourself?"

Her hand rested on her stomach. "I change my mind

a lot. I never think I'm really right. And now this. It changes things to have this going on inside. How could you understand?"

He sat on the bed and pulled down the sheet to reveal her nakedness. Her breath caught and she brushed her lustrous black hair from her forehead.

He placed his hand tentatively over the hardly noticeable swelling, as if trying to contact the life within. "Can I . . . I mean, 'May I?' "

"Feel it?" He looked so childlike, it broke her heart. At the same time, she wondered whether he wouldn't describe it later to Jeff with the same clinical detachment he'd described feeling the leg stump of a mutilated sailor he'd met in a Venice bar.

She laced his fingers with her own and took a breath. "You know what we're really talking about." She said, "You want me to kill our baby?"

He stood uncomfortably. "If we could have just got to know each other apart from all this."

Her smile was fragile. "I guess I thought you'd fight for me."

She opened her arms for him, but he knew he couldn't make love to a woman who was pregnant. He left. That was the end, eight months ago.

That night he began to have the Dream, always the same—driving along a highway and coming upon a car accident. Ambulance top lights flashed as curious motorists pulled over. The sight filled him with dread, but he stopped anyway to look down into the cockpit of a crumpled sports car where the broken body of a young man was stretched across the seat. The boy's neck hung over the door at a horrible angle, blood obscuring the face.

"Who is it?" he would ask.

A tall bald man with glasses would turn and say, "James Dean is dead."

He had seen her once more, at St. Timothy's where her storybook wedding to Vic Damone had taken place six months ago. As the newlyweds emerged, he was watching astride a motorcycle across the street.

Jimmy was roused from reverie by the pain of Liv grinding away on top of him. He sensed her irritation, as she took the indifference of his organ for personal defeat. There had been a moment when he thought he had a chance at getting his rocks off, and she had redoubled her sexual efforts to keep him inside her. But he thought of Pier, and withered away to roll over.

"So much for sexual magic," she said standing over him.

From his foreshortened view her brown gleaming thighs were pillars arching up to the darkness between her legs.

"I'm exhausted," he pleaded. "I'm on pills." He cradled his head in his hands, because it was splitting.

"You're losing touch with your own body, Jimmy," she said, lowering to a lotus position so the pyramidal triangle in her lap yawned. "And your body's your instrument."

He laughed sarcastically.

She was lighting a long Turkish cigarette, the cleft now the shape of a crocodile's mouth, saying, "Go on, laugh. The summoning was to have been the marshaling of sexual energy; the sacrifice would have been the giving up of your orgasm. Perhaps I could have appeased the demonic forces hovering around you. Because that's what's wrong, isn't it?"

"You think you know everything," he moaned.

Liv winked. "The great love of Jimmy Dean's life is

Jimmy Dean. There's a girl in town I think you should meet, Ursula Andress. You would like her. She's German and she looks just like you. A little boy with monthlies, everyone says it. She's your female double."

He lighted his own cigarette. "Where's your husband tonight? The producer?"

"He flew to Lone Pine to supervise some script changes on the Alan Ladd western. Alan thinks they spend too much time on horses. His leading lady's waist is long, and she looks taller than him in the saddle." She hesitated. "Tell mother. Is it the Dream again?"

"Car wreck. A boy is dead, and it's me."

"What do you want to know?"

"If it's real. That's what I want to know."

She paused thoughtfully. "We each have an animal soul. Mine is a wolf. I've always known that. As a small child in Norway I was shown wolves speeding over the snow. I had the most intense desire to run with them. Later I found the astral door, and my wish was realized."

He was interested. "The astral door?"

She knew him well. "In ancient Egypt processes of transformation were known to the priests. The energy lies buried inside us as a legacy of prehuman ancestry. I'll do it now."

She snubbed her cigarette, crouched naked with the weight of her body on her heels.

"How do you do it?" he asked curiously.

"I visualize one of the hexagrams from the I Ching," she said, flexing and extending her tongue. "I visualize it upon the surface of an imaginary door ... if you know how to open the door to the astral world represented by the hexagram." She closed her eyes, apparently mentally superimposing a hexagram over the door.

Nothing happened for a very long time.

"It's opening," she said finally. "I see it swing open. . . ."

Her features underwent a revolting change. Her lips drooled, her speech fading and ceasing until from her throat came only a hideous baying that rose and fell.

Jimmy was frightened. "What is it? What do you see?"

She looked at him with bestial eyes, and growled.

"I see a highway. Speed is the translation of matter into a higher form. The highest form is light. We are heading west and west is the direction of Death." She moaned in a disembodied voice, "It's a killing ground."

Her face swam in the shadows, his mother's face, and something else.

"Who are you?" Jimmy was asking. "Who's telling me this?"

Her voice was weird, chilling. "It's been consecrated to its purpose. It's a wasteland of space and spirit, wasteland of the eye and the soul. It is the Ground on which James Dean died, before he even arrives there. It has always been. Your soul will never leave that place, but will become part of it forever. And on that day, you will need me."

She began to tremble uncontrollably, then her eyes rolled up. She fell onto her side and shook for a while before she was still.

"Are you all right?" he asked, later.

She nodded weakly. "What did I say?"

"You don't know?"

Her expression changed. She spoke fatalistically. "You gave Greenspacht the box, didn't you? You trusted him more than me."

Jimmy did not answer. He did not tell her that he had suspected for months, and now more than ever, that she was Pontifex.

12

Tuesday, September 20, 1995
West Hollywood, 11:53 A.M.

"Bulova," the lieutenant of detectives said to Lou, "like the watch."

The gold badge read *Antoine Lefevre Bulova*, the man's features a strange cross of Semitic and Spanish. Early sixties? Lou saw immaculate silver hair above a tanned face and Brooks Brothers suit with impeccable silk tie. One of the Italian loafers was fitted with lifts— that leg a good three inches shorter than the other. Lou tried to relax in the chair, only to find that one of its legs also was too short.

He was in Pollack's studio, and through a door the artist's feet pointed in the air. Lou had no good explanation of why he happened to stop by—certainly not anxiety from a nightmare in which Pollack had appeared. When there was no response to his knock, he'd looked through the murky window to see Lysander on the floor with gaping mouth.

"You're a homicide detective," Lou said. He assumed the signs of struggle were from the painter crashing around as the stroke—or alcoholic dementia—took him.

"I was a friend to Lysander Pollack," Bulova said in a refined voice; he had no-nonsense eyes in contrast to fingers reflectively twiddling a cord with a strange knot. "Sometimes he would become involved with young men, and some of them were rough with him. He had been robbed in the past—even hospitalized."

"I didn't know," Lou said.

"I made a telephone call to the manager of your apartment. He hasn't known you to have a regular girlfriend in the three years you've lived there. It's an expensive address. Where do you get your money?"

"Tony—" a younger detective interrupted before Lou could respond, "we've got the pictures. We're cleaning up."

"Tony"—it rang a bell for Lou. He also knew the photos under discussion were of his own uncanny likeness chalked in a pentagram on the desk.

"I've had money from my family," Lou said. "I've been working on a degree."

"Yes, in a very leisurely way." Bulova nodded. "Did Lysander Pollack give you gifts? You mentioned a painting."

"I paid for that."

Bulova looked sadly around the room. "Are you a Dean fan, Lou? Belong to any of the Dean groups?"

"I met Pollack through a friend about three weeks ago."

"Yes—I saw you at the gallery."

Lou couldn't remember seeing him.

Bulova examined a canvas. "Lysander liked to say he painted for the subconscious eye, planted subliminal messages in his canvases. I don't have much of an eye—I could never understand." He turned to Lou. "I don't suppose you knew Larry Schmallhorst?"

"No."

"Did Ly tell you he believed that the hit-and-run was no accident?"

"He talked about it."

"Did he mention names?"

"He mentioned Jonathan Cottlee, I think because he was angry."

"Because Cottlee didn't come to his exhibition? Well, I wouldn't repeat that. It was just alcohol talk."

"I wouldn't have, if you hadn't asked."

Bulova replaced the Cross pen in his pocket. "You had a little trouble in Indiana recently. You were interrogated by the state police out at the cemetery in Fairmount?"

"They apparently had it under surveillance. I guarantee I had nothing whatsoever to do with what they were looking into."

"You were out there after dark?"

Lou felt stiffness spread up his back to his neck. Even dead, Lysander was a pain in the ass. "It was Pollack's fault I was out there at all. I had too much to drink, and he put me on a plane. I've tried to be helpful. Am I a suspect in anything?"

"That's all I have, though these other gentlemen may wish to continue. You should be careful for a little while."

"Why?"

The lieutenant smiled. "Lysander was a believer in reincarnation, and among his circle he broadcast that he had met a young man who had Jimmy's 'ka.' Does the term mean anything to you?"

"Egyptian, all that."

"Yes, and what I'm getting at is, because of some of

the things he said recently, you may find yourself regarded in some circles as the occult flavor of the month."

"What circles? I don't follow—"

"You told those Indiana police you had been directed to the cemetery by the very late Bing Traster. That was fairly occult on your part. Have you seen this before?"

He extended the Tarot card to Lou: Key 12, which depicted a man hanging upside down. Despite his awkward position, the man's face was radiant.

"No," Lou said. The many faces of James Dean stared at him accusingly from the canvases. "Should I? I don't understand all these questions."

"Maybe you don't need to," the cop said tolerantly. "You're probably a nice young man, and a friend to Lysander. His friends will appreciate that."

Lou started to shake when he was outside the studio.

13

Friday, September 23, 1995
West Hollywood

George had once told Lou he never went to funerals, so why was he at this one? Lou figured Bluestein was at Pollack's service on the off-chance that Donna, who was refusing to see him, might attend. Which she had, convinced Lou needed moral support. George squeezed into the already-crowded pew and started whispering intensely in her ear. Lou tried to ignore them.

The stuffy chapel of West Hollywood mortuary was jammed to the rafters, with standing-room-only in the rear. Lou was stifled, but couldn't get out without a scene. He didn't care for funerals either, and he was still unsettled by Bulova's interrogation. Wasn't allowing Pollack's cremation evidence that the detective accepted the pathologist's finding of a coronary?

It had been one weird week. Avidly morbid as ever, Patsy Polmquist had rushed into print a special black-bordered newsletter that contained maudlin testimonials to the "Dean Artist" from across the nation, and a special In Memoriam editorial, which captured none of the old artist's irreverence. In death he had become just another sacred cow, his wit homogenized.

The newsletter also contained a festive brochure inviting Lou to the International DeanCon on the thirtieth. It would be at Paso Robles, enabling Deaners to commute the thirty miles to the deathsite, where the film crew would be shooting the crash scene for the "Jimmy" film. A vivid picture was painted of the planned activities in the vicinity of the intersection, including deep-pit barbecue. There'd be a Dean lookalike contest, and a rock-lassoing competition in commemoration of the little rope trick Jimmy performed in *Giant*. Raffle prizes would include a role as extra in the Dean biopic. Fans the world over would be converging from major airports in Los Angeles and San Francisco.

A splendid time was guaranteed for all.

George's dissipated face was drawn around sleepless eyes, his entreaties attracting mourners' stares. "Just a chance," he was begging. "Just to *talk* for Chrissakes."

Donna was ignoring him, and Lou was proud. To his other side were Terry Marc Childes and Sheena. In the choicest seats were Patsy Polmquist and crew, while the Beverly Hills gallery owner came belatedly up the aisle with a train of elderly homosexual men sniffling in hankies. And Antoine Lefevre Bulova, in sunglasses. Were his eyes red?

"Do you know who he is?" Terry asked, explaining that Bulova was a longtime Hollywood fixture and anomaly: a rich cop. He'd made a bundle on judicious investments and real estate holdings; the unofficial reasons for his lack of advancement were his homosexuality, and an obsession with celebrity deaths—specifically James Dean's. Terry continued, "He's been into the

Dean crash since the fifties—and it wasn't even in his jurisdiction. And he was more than a "pal" to Lysander, they were on-and-off lovers for forty years."

It put Lou's interview with the detective in a new light.

"Why can't we just be friends?" George was pleading with Donna. "I'm asking you as a human being, another human being in pain. . . ."

Jonathan Cottlee wore a dark pinstripe suit, glossy cropped, dark hair in ringlets framing his face. Terry was frantically trying to attract the millionaire's attention as he scrunched Lou in an attempt to make more room; but Cottlee obliviously took an aisle seat.

"I didn't think he was close to Lysander," Terry said irritably. "What's he doing here? Schmoozing, probably. Damn. I need to talk to him."

The cloying funeral flowers were nauseating. At least there was no casket, just a self-portrait of the artist before a bouquet of black tuberoses. The burnished urn containing Pollack's ashes looked like a yachting trophy.

Liv Ermaine was taking the dais, tall and sepulchral in her black V-cut dress. Reaching into a wicker basket held by her attendant, the Hawk, she extracted a long black snake, which wrapped whiplike coils up her arm. As the chapel gasped, she began the eulogy in a smoky voice.

"In occultism the serpent is a symbol of wisdom, and for centuries magicians have devoted themselves to the search for the forbidden fruit which would bring fulfillment of its promise. The serpent said to Eve, 'Ye shall not surely die, for God doth know that in the day ye eat thereof, then your eyes shall be opened and ye shall be as gods, knowing good and evil.' . . . Lysander saw with the eyes of prophecy and expressed these visions on his canvases. He was certainly no angel—he could be a royal pain in the ass. But his defects were those of the eternal man-child of the universe, who dwells in a realm of wonder and innocence. . . ."

"Get a load of her," Terry was whispering. "She's using the poor bastard's funeral to make a comeback!"

". . . But all in all a generous soul—unlike others I might mention. Jimmy Dean never left a tip in his life, but he came by his stinginess honestly. Venus, Saturn, and Mercury in Capricorn. Capricorn uses people in his climb to the top. There's calculation in each cloven step. Preoccupied with contracts, there's your 'Rebel Without a Clause—' "

"Donna. Please—"

It was a weird memorial service even for Southern California. The bizarre ordeal drew to a close none too soon with operatic strains of Renata Tebaldi piped in, Ermaine stationing herself near the door to receive kudos for her performance.

Lou was loosening his tie and making long strides toward the parking lot, Donna's heels clattering behind him ahead of a distraught Bluestein. When George grabbed her shoulders, Lou would have intervened except he saw her eyes were impressed. Amazingly, she was weakening; Lou realized he knew nothing about women.

"Lou—" Donna was saying hesitantly. "I'm going to ride back with George. Do you mind?"

"Lou," Bluestein said with moist eyes. "This is a good day. I can see everything finally working out, for all of us. Please be happy for me." George grabbed him in an emotional bear hug, pulling Donna in, too.

Over Bluestein's shoulder, Lou saw the somber crowd filing out into afternoon sunlight. He noticed a shock of striking blond hair above dark glasses. Cherie stood at the bus stop like a cat ready to spring. There was a catch in his gut.

When he touched her shoulder, she spun. Then her mouth softened. "I thought I'd get away without you seeing me."

"You almost did. Why?"

She removed the sunglasses. "I feel awful about Indiana. It was so stupid, putting you on a plane the way you were."

"None of it your fault. Actually, thanks to you I even enjoyed it."

"Up until you got arrested?"

"That goes without saying. You're waiting for a bus?"

She made an indifferent face. "Terry was going off with Cottlee, and Sheena just disappeared. I'm staying with them a few days."

"They left you here?"

She laughed. "When you're always broke, you get used to it. Anyway, I like to ride around and see things."

"What kind of things?"

"Regular touristy things. Picture how it used to be like in the old days."

"Dean-days?"

She bit her lower lip. "We're all pretty predictable, huh? I know all the addresses where things used to be. Like Schwab's and the Villa Capri."

"Let me give you a lift. I'll show you whatever you like."

"Would you like to carry my books, too?"

He stammered. "I don't—"

"I'm sorry," she laughed. "It's just a line from *Rebel*, something Natalie says to Jimmy. Then she says, 'I go with the kids.'"

"What's he say?"

"He says, 'I bet.' Ignore me, something about funerals makes me act goofy. Like anytime you're not supposed to laugh, you get the giggles?"

"I wish it affected me that way. Hey, my car's just up the street."

It was almost sensual, the way she traced her fingers along the lines of the Porsche on her way around it. In fact, it was unsettling.

"Cleveland didn't come?" he said as they eased out into traffic.

She was tying a red scarf around her head. "Most of those fan club people can't stand him, so he's not comfortable."

"Is that the only reason?"

She hesitated. "I bet you see right through me."

"What?"

"That's another line from the movie. Jimmy says to Officer Ray, 'I bet you see right through me.' Weird, huh? 'Cause the director's name was Ray. Just like Jimmy raced against a kid named 'Buzz' in the movie. And 'Buzz' was the nickname of the cop who gave Jimmy a speeding ticket the day he was killed. Life is weird."

"Yeah," Lou said. "Weird."

"But I said it, because I figured you saw right through me. Why Cleveland didn't come. It's been kinda rough since that night they put you on the plane. Him and me, I mean. He didn't want me here today. But Pollack's the first person I actually knew who might've died from the curse. I guess it's kinda exciting."

"Wow," he said hesitantly.

"Are you making fun of me?"

"Why do you say that?"

"It's something Jimmy said to Natalie in *Rebel*. He's, like, joking with her."

"People besides James Dean say 'Wow.' Give me your best example of the curse."

She was pensive only a moment. "How about Rolf? He never recovered from the crash. He spent about eighteen months in the hospital and got addicted to painkillers. He had a bunch of nervous breakdowns, and was locked up after he tried to stab to death one of his four wives. He became an alcoholic. He was like Jimmy, in love with speed all his life. His love finally destroyed him, too."

"How?"

She got into the story. "One night in 1981 he's on his way home from a bar in Germany, and his Honda goes out of control on this wet road. He smashed into a house, and they had to use the jaws of life. But he was dead. He'd already survived wrecks besides the one that got Jimmy. I mean, he even raced at Monte Carlo." Her face fell. "And he'd just signed a book contract to come to America and for the first time tell the truth about Jimmy's crash twenty-five years earlier."

He wondered whether her regret was because she would have liked to have read that book.

She said suddenly, "I wonder who's going to get all his stuff."

"Stuff?"

"Lysander's, all his Dean stuff. Paintings and things. Everyone's wondering."

"Was there a will?"

She shrugged. "Cottlee wants to buy the whole estate. I think that's why he came."

"Now he's interested in Lysander's pictures?"

"Cottlee collects. Collects and collects. Lysander had a lot of stuff besides paintings. He had Jimmy's cummerbund from *Giant*. Life masks. Even a little fleck of paint he picked off Jimmy's death car when it was at a bowling alley. A lot of great stuff."

She turned and the seat belt bunched her breasts into small China moons. "Have you decided whether you're a fan? Besides your whatchamacallit, I mean."

"Thesis?"

"Right. Have you collected anything?"

"I did buy some stuff the other day. Before all this. Lysander, I mean."

She punched his shoulder. "You're a fan. Congratulations."

He tried to smile. "How long are you down?"

"I've been hanging out. Seeing the shooting sites from the films, and places where Jimmy lived. I'm so used to living near where he died."

"It's not far?"

"An hour and a half. You've been there?"

Only in my dreams, Lou thought. "I've been thinking about going. I think."

At that moment she half-rose in her seat with recognition. "Is this Mulholland Drive?"

"Yes," he said as they climbed the twisting road. "Like it?"

"Jimmy used to practice up here with his cars before a race." She looked enviously at the wheel of the Porsche.

"Would you like to drive?" he asked, already pulling over.

"You're kidding? You're serious?" Her eyes widened, then twinkled as they traded places. "Can I let her out? What's top?"

"She's kind of touchy," he began uneasily.

The car swerved out onto the road as she accelerated,

Lou gripping the door latch. He settled himself back into the seat.

"I've always wanted to do this," she said as she whipped the Speedster around a curve, the small tires spitting gravel.

Lou was pressed back as she went quickly through the gears. "I'm in a car with a maniac," he shouted above the engine whine.

She smiled.

Anything he might do would be more dangerous than riding it out; she needed to concentrate. "Now," he shouted. "Shift now!"

The odometer needle quivered upward from 70 as they came on a straightaway. At 90 Lou began to feel a certain relaxation, not bothering to fasten the shoulder harness. Were one of the Pirellis to catch a pothole, she would most likely overcorrect and roll. He had a plummeting sensation. But loss of control and nearness of death were balancing some sort of internal pain that had to do with Ernie Hockman; he actually felt pretty good.

The roadside blurred and the center line became a continuous thread. There was a hairpin turn ahead, and a precipitous drop.

He braced. Their best chance was if she kept the tires perfectly straight.

Instead, she was tentatively tapping the brake.

"No," Lou shouted. *"No."*

The car swung sideways, and they were off onto the shoulder of a cliff as she frantically twisted the wheel. They hit soft dirt and ice plant, but the car stayed upright in a screen of dust.

It was a moment before either of them realized the car was motionless. Lou waited for his stomach to catch up. The engine had died, and there was a deadening feeling as Ernie Hockman caught up with him, too. Lou realized he'd almost outrun him for the first time in five years.

Cherie was chalky, hands shaking. "Wow. Sorry."

Lou laughed. "You call that 'letting her out'?"

"I don't know what came over me," she said.

"My turn," he said. "I'll drive the rest of the way."

"How did I do?"

"I'm impressed," he said. "And you've never been on Mulholland?"

"Somehow, I just knew what to do," she said as she got out of the car.

He made no comment.

"My God," she said. Instead of walking around to the passenger side she was stepping toward the sheer drop.

"What is it?" he said.

She stood with her back to him, transfixed. "Somebody died here."

"Who?"

She trembled at the edge.

"Who?" he repeated quietly, getting out of the car.

"I think this is where it happened," she said in an eerie voice. "Where a boy died. Syd Kirkland—he was a friend of Jimmy's. A good friend. He studied with Strasberg before Jimmy did. They were very close."

He stepped cautiously forward, not wanting to startle her. Something told him she was going to jump. Not with premeditation, but on impulse. Or a compulse, if there was such a thing. He realized she was recalling that scene in *Rebel* after Buzz drives his car off the Millertown bluff, and Judy stands at the precipice.

"Come away from there—now." He held out his hand.

She looked at him strangely for a long time, wind rippling her short hair. She tentatively took his fingers.

He pulled her to him, relieved. "I'm glad that's over."

She was quiet a moment. Then, "What did you just say?"

The expression on her face made him ask, "What did you think?"

" 'Life can be beautiful.' Is that what you said?"

"No. But for a minute there . . ." he thought of her high school wrist-slashing, but now she seemed fine. He told himself it was in his head.

As they drove down the hill he said, "I think I asked you earlier, how long you were gonna be here."

"I didn't answer, did I? I'll call Cleveland tonight to see if he'll come and get me. Unless he's punishing me."

Lou's mouth was dry. "I could give you a ride tomorrow."

She laughed. "You're kidding? A hundred miles?"

"It's not really out of my way," he lied. "I told you I was thinking of driving out to the death site. I'll do it tomorrow."

"That'd be a good time," she said with approval. "I mean, next weekend it's going to be crowded with scads of people. I think it'll be okay if you take me halfway."

"You have to check?"

She looked away.

They were at Childes's house. "Terry's got your number," she said as she got out. "I'll call you tonight. Do you believe in the chakras?"

"I never thought about it."

"I have a third eye in my forehead. . . . You can even feel it with your finger—see?" She took his finger and touched it to her forehead.

His finger tingled.

"It's my psychism," she said happily. "It tells me that you've been sent into all this. It's no accident. I try to think that we all have, like, this oversoul that doesn't get any older, and that's what's really relating between people. The karmic stuff kinda makes everything shrink to ... insignificance. Right?"

Lou drove away. He was actually going to retrace the death route. Or was it "deathroute"?

He was surprised to see George and Donna on the apartment landing, concern on their faces. His front door was wide. The first thing he thought was "burglary."

"A little surprise for you," Donna said uneasily. "We just got here, and this delivery truck was pulling up."

Lou walked into his apartment, all suddenly unfamiliar.

"They just started unloading," Donna said. "From the executor. There wasn't a will, but you got 'em."

Yes, Lou thought. I certainly did.

Dark canvases were stacked leaning against the walls, all studies of James Dean: Dean in crucifixion pose, arms outstretched on the drive train and trans axle of a car; Dean in the bean field of *East of Eden*, a fertility god urging the sprouts to grow; and the unfinished *Last Supper*.

"I didn't know what to do," Donna said, "and the manager had already unlocked your door. You weren't here."

Yes, Lou thought. That was probably the idea. "Who was this executor?"

"The name was on the paper," Donna said. "Let me see, it was like a watch—"

"Bulova?" Lou asked.

Donna nodded. "That's it. It's a good likeness, by the way."

"Huh?"

In *The Last Supper* he saw his own face on the shoulders of the disciple next to Jimmy. As Thorpe rubbed apprehensively against his leg, Lou felt a tingling at the tip of the forefinger that had felt Cherie's third eye.

14

Saturday, September 24, 1995
Hollywood Freeway, 1:22 P.M.

Cherie apparently was in the habit of sleeping late; her eyes were still swollen when Lou stopped at Terry's in the early afternoon. She was quiet and withdrawn as they took the Hollywood Freeway exit north.

Despite a chill in the air and in the car, Lou found the hum of the engine and the highway beneath steel radials warmly transfusing. Even with the stop at Devereux's, he ought to arrive at the intersection about the time of Dean's accident.

He wondered whether the girl had had a fight with Cleveland on the telephone. "Is anything wrong?"

"I was thinking about Mulholland yesterday." She slid down the seat, shivering with macabre ecstasy. "It was a creepy feeling. I've had creepy feelings all my life."

"Is that all?"

She took a breath. "No. Cleveland said he's going to

talk to you, and it bugs me. He's got this idea that Jimmy was murdered by this crazy cult that paid somebody to bushwhack him on the highway."

"Why?"

"For magical power. Only it didn't come off right and the group sorta fell apart. Now he thinks Liv Ermaine's picked up where they left off. She's a connective link to the fifties. He thinks the fan club people are her slaves and they all plan to bring Jimmy back on Friday."

"The Second Coming?" Lou's laughter didn't relieve the creepiness. "What's supposed to happen then?"

She was embarrassed. "He thinks somebody has Jimmy's death car, and now they have his body. One week from today the accident's going to be duplicated by a film crew at the actual site. It's got some kind of magical significance. And there'll be blood sacrifices, or something. And finally the car and Jimmy Dean will reappear on the road. Cleve says Jimmy will run over everybody, and the highway'll be covered with blood."

A new Advent, Lou thought. "Lysander talked like that. It's so weird."

"I just don't want you to get sucked into this is all. Because that's what he'll try to do."

"Why?"

"He says he needs somebody like you. Somebody straight, and from the outside. Who's not looney tunes."

He wanted to steer her away from haunted shoals, but gray sky oppressed as they climbed the mountains. She chain-smoked and fiddled with a transistor radio, more tense with each mile.

At the top of the Grapevine he saw a dirty blanket covering the valley, fog rolling in to cloud their entry into Bakersfield. Cherie insisted he stop at a certain telephone pole where Cleveland had erected a homely aluminum plaque. Because Jimmy had been ticketed there for speeding on his way to eternity, Devereux designated the site one of the Stations of the Cross.

The muck reflected the headlights back at them as Cherie guided Lou to a dilapidated area in the unincorporated outskirts of town, and a dead-end street. They pulled to the curb before a modest and sullen-looking house. The pony-tailed Bill Bario came out barefoot to meet them. "He's been worried about you," was all he said to Cherie.

Cleveland appeared unshaven in the doorway to intercept her, and there was a brief skirmish before she disappeared curtly inside. He walked to the car, trying to manage an amiable smile. "She says you're going out to the crash site."

"That was the plan, until this fog."

"It's dangerous to drive, and you won't be able to see anything. What I'm saying is, you'd better spend the night."

Lou hesitated, surprised. "I can get a motel—"

"Nonsense, it'll be my way of making up to you, about before. The Indiana thing. You're not going to punch me in the eye, are you?"

"I'm trying to decide."

"Believe me, I'm really sorry. I didn't know who you were."

"Who am I?"

Cleveland smiled inscrutably, irritatingly. "Come on inside."

Lou followed with misgivings but curiosity, noticing there were actually two doors, the outer a heavy iron-wrought security number, which Devereux dead-bolted behind them. It was dark inside, but off the hall Lou saw the front room described in Devereux's book, the Holy of Holies.

"All my Dean stuff," Cleveland said self-consciously.

The walls were covered with photos and posters. An eerie life mask of the actor, like those in Pollack's studio, stared down with vacant eyes from over a piano. There was an easel with a half-finished portrait of Jimmy in the red jacket, a good likeness.

"Cherie's the painter," Devereux said. "I think that's why she wanted to go to Lysander's funeral."

Lou was jealous; he hadn't known she painted. There were also a half-dozen rumpled sleeping bags on the floor. Devereux was waiting, and he followed. "Looks like you've already got company."

"There's a bunch of fans who'll be staying here until the end of the month."

"Yours, or Dean's?" The sarcasm was made feeble by Cleveland's indifference.

"Jimmy's," Devereux said distractedly. "Everybody's out to the market getting food." He indicated a chair at the kitchen table. "The intersection's an interesting place, apart from Dean. A lot of motorists besides Jimmy have been killed there, especially before they put up the safety lights. Coffee?"

"Decaf? Fine." Lou noticed iron bars over the window, and Bario sitting moodily in a sunken den with more sleeping bags on the floor. He was cleaning an automatic pistol.

Cleveland started the coffee maker among the pile of unwashed dishes before seating himself. "And ten thousand years before that, the ancient Chumash Indians believed that spot to be the unifying center at the heart of all creation. And when you died there, your soul did not leave but was imprisoned in the rocks and hills forever."

Lou indicated Bario. "He's got a gun."

"Yeah," Cleveland said, embarrassed. "Everyone's upset since what happened to Lysander."

"The coroner said Ly died a natural death."

"But by supernatural means. His heart was burst by unhuman hands. There are folks who've taken fandom way beyond . . . this." He indicated his Dean collection in the other room.

"How far?"

"I think there're darkened houses in this country which've been turned into private museums. You go from room to room, and you'll see more than commemorative plates and pencil sharpeners. You might see the death car. And now, you might see the body of James Dean mounted like an exhibit at Madame Tussaud's . . . as you know. Do you believe in magic?"

"I believe that some believe."

"So do I, and they worry me. I think Lysander had a guilty secret, and it got him killed. Forty years ago he was on the outskirts of a cabal which planned and executed the death of James Dean for magical power. They wanted to create their own designer god in the middle of this century." He seemed disappointed Lou was not shocked. "Jimmy was killed on schedule, but for some reason the plot went haywire and never came to fruition. But now I think it's been reactivated by Liv Ermaine."

"Is that why you're all holed up here? Waiting for the end of the world?"

"Just until next Friday. That's when the movie crew will reenact Dean's passion. It's the prerequisite opening of the mystic door. There'll be a ceremony and a sacrifice. Hundreds of people will be out there at the intersection of 41 and 46 that night. Dean's car will be hidden somewhere nearby, and even his body. You're the religions expert. What do you think comes next?"

"Remember, my work's merely 'in development.' "

"Body and car will be *reunited* at a certain point in a ritual. It will be like touching the hot wires of a battery. There'll be a 'spark' and a god will become *ensouled*. Right now, Dean is merely a cultural icon. They need an *actual* resurrected god with all the powers a god can command and bestow. They intend to inaugurate a new eon in which they'll be the elect priesthood."

Lou was glad Cherie had braced him for the pitch.

Devereux lit a cigarette, drawing a skull-and-crossbones ashtray closer. "I'm trying to quit. Why am I blurting all this out on you? Look, I'm a James Dean crackpot. You're a perfect complement to my personality. You have something I don't. Credibility. You can get entrée to people I can't. Together we could smash this ring by next Friday."

"What people? Cottlee?"

Cleveland started. "Did Ly mention Cottlee? Jonathan certainly has the money and connections to pull off all the media manipulation."

" 'Media manipulation'?"

"Stir up the psychic energies in the collective unconsciousness to critical mass. That's the force occultists want to harness. Black arts is all about power. Cottlee I can get next to. He likes me. But Liv hates my guts."

Lou paused, dizzy. "Where does Cherie fit into this? Is she just another fan as far as you're concerned?"

The other man crushed out his cigarette. "She's real fragile, but stubborn as hell. If I told you who she was, you'd never look at her the same again. If I'm right, you may be in danger already, but you've got no idea what you'd be getting into with her. Do you really want to help her?"

"You think she needs help? What kind?"

Devereux leaned back. "I told you. Break up the plot by this Friday."

Lou was relieved of having to reply, because there was commotion at the front door, Bario rushing to undo deadbolts.

Dean widows Amy and Vonda seemed glad to see Lou, but Sharon was sulky beneath headphones. Ruiz's eyes were evasive as he set the armfuls of groceries on the sink, followed by several high-school age Dean knock-offs of both sexes whom Lou had never seen. Cherie reappeared to greet Amy and Vonda with hugs. Bario scrounged hungrily through the supplies.

Lou had a hammering headache. *Death cult. Death car. Death route.* He wanted to leave the house, but not until he had a chance to talk privately with Cherie. But the chance didn't come. Not only were they never alone, but she seemed to be avoiding him. Devereux's Deaners ate junk food for dinner, and afterward settled in for a James Dean Theater. For hours the little TV illumined their faces in the shadows as Jimmy's three testaments were rerun, while Lou played solitaire obstinately in the kitchen.

It was late when someone popped into the VCR a cassette of a defunct TV show called *What Happened?* in which investigative experts reconstructed Dean's crash via computer simulation.

"Look at that," Cleveland said as he froze the tape and knelt before the screen. "See, in the eastbound lane? The Ford leaves two sets of skids thirty feet long, with a ten-yard gap in between. What's he braking for clear back here? They talked at the inquest of how the Spyder blended into the road because it was silver. But what about these big red numbers on the front? And Rolf's wearing a red shirt."

"We've gotta try to get to him again," Bario said. "The driver."

"What?" Lou was roused from the cards for the first time. His vehemence surprised himself as he said, "You mean you've harassed that poor guy?" He felt the stares. "I just mean, the guy in that other car has to be miserable enough. You people are inhuman."

Cherie seemed to be avoiding Lou's eyes, lost in cigarette smoke as he stared blankly at the frozen image of computerized cars.

Devereux's voice was slyly conciliatory. "What if a full disclosure of the facts would exonerate him of any guilt? What if it could be proved after all these years that he was entirely blameless in the death of James Dean?"

"Forget it," Lou said hoarsely, tired of Byzantine scenarios. "It's been a long day."

"For everybody," Devereux said diplomatically.

Cherie disappeared, and Lou wondered whether she retreated to her own room. No, he corrected, I'm wondering whether she's sleeping with Devereux.

The walls of Lou's assigned bedroom were overlaid with Dean stuff. Or "Deanstuff." Fog pressed against the window as he tossed on the mattress, his mind running in circles and telling him the coffee wasn't decaf. His defection had revived the party, and he could hear them playing the accident over and over again.

He woke with a convulsive breath, a nameless chaos, to realize his cheap watch had stopped at midnight.

He lay in the dark with eyes open. Hanging crookedly on the opposite wall was a Lysander Pollack canvas. Lou had to get up and right it compulsively, staring for a moment into Dean's ghostly face superimposed on clouds above the intersection.

On one of the curves that snaked up into the hills was a small silver cross, which seemed to glow as if the paint was luminescent. And the spot it marked was exactly where Ernie had been standing in the dream.

Some states marked highway fatalities with roadside crosses, but California wasn't one. And this cross was on the old road, above the intersection. Looking closely, he made out an actual inscription, picturing Pollack working dementedly in miniature with the finest of sable brushes to print in phonetic Greek:

ϑαμεσ Δεαν Διεδ Φορ Ουρ Σινσ

"James Dean died for our sins."

"A tool for meditation," Pollack had said.

The insistent cross floating in the dark kept Lou awake. What happened there? What was Pollack trying to say?

After an hour, he resentfully slipped on his jeans and walked quietly up the hall and into the front room for his own unguided tour of Devereux's Dean shrine, stepping gingerly over the bagged and snoring bodies.

On the piano was a small framed photo of a pudgy, acned kid standing awkwardly at the intersection. He had to look closely to recognize Devereux at the age of sixteen.

The hand on Lou's shoulder startled him.

Cleveland smiled apologetically in Levi's and bare feet, cigarette aglow in his fingers.

"Jesus," Lou said as he caught his breath.

"I couldn't sleep, either," Devereux whispered. "I thought I heard somebody rustling around." He embarrassedly turned the picture to the wall.

Lou realized the other man was drinking.

Cleveland spoke with a soft slur as he waved his cigarette. "Are you beginning yet to understand what people like Cherie and I are all about, what draws us?"

"Not entirely. No."

"I'm sure part of it's the mystery." He indicated a framed Roth photograph of the attendants loading Jimmy's blanketed body into the ambulance. "For instance, that ambulance did not go straight to the hospital. It stopped, supposedly after a minor sideswipe with another car. What if Jimmy was still breathing, and they stopped so Jimmy could be given a lethal injection? Or maybe even broke his neck? 'Snap!' Just like that."

"You all want it to be anything but an accident," Lou said quietly. "You think that's not dramatic enough, but maybe accidents are the most frightening things there are."

Devereux continued obliviously.

"What if there was a witness? Rolf was in the back of that ambulance, too. What if he came to for a little bit and saw something? It's documented that important representatives from Porsche went to see Rolf in the hospital where he was in traction. But what if they weren't Porsche? What if they were the ones who spirited Rolf out of the country within a year and saw to his upkeep all the rest of his life? Until his alcoholism and instability made him a danger. Until he threatened to have his memoirs ghost-written. Then, a second crash is engineered to silence him in 1981."

Lou found himself listening, despite himself.

Devereux's face was closer. "Or, what if Rolf's involvement in the crash was more incriminating?"

"Some kind of tampering?"

Devereux poked Lou in the chest for emphasis. "Why else would the wreck be towed secretly to Hollywood under a tarp, only to be stolen for good and ever in 1960? What might a close inspection of that car have revealed even five years later? What did Jimmy know about his killers? Why is his house burgled that night? To eradicate what traces?"

"But Rolf was as likely to die as Jimmy if there was a crash."

"But maybe he was a fanatic whose belief system didn't recognize death."

"More intriguing," Lou said uneasily, "the only two eyewitnesses at the inquest—Fredericks and Dooley— were unshaken in their claims that Jimmy had been the passenger and *Rolf* the driver at the time of the wreck—" He stopped when he saw Devereux smiling a sort of prick-tease smile, and knew he had been had.

"See what I mean?" Cleveland said more casually. "But I had started to say it's more than the mystery which pulls people like us into the enigma of Jimmy's life and death. It's really a sort of . . . religious yearning. You're a young guy. You're also searching, looking for something. Evading that inner emptiness has brought you right here—no accident—to James Dean. And people like me, and Cherie. Do you realize you're already involved? Deeply?"

"I don't know about that."

Cleveland smiled as he leaned against the wall. "Dream on. You're hooked. I know the look."

Lou's face stung. "When I got here today, you said you didn't know 'who I was.' What was that supposed to mean?"

Devereaux's smile was appreciative. "I mentioned events coming into alignment. But what if there's an avatar? I'm sure you're familiar with the term."

"To the Hindus, the human incarnation of a deity."

"Or, a variant phase or version of a continuing, basic, entity. The individual could be blood-lineal, or spiritual-lineal. Like a reincarnation."

"That 'ka' crap?"

"Whatever. Any sort of heir to James Dean threatens to disperse the psychic energy they're trying to concentrate. He, or she, would have to die, ideally by sacrifice. The highest symbolic act."

"I'm going to bed," Lou said, turning.

"If you're not with us, you're against us. And if you're against us, you shouldn't go out to that intersection tomorrow. You won't have the safety in numbers."

"I'll take that chance."

"Lou," Devereux said more quietly. "Is it Cherie? If it is, you'd be better off getting it out of your system so you can move on. Would you like to take a shot at her?"

Lou turned. "What'd you say?"

"She's in my room right now. Get it over with, then go back home tomorrow. Tell yourself what a silly bunch of people we are."

Lou was stunned. "No. And you get the fuck away from me."

He closed the door behind him and slipped between the covers of the strange bed without undressing.

Would you like to take a shot at her?

He punched his pillow, but it didn't help. The little cross glowed in the dark. Did it commemorate something? Or was something buried there?

15

Sunday, May 1, 1955
Minter Field, Bakersfield, California

Jimmy squinted through the drizzle beneath bleak skies at the other sports cars stacked along the airport starting line, 8,000 spectators watching from beneath umbrellas or black plastic. The runway course was demarcated by 1,200 bales of hay to cushion slides at the corners, but the talk in the pits was how the bales had soaked until they were hard and dangerous. The drivers in the 1,300–2,000cc production competition nervously awaited the starter pistol of the 14-lap race.

To Jimmy in his Speedster there was something about high speed which was more than freedom. Acceleration translated you into a higher form of energy. He was remembering his first motorbike, a Czech Indian. He flexed his hands around the steering wheel.

He was looking for respite from Hollywood a hundred miles away, but seemed to have brought it with him. *Rebel* was running four weeks behind schedule, and George Stevens was waging a desperate campaign by memo trying to wrest Jimmy free by the end of the month so he could be rushed to Texas, where *Giant* would already be in production. A studio edict forbade racing, but Jimmy hoped to sneak in at least two more before he left.

He already had a retinue, though only one of his films had been released. This was the best time to catch a star. He saw Liv Ermaine down the fence line, stark as a black crow with feathers shiny from the rain, Frank Saunders holding a program over her head to protect her coiffure while he described the fine points of racing.

They were a striking couple. Saunders was one of the Austrians who had expatriated to sell and service foreign cars in the American market. A group had formed around the racing circuit, and their communion with speed and engines appealed to Jimmy. The 6'5" Saunders, blue eyes piercing beneath a blond mane of hair, was a successful salesman at Racer's Edge Motors, southern California's most visible foreign car dealership. He was married, and Jimmy was disappointed that one of his heroes would succumb to Liv. But he was more interested in one of Saunders' fellow employees.

Jimmy had met Rolf Weutheric that morning and was immediately drawn to the wounded quality, and the romance of a Luftwaffe pilot who as a teenager had been sent on suicide missions by a desperate Hitler the last year of the war. Rolf had black ringlets of hair and haunted eyes. He was loud and boisterous in the pits, but Jimmy knew the engaging grin covered insecurity. Rolf also had trouble with English, and Jimmy had been too glad to help as Weutheric looked over the Speedster's engine. He had magic hands.

Jimmy knew how to make someone feel like a prince, and talked about teaming up for Monte Carlo—

style racing in the future. He also promised to dedicate the race to him like a toreador dedicating the ears of a bull, but wasn't sure Rolf understood.

He caught Weutheric's eyes in the pit, and the other man smiled broadly and signaled thumbs-up. Jimmy psyched himself into a heightened state of concentrated awareness.

That was what racing was about, the next best thing to bullfighting. It demanded the mode of mind of a warrior facing death, extremely alert without being distracted by anything going on around him. He intended to take a martial arts class in kendo, *the way of the sword*. Like racing, it would combine violence and spiritual discipline—

The starter's pistol sounded, and the cars lurched forward with whining engines.

Heading into the first curve, a racer slipped in front of Jimmy to throw sheets of water across his windscreen. He felt self-contempt and determined to make up distance on the straightaway.

He did over the next eight laps, breathing hard and high in his chest as he led the howling pack of nudging machines. Then a red MG drew even, its chrome-spoked wheels a blur in the misty wetness. Jimmy could not see the other driver's face. They were alone behind a curtain of drizzle as they battled it out. Turn Three would decide.

There was the clap of thunder, and the flash of lightning blinding with weird brilliance on the oily sheen of tarmac. Jimmy heard DeWeerd's voice. *"It is the Magician who controls earth's major forces and draws the fire down from heaven. With the symbol of infinity over his head he wields the magical weapons with which he shall conquer the—"*

The red MG closed in front. For the instant Jimmy

lost him in the mist. When the other car emerged, it was losing traction in the slickness to hit the hardened bales like a wall of concrete. The concussion was terrific. The racer broke in pieces.

Jimmy saw the engine and cockpit rolling over and over, buffeting the harnessed driver like a rag doll.

The yellow flag was out, cars slowing and skidding in the downpour as the lights of the ambulance sped across the waste. Rain made it vague.

The engine thrum was still in Jimmy's limbs as he unharnessed himself to run to the wreck, the only driver to do so. There was a gasoline explosion from the ruptured tank, and flames flowed over the car. The other driver screamed, his arms jerking like sticks as his flesh crackled.

The heat drove Jimmy back. He thought the victim looked directly at him from two melted eyes, as hissing raindrops washed away the steaming face in black rivulets.

Competition resumed when the ambulance was gone. Jimmy hoped it would clear his mind. It didn't. He was mentally lost. He could have placed first, but held himself to third. The announcement from the hospital came after the race. Of course, the boy was dead. At the same time, Jimmy felt in his pocket and realized Syd's mezuzah was missing.

That night at the awards banquet there was a moment of silence for the victim. Jack Drummond, a loan officer and service veteran from Arizona, left a wife and two small children.

Jimmy received his trophy and began to get drunk. Liv was in fine form, her tongue dipped in acid. She was relentless in her needling, and he knew why. When the tabloids had come out with stories about his possi-

ble romantic liaison with the TV actress, he'd countered
with his own barbed quote planted with Hedda Hopper.
"I don't go out with witches, and I dig dating cartoons
even less. I have a fairly adequate knowledge of satanic
forces, and I was interested to find out if this girl was
obsessed by such a force. I met her and engaged her in
conversation. She knew nothing—"

Liv had decided to save face publicly with a pretense
they were engaging in a good-natured feud through the
press. But she was venting her spleen this evening. He
let her go on, even deriving a masochistic pleasure.
Rolf's confused eyes were defensive and protective, and
Jimmy enjoyed that.

The post-race party was in his room at the Bakersfield Inn, "The World's Largest Motor Hotel."

It wasn't the evening Jimmy had planned, and he
slumped on the floor against the wall, cigarette dangling
from his lips as he pounded desultorily on bongos. Photographer Sandy Roth had shot Einstein and Picasso,
and now installed a fish-eye lens on his 35mm Nikon to
search out dramatic shadows on his new subject's face.
Jimmy had arranged paperbacks on the nightstand so
their titles showed—*Pain, Sex and Time* and Cassio's
Los Toros.

Racing friend Bill Hickman sat on the bed awkwardly next to Rolf and asked mournfully, "What's the
matter, Jimmy? Is it what happened today?"

Jimmy blew a stream of smoke up into the corner of
the ceiling.

"You shouldn't have gone and looked," Bill was saying as he worked the cap off a beer. "I'm superstitious.
It's bad luck in a race."

"Oh?" Rolf said a little drunkenly. "I always look.
And I place first."

"Yeah," Bill said. "I know you, you're an insensitive

bastard. It's not fair, but they don't have much bad luck."

Rolf laughed, and when he lay back the leather of his boots and jacket squeaked. He smiled at Jimmy across the room and upended his bottle. The currents in the room were becoming intense. Jimmy noticed Rolf's English improved with alcohol. But when he thought about the dead boy, it was like cold plaster poured into his guts.

He was reminded of the little ceremony that had been performed over his racer before he left town.

It had started on the *Rebel* set, where everyone knew Nick Ray was romantically involved with seventeen-year-old Van Nuys High School senior Natalie Wood even before the picture began. He'd lobbied with Jack Warner to cast her as Judy, finally gaining the concession with a promise to work closely and personally with her on voice, wardrobe, and hair. Still, it was shattering for a love-struck Dennis Hopper to catch her in the shower with the grizzled forty-four-year-old director at his bungalow at the Chateau Marmont.

Nick had encouraged a tight-knit *Rebel* gang since preproduction, but now it backfired. They felt betrayed by the man who'd come on like a surrogate dad, and closed ranks against him. Not Jimmy. He was aloof, and he'd also bragged to Jeff and to Joe Hyams about having Natalie in the front seat of his Speedster.

He had grown to respect Nick, a visual but erratic director who played by nobody's rules but his own and had done better than most in keeping his artistic soul intact in Hollywood. Everyone said Ray was very good with Jimmy, who was developing a bad reputation for eccentricity and unmanageability. Nick involved him in every phase of production, and accepted suggestions and improvisations. Jimmy's winking at Ray's peccadilloes drew them closer.

"You've got to see it," Nick said to Jimmy on Friday, describing his new Malibu rental. "You're racing tomorrow? Come around tonight, I'll give you a little boost."

Jimmy did not know whether he meant drugs, a pep talk, or another rambling monologue about the proposed picture after *Giant*. He humored Ray. What was one more talking commitment? He was also looking at *Somebody Up There Likes Me*, *The Left-Handed Gun*, and a remake of *Dr. Jekyll and Mr. Hyde*.

Arriving at the beach house that evening, he was unpleasantly surprised by the Cadillacs, Mercedes, and small foreign jobs lining the coastal highway. He hadn't expected a party, but knew he could beg out early by saying he had to practice power turns in the Hills. Fortunately, he had fortified himself with a few drinks.

Nick met him at the door, glass in hand.

"Look," Ray slurred, "we're going to have a little ritual over your car, and I'll be goddamned if I'll apologize to anybody about it." His stance was belligerent as he took the keys from Jimmy's fingers. "Lemme pull your racer in the garage."

Jimmy stepped into the dark house and an atmosphere tense as an illegal cockfight, nodding coolly to some producers and directors from his CBS days. Jazz played on the stereo, and he perused some of the books on the coffee table before curling up in the corner with one of Ray's antique pistols.

"I've got a financial adviser," Nick said when he returned, as if Jimmy was the only person in the room. "I've got a tax adviser. Why not a spiritual adviser? That's how I got involved in this. I know about those Maleficarum faggots that left a bad taste in your mouth, but this is different."

Ray's words stung. Jimmy was self-conscious about the reputation he was acquiring, the rumors about pre-stardom hustling, and his underground reputation as "the human ashtray." More than the deviance, he was bothered by whatever threatened his own insistence that he was self-made and owed nothing to anyone. He got his own drink from the bar.

Nick saw the hurt. "You didn't think I knew? I understand. You and me are alike, we're experimenters. Just suspend your disbelief for a little bit."

Ray's excitement was contagious, and Jimmy was cautiously curious. "What's the ritual for?"

"Victory," Nick said as he replenished his drink from the bar.

"It works?"

Nick winked and punched his arm. "How do you think I got you to sign for *Rebel*? Let's go down to the garage."

Jimmy gulped his drink. It was dangerous and he didn't care for these strangers to have anything on him, but he already had some practice at disavowal via press manipulation. Hedda was in his corner, he'd charmed her out of her panties.

"Who's this 'spiritual adviser'?" he asked, aware of other men following down the stairs.

" 'The Goat,' " Nick said obliquely, playing the mystify game of which Jimmy was also master. "There's a lot you have to go through before you're admitted to secrets—but you be the judge. Watch your step."

Jimmy saw his Speedster in the middle of a pentagram on the oil- and grease-spotted concrete. He was surprised at the number of old and young men crowded into the small carport. There were no women. There was a poignant bleating noise from a door, and a shining man appeared in a robe the silver Porsche racing

color, his lower half clothed in black. He led a white
goat protesting on a tether. Doctor Greenspacht didn't
even nod recognition.

Jimmy's shock crawled up from his socks and did a
lot to part the alcohol curtain he'd drawn across his
brain. Not only was Greenspacht made up like Brackett
had been at those long-ago coven meetings, but now
Greenspacht had the box.

Jimmy recovered **and tried** to mentally condition
himself for the scene shaping up. Nick was always testing people.

"I'm proposing we dedicate this car to victory up
north tomorrow," Nick said as he put his arm around
Jimmy's shoulder.

Jimmy raised his brows. "The last time I ran, I threw
a rod and didn't finish. What can it hurt?"

"You're with me?"

"It looks like kicks," Jimmy said easily as the others
assumed positions around the car. He was still drunk
enough, and he didn't care for his psychiatrist to see
any fear.

Greenspacht raised his arm high and brought a knife
down hard across the animal's neck, then hurried to
catch the blood from the artery in a chalice. The blood
ran down his hands and his wrists until someone helped
him by supporting the animal's limp head.

Nick drew on his unfiltered cigarette, then dropped it
to the floor so he could take the chalice and hold it over
the car. He looked odd in his open polo shirt as he intoned, "We're here to consecrate a Porsche. Tomorrow
will be Jimmy's race in this beautiful machine. Men of
speed and light know that the man and the car must be
one, they have to share one heart and one soul. Let it be
so with Jimmy and his car. What do you say?"

There were smiles, and murmurs of assent as Ray dribbled the blood onto the aluminum hood.

"You're crazy," Jimmy said. "We'll see if it works."

Nick winked. "There's two parts to any ceremony, and the most important one is the expectation it'll work. Racers are a superstitious bunch, anyway. And you'll do *Blind Run* with me."

"You killed a goat over that, too?" Jimmy asked.

"If it works, why fix it?" Nick smiled as he wiped the rim of the cup with a hanky he returned absently to his pocket. "I feel like a drink, let's get upstairs and talk about that production company you and I are gonna form. Did I ever tell you my theory how this whole industry is based on magic?"

It was getting late in Jimmy's suite at the Inn. He continued to drink, and relaxed more when Bill and Sandy left. Rolf seemed tense, drinking more and squeaking his leather as he walked nervously across the room.

"Sit down," Jimmy said, touching the floor.

The sounds of lovemaking through the wall of Saunders's room next door added piquancy. "Looks like Liv's made a conquest." Jimmy giggled.

Rolf smiled as he slid to the floor, but did not completely understand.

"What they ought to do is put on some music. See? Then they can make all the noise they want." Jimmy placed a reel of tape on his German recorder, the voice of Renata Tebaldi filling the room.

They talked haltingly, Jimmy exploring Rolf's personality and tightening the threads of intimacy, alternately impish, seductive, and purely manipulative. It was a subtle testing, a teasing and withdrawing that slipped back and forth between racing bonhomie and girlish giggliness.

Rolf would only talk about the engines of the planes he flew in the war, not talk about whether he had shot anyone. He did not want to talk about any friends going down in flames, or burning cities. He did not want to talk about the feeling of pressing a machine gun's trigger, or whether you could see another pilot's expression as you fired on him. The German just drank more. But the game served to push Jack Drummond from Jimmy's mind.

"No, it's got to be the Spyder," Rolf said with sudden vehemence when Jimmy told of his intention to order a Lotus to compete in a bigger-bore car. The other man's sudden intensity amused him.

"You think so?"

Weutheric's nod was passionate. "We have a saying, 'If you don't own the Spyder, a Spyder will eat you.' And I can do things with the engine to boost it, I know what it can do and how to get maximum."

"And you'd do that, for me?" Jimmy's voice was intimate.

Rolf sipped suddenly and self-consciously on his beer when Jimmy's face came very close, but eventually the bottle was undeniably empty. Jimmy put a finger on Rolf's lip. "Have you ever kissed a man?"

Rolf smiled hazily. They kissed for a while. His hair and hands smelled of gasoline, and Jimmy imagined punctured fuel tanks in Foch-Wulfs.

"Can you be fucked?" Jimmy breathed.

"I don't know," Rolf said with fear in his glassy eyes.

They kissed again, and Jimmy played off the other man's resistance and confusion as they lay back on the floor. He made it a game, a playful physical contest. He wove glamor around himself with the calculated dropping of names. Jimmy was too deft, and Rolf was compromised before he knew it, and too befuddled to know what to do. There was pain.

Jimmy turned up Renata Tebaldi, and her voice covered the cries. The tears Rolf cried later were not woman's tears, but those of a man who had seen a friend die violently. Jimmy helped him through it.

Afterwards they lay together, and Jimmy kept seeing Jack Drummond of the wife and two kids, fire peeling the flesh back like a banana around his lidless eyes. Just the staring eyes like golf balls and these incredibly white teeth in a black—

Rolf stirred. "What's that smell?"

"It's a matador's cape," Jimmy said as he pulled it from beneath the hotel bed. It smelled of bulls and blood.

"My security blanket," he said as he pulled it over them in the dark. But he couldn't sleep.

16

Sunday, September 25, 1995
Bakersfield, California

Lou awoke at dawn feeling he'd hardly slept, but was galvanized when he saw the cross on the picture and recalled his intentions at the deathsite. He went through the house and found none of the fans stirring yet, which was fine. But Cherie, in sweater and sneakers, was fixing coffee in the kitchen. As soon as he saw her, he remembered the dream.

There was a traffic accident and smell of leaking gasoline. But his feet were caught in the wreckage of his car, until rough arms lifted him up and pulled him free. They carried him like a baby across the highway. He looked up at the face that had saved him, and saw Ernie Hockman. "Don't look back," Ernie said.

Lou saw Cherie still in the car, unconscious. A small orange flame became visible underneath the car. She would be incinerated. Hockman said, "It's no use, Lou."

The orange heat flowed over her like napalm, sucking the air from his own lungs.

Now in the kitchen, Lou was staring. He barely heard her question of concern. "I'm fine," he answered.

She said uneasily, "Do you mind if I go with you? Today?"

It jarred him wider awake. "I hadn't planned to come back on the inland route."

Her own eyes were tired. "I was thinking of going back with you. I could stay at Sheena's. Cleveland's going up in a couple of days, I could come back with him then."

He tried to pull his mind together. "So, you checked with him?"

"I told him I felt like going, anyway." She averted her eyes.

What are you getting into? he asked himself. "Sure. If you want."

He left a terse note on the sink thanking Devereux for his hospitality—after accidentally spelling "hostility."

He was glad to be on the highway driving north. She was very quiet, and he noted how a single night with Devereux had changed her. Twenty miles later they took an exit west onto Highway 46, just like James Dean forty years ago when it was still 466. Lou had the sensation of going back in time.

George had told Lou once that he must be a very old soul who had been on the wheel of life many times. Now he played with the idea. Could life be a cosmic checkers game in which the pieces might be removed from the board, only to play another day? Perhaps this plane was the death and the darkness.

"Next weekend it's going to be a mess," she said quietly.

"How do you mean?" He wondered whether she was referring to Cleveland's little apocalypse.

"So many people out at the crash."

He nodded. Vendors would be constructing booths for fast food. There would be a myriad of specially commissioned Dean souvenirs commemorating Jimmy's death. The licensing agent representing Dean's family would probably be omnipresent, handling endorsements and slapping injunctions on unauthorized products. Not to mention the movie crew shooting the "Jimmy" film.

She closed her eyes. "I know what Cleveland says. It's getting pretty heavy. It used to be fun, but sometimes the last couple of days, I wish I'd never heard of Jimmy. There is a curse, Lou. Whatever you think."

"Meaning . . .?"

"All the victims don't just die, like the people who were killed by the death car when it went around the country. Or Natalie. Or Sal. Some just fall apart and go crazy, like Nick Ray."

And Pier Angeli, Lou thought, whom Cleveland claimed was the mother of Dean's secret baby. Her career went into a slide after Jimmy died, and she killed herself saying he was the only real love of her life.

"Who else?" he asked.

"Nick Adams committed suicide. And Albert Dekker; he was in *Eden*. They found him hanging in his bathroom, with all these dirty words written all over his naked body in lipstick. It's called 'auto-erotic" something, people get turned on by hanging themselves. Even Cleveland. I don't mean he hangs himself. But like, if you think about it, he's lost a family. He's pretty lonely, and he's started drinking a lot. He'll sit and drink and listen to that cemetery tape."

Lou nodded. "Ly said something once. He said once Jimmy crossed your life, it was never the same." He realized it was true for himself. His palms were sweaty and the needle on the odometer kept creeping past eighty with his eagerness to finally see the fatal spot.

Ahead was little Blackwell's Corners beneath a billboard boasting JIMMY DEAN'S LAST STOP. Lou pulled in and gassed up. He also bought a shovel.

He knew brightness showed in his eyes when Cherie asked in alarm, "What's that for?"

He felt the lopsided smile on his lips, wondering why a little obsession on his own part should upset her. " 'You gotta do something.' "

If she recognized the quote from *Rebel*, she didn't respond. Just settled back into the seat and watched the haunted highway as he took off once more.

"Don't worry," he said, "I'm not going to dig up another body."

She respected his silence. Wasn't that the point of the James Dean experience? Individuals doing their own thing?

Everyone's entitled to his own obsession.

A half hour later, they were heading down a straightaway out the hills, and Lou had the strangest feeling: he knew this place. There was a concrete chunk in the bottom of his stomach as he tamped on the brake to try and slow the weird premonition coming with each revolution of the tires.

"What's wrong?" Her face was disturbed.

To the left was the old highway, and at the bottom of the valley in the distance was Jimmy Dean's intersection. He shook his head and tried to relax his breathing, but the anxiety was mounting almost to panic. Everything safe and familiar was far away.

"You're not stopping?" she asked.

He did not stop at what the fans familiarly called "the deathsite," not yet. A half mile further around a broad

curve to the west was the little spot on the road called
Cholame—just a restaurant and post office. Parking by
the James Dean monument, he felt he had crossed a
time warp into the American 1950s.

*Who were the gods of these people? If Dean had not
died when and how he did, things would have been different. No idol, no cult. It had to be violently, at the
wheel of a speeding sports car, for there to be a myth.
Timing was everything, his death the greatest publicity
coup.*

He stretched his legs to read the tablets installed at
the base of the monument. Between them a little bird
was dead, as if it had just fallen. Then he realized it was
sculpted of bronze and part of the monument.

He read aloud from the tablets, " 'His name was
James Byron Dean. He died just before sunset eight
hundred meters east of this tree, which has long been
called the "tree of heaven." . . .'" He paused.

" 'Tree of heaven,' " he said as he looked up with
new interest at the leafy canopy. "I never saw one, that
I know. It's strange."

"It's just a tree."

"No, he's saying it's a *bodhi* tree, the tree of enlightenment. It was under one of these that the Buddha became the One Fully Awakened. His disciples venerate it
to this day. In the course of a night, he acquired three-
fold knowledge. He had his breakthrough, a sudden
transformation to cosmic consciousness."

Lou removed the shovel from the trunk.

"What are you doing?"

He replied, "Walking to the crash sight. I don't suppose you want to come?"

Her face was chalky. "Why do you say that?"

"Well, you didn't want to go to the grave. And up
there's where he actually died."

She nodded dully and sat by the tablets. "You're right. I just wanna think. Maybe I'll get some enlightenment. It's going to be so crowded this Friday, there'll be hundreds of people." Then her hand was on his arm. "Don't go."

"I've got to," he said, unclasping her fingers.

He started to walk the quarter mile back along the highway toward the crash site.

The original intersection had been obliterated long ago by rechanneling and the addition of caution lights. In 1955 Highway 466 had been single lanes in both directions, each only ten feet across. But this was the spot, marked only by a few beer cans and a soiled condom.

It was a strange and lonely place.

There are vibrations here, Lou thought, a resonance of things which have happened before. He was thinking of bioenergy. The ancient Chinese believed that every man produced "life force," and that this force continued into space. The Hindus called it *"prana."* Perhaps Dean's escaping life force had ionized this spot. It was in the earth and the rocks.

A strange energy. There was no scientific proof for the theory of the existence of stimulus zones based on earth radiation. What were those hot spots on the earth called? Ley lines? Geopathological zones? In Germany there were many "streets of death" where extraordinary numbers of accidents occurred. Clairvoyants had discovered a powerful disruptive source of earth radiation at those spots. Lou knew that his own mother had cured her chronic insomnia once, just by moving the bed from one place to another.

Which was another way of saying to himself: I'm not crazy. There is a weird psychological noise here, like the ping of a harp string just out of the range of human hearing.

He took off his sunglasses, squinted through the burn on his face. He had the sensation of arriving at his own dream. That was the barbed wire fence where the hit-and-run victim's crumpled body had come to rest. Over there was where the impact had taken place near sundown on September 30, 1955. In a way, James Dean was born the day he died, and this was his matrix.

He walked east up the new highway to where the old bypassed road came out of the mountains, its faint outlines in the dry pasture grass; abandoned now, it was the only original road surface still in existence on which James Dean had driven. Walking was a totally different attitude than driving, he thought as he looked both ways to cross the highway at the point where a tree stump marked the ghostly merging of the old with the newer bypass.

The bulls and all the cowflop discouraged him from joining the old road at that point. He continued to trudge up the incline of the bypass, feeling anxious at all the cars roaring toward his back. Near the top, he crawled up the dirt shoulder and slipped through the barbed wire. Clods of dirt dislodged under his rubber soles as he slid down the hill on the other side, and onto the old road.

What a change—suddenly it was the new highway and its cars which were invisible, their rushings distant.

Quiet descended. Only grass whispered.

Down the direction he had come, the intersection was visible in the distance. He stood for a moment in stillness and felt the haunted quality of the place. He also felt eyes on his neck, but shook off the sensation.

Up ahead the old highway zigged and zagged in triangulating lines through the pass, marked in spots by white bones of an old guard railing. In several places the roadway had given way entirely, a jagged scar marking where it had collapsed down the hillside. Underfoot were rusted highway markers, and glass conducting insulators fallen from the decrepit phone poles; but mostly, there was the wheeling of crows overhead and the sound of gravel under his tennis shoes.

He began to sweat, and his neck was reddening from the merciless sun baking the brown hillsides. Suddenly he came upon it: the perspective of Lysander's painting. The painting that told him to dig, and where.

His heart beat fast and rushed through his ears. He felt lightheaded and woozy, as if everything was radioactive. He was standing on some toxic Ground Zero.

This is a mistake, he thought. He had to get out of here, and fast. There was no cross on the side of the road—but there was a rusted highway marker laid over another. An accident, the foreshortened T they formed? The Hebrew "Tau," the most ancient form of the crucifix. *There are no accidents,* he reminded himself.

Suddenly the ground moved beneath his feet. He crouched down with hands extended to steady himself. The temblor stopped just as quickly. He reminded himself that he was in the earthquake capital of California, the hills around him seismic dominoes, which experienced such regular shocks that the government had placed a monitoring station in nearby Parkfield.

Standing again, he moved the markers aside and began to probe the hardpan with the shovel, unsure whether he had the strength to dig, or whether, having dug, he would be able to make it back to the car. Sweat fell into his eyes, stinging.

* * *

Cherie knew something was wrong as soon as she saw him. "Did you feel it? Are you all right? What happened up there? You look like shit."

"I don't know, I feel kind of sick."

'What's that—?"

It was a metal strongbox eaten with rust, though the industrial lock still held. It wasn't heavy, and something rattled inside. A box within a box just like James Dean? He would need the tools at his apartment to work on the lock and hasp, so he opened the hood and set the strongbox beside the battery cables.

Cherie's breath was coming fast. "What is it? Where did you get—?"

He shook his head. His ashen color cut short the question.

"Come where it's cooler," she said worriedly, and led him by the wrist through a broken door and into the musty shade inside the old abandoned garage. Dead-smelling slices of light came through boarded-up windows.

He did feel better out of the sun, though he wondered why they hadn't just gone into the restaurant.

He took deep breaths. "I don't know what came over me." He didn't think she was listening. She was transfixed by the old shed.

"This is where Jimmy's car was brought after the crash," she said as if in church.

She turned and smiled uncomfortably. "It's kinda funny, isn't it? You've seen the pictures? The wheel was all bloody and bent out of shape. He was gored on the 'horn.' Get it? Car horn?"

"Yeah," he said, sweat running down his back. "Funny. And this was where they kept the ambulance?"

"He was dead on arrival at the hospital," she said. "Did you know that? The left side of his face was dam-

aged a lot more than the right. Everything about him
was broken. His upper and lower jaws, his arms. Legs.
His neck. They called it a 'basal' skull fracture. When
the doctor moved his neck in the ambulance, he could
hear the rough splinters creaking. There was glass em-
bedded in his face."

Her eyes were strange. "There wasn't even enough
blood left for an alcohol test. Life is so . . . cold. Isn't
it, Lou? The towing service charged $175.37 to bring
his car here. His dad was charged 731 dollars by the funeral home for doing what they do to a dead person.
Jimmy and the casket together weighed five hundred
pounds, and it cost $165.93 to ship him to Indiana. . . ."

There were tears in her eyes, and her voice quavered
as she turned away. "Plus, the ambulance guys rolled
his body before they dropped it off at the morgue."

When she turned, he knew she was going to do
something. She took a breath, then stood on tiptoes to
kiss his lips.

His own mouth was dry. He put his arms gently
around her. "You didn't really feel like doing that."

She sighed in his ear. "That's the way it is with me,
if I wait to feel something it's never gonna happen."
She was up on her toes again, a kiss more confident.

His stomach was queasy, throat parched as he loosed
her arms. "I guess I'm not up to it right now," he said.

She turned quickly, hurt. "Are you gay?"

Shock drained him. "What did you say?" But he
knew he'd heard right.

"It's no big deal," she said offhandedly. "I've wondered about myself."

"It's not that," he said with deliberation. He hesitated. "Now, I'm going to make you a speech."

His throat was trying to close. "Five years ago I
threw a hammer in a competition, and I hit a man

named Ernie Hockman in the head. I heard the crack.
Everybody heard it. He went down and he never got
back up. I'm saying he died."

She faced him.

"He never got back up," Lou said. "He was feeling
no more pain, but I felt like I had to . . . pick his pain
up. It's my responsibility to feel it for him. I feel
ashamed when I laugh, I feel guilty if I find myself lik-
ing somebody or having pleasure. I'm his ghost, I re-
fuse to talk to his parents and confront this, though I
know that might set me free. I don't know if I'm more
afraid to talk to them, or afraid to be set free, because
then I'll have to—

"I don't know *what* I'll have to do. The same things
you're afraid you'll have to. Do you understand? I think
you understand. I think you're the only person who
would."

"Yeah. I get it," she said, taking his hand.

He felt the stirring inside of something he had
thought was dead, felt his knees trembling. The next
kiss was deep. She peeled off her sweater.

"Why?" he asked breathlessly. "Why this way? Why
now?"

"Our big chance, I guess," she said. "I want it behind
us so we can get on to whatever's next."

He felt the confusion through her body.

"Do you want to?" she asked, pulling his head to her
small sharp breasts.

His hard breathing was the answer. Then he saw the
bruise close to his eyes, the red bite mark around her
nipple. Sickened shock went through him. She felt it.

"What happened to you?" he asked.

She pushed him away, and he was looking at her
tense shoulders.

"Cleve was kind of a bad boy last night," she said.

Then, as if to explain her rejection, "It's not that long ago that your parents died, huh?" She lighted a cigarette from the crumpled pack in her jeans.

"Right," he said uneasily. "It's not."

She nodded, satisfied. "I think I know how that feels."

"Maybe we better go, now."

She shrugged nonchalantly, smoking the cigarette.

His stomach relaxed as the Dean monument receded in the mirror. It was a weight lifted, leaving the radius of the emanations of the death site. His nerves were ragged with confusion. Not just by the haunting gravity of the intersection. The whole business. His feelings weren't making sense.

She reached over, touched his arm and squeezed, left her hand there.

Something rose in his throat, and he couldn't talk.

17

Sunday, September 25, 1995
Westwood, 4:30 P.M.

"It's you that got all the paintings," Cherie said in
amazement when she saw the apartment. "Lysander left
all his stuff to you."

Lou was eager to open the strongbox. He proceeded
to arrange newspaper on the front room carpet to catch
rust flakes, kneeling before the corroding relic with a
screwdriver in his hand.

"Don't," Cherie said suddenly. "Let's take it back."

He pushed the curious and lonely Jim Thorpe aside.
"Why?"

"A feeling," she said as she crossed her arms against
gooseflesh. "If it was buried, there was a reason."

"Can you do any better than that?"

She lowered herself to the floor. "What if there's
something horrible in it?"

"Like?"

She took the cat in her arms. "Like ... Sal Mineo's

knife wound, who knows? It just scares me. Why do you have to do this, after I've told you how I feel?"

He felt the entreating and sensitive faces of James Dean staring from the canvases. "What's the real problem? The curse?"

"It's the way you look."

He was defensive. "How's that?"

She paused. "Like Cleveland. Like the rest of them."

"Like you?" It hurt her, and he felt bad. "Did something else happen last night?"

She hugged the cat close. "What happened last night was, I realized I really like it, that you aren't like them. Like us. Look—your hands are even trembling."

She was right. "If you're uncomfortable," he said irritably, "I'll take you to Sheena's."

"No." She shook her head, the cat jumping suddenly from her arms to vanish under the sofa.

Lou had a tension headache, his cramping leg quivering beneath him as he set to work. The rusty lock gave quickly. The smell of mold and age came up, and he tried to control his heart as he looked inside.

"What is it?" Cherie asked.

He was disappointed. "A bunch of old crap, odds and ends."

He felt her press closer as he sifted the contents. "An old book of poems. Emily Dickinson? *The Beginner-Mind of Zen* by D. T. Suzuki. I guess Jimmy had pretensions to intellectuality. 'If you encounter the Buddha on the road, kill him!' "

She bristled protectively. "It says that?"

"No," he said as he set the thin book aside, "it was a Chinese Zen master about two hundred years ago. He was trying to push his students beyond the rational, to true enlightenment. I just thought it was ironic."

"Because Jimmy died on a road?"

Lou didn't answer, engrossed in a scrapbook he'd found. She looked over his shoulder as he leafed through color pictures of needlepoint samplers, and a dozen photos of babies laughing. There was an old traffic warrant, poems about children, and clipped country scenes of winter and summer. And a folded envelope full of 35mm negatives.

He held them up to the light, let his eyes adjust to the sepia monochrome. They were all of a young man, but not Dean. The hair was too dark, the classical features blunter.

"It's Rolf," Cherie said as she squinted over his shoulder. Lou saw that Dean was in none of them. Cherie read his mind. "Because he musta took 'em," she said leaning back.

Lou took a breath. Some shots showed Weutheric covered with oil and bronzing on a flotolounger in a swimming pool, laughing with hand upraised in protest at the camera. But others were more intimate and lingering. Rolf seemed uncomfortable posing open-shirted or bare-chested in sensual shadows. Lou felt the voyeur examining them. Lighting was arranged to outline the definition of Rolf's pecs, or the corrugation of his hard belly.

"Jimmy's house was burglarized right after he was killed," Lou mused. "Could this have been his stuff?"

"Cleveland says Jimmy recorded the story of his life, and the plot to kill him, on his Telefunken the night before he left for the race. He thinks that's why the place was robbed." She removed a charred glove from the box to sniff it tentatively. "It's been in a fire. There's no fingers."

"A racing glove," he said as he took it.

There were also two black and white eight-by-ten photos which had certainly not been among Dean's possessions. They showed him splayed bleeding across the rear cowling of his sports car, arms outstretched and feet still entangled in the clutch and brake.

"The Roth photos," Lou said, "the ones he took of Jimmy in the car at the accident. The ones that were never published."

Cherie was shocked. "Roth's widow said he didn't take any of Jimmy's body, just the cars. For insurance, or something."

"Right, but you're forgetting that she became a professional 'Dean friend'—until she sold the whole lot for a quarter-million dollars to the Japanese guy who built the monument. She didn't want her husband, or herself for that matter, to appear too mercenary."

"I guess," Cherie said, transfixed by the pictures. "Who do you think put this stuff out there?"

"Isn't there something else you want to know?"

She was uncomfortable. "What do you mean?"

"Like, how did I know where to dig?"

She flushed and began to stammer, but he interrupted. "Pollack," he said. "Last night I noticed that painting in that bedroom at Cleveland's house. A little cross marked the spot."

"Nice work, Sherlock," she mumbled.

Her sarcasm penetrated. "Doesn't it mean something, the possibility this stuff belonged to James Dean?"

She was tense. "It doesn't mean I have to know everything. It's so sad and personal, I feeling like we're violating him."

"That's what Cleve loses sight of, huh? And now, me?"

"Maybe the important thing is who he was, and what he did. Maybe that's why there's a curse, to remind people."

"Well, lightning hasn't struck me yet," Lou said distractedly. "Let's see what's left."

The answer was hundreds of moldy pages of typescript, all dialogue. His disappointment did not escape Cherie, who said, "You were expecting a treasure?"

He checked for a false bottom, then examined a title page. "It looks like a movie script. 'Blind Run.' Heard of it?"

"Maybe," she shrugged. "It looks too long for a movie script."

He stole the cigarette from her lips, took a drag. "I know, but that's what it is. What about a production company called 'Pontifex'?"

Her fingers traced the embossed letters, but she shook her head.

"I've got to put them in order," he said finally. "Are you going to help?"

She seemed to resign herself, scooting determinedly beside him. "If you have to do it, let's do it. But do you have any air freshener? The mold gets my asthma."

"By the kitty litter," he said as he began separating pages on the floor. "I didn't know you had asthma."

He arranged stacks by hundreds, and in a half hour there were ten. By the time he finished carefully collating the pages with brads from his computer desk, there were three plump volumes.

"You've got to be starving," he said unenthusiastically. "It's almost six."

"You're dying to read," she said, massaging his back. "So read."

He didn't object when she offered to make coffee. He passed her the first volume when he was finished, but she was still conflicted about invading the dead Jimmy's privacy.

"I've got dyslexia," she said, slumping tiredly against his shoulder.

He read on through the evening, pausing only to look at her face and wonder whether Cleveland was calling Childes's at that moment to see where she was. Through the opening of her bunched blouse, he saw the impression of Cleveland's teeth on her breasts. The welter of pain and pleasure was confusing.

He read on into the night.

At midmorning on Monday, George and Donna stood in the doorway in coveralls spattered with the paint that also flecked their hair.

Lou leaned back on the sofa and rubbed his eyes against the streaming sun. "I didn't hear you knock," he yawned hugely. "What time?"

George glanced uneasily at the unaccustomed mess, spotted the burgled strongbox on the floor.

"Lou ... we were working downstairs in Donna's apartment so she can recover her deposit. We've been getting kinda worried about you, your light's been on all night—" Noting Cherie, his brow arched appreciatively.

Lou cut off the prurient thrust. "I've been reading. Deposit?"

"Reading that?" George nodded at the script.

Cherie stretched awake with a drowsy smile, until she saw the strongbox and remembered.

"There's been a millionaire coming by looking for you," Donna said as she stopped stroking Thorpe long enough to pick up a Roth photo. "My God. This is grisly. Where'd you get it?" She held it at a distance with fingertips.

"How do you know he was a millionaire?" Lou asked

with instant alertness. All of Pollack's accusations against the Frenchman came to mind from the grave.

"He had a Rolls," George said, still awaiting introductions. "Jonathan Cottlee—the perfume guy."

Lou attended to the niceties. "George—I'd like you to meet Cherie Lowe. George, Cherie."

"We've met," Donna said, a trifle icily, Lou thought. A girl thing?

George gathered Donna close with a bearlike arm. "Lou, we have an announcement. We wanted you to be the first to know, because it was you who brought us together. Donna and I are going to get married."

Lou felt shock. "Congratulations," he said. Donna couldn't meet his eyes. "Have you set the date?"

George was more confident. "Not exactly, but probably around Thanksgiving. We realized we were two people who'd been injured by life. We've got our problems, but our karma wants us to heal each other. It's no accident Donna showed up when she did. I was tired of running around—all the bullshit and macho pretense."

"I'm happy for you."

"Donna," George said easily, "would you mind fixing us a cup of java?"

Was that a twinge of resentment on her face? She better get used to it, Lou thought.

"Now," George said. "What's all—"

"I want to talk to you," Lou said. "These pages were buried on the old highway near the intersection where Dean was killed. I dug them up."

"Out of the *ground*?"

"There was this little cross in one of Pollack's paintings showing the old road—that was the clue."

"Buried? You're kidding. Which painting?" George looked around.

"Not here. Look at this, it's a movie script."

"No shit," George said as he accepted a volume.

Lou stood and paced. "A script for a movie that was never made. Instead, it all happened in real life."

Cherie looked disturbed. "What do you mean?"

Lou stopped.

"It opens with this kid in Iowa, who dreams about movie stardom. 'Jamie Starr' comes to Hollywood and hits it big. But the real story is what happens after he's killed in his speeding car at this big race. He becomes a god. Death sort of crystallizes him, and millions all over the world organize into a sort of . . . community . . . with him as the psychological nucleus."

Cherie put a lighted cigarette in his animated hand, and he nodded thanks before continuing.

"His fans attach great significance to his sudden death. . . . The smashed car becomes like the Cross is for Christians. It even tours the country, the world."

"Obviously based on the life of Jimmy Dean," George said blithely, "to cash in on the craze."

"That's what's fascinating. Because if the January 1955 date on this script is true, the James Dean death cult started *before* he was killed. And what you're holding in your hand is more than a script."

Donna, back from the kitchen, rubbed her arms. "You gave me goose bumps—"

George was uncomprehending. "That's interesting. It could be good for your thesis."

Lou was frustrated. He was thinking way beyond any thesis. "It's more than interesting! I mean, there's differences, but a lot of it parallels what happened after he was dead. Jamie Starr made three films in sixteen months, films which depict allegorically the cycle of the hero translated into modern cultural terms—filling a void left by the dead, irrelevant and obsolete gods of contemporary religion. Including James—"

He snatched the book and riffled pages. "There's all these . . . insertions, and addenda. It looks like it went through stages—and kept growing into over a thousand typed single-spaced pages. It's so documentary, it's almost a technical manual."

"What do you mean, 'manual'?" Donna asked warily.

"On how to maximize publicity, after the death of Dean . . . or, 'Starr' . . . and this meticulous description of its aftermath."

"Who wrote it?" George asked.

"And what was Ly doing with it?" Lou added. "Because he must be the one who put it there, right? There aren't any names—just something called 'Pontifex.' Look on the front."

"Lysander?" George said as he examined the logo.

"It looks like a Christmas tree," Donna said over his shoulder, "a tree with ten big ornaments."

"Arranged in three triangles," Lou said, "the topmost pointing upward, while the lower two point down. Do you recognize it?"

"Yeah," George answered. "Do you?"

"It's the qabalistic Tree of Life. The Cabala."

Donna said, "What's a 'Cabala'?"

"Jewish mysticism," George said, "an ancient blueprint of the universe and creation that concentrates all the mystical teachings. And the basis of all western occultism. Thick veins of magic and sorcery have always been just under the surface. Nowadays, modern gnostics use it as a meditative discipline to gain access to the higher planes of consciousness." He saw he was making an impression on Cherie, and smiled. "True adepts take the tree as an actual map which points to the way of spiritual attainment for the individual. Its diagram of symbols enables the everyday consciousness to communicate with the subconscious. Through meditative exercise, one can ascend up from this plane to the higher worlds—"

" 'Adepts'?" It was Donna.

"Magical adepts. 'Pontifex' means 'Bridge-builder.' "

"Bridge to what?" Lou asked.

George shrugged. "I'd have to read it. Ly had all these pages hidden?"

"He believed that in the last months of his life James Dean himself believed he was going to be murdered."

"Right," Donna said with unwonted derision, "and he also said there were crazies who believed Jimmy Dean was returning from the dead next Friday."

"He was right about the crazies—" Lou said, and regretted the words.

Cherie smiled wryly, hugging a cushion to herself.

He tried to apologize with his eyes. "I mean, maybe it's not crazy to think there could be people out there who want to perform some sort of ritual this Friday. There are facts, including the theft of Jimmy Dean's body."

"His *corpse*?" Donna said with disgust.

"I ought to know. I sort of ran afoul of a police surveillance at the cemetery back in Indiana."

"What do you mean, 'ran afoul'?" Donna asked.

"Arrested? Suspicion of grave robbing?" Lou smiled, then winced as George seated himself on the sofa in those painted overalls.

"You've been holding out on me, sport," Bluestein said. "I heard you went to Indiana, but you were *arrested*?"

"This Friday a movie company's going to re-create Dean's death at the intersection, and that's supposed to be the final ingredient to bring about 'The Second Coming.' "

"What?" Donna said.

"It'd be like a passion play," George said, "to stimulate reopening of the door to the god. And Lou's right about the body. Something like that would be heap mucho magic to a cultist. Let's suppose there was some sort of plot in the fifties. You're not implying contemporary cultists were involved back then? I mean, they'd be in walkers by now."

"I've met a guy who believes that the torch was passed at some point. And that Cottlee might be one of the receivers."

Donna said suspiciously, "Lou, I've never seen you excited."

George rose to clap him on the back. "Hell, I've never seen him *interested*. Why's there mold on your Suzuki?"

"Not mine, Dean's."

The book fell open in George's hand. " 'The Buddha is a dried shit-stick,' " he read, and guffawed.

"George!" Donna reproved.

"No," he defended himself, "it's underlined, right here. It's a famous 'koan.' The whole thing goes, 'What is the Buddha?' The answer is, 'A dried shit-stick.' The point was to overcome all distinctions, even between the sacred and the profane, by shock. You concentrate on solving it, until you realize the insufficiency of reason. It forces you to try to open another door in your mind."

"Then Jimmy's life was a koan," Cherie said softly.

George looked at her, impressed. "That's a damn good point. The koan's enigmatic and resists a logical solution. It gives rise to a search, which seems to want to show the futility of intellect. It points beyond the rational, to another dimension of—"

"Tell him why else we came by," Donna interrupted irritably.

"Why—?" George said. "Oh, yeah. We want to invite you to dinner tomorrow night at my place. It's a going-away thing for Donna. She's flying to see her folks once before the wedding. You can bring your friend, too."

Lou looked at Cherie, but she was noncommittal. "We'll talk it over," he said. The evening would tell, whether she left or decided to stay.

The phone rang. Donna said, "That would be that guy, I bet. Cottlee."

"What's a millionaire want with you?" George asked, impressed.

"Maybe he wants to buy Pollack's collection," Lou said as he walked to the phone. But he suspected it was more than that.

18

Monday, September 26, 1995
Westwood, 3:30 P.M.

"You'll be fine here?" Lou asked as he left.

Cherie's eyes were enigmatic. She'd probably had her fill of possessiveness, under the guise of protectiveness, from Cleveland.

When he said, "I'm just worried you might get bored," she put her arms around his neck unexpectedly.

"You're worried I won't be here when you get back?"

He faltered. "I know we haven't talked about what we're doing. You're someone I'd really like to get to know apart from all this Dean stuff, and since yesterday I've been acting like . . ."

"Cleveland?"

He nodded. "You know, you were right. He wanted me to get involved with him on breaking up the plan of his so-called conspiracy by Friday. He said you're in danger from Liv and Patsy's fan club. Maybe from Cottlee."

"Maybe Cleve said that because he wanted to hang on to me." She kissed Lou's chin and nose. "Well, if I'm in danger from Jonathan, I'll be safe this evening. You'll be with him." She kissed his lips. "And you're really nothing like Cleveland. Trust me on that."

He walked down to his car, somewhat reassured.

A half-hour later he was in a glass-enclosed restaurant overlooking the Mesa Marin Race Track, seated across from Jonathan Cottlee, his dark hair moist, while brightly painted cars zoomed on test trials around the black surface of the course below.

"I understand you wound up with all of Pollack's art," Cottlee began. "You must be very proud. I would love to see and catalog it. I'd consider buying certain items, or the whole collection as a lot, and cataloging it later."

"I really haven't thought about what to do with it," Lou said. "I don't even know why Bulova dumped it on me."

"My opinion?" Cottlee asked. "I think it was jealous pique. He found this little shrine to you at Lysander's studio, and I think that hurt him."

"I'd hardly call it a 'shrine'—and how do you know about that?"

"Liv Ermaine told me, I think she's close to Bulova. I'm trying to get to know her before it's too late."

"Too late?"

Cottlee was diffident. "Well, I always intended to meet Lysander Pollack, and now he's gone. These are people who were actually around in the nineteen-fifties in Hollywood. They form a link to the past, which fascinates me."

Link to the past, Lou thought. "Why?"

Cottlee smiled.

"What you've got to understand about me is I'm very involved in my hobbies. I've got time—my company runs itself. I grew up on American music and films, so there's this fondness. I think it's worthwhile to try to re-create the past before it slips away. That's why I'm interested in Lysander's collection. But you think about it, there's another matter I want to discuss."

"What's that?"

Cottlee's expression was sincere. "It's Liv Ermaine. She's fairly eccentric and unusual, but a fascinating woman. She's also quite smitten with you."

"I hardly met her—" Lou objected.

Cottlee placated him with a friendly hand. "You know how it is at that age. A lot of fantasy. I don't think she'll ever write her memoirs on her own, she can't organize and all that. I think it would be a significant contribution to Hollywood history if somebody like you would be her ghostwriter. It would give me pleasure to be associated with that."

"What kind of pleasure?" Lou asked as he sat back in the booth.

"I would just like the story of Jimmy's last months told properly and believably by a true scholar. She was impressed with you, and seems convinced you're the man for the job. Jimmy's very big in Europe, you know. I should think there would be a lot of interest. Personally, I'd be fascinated to read it, put together professionally and coherently."

"I'm hardly a professional writer. The jury's even out on the scholar part."

"Even if you could have access to all her recollections? She would help you every step of the way. Give you entrée to people like Jeff Hackett."

"Who?"

"He's in the biographies—Jimmy's friend. He's remained aloof and uninvolved as far as the idolatry and craze is concerned. I think there're significant psychological insights into Jimmy, yet to be revealed." Cottlee's smile was portentous. "Like the possibility he was mentally unstable those last months. You know he had this frayed noose hanging in his rafter? And he shot out the windows of a rental car on location in Texas."

"Is that all?"

"No. One day he actually exposed himself and took a piss in front of all the locals on the set, including women and children. Something was driving him over the edge. He believed someone was out to kill him, and so do I. I think it was executives at his own studio."

"Warner Brothers?" Lou asked incredulously. "Why?"

The millionaire leaned across the table. "Rolf Weutheric. A Vine Street mechanic invited on a weekend jaunt with a movie star? That relationship is an absolutely unmined facet of Jimmy's life."

"More than driver-mechanic?"

"More pertinently, would the studio have considered the revelation of a liaison with a Vine Street greasemonkey a threat to their investment, the two unreleased pictures? Wouldn't it be typical of Jimmy to be indiscreet and not observe the conventions of that sort of relationship? Would they perhaps want both Jimmy *and* Rolf out of the way?"

"Why—?"

"Because their wunderkind was losing control. Liv is an encyclopedia of what was going on. But what's in it for you?"

Lou let himself be worked by an expert "closer."

"I would appreciate it if you would allow me to put you on a retainer while you work on this. I believe you can come up with a product which would satisfy your academic requirements, your thesis. And also be commercially viable. So I'd recoup my investment at that end, you needn't feel badly if nothing came of it. . . . I'll assume the risk. Do you think you would consider that sort of arrangement? I mean, in your situation?"

"What's 'my situation'?" Lou asked with foreboding.

"Forgive me," Cottlee said, "but as you know, I've been conducting my own search for Jimmy's death car. I've had a full-time investigator out in the midwest tracking down leads, and it was a small matter to have him look into your own background. He's told me about the rather unique stipulations in your parents' wills. I don't know how far along you've come with an actual thesis, but my proposal would seem to benefit us both."

Lou felt violated and embarrassed. And angry. "Tell me more about your search for the car," he said to see the millionaire's reaction. At that moment it was not difficult to believe Cottlee capable of all sorts of covert activity.

Cottlee leaned back. "That would be quite a find, that. It's how I met Terry and Sheena. I feel myself drawn into this more and more. See, the occult's fascinated me since I was a lad. I've retained this reputable investigator to look into all the car stories. If I found it, I probably would just contribute it to a museum." He smiled disarmingly. "You're suspicious?"

Cottlee spoke shyly as he turned the frosted beer glass in his hands. "There's a picture which says it all for me. It's a Highway Patrol photo taken the next day, and it's of the crash site the precise time the accident occurred—to show where exactly the sun was in Jimmy's eyes as he drove to his death.

"There's the highway in the foreground, and the sun going down behind the hills to the west. Its rays wash

the intersection in light, a shimmering mirage so that
the old highway seems to join the river of light and
flow up into the sky and into the sun. The light is so
bright the eye cannot follow. There's that sense, for
me—the 'Little Bastard' never stopped. It changed form
and kept on going on a highway of light with Jimmy inside it. It's not about death. It's about life. Each day
Jimmy lives a little more."

He was self-conscious. "So," he said more business-
like, "would you consent to meet with Liv if I arrange
it?"

"Sure," Lou heard himself saying. "But for my own
reasons."

"Excellent," Cottlee said cheerily. "That's all I ask at
this point. We're going to meet out at Griffith Observatory tomorrow morning. The occasion is the posthumous unveiling of Lysander's statue of Jimmy. Fitting,
don't you think? Will you be there?"

Lou considered. "I can do that."

Cottlee looked uncomfortable. "One more thing I
want—if I was better at this, I would probably be more
canny than just to come right out and ask. But among
Lysander's things I am interested specifically in a
movie script I've heard rumored. Have you found anything like that?"

Lou hesitated. "I've only just started to go through
the stuff. Is it important?"

"It's probably not bright of me to tell you, but, yes,
it'd be awfully valuable. Jimmy Dean might have written it. He had aspirations in that direction."

"He did?"

"And that it was autobiographical. Now, that would
be amazing. It would also be tangible evidence as to his
actual state of mind. Well," Cottlee said as he stood to
shake hands, "tomorrow?"

Lou was thoughtful all the drive back to Westwood. "I've been interested in the occult since I was a lad," Cottlee said. "Each day Jimmy lives a little more. . . ."

Lou had to pull over and think for a moment. What the hell was he doing? What had he meant when he'd told Cottlee he would see Liv, but for his own reasons? What reasons? "You're hooked," Devereux had told him. But by what? What was the excitement he had been feeling since unearthing the strongbox?

He realized he had entered a scramble to piece together a jigsaw, a regatta of egos. Maybe he had an ulterior motive for not aligning himself with Devereux, and now Cottlee. If Dean had actually been murdered, then the first person to arrive at the proof and solution would become an inextricable part of Jimmy's story. It would be union with the godhead—

At that moment a car pulled in behind his own, cut its lights. When no one got out, Lou shuddered and drove off. The headlights around him were so anonymous, shifting sinisterly in the rear mirror. Cottlee and his money. His operatives. Lou began to speed up, worrying about Cherie alone in the apartment.

It was all about one-upmanship, and now Pontifex was his own entry in the Dean murder sweepstakes. But he could not stop thinking about the murky figure who had come to the fore: Rolf Weutheric. Who was he? Why had Ly *really* made him Judas in *The Last Supper*? What if the men who had visited him in the hospital after the wreck weren't Porsche representatives? What if they were Pontifex?

What if, what if?

The windows of the apartment were dark when Lou arrived. It was with trepidation that he unlocked the door. And momentary panic. He couldn't find her until he went into the bathroom.

She looked up, startled from where she was on her knees before a Tarot card mounted on the toilet seat.

He realized he'd been holding his breath.

"I got scared," she laughed. "I've always hidden in bathrooms. Is that crazy?"

"There's probably a deep-seated psychological reason," he said embarrassedly, "but that's not my major. I didn't mean to interrupt—"

"I know what it looks like," she said with chagrin, "but I'm not praying, just meditating. Something I do every day. This card's called The Star—it's Jimmy's card." She handed it to him. "It's the sign of Aquarius, the water bearer. She showers stars on the earth, she's a way-shower for men."

He sat on the bed. "What comes to you when you meditate?"

She bounced lightly onto the bed and assumed the lotus position next to him.

"Well, I see Jimmy. These double rays of light shine from his eyes, and there's a star behind his head. I feel like we're caught in dreams and images, these self-created fantasies preventing us from seeing the world as it actually is. I always feel like we're all gonna plunge to our death, or something. I talk to him."

"Does he answer?"

"Maybe. I have 'Jimmy' dreams all the time. When I was younger . . . they meant a lot to me. I never told anyone. Sometimes I'd be walking in a big cemetery, studying headstones and looking for Jimmy's grave. Or, I see a casket all wrapped in the roots of a tree."

"And the recent ones?"

That got a blush. "I'm waiting for the Spyder on this dirt road in the middle of nowhere. It's like I'm there alone and everybody's just left. Then comes the stupid part." She hesitated. "I wish I hadn't started this."

"I'm listening."

"Okay," she sighed. "Then, there's a light like a stained-glass window. It's the Spyder and it's made out of light. Jimmy's behind the wheel, and he shines."

She did look beatific. He'd put one of her cigarettes backwards in his lips, and she corrected it and continued animatedly.

"Then there's a bunch of us and we're all walking into the light like zombies, and suddenly I'm not afraid of dying—death's always scared me. I can't believe I've ever been afraid. Then Jimmy just sort of motions for all of us to get in the car. The next part is like a miracle, because we're all filing into the car and somehow everybody fits."

He lay back on his elbow and tipped the ashtray, had to dust the embers to the floor. "Where's he taking you?"

She smiled. "Cancún."

"Mexico?"

"Goofy, huh? I used to have this calendar with pictures of it. It was like heaven to me."

He hesitated, crushing out the cigarette because it tasted so rotten.

"Look, I'm sorry I was pushy about that dinner thing tomorr—"

She shook her head. "No, that was nice. I guess I'm not too used to being around 'normies'—that's what Cleveland calls them. I want to go." She wrinkled her nose. "I think."

She looked an uncomfortably long time into his eyes. "You blinked," she whispered. Then she kissed him.

He put his arms around her, and her tongue was sweet despite the nicotine. She was pulling on the belt of his pants at the same time. "I guess I won't be going to Sheena's tonight," she said.

Lou's heart beat fast, and he covered her mouth again. Their clothes were off, when she asked whether he had a condom. "What?"

"I left so fast, I forgot my diaphragm. This ain't a safe day, calendar-wise."

He stammered, because he didn't.

"It's cool, I got an idea," she said as she rolled over.

He objected that she would hurt, unable to admit his own discomfort. She wagged her buttocks against him, impish and insistent until strain told in her voice. "I want you inside me."

She hadn't told him the truth, because he knew by her tense back and the noises from her throat that it did hurt. But there were noises of excitement too, and she urged him. By the time the noises became all pain he was too committed to stop.

Afterward he felt love and repulsion, happiness and fear. It was confusing.

But she fell asleep in his arms and seemed satisfied, very small against his chest. His own disturbance probably contributed to the dream.

It was not about Cancún.

It was about night at the deathsite. Schmallhorst was outstretched on the barbed wire fence, arms outstretched and head wobbling loosely on a broken neck. The dust beneath him drank up his blood.

What happened to the precious blood? Lou wondered, and had a revelation.

We are all James Dean. The blood is in me. I am the Grail and the vessel. He has made of me his chalice, and I look to the day of his coming. His death gave us birth and his second coming will liberate—

Then he saw Cherie at the intersection among a crowd arranged like the cover of *Sgt. Pepper's Lonely Hearts Club Band*. Devereux, Polmquist, Ermaine, the Dean Widows, Cottlee, Pollack, Sal, Natalie—

We are all here. It is night and we are waiting for the summoning and the sacrifice. The stars are out, and we all bear on our flesh the scars of a car wreck. The stigmata.

He looked down at his palms and they throbbed with blisters, which he knew were from the shovel.

How hard was the ground? Permafrost? The car we have hidden forty years. The driver is back in his car. The car is ensouled and calling the fire down.

A star was becoming brighter in the east, closer and brighter until its single piercing ray shone down like a sword on the intersection.

There is the Spyder and it is made of light, whole and one piece again. Jimmy is behind the wheel and his face is shining and he is light, too. . . .

Suddenly Ernie Hockman in his orange Caltrans uniform was setting sizzling warning flares across the highway between Lou and the fans, who recoiled like vampires from the hissing flames.

19

Tuesday, September 27, 1995
Griffith Park, 11:32 A.M.

Cherie slunk down in the bucket seat as the growling Speedster climbed Observatory Drive to Griffith Park. She'd been sullen since he dropped the script off at George's. "Yesterday," he said, "you were all for me getting rid of it."

"I was for you putting it back where you found it."

He did not feel like telling her it was just for safe-keeping, or that he had been wondering seriously whether Cottlee merely wanted him out of the apartment so he could search it. Didn't the man have investigators in his employ? "I trust George and Donna. In fact, they comprise my entire circle of friends. We'll pick it up tonight when we see them for dinner."

As the planetarium dome came into view, Lou was startled by a festive crowd in Dean shirts, television crews hustling for interviews, and vendors selling souvenirs.

And on the periphery was Tony Bulova, talking to Jonathan Cottlee, who was astride a Silver Ghost Harley-Davidson. Lou wondered what that meant.

"It's a zoo," he said as he pulled the emergency brake.

"You're surprised?" Cherie said as she flicked her cigarette. "C'mon."

Gasps came from the faithful as the shroud was pulled to reveal a bronze Jimmy Dean, his hair immortalized in a peak like a Pentecostal tongue of fire. There was a whir of cameras, multilingual oohs and aahs. Patsy Polmquist and a score of Deaners laid a wreath at the base, then obligingly posed for pictures. Liv Ermaine became queen bee at the buzzing center of a hive of autograph seekers.

But Ermaine saw him, and broke regally from her admirers. "It's you," she said. "See? I have goose bumps on my arms. I knew Jimmy would—" Her black hackles rose at the sight of Cherie.

An awed fan approached to say huskily, "I've seen *Vampires from Outer Space*, like, dozens of times. I stay up whenever one of your old movies is on. Really."

Ermaine's smile was brittle. "I haven't had a sweeter tribute since I was carbon-dated. Now, fuck off."

It was certainly not the place to talk, and Lou was angry that Cottlee must have known that. Not in the mood to swell a crowd scene, Lou was unaware of the television crew diverting its attention with shouts, "Hey. Isn't that . . . him? You know, the *one*."

Someone adjusted a sun reflector, a blond woman confronting him with a microphone. "You're the one, aren't you? What are your emotions on this day?"

"What are you talking about?" he asked. "Who do you think I am?"

"You're kidding?" she smiled with feral teeth. "Lou Ehlers, who do you think *you* are?"

The guy from *Entertainment Tonight* edged himself into the rapidly forming circle. "When did you first come to believe you were Jimmy Dean? Is it why the artist left you the paintings?"

The nucleus of the crowd shifted, pens extended toward Lou.

"If you didn't want this, you shouldn't have made the tape," the *Entertainment Tonight* guy was saying.

"Tape?" Lou had lost Cherie in the confusion.

The next question stunned. "Were you ever arrested in investigation of the theft of the body of James Dean?"

The crowd hushed in freeze-frame, then a tumble of questions about grave robbery. Lou stood in shock until a strong arm took his own. "Let me help you out," Bulova said irritably, holding Cherie by the wrist and escorting them firmly through the hubbub.

"What are they talking about?" Lou stammered.

"You in the Spyder," Bulova muttered, letting the dangling cigarette fall from his lips. "All the stations got a copy this morning."

"Copy? I haven't made any tape."

"Of course," Bulova said sardonically, quickening their pace. "I'm sure you just posed in the car, and somebody caught you on *Candid Camera*."

"I haven't seen any—" Lou began.

"Then watch TV this evening," Bulova panted as they reached the Speedster. "It's slick, like a press release." He held the door open. "Poor Ly, this should have been his day."

Cherie's eyes were amused by the gaining crowd, and she turned her head to watch and wave as a bewildered Lou burned out of the parking lot.

* * *

"Very Hollywood," Cherie said raptly that evening as she watched the television coverage of Lou fending off media.

"Also on hand at the unveiling," the newscaster was saying, "was the young Westwood man whose identification with Jimmy Dean has taken supernatural form. If James Dean happened to be reincarnated, who would he pick? Many Hollywood insiders believe twenty-five-year-old Lou Ehlers knows the answer—"

There was a clip of a sullen Lou in the Spyder on the convention floor, perfect lead-in to the big story.

"File this one 'Beyond Belief.' Indiana State Police will neither confirm nor deny that the late idol no longer rests easy in his grave. 'No comment,' is the official response to reports that the earthly remains of James Dean have been hijacked from an Indiana grave. And whose name keeps popping up in rumors of the ghoulish shenanigans? If you guessed 'Lou Ehlers,' you're right. What's next? Here in an editorial comment on the posthumous goings-on is our own—"

Jesus Christ.

The bit was hardly over before the telephone started ringing. Some were Deanfans, others amateur occultists. Lou listened to Cherie fielding the calls, and was on the verge of unplugging the damned thing when she cupped the receiver to say, "It's Terry—"

His hands trembled as he snatched it.

"What do you think, buddy?" Childes was saying brightly. "Is this great publicity for our documentary, or what?"

Lou tried to stay calm. "You had no right. It's a major disruption of my life. I'm a private person and it's an invasion. Do you realize I could sue you? Sue the shit out of you?"

Cherie switched channels, but Lou could still hear it in the background.

"The new Dean biopic in the works? Budd Kunstler has already built six replicas of Dean's two-seat Spyder. On September thirtieth, Dino Shackleford and crew will shoot at the intersection of California highways 41 and 46. . . . Attention to detail is the trademark of both Shackleford and Kunstler, who've been working with top industry stunt men on the complex calculations and precautions necessary for any high speed—"

"You signed a waiver," Childes said with faint bravado. "You're looking at this all wrong. It's just an angle for a little hype and hoopla, it won't last. In Hollywood you're famous for about fifteen minutes, and then it's you like you were never born. Once the anniversary's over—"

"Where *are* you?" Lou asked.

Terry said warily, "At a friend's house—in fact, he wants to talk."

The phone was passed at the other end.

"Lou? Jonathan here. Terry's a bit thick, but I'll try to impress on him your displeasure. It took everybody aback, the crowd out there today. It's no doubt the craziness with the anniversary. Liv was disappointed she didn't get to chat with you. Have you any time this evening? I could send a car—"

"Did you set me up? How do you know Bulova? What were you two talking about?"

Cottlee bridled. "The new movie, actually. Are you paranoid? I'm sorry if what happened today upset you. Liv is sorry—she's quite anxious to talk with you, and would have called but I think it flatters her to have me run interference. She's sort of off-putting, but a warm person underneath for all that."

Lou seethed. "I have a dinner engagement." Not that he had any appetite.

"Afterwards?"

Lou walked to the window and parted the curtains, half-expecting to see a scraggly crowd of Deaners below. But the street was empty.

"Do you know who you are?"

"It'll be just her and me?" he asked.

"Honor bright. But I know she doesn't receive at her place—you know, she lives over a garage? She's self-conscious about her humble digs, has so many cats you can hardly breathe. Wait—how about the corner of Santa Monica and Gower?"

Cherie changed to another station where the local anchor intoned cynically, *"Speaking of supernatural sidelights to the death of James Dean, tonight we can add another mystery. Do you believe in reincarnation? Some fans of the late James Dean, do—"*

"Let's get out of here," he said as he got off the phone.

"We've been watching you on TV," George said as he came out to meet them, beer in hand. He said to Cherie, "Donna's in the kitchen. I'm sure she'd appreciate the company."

"I'm sure," Cherie said, sarcasm lost on George as she walked stiffly into the house.

"You weren't shitting about this grave-robbing business, were you?" Bluestein said solicitously. "It was pretty intense, all the stations—"

"Intense isn't the word, it's crazy. I thought the Dean hoopla would build gradually toward Friday, but today it seemed to increase exponentially. Today it just seemed to blow up."

Bluestein sucked foam off·his beer. "That's because you were in the middle of it."

"That's an understatement ... and now I'm on TV. One station interspersed clips of me and Dean, a montage, as if I was claiming we were some sort of combined entity."

George was philosophical. "If fame is inevitable, relax and enjoy it."

"Not like this. What happened today was the result of somebody's calculation. A guy named Terry Childes took the film, but he's not that bright. I think somebody manipulated him."

"Any ideas who or why?"

"Maybe the same person who lured me out there today for the television stations. Jonathan Cottlee."

"Your millionaire?"

"I saw him at the planetarium where all this was going on, and he was talking to that 'Dean accident cop' you told me about. His name's Bulova, and it turns out he's some sort of spurned lover of Pollack's whose been carrying a torch for forty years. He hassled me the day I found Ly's body, then turned around and gave me all the paintings."

George emitted a low whistle.

"Cottlee was Pollack's pick for robbing Dean's grave. And Devereux thinks he's got the death car."

"Devereux is ... ?"

"A self-proclaimed premier Dean conspiracy theorist. He's already done one book. He was also Cherie's 'boyfriend,' or whatever you want to call it."

George's eyes widened. "You stole her?"

"It wasn't like that," Lou said impatiently, "it was this sick scene, he feels Jimmy's his own little corner of history. Christ, I must need to talk."

"I can't believe you stole her," Bluestein clapped him

on the shoulder. "I didn't know you had it in you. Anyway, you've got some suspicions about Cottlee. But what about the 'why' part?"

"All I can figure, it might have something to do with the business Ly was spreading around about me being Jimmy's 'ka.' The occult 'flavor of the month,' that's what Bulova—"

Donna called from the kitchen window.

Dinner was difficult. Cherie's few remarks seemed to have an undertone of ridicule, probably the same Cleveland reserved for 'normies' or non-Deaners. Or maybe he was just tense. Afterward, George got two beers and drew Lou into the front room as Donna detained Cherie in the kitchen with strained chatter.

"She's a beautiful girl. I'm happy for you, Lou," Bluestein said without enthusiasm when they were ensconced on the worn sofas.

George began hesitantly. "Lou, what you were saying about reincarnation? Have you ever considered a past-life regression?"

It hit Lou out of the blue. "A hypnotist? Not you, too."

"A hypnotherapist. You're in a lot of confusion. Why not just find out? The message from deep trance is that most of us have taken up residence in this life many, many times as disembodied entities. Past-life memories brought into awareness have resulted in some rapid healings. You're in pain from your consciousness dividing into two streams—those dreams of yours, for instance. Did you ever get into *The Tibetan Book of the Dead*? There's a concept called *bardo*—it's the space of consciousness between these islands of—"

"George!"

"We'll drop it. I just meant this must all be happening to you for a reason. But there's something else I want to put to you." Bluestein became uneasy. "I'm in a bit of a jam—"

Money, Lou thought.

"I've got some enemies on the faculty. I'm coming up for a review and they'd like to get rid of me on any pretext—we both know it. My problem is I'm kinda vulnerable right now. I've been distracted and sort of a mess the last two years, right up until I met Donna. It's the 'publish or perish' thing. It's been a long time since anything's come out under my name and I'm feeling a lot of pressure."

"So?"

"So, I wanna make a proposition—and you just stop me if it's not good for both of us. I'd like to develop your material and publish something. It'd come out under both our names. I think I could do it pretty fast, and it would bail me out of a spot. I've read the script—and I've got some theories."

"Like what?"

"Like what you said yesterday about the torch being passed, and some modern-day group being responsible for all the weirdness coming down. Jimmy's body being stolen, talk about occult doings out at the intersection this Friday. And now what's happened to you today."

He wet his lips. "What about this cop, Bulova? It occurred to me that his ongoing investigation over four decades would be the perfect blind to keep abreast of any other investigations into the death of James Dean. Ly hid the strongbox out there, and you just said Bulova was some kind of spurned lover. Maybe he's where Ly got the stuff. Anyway, I'd like a shot at him. You've got nothing to lose, plus I'm good with cops."

"What makes you think he'll see you, or tell you anything?"

"That's the beauty part, and one way to test my theory: dangle this script in front of him. If he's afraid it could implicate him in any way, he'll want to recover it."

Lou blanched.

"Is there a problem?" George glanced to the kitchen. "The chick?"

Lou confessed, "I told her I'd pick up all the material tonight. She's emotionally involved with Dean's memory, and I think it bothered her that I put it in unconsecrated hands today. Something like that. I promised her I'd pick it up tonight."

Bluestein smiled conspiratorially. "Women are a species unto themselves, huh? Donna's really spooked by all this dead movie star-stuff, too. Look, you take the strongbox tonight. Nobody has to know it's empty—and I'm talking about Donna, too. She's leaving tomorrow and I don't want her to worry."

George saw Lou's reservation about the dishonesty. "I want you to feel good about this. I'm bright, and know cults and occultism. I'm your thesis adviser, remember? So let me advise, now."

"Okay," Lou said with mingled relief and guilt.

"At dinner you said you were meeting with this Liv Ermaine, tonight. Cottlee set it up?"

"Devereux believes Liv would also be involved in any contemporary cult activity."

George's smile was cryptic. "Well, I wouldn't put too much stock in that, if I were you." Then he whispered hurriedly as the women came in from the kitchen. "Thanks, Lou. I won't forget this."

Lou parked at Santa Monica and Gower, realizing with annoyance that Cottlee had arranged the rendezvous beneath the dun-colored walls of Hollywood Memorial Park cemetery. A hearse was gliding to the curb across the street.

"That's her," he said. When the smoked window rolled slowly down he saw "the Hawk" beckoning him.

"Get in," Liv Ermaine's brittle voice came from the barely-cracked jump-seat window.

The Hawk opened the door. Lou slid in next to Ermaine, and felt Cherie pressing close before the door shut with finality. At least there was no casket in the back bay. The hearse moved away from the curb.

"Hey!" Lou said as he turned in the seat. "I'm not sure I want to leave my car out there!"

Ermaine laughed so the black pearls jiggled on her bosom; something about the smell of her reminded Lou of a Chinese restaurant.

"It'll probably be okay," Cherie calmed him, which drew Liv's baleful attention.

"Are you two joined at the hip? Aren't you one of Cleveland's elves? Why are you people so interested in the death of James Dean?"

Lou started to intervene.

"No," Cherie patted his hand. "It's okay. I think of Jimmy's death and it's like . . . something that happened personally to me."

Liv snorted with condescension. "That's a prerequisite for perfection, isn't it? You Dean Widows are like the brides of Christ. The dead Jimmy can never disappoint, and he never threatens."

"Where are we going?" Lou asked irritably.

Liv looked straight ahead. "You know, I went out there as guest of honor to Cleveland's festivities one year. The death site. I said only, 'When are you ghouls going to eat?' It effectively ensured I'd never be invited again. Have you been talking to Cleveland?"

Cherie was looking out the window. "This is Baldwin Hills, isn't it? Where they shot *Rebel*?"

Lou noticed that now the neighborhoods were predominantly black.

Liv said, "Why did you come, Lou? And don't say 'Cottlee,' that was *his* reason. But your reason is you're trying to find out who you are. That, I believe I can help you with. It's time you met someone. You've put it off long enough."

"I don't care for surprises."

She smiled. "Oh, there's no preparing you for this one. What do you know about Jimmy's ambulance ride to the hospital after the accident?"

"There was a minor fender-bender. The driver pulled over to check the damage."

"True. An unscheduled stop. What if Jimmy was switched with someone else at that point? Someone with a face so damaged as to render him unrecognizable. Face disfigured, closed casket. No autopsy. Who would know the difference?"

"You mean," Cherie asked, "Jimmy might have survived the accident?"

The hearse turned into a dark cul-de-sac and parked before a rundown two-story with a lawn gone to rank weeds. "Get out," Liv commanded when they hesitated.

She paused portentously at the curb. "There's been a single occupant in this house for forty years. He never goes outside and he never talks to anyone. Except me."

Cherie crossed her eyes as soon as Liv's back was turned, but Lou didn't feel they were on a lark. He was getting bad vibes from the secluded house with its boarded-up windows and broken streetlights. At least the Hawk stayed in the hearse.

Ermaine unlocked the door and once inside lighted a black candelabra. "No power," she said. The house was

empty and the floors bare. She paused at a door en
route to dark stairs, extending the candles within so
light swam on the walls like floating highlights of an
aquarium. "Look."

A flickering anteroom was filled with Dean memorabilia. But on second take, it was not the standard fan
club accumulation. There were wardrobes in plastic on
hangers.

"That's the coat Jimmy wore in *Eden*," Cherie
breathed. "And I recognize that sweater."

"Angora," Liv said, like a sensual invocation. She
began a weird glide to the stairs.

"Who owns this house?" Lou demanded.

"You don't know him," she said haughtily. "A New
York fan who wants to open his own Jimmy museum.
I'm surprised he hasn't mounted old Aunt Ortense. I
don't mean 'mount' in the sexual sense." Her mouth
was quizzical. "Or do I?"

Cherie clutched his hand as they climbed the stairs.

Ermaine paused on the landing before a closed
door. "You," she whispered to Lou. "Go in." She stood
aside.

Lou recalled those old fan magazines. *Come out of
hiding. Your fans love you—will always love you, no
matter what you look like. . . ."* He barely touched the
door.

It swung by itself.

The room was bare except for a rocking chair where
a seated figure looked sadly out the window, head
thickly wrapped in dirty bandages.

"Jimmy?" Liv said.

The mummy-head rotated.

There was a plaintive and almost agonized expression
barely discernible on the bandages, the mouth moving
as if trying to speak.

Cherie gave a hysterical cry, then slid to the floor. Her sobs were convulsive.

"Christ, Liv," the bandaged form moaned, "I told you this wasn't funny!"

The figure was unraveling the wrapping to reveal gray hair neat around a burned and jovial face.

Liv said indifferently, "Lou, meet Jeff Hackett."

A seething Lou supported Cherie as she regained composure, shoulders still shaking.

"Jeez," Hackett was saying, "I saw him come in, and for a minute I thought—"

"We know," Liv said, "they say he's Jimmy's reincarnation. Personally, I think Jimmy has elected himself Lou's spirit guide. Jimmy's not hiding here, only Jeff. He has a little trouble with parole violation and he's avoiding a warrant. Jeff's plagued with guilt that he didn't accompany Jimmy."

Hackett spoke with self-recrimination. "It was too much car for him. I shoulda gone with him to the race that Friday, he wanted me to. But I had a party at my sister's—" His eyes were red.

Liv ensconced herself on the floor and lighted a Turkish cigarette. "All the people who claim Jimmy invited them along that day? Now, they'd fill a bus."

Hackett continued to plead with Lou for expiation. "I told him not to go. He died on the highway, and there wasn't anybody with him who was close to him. Like a dog, all alone and surrounded by vultures." He reached for a bottle of Cutty Sark.

"Jeff's in a sort of time warp," Liv explained. "He's not quite clear on the fact forty years have passed."

"He shoulda got the Lotus," Hackett blurted. "I wanted him to get the Lotus Mark Nine, but he had to have the Spyder. I says, 'What about the oversteer? And you're gonna enter a race with a new car with only eight hundred miles on it? And with just two weeks practice time behind the wheel?' But he wouldn't listen."

"That's enough, Jeffrey," Liv said brusquely. "It wasn't the Spyder Jimmy had to have, but Rolf."

"Oh?" Lou was pricked by interest.

Liv's nod was knowing. "I knew Frank Saunders, the salesman at the Porsche dealership. As a selling point when he sold a racer, he promised to send one of the mechanics along to the first competition. Rolf was trying to break off their relationship, refusing to see Jimmy. So Jimmy bought the car with the stipulation that Rolf be the mechanic Frank sent along."

She made a dismissive gesture with the cigarette. "The relationship with Rolf threatened Jimmy's career, so of course he had to have him. Just another form of suicide. Rolf was devastated by his discovery of a latent homosexuality. He'd been quite the ladies' man up until that time. He discovered a part of himself he didn't want to know. He had a love-hate for Jimmy for seducing him and wanted them to go out together. He would make Jimmy pay, and unite them in a marriage of death in the same stroke—That's why he killed Jimmy, and tried to kill himself. Maybe a little tampering at Blackwell's Corners, their last little stop thirty miles before the accident site? Who would be suspicious of the mechanic monkeying around with the brakes?"

Lou said, "Cottlee thinks the studio killed Jimmy, and tried to kill Weutheric."

She smiled. "Then he's an idiot."

Lou took a breath. "What about 'Pontifex'?"

She seemed a little startled, but recovered with a snort. "Pontifex was merely Jimmy's imaginary mommy. A superego to punish him for being a bad boy. He was extrajecting his personal demons on the real world."

"He made it up?"

"He made himself up, didn't he? He told me all about Pontifex. It was this demonic fraternity behind the Maleficarum coven Rogers involved him in. He said they wanted him dead, they were trying to control him magically. The studio already had him seeing a psychiatrist, but I therapized him my own way."

"How?"

"By sending him to Indiana on a magical goose chase so he would regain control of his life again. Fighting black magic with white magic, using his own belief system."

"Jimmy wasn't crazy," Cherie said protectively.

"Be the judge. Lou, did Cottlee tell you about my phone call from Jimmy the night before he died? No? Jimmy wanted me to send someone back to the land of death. At first I thought he meant his mother, but he swore it wasn't. I eventually got the truth." She savored the suspense.

"Who, then?" Lou asked with irritation.

"It was a boy killed in one of Jimmy's races a few months previous. I believe his name was Jack, and Jimmy apparently felt his presence. I was flattered, it wasn't every day somebody reposed that much occult confidence in me. Jimmy was cuckoo—that's why he wanted to play Nijinsky, the crazy ballet dancer. He identified with the artist losing his mind."

"To the extent of writing an entire movie script?"

Liv smiled. "The height of hubris, but ultimately a self-portrait of his own dissolving mind. And not even original—it was based on some flaky idea Nick Ray gave him. Why do you think the studio broke into his house after he died? To retrieve any evidence of his homosexuality and craziness. They had to protect their investment, with two major unreleased pictures in the can."

Jeff interrupted morosely, "And now they got his body for Chrissakes!" His eyes were wounded as he tugged at Lou's sleeve. "I hear you got busted out at the cemetery. You didn't steal Jimmy's body, did you, Lou?"

Lou's face heated. "No," he croaked.

Liv smiled. "Jeffrey, there are fans, and there are *fans*. The little necrophiles have their own logic—unless Lou subscribes to the 'black magic' scenario?"

Lou said, "Pollack did."

"Poor Ly was almost as bad a drunk as Jeff here. And Devereux? You tell Cleveland I think *he* killed Jimmy Dean."

"Jeez, Liv," Hackett said uneasily. "You could get sued."

"For what? My trousseau and a single room over a garage? I'm the one who has the skinny on everything, Lou. The famous missing death car? Elvis was obsessed with Jimmy to the extent of dating both Natalie and me, because we'd known Jimmy. He used his power and influence to get the car for his own Dean collection. That's why I brought you here, Lou—to see for yourself that I know where all the skeletons lie. Jimmy wants his story told. By you, through *me*."

"And Cottlee?"

Her smile turned derisive. "He's a *bore*. An *infantile* bore. I've known so many of his ilk, who flatter and wheedle, and when they are through with you—"

"Christ, Liv," Hackett said, "you always turn on everybody."

"It's forty years since Jimmy died," she said imperiously, "and of all his friends, I have nothing. Even though I've kept my promise to Jimmy. I told him I would light the candle for him and would guide his soul. I'm still closer to him than any of them. Any of you."

She held the candelabra below her arch face so shadows crawled across it like rippling spiders. "You see, I lead him back when he gets lost. Back to the light. He is held prisoner. You see, Jimmy and I were soul-mates. We both wore dental plates."

Her chilling smile once more revealed the black gap of her front teeth. She suddenly rested the weight of her body on her heels, her eyes rolling up.

"It's opening," she groaned. "I see it swing wide. . . ."

"Christ," Jeff slurred. "Channeling. The wolf's talking to her. She does this sometimes."

Her features were undergoing a revolting change. From her throat issued a hideous baying. Then words came in a hellish groan.

"It's no use, Lou," Liv moaned in a man's voice. "Don't come any closer. Beware the killing ground! Beware those weird and timeless reaches! It's a wasteland of space and spirit, of the eye and the soul. Don't be there on Friday!"

"Who are you?" Lou asked hoarsely.

"You know."

"No," Lou said. But the voice was familiar. Distorted, but a voice he knew from dreams.

The voice from the woman's throat said, "Your soul will never leave, but will become part of that place forever!"

Her chin collapsed against her chest.

"She says you know who it is," Cherie whispered to Lou.

He shook his head. "I don't," he insisted.

Ernie. Ernie Hockman.

Back at his apartment, Lou grabbed a Heineken and sagged exhausted on the couch, leaving Cherie to get the string of messages off the blinking answering machine. He realized he was crestfallen. He had hoped Pontifex was real, that there was some sort of super-villain mastermind behind what had happened in the fifties, and that he would be the one to discover his identity. Instead, he had found only another sick and angst-ridden kid: Jimmy Dean. Excitement had left Lou's life, and he had not realized how much he had come to depend on its narcotizing effect the last few days. Anything to relieve him of himself.

"More nuts?" he asked as Cherie sat beside him.

"One from George," she said, brushing the hair from his forehead. "He wanted you to know he has an appointment with that doctor you recommended. Tomorrow afternoon."

Today, Lou corrected to himself. It was already Wednesday.

"Was he sick?" Cherie asked. "Is that what you two were talking about for so long?"

But Lou did not answer.

20

Wednesday, September 28, 1995
Westwood, 2:32 P.M.

The jukebox in the West Hollywood bar was blaring
"James Dean" by the Eagles as George caught the eye
of the girl on a far stool nursing a beer. She wore black
leather shorts and had a beautifully brutish face beneath
pink hair moussed into a spiky fantail. Then he shook
the webs of fantasy, reminding himself he had put
Donna on the plane—

He tried to get his mind on track. Actually, he was
hoping Lou would lose interest in the whole project.
Wasn't that his pattern? The resultant book would be all
his own—

A hand on his shoulder spooked him.

"You were easy to find," Bulova said as he took a
seat. "Like you said, the only Anaconda-skin boots in
the place. You said you're a friend of the Ehlers kid?"

George's eyes were appraising. "In fact, he introduced me to the woman who's going to be my wife."

"You said you wanted to talk about a script," Bulova said. "That was the carrot. Something about an independent movie company called 'Pontifex.'"

"I didn't say it was an independent movie company," George said slyly.

"You didn't?" Bulova ordered a Tom Collins, explaining, "I'm off-duty. But it doesn't mean I want to waste my time."

George was defensive. "I'm not bluffing," he said, resisting the impulse to run out to the trunk of his car and get the thing.

Bulova pursed lips judiciously. "What's the Ehlers kid's interest in all this? And yours?"

"Why did you send Lou all of Ly's paintings?"

Bulova sipped his drink contemplatively. "I really thought that Ly would want him to have everything."

"Except for his ring?"

Bulova raised his hand, musing as he fingered the ring. "I was about to say, it was the one thing Ly gave me, but he didn't really."

"You just kept it? You sound bitter."

"George, what can I do for you? I don't care for the ambience here. This isn't a bar I'd frequent."

"That ring's Baphomet—the goat-headed god. He was worshiped at Mendes in Egypt."

"You're quite the expert on the occult."

George started to enjoy the game, feeling his drinks. "It's hard to read you guys."

"Cops?"

"No, you closet guys of your generation. Existential guilt. That's what I liked about Ly. He didn't have that."

"Then you didn't know him. Everyone has secrets—even you. I did some background. Wasn't there a divorce ten years ago—a very ugly one? Your wife claimed your sexual requests were a little out of the ordinary . . . some of them pretty extraordinary. Is the university aware of these less savory milestones—?"

George went rigid. "Arizona was a long time ago."

"Or, for that matter, your bride-to-be? Have you shared details with her?"

"Shut up!" George said. "You've never been married. What do you know about anything?"

Bulova raised his brows. "Where's this script? In your car?"

George, rattled, ordered another. "I'm coming up with my own theories about that script. Like maybe this forty-year investigation of yours is just a blind, to cover your own involvement."

"In what?"

George paused dramatically. "The murder of James Dean. You were the middleman who hired the kid to ambush Jimmy's car."

Did Bulova look startled? Or just disgusted? "George," he said with disappointment, "you've been listening to that goddamn Elvis tape, haven't you?"

It was George's turn to be shocked, again. He had not told Lou how he had dipped into Donna's meager savings to purchase a set of the bootlegs.

"Let me tell you what they say," Bulova said comfortably. "Elvis says he dated Liv in the late fifties, and one drunken night she confessed how she knew that this all-male occult cabal, including myself, engineered the murder of Jimmy Dean on that highway to get some sort of magical power. The tape's totally bogus, George. Every other sucker on Hollywood Boulevard has invested in his 'exclusive' set. I can't believe a man of your education fell for it." He shook his head and sipped his drink as if to wash a taste out of his mouth.

George felt the floor drop out from under him, glad Lou was not there to see it.

Bulova said, "You have no idea what you're getting into. If you actually have that script, the smartest thing you can do is give it to me."

"Oh?" Bluestein laughed with fragile bravado. "Is that a threat?"

Bulova shrugged. "Take it like you want. Not playing? It's on me," he said quietly as he left bills on the bar.

George could not think of a rejoinder until Bulova was at the door. "If it's all so bogus, what brought you down here?"

But Bulova did not deign to respond. George continued to drink, thinking about Donna and Arizona.

Lou sat drinking behind the louvered blinds watching straggling Deanfans milling on the sidewalk below, drawn by the entertainment pieces which had appeared on the television.

Was George right? *"Past-life memories brought into awareness have resulted in some rapid healings. You're in pain from your consciousness dividing into two streams—those dreams for instance."*

Something Jimmy said in *East of Eden* kept going through his mind. "I got to know who I am." He had tried to sleep, but the Ohio number of Hockman's parents was emblazoned on his memory in the neon of self-contempt. He heated up his cigarette, sharpened the hot point on the lip of the ashtray, and absently held the hot red tip to the sensitive skin of his forearm.

"What are you doing?" Cherie startled him.

"I thought you were asleep," he said beet-faced. "What time is it?"

"I saw what you were doing," she said as she took the cigarette from his hand, put it to her own lips. She was wearing one of his old shirts, and he wondered whether she had anything on underneath. He said, "You don't understand."

"No? Sometimes you have to hurt to heal, I know all about that." She bit her lip. "You know, if it really helps, I can do things for you."

"What things?"

"Uh, I don't know. Spank you? Whip you?" She made a mock pass at his jaw with her fist. "Beat you up?"

He had to laugh. "I don't think that'll be necessary."

She seemed relieved, but sober. "Is it the gay thing that's tearing you apart?"

He flinched. "That's twice you've brought that up. Why?"

She hesitated. "I didn't mean to piss you off. Cleveland saw it right away, and he never misses. So I had my eyes open."

He was disbelieving. "Cleveland never misses? Jesus Christ, we've made love, haven't we?"

"Sure," she said wryly, "whatever that means. Since last night, you've been like somebody else."

He put the cool bottle of Heineken against his throbbing temple. "I've been trying to sort out where I fit into all this. I have dreams about Dean and the intersection. I spend so much time there in my sleep, I qualify for frequent-flyer miles. But I suppose Cleveland saw that, too."

Her voice had a dead sound. "Yeah. I just didn't know it was ... a problem. I guess. All the 'ka' stuff's not like possession, or anything. I figured it was just like discovering there was more to you than maybe you thought."

"George says I need a therapist. Don't say it— 'Cleveland doesn't trust 'em.' " He made a contemptuous noise.

"Look," she said quickly, "if you're uptight, maybe you need to back away from all this stuff. Obsessions can get sort of ... unwholesome."

"You're right," he breathed. "Sitting here in the dark, obsessing. First about the murder, and now ... I wouldn't have thought I was so suggestible. I don't even believe in reincarnation. Watching myself on television in that Spyder ... then the deal with Liv. Not to mention George."

"George?" she asked. "What happened with George?"

He took a guilty breath. "I didn't want you to know. I was ashamed of how wrapped up I was getting. He said he wanted to get involved in the Dean business with me."

"Get involved, how?"

"So he could publish something. I guess I've been alone so long it's pretty natural to have secrets. It's stupid, I'm sorry."

"And ... that's all?"

"Did you think he was telling me I needed to find another girl?"

She sucked deeply on the cigarette, eyes sardonic. "I guess it crossed my mind. It wouldn't be the first time."

She was pensive, then intense as she said urgently, "Look, it's not too late for either of us. We can cut ourselves off from this crap ... maybe go away for a few days until this all blows over. Put it behind us."

He saw the fear in her eyes. "You think I'm falling victim to the Dean curse?" He regretted his words.

The look on her face broke his heart as she said, "I've already watched one man fall apart, sitting in the dark and drinking. Hoping Jimmy was murdered. Because if he was murdered, then Jimmy isn't just a dead end where you finally have to confront yourself."

"How do you mean?" he asked, concerned.

"If I have to explain, then you can't understand. . . . Look, I know how many ways all this can pull at you. It's brought you into my life, and that was good. But if I don't know where to get off, it'll take me right on through to the other side. Away from you."

He watched her struggle for more words, until he couldn't stand it.

"I think you've got a good idea," he said, "about getting away. Maybe I've got an idea. How about Cancún?"

Her eyes widened. "You're kidding?"

"I'm not. I can make reservations, and—"

Her eyes had welled with tears.

"What's wrong?"

"Nothing," she said as she dabbed at her eyes. "Really. Would you believe I've hardly ever been on a date? And now, flying to . . . *Cancún*."

"What about a boat? A slow one. But it might take me twenty-four hours to put that together, plus we'd have to—"

She kissed him suddenly. And deeply.

"Wow," he said.

She bit her lip, looked in his eyes. "And I've got a plan, too. For the next twenty-four hours. We go to bed. No expectations, no pressure. Nothing to prove. And we pull the covers over our heads."

"Disconnect the phone?"

She giggled conspiratorially. "And don't answer the door."

"Nobody mentions Dean, DeanCons or Deanfans? No more talking about Deathcars, or Deathsites?"

"Or 'Deaners.' Just us and who we are."

"I think I like that plan," he said. "In fact, it's the best idea I've heard in a month." He hesitated. "But maybe I ought to leave the phone on for George. If he doesn't get hold of me, he'll probably come over—"

She kissed him again, and her voice was smoky. "And we wouldn't want that."

Goddamn me, George cursed himself over the next three hours, *but she's a wild-looking bitch in that black leather.* He sat too long drinking beer, and then Wallbangers to cut the bloat. He had struck up an acquaintance with the leggy gal. *Goddamn me*—

There were little silver doodads on her necklace which dipped into braless cleavage, the air conditioner hardening nipples for his inspection. That was all she wrote. George let her know he was a professor, Professor *Lou Ehlers*.

Goddamn me. He was mad because she made it so easy by saying her apartment was nearby.

Outside, it was darker than the interior of the bar. He pulled over once in his Caddy en route, to walk up to her champagne VW Bug and deliver a little prepared speech that went, "Look. I think I mighta made a mistake. There's a significant someone in my life now. . . ."

But as he dipped his head to her window, there were hard breasts hanging loose against squeaky leather.

She read his mind. "Look—if this is a bad idea . . .?"

He smiled. "You say your place is just around the corner?"

He followed her through twisting streets of squalid apartments beneath palm trees dying of smog, and condos built during the boom; their scant lawns were burnt with insecticide. It gave him a sense of safe anonymity. Parking, he wobbled and navigated a tricycle to follow her inside the door of a dark rental house. The drapes were drawn; she led him through a beaded curtain.

"You're really into him, huh?" George asked. Covering an entire wall was a huge silkscreen of James Dean.

"Jimmy? Yeah," she said, setting her purse down. "Right."

"I'm writing a book about him now," George said.

Sex was inevitable in the air, and he was getting into the resigned mode where he might as well enjoy it. She was taller than he had realized as she wrapped long arms around his neck to mash her lips to his own. She detached with a squeak of leather, turned and peeled off shorts. When the jacket fell, George sucked a breath. "Wow," was all he could say. Between her shoulder blades and extending down the small of her back, was a tattooed outline of the state of Indiana framing Jimmy's soulful face.

Are you up for this? her blue eyes teased as she clicked her tongue. She lay on the rug with legs spread.

"You believe in gettin' right to it," George said, impressed. He also noted she wasn't a real redhead.

He was halfway down the buttons of his Levi's and already she was strapping him on. He got off to a slow start then felt he was doing well, working some of that sexual yoga Donna had taught him, the chakra deal where the male seed shoots up the spine. It broke his concentration when she tensed her thighs to roll over on top. He could hardly restrain himself, yoga be damned.

She slid off him to work his organ furiously with her hand. He exploded, trying to catch his breath. She smiled with the viscous spider web between her fingers.

"Nasty," she winked, wiping her hands on his thighs, not even breathing hard.

"Jesus," he gasped.

She patted his sweating belly. "Hang on. I'm gonna be in the can for a while."

She was gone a long time. He was feeling that conquistador thing: in conquering the woman he had conquered her space. This gave him right to look around, at least as long as the water was running in the bathroom. There was a walk-in closet, and he opened the door quickly so it would make no noise. He had the idea of inspecting a wardrobe, expecting to smell oiled leather. Instead, there were shelves.

On the shelves were jars.

There were ten little fingers all in a row swimming in some sort of preservative. Neatly coded, the arrangement was apparently chronological. Some fingers were forty years old; those were gray and shriveled. He was shocked, reached up to touch a jar and make sure it was real. *What the—?*

A sting on his naked freckled back made him turn in pain.

She was smiling, holding a stained knife. The jagged blade looked to be a shard of some kind of metal alloy, perhaps aluminum.

"Hey," he said.

Her breasts bounced as she made another sweep with her arm, meaning to cross his groin. But he jumped, and the rough metal caught his inner thigh, femoral artery. Blood spurted everywhere.

"Hey!" he said with real anger.

His racing heart made the blood shoot more as he clutched at the big artery like it was a severed air hose. Amazed at the lack of pain, he racked it up to shock. "Get away from me," he said desperately, scooping the floor for his shorts. He had to get to a hospital, hobbling on one leg trying to pull on white briefs turning red. This could be ugly.

She was on him fast, as he thought of trying to explain to Donna what had landed him at Kaiser Permanente. She slashed his inner arm, severing tendons. Arm useless, he tossed the shirt at her with an angry toe, running and spurting toward a door. Wrong door, no beads.

He fell into a garage, where his own blood made little splats on the concrete.

There was a hospital gurney with something like a brown cocoon of wrapped plastic. Slipping on his own blood, he stumbled into it, and it rolled eerily into the wall. He staggered heavily against it, and the plastic separated.

He saw a decomposing dress shoe, encrusted with mold. There was a foot in the shoe.

Jesus Christ. The question was in his stunned eyes as he turned to see the doorway filled with the woman and her upraised blade. Just like Anthony Perkins in *Psycho.*

"I guess you *are* into James Dean," he said.

She swooped with the silvery blade, the aluminum fang hitting between his shoulder blades like a fist. On his way down he passed through a mist of his own blood. He scooted backward on white legs, saw a smeared track of redness in the shape of his own buttocks. Each cringing movement exposing some vulnerable target.

"Shit," he tried to say. The sound of blade into flesh was like a plum squashed by a boot.

21

Monday, July 5, 1955
Marfa, Texas

The Gothic house was a stark anomaly on the west
Texas plain—a facade propped with timbers and existing in only two dimensions. Sweating cast and crew felt
they had been forever, and would be forever, at the
movie set which had become Jimmy Dean's private hell
as George Stevens endlessly shot and reshot each scene
with multiple cameras.

At blaze of noon hiatus the sun beat down on the al-
kali flat swarming with technicians and extras, bare-
chested carpenters swapping jokes and fighting over
shade. Jimmy was remote as usual, on his knees with
cowboy hat on sideways so he could peer through a
viewfinder. Liz Taylor and Mercedes McCambridge,
both of whom had soft spots for strays, were his only
friends but neither was on call today.

Jimmy was angry. The desert through the viewfinder
excited his imagination as he visualized himself direct-

ing and starring in a vast cinematic epic about Lawrence of Arabia, who "drew tides of men into my hands
and wrote my will across the stars" for love of the Bed-
ouin water boy to whom he had cryptically dedicated
Seven Pillars of Wisdom. Sal Mineo would be perfect as
the seductive Dahoum if Hollywood didn't first corrupt
his innocent features.

What fascinated Jimmy was how the shaper of Arab
nations turned his back on the world and consigned
himself to degradation and hardship as an anonymous
airman whose tormented last years were enlivened only
by sessions of flagellations inflicted by a young soldier.
Jimmy envisioned a final scene with Lawrence behind
goggles on his speeding motorcycle. A mysterious
black private motorcar approached on the lonely road.
A collision, and the bike twisting and turning over and
over again. The clear implication would be that the accident was no accident.

Jimmy was angry because the film would never be
made by him. *Giant* would be his last, because it completed the mythic tryptich.

East of Eden had started the cycle in an idyllic agrar-
ian paradise, carrying the hero up to his expulsion from
the Garden. *Rebel Without a Cause* transformed this
same hero into an urban Galahad, chronicling his trials
and descent into darkness before emerging victorious
and reborn from the belly of the cosmic whale as dawn
appeared over the Hollywood Hills. *Giant* completed
the cycle in the existential deathscape of the crippled
Fisher King of Grail Legend. In it Jimmy would come
full circle and become himself the corrosive elder
Father-King whose defeat in *Eden* commenced the cycle.

But now everyone was creeping from protective umbrellas to squint into the sky where a loud buzz was

taking shape as white and green Beechcraft Bonanza N 3794N. It was no courier with some high directive from Warner Brothers in Hollywood. The plane set down roughly on a dirt road.

James Dean approached in the lock-kneed gait of a wrangler.

Jeff Hackett, who had a pilot's license, stood awkwardly next to a wing. "I didn't spoil a shot, did I? Tell me I didn't."

Jimmy pushed his sunglasses up his nose with a forefinger to acknowledge an uneasy Rolf Weutheric.

"We've got to talk," Jeff panted.

"Later," Jimmy said. He looked at Rolf. "What've you got for me?"

Weutheric shifted under the gazes of technicians, but reached into his jacket pocket for a crinkled cellophane bag. Jimmy took one of the pills, washing it down with the remainder of the Coke in his hand.

"Christ," Jeff said disgustedly, "those things are gonna kill you. You won't sleep for two days."

Jimmy winked. "I got pills for that too. Take him to my trailer and wait."

The interruption did not endear him to a glowering Stevens, who had already severely reprimanded him before cast and crew, and was painstakingly documenting the actor's chronic tardiness. There'd be another confrontation tomorrow over Jimmy's bizarre insistence that Jett Rink carry a shotgun across his shoulders in blatant crucifixion symbolism.

Not Stevens, not anyone, could understand that artistic creation was Jimmy's only means of salvation, reconciling the finite with the infinite. It was what he had instead of God. When the vision was pure and the creation was pure, there was always joy. That was why lostness was swallowing Jimmy as the film drew to a close.

The gusher came in that afternoon as Jett Rink struck oil on the Little Reata, Jimmy awash in the black paleolithic blood of the Earth Mother. Stevens again shot hundreds of feet of color negative which would be airfreighted to Hollywood that evening for development and preview by studio execs. Most of the crew debarked for the nearest town of Marfa and the bar of its single hotel, the El Paisano.

Jimmy was exhausted as he walked to the trailer. Studio doctors had given him a complete physical and placed him on a high-protein diet, but he could not shake the fatigue.

"You look like shit," Jeff Hackett said nervously as he mopped his face with a handkerchief.

"I'm covered with oil."

Hackett said, "I don't mean that. I talk to people who say they don't even recognize you."

"Maybe they never knew me anyway." Jimmy lit a hand-rolled cigarette.

"Is that stuff flammable?" Jeff asked. "Do a favor, drop the Texas accent with me me, okay? Was this 'Pontifex' deal some kinda goose chase? Because I can't find 'em on any coast, under any rules of incorporation. Nobody's heard of 'em."

"You think I'm making them up?" Jimmy bristled.

Jeff was flustered. "Say they're for real. Your participation would be the sole asset, and Warner's got no incentive for a loan-out. They'd have no chips. I read that script—"

"I only asked you to find out who they were, not read the script."

"But you knew I would, didn't you? I don't want to queer anyone's deal, but if there's a picture in it, I

couldn't find it. Or a plot. It's either car races, or end-
less yakking. This Jamie Starr guy is killed off halfway
through, and the rest of it—"

Jimmy's smile was bemused as he quoted Nick Ray.
" 'He's like Hamlet and Jesus together, he's the role of
a lifetime. It's a comment on the film industry, an in-
dictment of society."

"Whatever," Jeff said in confusion, "I can see the
trailers—'There's never been a picture like this!' Goddamn right, and good reason. It's like *Heaven Can Wait*
and the worst board meeting I ever sat through. How
can you not know who wrote it? Jimmy?"

But Dean was eyeing the trailer where Rolf waited.

Jeff knew what he was thinking. "You gotta be crazy,
bringing him out here. Everybody knows what's going
on, and I'm not just talkin' about the pills. I hear you
been workin' on your German, and I tell everybody it's
for Ursula Andress. What am I supposed to say?"

Jimmy hot-boxed the cigarette, then ground it under
his boot. "Tell 'em I'm still a Texas virgin, and it's getting to me." He closed his eyes, an electric ampheta-
mine arc tracing across his brain.

The script was just the method by which consummate
method actor Jimmy Dean was being prepped for his final and greatest role. Life imitating art. Since his earliest years he had been groomed and fatted not just for
martyrdom but synthetic godhood.

Jimmy entered the trailer. Rolf looked up fearfully.

"Find anything interesting?" Jimmy asked. Tacked to
the wall was his drawing of Marlon Brando as Buddha,
and others depicted lounging matadors with oversized
genitalia.

"I didn't go through your things, if that's what you're

getting to."

Jimmy's shirt was open and the oily towel around his neck. The air in the trailer was the moist from the sweating air conditioner in a window. "I missed you. Stand up."

Rolf obeyed, but resisted the dry lips which brushed his own.

"What's wrong?" Jimmy asked. "Don't I get a kiss?"

"Here's your pills," Rolf said as he turned away to scratch the blue tattoo on his forearm. "The police came and searched my place. I think the studio sent them."

"I'll take a couple weeks off in Palm Springs and clean out," Jimmy said, "that is, when I've finished my other commitments. Like 'Blind Run.'" He snaked his arms around Rolf to feel the firm lines of belly.

The sexual encounters were little ballets with separate movements. Rolf turned and their mouths closed, until Weutheric made a noise of protest in his throat.

"I love you," Jimmy said in Rolf's ear. "Why wouldn't you see me before I left town?"

"You don't remember?" Rolf said bitterly. "You said things the last time I saw you. You accused me, you said I was one of 'them.'"

"That's why you wouldn't return my calls?"

Rolf broke away to light a cigarette, looking nervously around. "You're like a house I can look at, but can never live in."

"Or maybe you didn't like what Pontifex is doing. Maybe you didn't want to be a part of it anymore."

Rolf snapped the lighter shut, dark jaw line tense. "You talk crazy, and I don't like how I feel after we're together."

"So why did you come, now?"

Weutheric's eye twitched as he said thickly, "I don't know. Frank says they give you seven thousand dollars on the Speedster. I brought contracts."

"That's the only reason?"

"It kills me to see what's happening to you. Why did you send?"

"Maybe I can't stop."

Rolf looked hopeful. "Then you trust me?"

Jimmy smiled and practiced his Texas drawl. "Well, I didn't say that. No sir, I wouldn' go all that far."

"Bastard," Rolf said angrily. "It wasn't just the police! A guy from the studio came. He wanted to pay me to go home to Stuttgart, other money. A lot. I should have took it!"

Jimmy stepped closer, their faces almost touching. "But you didn't."

"No," Rolf said, face gray.

Jimmy turned and picked up an old guitar. He indicated with a nod the scuffed black flight jacket on the unmade bed. "Put it on."

Rolf said, "That's something else I don't like. Things you want me to do."

Jimmy strummed the guitar once, then dropped it to pick up the jacket. "You look good in leather, like a Nazi. You were a Luftwaffe pilot, weren't you? You flew for Hitler, bombed little kids. Weren't you a Nazi?"

Weutheric flinched. "I see, now comes the part you start to hate."

Jimmy tried to drape the jacket on Rolf's shoulders. "I think I hated you 'cause I hated myself. You can do better than them. So can I."

"Who is this 'them' you keep talking about?"

"Pontifex. Whoever wants to control Jamie Starr. Together we can break away, I'll show you."

"By fucking me?" Rolf's harsh laugh turned into a
cough as he shrugged away.

Jimmy said quietly, "Let me talk and you don't have
to say anything, unless I say something that's not true:
they want you to get inside my head and tell them what
I'm thinking. They want to use you to blackmail me,
they want you to hook me on dope. They want to know
who I'm talking to—"

"I'm not playing, Jimmy," Weutheric said tiredly.

"—and the car. It has to be the Spyder, doesn't it?
Because that's what Jamie Starr drives."

"You twist everything around. You think I care what
car?"

Jimmy's face was close. "Oh, you care all right. That
was something you didn't count on, huh?"

Rolf's eyes were moist. "You're not talking about the
car now." He saw his own gaunt reflection in the bureau
mirror and didn't like it. "I don't know who I am anymore. What do you want from me?"

"I want you. Now."

Weutheric's handsome face was disjointed and per-
spiring. And hopeless. "Okay, Jimmy. You win."

Dean raised his brows. "What?"

Rolf hesitated, conflicted and angry as he unbuckled
his belt. "I said, how do you want me? Like a woman?"

Jimmy stopped Rolf's hand. "You're telling me I can
have you now, any way I want?"

Rolf nodded.

"I want you to say it," Jimmy said relentlessly. "It's
very important to me that you say it, and mean it. And
not because you feel sorry for me. Though I suppose
it's nothing compared with what you're asking me to
do."

Rolf repeated the words with difficulty. "You can have me."

There was a tense pause in which Jimmy tried to stop himself. But he couldn't as he demanded, "Who's behind all this? I feel him all around me but I can't see his face. There has to be a mastermind. Just tell me that."

Tears welled in Rolf's eyes, his teeth clenched in frustration. "You're crazy and you make me crazy." He started to quake as if something inside him had broken. He didn't resist when Jimmy put his arms around him and said soothingly, "Okay. It's okay. I just had to know, that's all. This'll never happen again."

Rolf looked incredulous, then furious. "This was a game?"

Jimmy put his finger to the other's lips. "No. Just the difference between wanting you and not having you, and being able to have you and deciding not to. Just the decision, that's all."

Weutheric's eyes were uncomprehending. "I don't get it."

"You don't have to," Jimmy said as he turned indifferently away. "Now you better go. But first I want to give you something."

Rolf's lips tightened as Dean took his finger. "Jimmy—" he began hoarsely.

"It's just a cheap ring," Jimmy said, "a Pan Am flight ring."

Weutheric's face was divided. "And I brought something for you. I was going to leave it here, but I give it to you now." He went guiltily to his knees, groping under Jimmy's bed to retrieve something.

"What's this?" Jimmy said as he accepted a charred racing glove.

"I'm sorry, Jimmy," Rolf panted. "It belonged to that

man who was killed in the race in May. Get rid of this. Get rid of it, now."

Jimmy looked at him quizzically.

"You bastard," Jeff said rising from the canvas chair as Dean emerged from the trailer. "You wanna tell me what's going on?"

Jimmy looked across the dusky flatlands with his secretive smile that infuriated Jeff. "Do you know someone who sells life insurance? I want some. A hundred-thousand-dollar policy to go for Markie's college fund." Markie was his eleven-year-old-cousin, perhaps the person most important to Jimmy in the world. There was a purity to kids. They were so innocent and uncontaminated.

Hackett said, "You talk like you're dead, Jimmy."

"Maybe I am."

"What're you gonna do?"

Bob Hinkle, Jimmy's dialogue coach, was approaching with .22 rifles and flashlights.

Jimmy said, "Hunt some jackrabbit."

The lean Texan Hinkle was silent as Jimmy followed him into the brush. The dark set receded. Now there were only the stars overhead.

The Beechcraft took off in the night a quarter hour later, Jimmy watching until its taillight winked out. It flashed him back to another movie idea.

He wanted to play Baron Manfred von Richtofen, Germany's Red Knight of the Sky. He could see himself as the blond and tragic young aristocrat in the deadly Fokker triplane that had killed almost eighty men. It was even the sort of thing Pontifex might want to produce. Weren't there obsessed fans of the dead Rittmeister, even private collections of what they called

'Richtofania' including tattered red fabric from the plane?

Rolf could have done the actual flying. Jimmy had even dreamed about it, but in the dream the plane was a two-seater and Rolf was behind him in the cockpit.

And in Rolf's lap was a teakwood box.

22

Thursday, September 29, 1995
Westwood, 10:30 A.M.

"That might be the pharmacy about my pills," Cherie said as she zipped Lou's travel bag and padded hastily across the floor to answer the phone, scooping up the neurotic Thorpe in the same motion.

Lou admired her lithe body as she pressed the cat's soft fur to her face, receiver between her ear and bony shoulder. He glanced around the apartment; anything he might have forgotten could be purchased by credit card.

Then he saw Cherie tense and shrink. "It's that cop, Bulova. You better talk to him."

He was quiet for a moment after he hung up.

"What is it?" she asked in a dead voice.

"George is dead."

"Where?" Her face was stricken.

"Park rangers found him at the base of the Griffith Dean statue at six A.M."

"Maybe it's a mistake," she said in a voice that sounded drowned, far away.

"That's why he wants me to identify the body," Lou said as he slid down the wall to the floor. For a while he didn't hear anything else she said. . . . *In the hammer throw, a competitor makes three full, quick turns of the body before flinging the weight. The ball is solid iron.*

Her incongruous smile came gradually into focus.

"I guess this means we aren't going to Cancún?" She laughed one hopeless bark which startled him, and flopped onto the couch with eyes already shiny.

"Where?" she asked. Not, "How?" Lou saw Dean staring at him mournfully from one of Pollack's canvases. He hesitated only a moment before kicking his foot through Jimmy's face.

Lou was in for another shock as they walked numbly across the parking lot: the chrome striping and Porsche insignias were stripped from his Speedster. "Vultures!" he shouted at the listless girls milling on the sidewalk. But maybe they had nothing to do with James Dean at all, or the pirating of his chrome for souvenirs. Maybe he was just out of hand.

Cherie got him into the car and slid behind the wheel. "Say something," she said tremulously as she threaded traffic.

"This puts me two-for-two," he answered with a mirthless smile. *What am I going to say to Donna?*

"Pull over," he said when he saw a kid selling star maps on a corner, a kid who watched indifferently as Lou vomited his guts into a potted sago. It felt like George coming up through his craw. He returned green and shaky.

"It's not your fault," Cherie said.

"Maybe I'll have to do, until I know whose fault it is."

George had talked about heaven, he thought as they drove to the morgue. *"The Great American Dream, this beautiful celestial city with freeways and autobahns. If you had learned the lessons well, you got a really good car. If you were so-so, you had a midrange economy thing. . . ."*

"Pull over again," Lou said hoarsely. "Quick."

Bulova wasn't there to meet them. The viewing was surprisingly antiseptic, George's shrunken face televised over a monitor as as if he'd been translated to some orthicon plane of afterlife, a remote and angelic image of light. Like James Dean.

The phone call to Donna hung over him as they returned to the apartment; he had her Nebraska number somewhere. But on arrival he saw a yellow police ribbon across the steps. When he tried his door, it was unlocked.

"Stay here," he said to Cherie before stepping inside.

Bulova's eyes were red-rimmed from tiredness as he sat at the table in the kitchen.

"What are you doing in here?" Lou demanded, making a cursory check of the apartment.

"Your manager let me in when I showed my badge," Bulova said casually. "The ribbon downstairs is a consideration to keep the little ghouls at bay. They're just the advance. The rest will come when they get wind of what's going on."

"And what's that?" Lou asked angrily.

"A body at the base of the Dean altar two days before the death celebration. 'Dean Curse,' 'Chain of Death,' 'Unsolved Mysteries'—somebody'll connect the dots. This on top of that leaked tape of you in the

Spyder, not to mention your grave-robbing escapade."
He shook his head, impressed. "The placement of the
body was a stroke—Ly's statue. Plus, the way the body
was arranged."

"What position?" Lou really didn't want to hear the
answer.

"Quite decorative—he was upside down, one ankle
tied with this cord around Dean's neck. I mean the statue's. The other leg was crossed so a right angle was
created. Sound familiar?"

Lou thought of Schmallhorst on his rack of barbed
wire. He had to sit down.

Bulova stood. "It's a nice apartment. We have similar
tastes."

"Why didn't you meet me at the morgue like you
said? Did you just want to pull me down there so you
could search through my things?"

Bulova looked hurt. "No thanks for the ribbon? I
strung it myself. Actually, right after we got off the
phone I was pulled from the case. My history with this
thing gives them a crisis of confidence." He indicated
Cherie with eyes curious over the half-glasses on his
nose. "Miss, don't be shy. Won't you have a seat?"

Lou saw she was transfixed by something in a chair,
her face betrayed and shocked: the three volumes of the
script. Then she walked stiffly through the other room
where he heard the bedroom door close with finality.

Bulova pursed his lips, then his face was illuminated.
"I'll be damned. That little girl—it's her, isn't it? The
one who thinks she's Jimmy Dean's love-child?"

Lou felt color rising. "You leave her alone. She's trying to get her life together. We both are."

Bulova laughed convivially. "You're a soft-hearted
guy, aren't you?"

"That's enough," Lou said. "How did you get the script? George had it."

"It was on your doorstep, I just brought it inside before your 'fans' carted it away."

"You said you weren't on the case," Lou said. "I think I need to talk to someone who is. Because as far as I know you were the last person to see him. He had an appointment with you."

Bulova examined some of the canvases, standing back for perspective. "You don't have enough room, here. You'll probably have to put them in storage." Bulova spoke quietly. "You know, you're not the only one whose only friend was murdered. By the way, here's something you might want to have."

Lou was speechless as the other man handed him a mezuzah. He hadn't even known George wore one.

Bulova said pleasantly as he made to leave, "You're welcome for the tape downstairs."

Alone, Lou closed his eyes against the headache before trying the bedroom door. It was locked, and he imagined her sitting against it on the other side riffling through Tarot cards for consolation.

"Hey," he said softly. "Everything I told you was true. . . . I just left part out. I don't know why, maybe I was ashamed."

No use. There were weights on his calves as he trudged to the refrigerator for a Heineken. When he closed his eyes, George was a grisly pendant hanging upside down from James Dean's neck.

The Hanged Man. The card Bulova had found in Lysander's studio. Liv had cards, too.

He felt ashamed as he unzipped the carryall Cherie had packed. He found a little book, *Key to the Sacred Tarot.*

Anything but call Donna, right?

He settled on the couch and found the picture of the Hanged Man. Also called the Dying God, a crucified man hanging upside down with foot bound to an Ankh of Immortality by the serpent of life. The legs are crossed so a right angle is formed, and the arms are stretched out at an angle of sixty degrees—

He recalled Pollack. *The same angle formed by the conjunction of the highways.*

The limbs form the symbol of a triangle surmounted by a cross, the descent of light into darkness. Why 'the Dying God'? *The god must die. That's where he gets his power to save.*

He was the mediator or redeemer striving to balance his kingdom by uniting the higher and the lower realms. The victim hangs from a branch of the Tree of Life that grows through every plane of the cosmos; his smiling face reveals that his sacrifice has not been in vain, and he has his reward. Torture has been transformed into ecstasy. His abode was Tiphareth on the Tree of Life.

Incarnated gods were sacrificed for their people in order that the tremendous emotional force set free by the act might bring about an equilibrium of forces.

"Cherie?" he said aloud, to no response from the door. The telephone taunted him. He wanted to run, and think. He wanted to be somebody else, but all he did was have another beer. And another.

He kept seeing Jimmy Dean picking his way among the rubble of a temple filled with ancient idols and obsolete gods. Rotting Attis and Osiris. The corpse of crumbling Jesus on the Cross.

"Cherie?"

He closed his eyes and saw the gods on a great spinning mandala. Above them all loomed Jimmy Dean in his shining car.

* * *

The phone wakened him, but Donna's voice sobered him up.

"I had to hear it on the television," she quavered. "My mother has a dish. Lou, I just happened to be watching L.A. because I was homesick."

He was ashamed of his cowardice, doubly guilty at his relief. "I couldn't find your number," he half-lied. "Donna, I'm so sorry." He checked his watch: 2:48. The door to the bedroom was open, and he walked towards it until the umbilical of cord brought him short.

Her voice tore angrily around the sob. "What happened, Lou? What really happened?"

He took a breath. "We don't really know, yet. It's horrible, Donna. Worse than horrible." He held the phone at arm's length to quickly glance in the room, but Cherie was neither there nor the bathroom. *Where is she?*

"I'm sorry," he apologized. "I didn't catch that."

"It all started that night, didn't it?" Donna was saying. "When you and that girl came for dinner."

In the dim kitchen he checked the sink for a note. Nothing.

"Maybe it did," he said. "I feel horrible, I can't tell you. He wanted to be involved on this James Dean deal. I really don't know if it had anything to do with that, or not." *The hell you don't.*

She sniffled, "I'm flying back."

"Alone?" He saw impressions of doodles on the scratch pad. If Cherie had gone anywhere, she would have had to take the bus. *Unless someone picked her up.*

"I think my mother will come," Donna said. "This is too much, too fast."

He ran a pencil over the indentations.

"Lou?"

A phone number appeared above *H. Wood Mem P.* Hollywood Memorial Park.

"Of course, I'll meet you at the airport."

"Wait a minute—my mother's saying something. She thinks I should wait. Lou, can I call you back?"

"Sure," he said gratefully and hung up.

Shadows loomed across the old cemetery as Lou pulled the Speedster through the iron gates. He despaired of finding her in the sepulchral vastness as he navigated gravel drives. But there was Bill Bario stationed before the huge Baroque mausoleum with arms crossed like the bodyguard of a banana republic dictator.

Lou parked, yanked the emergency brake.

"Hey!" Bario cried as Lou dodged past him up the steps of the Court of the Apostles.

Bario followed him into marble dimness, Lou pushing him aside once more. "Get away!"

"It's all right," Devereaux's voice echoed.

Lou saw Cherie peering from a niche of crypts lighted by murky stained glass.

"It's not her fault, Lou," Devereux said, making a calming motion to Bario.

Lou realized with a start that Cleveland was standing before the vault of silent star Rudolph Valentino.

Cherie looked guilty and conflicted, betrayed and confused as she started to move toward him.

Cleveland told her, "Give us a minute, Cherie. Go with Bill, okay?"

She walked reluctantly away with Bario, throwing concerned over-the-shoulder glances.

Devereux was placating. "Lou, I don't have any hard feelings about Cherie. I never looked upon her as a possession, and nothing could make me happier than that she's found a real relationship. I never had illusions that she was going to spend the rest of her life with me—or even that I wanted her to."

Lou tensed. Through the Gothic arch in the distance, Japanese men were entering with red roses. He had no idea where they were going.

Cleveland began to plead urgently. "But you don't realize what you're getting into—maybe you do. I heard about your friend, and I'm sorry. It's true Cherie called me, but I had to beg her to come. She's in danger, and you won't know what to do. I've seen you on television, I know what's happening."

"And what's that?"

Cleveland wet dry lips. "The power of the collective unconscious, millions of minds focused in a single direction. A mental representation's built up by repeatedly adoring it. If the process if successful, the god becomes tamed. It can be invoked into a form that's been built up out of mind-stuff."

"Bullshit."

Cleveland grimaced. "You've had the same thoughts, she told me."

Lou shot a betrayed glance in the girl's direction, but she'd disappeared. "Anything Cherie hasn't told you?"

"She says your friend went to see Tony Bulova and never came back. What do you think you can accomplish by yourself?"

"What makes you think I want to accomplish anything?"

"Now that your friend's been murdered by these people . . . I just imagined it would be hard to disengage yourself emotionally at this point." His face became pained. "You don't like me, but remember, I've been involved in this thing since I was twelve. One crummy day of the year I'm a big fish in a little pond. But the pond gets bigger, and the fish smaller, every year my book's out of print. That's *not* what I'm all about."

"I know what you're all about—gurus, sex, and people who are emotionally vulnerable."

Cleveland flinched. "But even a broken clock is right twice a day. Do you know who Budd Kunstler is?"

"I'm in no mood to play Dean Trivia."

"He customized Dean's Porsche, worked on the paint right before the race. And he had the death car before it disappeared. He's the car guy who's going to re-create the accident for the film company tomorrow. There was an article about it in the *L.A. Times*—and a picture. It was grainy, but clear enough for me to see his hand was bandaged."

"So?"

"Someone cut his finger off!" Cleveland said, exasperated. "Somebody who believes that by controlling some part of a person, he can control them! Kunstler was refusing to participate in the film. The picture's been an on-again-off-again proposition for a year because of financing. Last week they suddenly came up with an angel. Guess who?"

"You tell me."

Cleveland bored in. "Jonathan Cottlee. He's apparently diversifying. Did you know Cottlee lives in the mansion built by Frank Saunders?"

"Who?"

"The head salesman at the dealership where Jimmy bought his Spyder. Rolf's employer, who was also fucking Liv on and off. Can you imagine anyone buying a house for that reason?"

"You, if you had the money."

Cleveland winced. "Saunders and Liv. Now, Cottlee and Liv. And he has a replica Spyder which could've killed Schmallhorst. I want to get into that house. I think he's got the deathcar. Maybe even Dean's body. Wouldn't that be proof? I think he's had the wreck all along and this search for it is just a ruse. He's been moving it around, but I believe it'll be at his house tonight to be 'prepped' for a ceremony tomorrow. And he's called a little party this evening. He wants you to come. So do I."

"A get-together on the anniversary eve?"

"A tradition for the people who are going to retrace the deathroute—he says Liv'll be there."

Lou started to turn away, but Cleveland grabbed his shoulders.

"Let go," Lou said, "or I'll do what I felt like doing when I saw you."

Cleveland released his grip. "You don't think I'm crazy. Otherwise you'd have walked off ten minutes ago."

"I should have," Lou said as he turned to find Cherie, leaving the other man standing there.

Cherie finally spoke on the drive to Westwood. "The two of you arguing about me, like I was some kind of nonentity. And you think you're the injured party."

"How did you know where to find him? Have you been in contact with him all along?"

"You're paranoid," she said bitterly. "He's always in town this time of year. Always."

"I thought you were gonna put this shit behind you."

"Behind *us*, remember? Who decided to stay in town when we could have been on a boat to Mexico right now?" she said angrily.

"Things have changed," he said uneasily. "It wouldn't be right to leave now."

"You're using George," she said. "You used your guilt over the guy you killed in Ohio, and now you're using guilt over George."

"What do you mean I used guilt about Ernie in Ohio?"

"As an excuse to run away from yourself. And now that both of us have a chance, you're gonna use what happened to George as an excuse to keep on this thing until something happens to us. Just when we should be as far away as we can. That's why I went to Cleveland, I wanted him to leave you alone. I knew what he'd do. He's pushing all your buttons."

"You didn't even tell me you were leaving the apartment."

"You were passed out on the couch."

"I fell asleep! This hasn't been the easiest day of my—"

She was in his face. "And you lied to me about that script! Just when I was trusting you more than anybody ever in my life."

He was quieter. "Why'd you go to him?"

"I was worried about you. I know him. I wanted him to leave you alone, keep us out of this. But I know what you're going to do."

"And what's that?"

She pressed her temples with her hand. "You're going tonight, aren't you?"

Depression settled over him, because she was right.

If he wavered at all, what he found hanging over the door outside of his apartment steeled him. It was a squawking white chicken which flapped with terror at his approach, and scratched his arms as he untied the leather thong holding its feet. He looked at Cherie with furious eyes, and neither had to say it was a reference to the scene in *Rebel* when the gang taunted Jimmy by hanging a chicken over the door of the Stark residence in a weirdly anomalous allusion to voodoo—or so Ly would have said.

Things had been so simple when the only ghost haunting Lou was Ernie Hockman's.

23

Thursday, September 29, 1995
Hollywood, 9:30 P.M.

Antoine Lefevre Bulova knew there wasn't much time—twenty-four hours, to be precise. That was why he'd broken the door to this single room above a storefront despite the fact that he didn't have a search warrant. He'd surveyed the place on and off for a week without success, and now he found it hastily abandoned.

He tried the light switch, but the electricity was off. It was just as well. Perhaps he wasn't the only one watching this room. The shadows on the drab wall behind him were made colorful and flashing by the neon from Melrose. Bulova was not sure who belonged to this apartment—because an altar possesses its curator, more than vice versa—but it was a bird which had led him here: a Hawk.

Many owed their careers to James Dean, but only one owed his nose. The Hawk was Jimmy's friend from the fifties, and Liv's slavish sycophant in the nineties. The

Hawk had made furtive deliveries to this address for the past week. It did not seem likely a wrecked car could be concealed there, but Bulova would not rule out a forty-year-old corpse.

Poor Ly, finagled by a man who used him into making that damned paint forty years ago. In the cabalah, not only numbers but colors have magical significance. In sympathetic magic relics of a victim—blood or body hair—can be added to a medium and imbue it with further magical properties. A medium like paint.

Because everything about Dean's car had significance, down to the serial numbers. After the crash it was taken away under a tarp so no one could examine it until it had been "sanitized."

Bulova crossed to the walk-in closet and flicked his lighter for illumination. Sal Mineo's knife wound swam before his eyes in a gallon jar of formalin. It had been utilized as a bookend for large scrapbooks—neatly arranged volumes of yellowed clippings chronicling a posthumous craze. Something fluttered to the floor, and he knelt to find it was James Dean's natal horoscope.

Also on the floor were several cardboard boxes. The first contained yellowed documents neatly filed, including Highway Patrol diagrams of the crash. But the next, tied with brown string, was labeled *Pontifex*. He reached for his pocket knife, wishing he'd brought a flashlight.

He recalled Ly's coquettish smile forty years ago, even before the death of James Dean.

"Pontifex? Purely philanthropic. Their anonymity? The ventures which attract them are controversial. They want to make sponsorship decisions based solely on the merits of projects, without impacting the public aspect of their careers. Pontifex is only their avocation. A fo-

rum of like minds, who find it relaxing to sponsor pet projects from a remove—"

Bulova had said, *"And you think they'll sponsor you? For what?"*

Ly raised his glass of claret. *"I know what you're thinking. It's the money. The entrées, the cachet of being one of an 'inner circle.' I'm one of those little blue fishies swimming in and out of the shark's jaws, hoping for dribbles from the table—it's the aura of wealth, of glamour. And I'm attracted like a moth to the flame."* He drank deeply and giggled, *"Everything I'm telling you is secret. I'm talking out of school, Tony."*

"When I think of you with that bastard—" Tony began.

"The Goat? Tell me," Ly had said. *"Is it because you're Jewish?"*

Ly could be cruel.

Tony had seethed, *"I spent four years in the Air Force fighting his kind. That's hard to forget. But it's more than that. By letting him keep you, you're destroying your talent. Look at you."*

Ly's intoxicated grin was blithe. *"Oh? Are you applying for Knight in Shining Armor? Make an honest woman out of me?"* He had stroked Tony's hair, and spoken softly. *"Do you want to install me in your little apartment on Franklin? Do you think you could keep me in the manner to which I've become accustomed? It's too late for us, Tony."*

Ly was a weak link, a complex guy whose conscience bothered him for forty years. A conflicted man, he had looked for absolution as best he could. He wanted to be found out, but just didn't have the moral courage to confess. So he dribbled hints in his paintings and all that drunk talk. So he hid the script, but left enough clues so someone would find it one day.

Bulova knew who had killed James Dean, but it was exactly that secret he had tried to protect. It was where Ly came in, and why he had continued to pursue his investigation privately: he did not want Ly's name dragged through the mud, did not want him remembered only as one of the people who helped murder James Dean. He had paid for his crime, which really consisted only in his weakness in becoming romantically involved with the mastermind behind the death of a movie idol.

But the Goat had been dead some thirty-five years. The pertinent question was, who was the mastermind today? Because that was the individual who had killed Ly.

Bulova cut the string and it snapped to the floor.

There were phone numbers and addresses of some of the biggest names in the film industry of the fifties, a roll call of Hollywood movers and shakers long-dead or vanished. He saw flow charts, and time lines charting a posthumous publicity campaign. There were notes on proposed documentaries on the late Jimmy Dean, carefully worded formulae painstakingly calculated to implant suggestions in popular consciousness.

He found psychological profiles of the typical James Dean fan, and memoranda on broadening the base of the dead icon's magnetism to infiltrate wider cross-sections of the country. There was correspondence in foreign languages on Pontifex letterhead, outlining simultaneous programs across the globe. There was a detailed charter for proposed fan clubs, and assignments for sponsorship of various nonprofit foundations bearing the name of James Dean, all dedicated to keeping his flame burning brightly.

But something had gone wrong. The Dean myth had taken forty years to reach the peak of intensity which the carefully engineered time lines and rigid tables scheduled for five. What did it mean?

The corner of a manila folder caught his eye, and he unfolded a large diagram on the dusty floor, a detailed map of the race course at Salinas Airport. The neatly lettered legend at the bottom was dated October 1, 1955.

He knew that wasn't the date of the diagram's execution—it was probably months in advance—but the date of Jimmy's scheduled race the weekend he died.

He traced painstaking notations in pen and pencil, mostly in English but some German. Of special interest were the projections and calculations in Turn Number Three, all in ballistic precision. Jimmy's Porsche Spyder number 130 was depicted to scale on three places, always in relation to a second racer. That mystery car was plotted to collide with Jimmy's Porsche going into the third curve.

A detailed internal schema of the "Little Bastard" answered his next question: there were to have been two components to the crash. Number 130 was displayed in cutaway so that the trans axle and brakes were clearly shown, along with mechanical modifications. A simultaneous failure of steering and brake mechanism would hinder Dean's power to correct, or ensure he would over-correct.

Bulova could imagine who would have been driving that second Spyder. Ly's ring on his own finger served to remind him of a man long-dead whom he had never met, but whose brainchild was spread on the floor before him.

Bulova shook the dwindling lighter for more fuel, strained his eyes to read in the fluttering light.

Equally explicit were the placements of both film and still cameras. The carnage would have been captured from multiple angles and perspectives. Had the execution and timing been flawless, it would have been the best-documented death in history. Played and replayed, it would provide the impetus to set in motion a cultural juggernaut. The snuff film would accelerate the cult, Jimmy's public death witnessed again and again. Jimmy's fans would all participate vicariously in his demise.

And the driver of the mystery car?

Bulova consulted the timetable and noted the acquisition schedule for visa and passport to coincide with critically planted news stories. The leaks were in rough draft, and calculated to focus the anger of grieving fans on one man's head. The Goat, again. Because there had to be a nemesis, Jimmy's death had to be emotionally polarized into black and white, light and darkness.

Other addenda included contingency plans in case the Jimmy Dean hysteria threatened to abate, or burn out.

On cue, the lighter guttered and died. Bulova stood and flexed the leg that had fallen asleep.

What happened? Why had Dean died on the highway en route, instead of at Saturday's race—a day ahead of schedule? Where was—

There was a creak of hinges as the door to the walk-in closed, and Bulova was shut in absolute darkness.

The neatly blocked white hairs on the back of his neck went erect as he recalled the knife wound swimming on the shelf. It had been a little too easy, hadn't it?

He drew the pistol from the ankle holster around his Angora socks, and took a breath as he reopened the door.

Nothing.

The breath released, but he didn't replace the gun.

He became aware of the swirling in the corner of his vision. A swirling like mist.

It's not real, he prepared himself. *Think of it as a broken image revived from the clutter of the collective unconscious, energized with mind-power for a limited purpose.*

He turned. The tenuous image of Jimmy Dean was materializing out of the shadows. It wore jeans and boots, slouching in a red windbreaker against the blistered wall.

Jimmy looked up, and their eyes met. Dean smiled seductively.

Bulova had no sense that he was looking at a person, or that there was any real consciousness there. He glanced around the room, certain that somewhere in these shadows was a talisman or magical weapon, whatever had been used to focus the energy creating the manifestation.

Jimmy Dean winked, dropped his spectral cigarette and ground it underfoot. Then his transparent image was walking toward the detective.

Bulova did not move, trying to resist the insistent half-reality of what he told himself was a thought-form that drew on his own mind as much as anything else.

Then Jimmy Dean's hand was reaching casually into Bulova's chest, disappearing up to the wrist.

Bulova felt fingers close around his heart. The shooting pain was awesome. He'd never even had angina, and the cardiac agony stunned him to his knees. The hardwood floor was coming up to meet his face when the fingers relaxed slightly.

A gasp escaped Bulova's lungs.

Then the knot around his heart tightened again, his left side suddenly useless as he crumpled.

He saw periphally through the dust bunnies beneath

the unmade bed a small something neatly tied with a
ribbon. Hope came alive. He stretched out his right
hand, flopped and inched toward that something, fighting the pain for each millimeter.

It was nearly all over by the time his fingers closed
over the vial tied with a single ribbon. The vial he'd
seen at Lysander's, inside it a fleck of paint from
Jimmy Dean's Spyder. Another vial with its dark sedi-
ment he hadn't seen before, but he could guess what it
preserved.

His tingling fingers slipped inside to loosen its knot.
The vial fell to the floor. He clutched it, and pressed until the glass tube broke.

The pain stopped, and the room stopped turning. Best
of all, Jimmy Dean was gone.

Bulova rolled onto his back, panting.

It was a quarter hour before he looked at the cuts on
his palm, and the dark powder. He knew what it was.
The precious blood. And he thought he knew when it
had been siphoned out of Jimmy Dean. That minor collision of the ambulance, when it had pulled over on the
roadside and delayed arrival at the hospital? One attendant had been in the back with Jimmy and Rolf.
Exsanguination could have been performed even as a
Highway Patrolman stood outside.

Bulova blew on the powder and it wisped across the
floor. He sat up anxiously, wishing he could torch
the place. But that could be a problem, especially for
the other tenants of the floor.

He took the jar of sloshing formalin into the decrepit
bathroom and unscrewed its lid, the fetid smell as-
saulting his nostrils. Sal Mineo's knife wound went into
the toilet bowl. Flushing, Bulova watched it swirl away.

Then he leaned against the door jamb, pinched the
bridge of his nose between thumb and forefinger with

exhaustion. *Jesus Christ.* He massaged his aching chest and turned to leave.

There was Ly was sitting on the bed with poignant eyes, raising his hand in vague greeting.

"Ly—" Bulova began, until shock cut the words.

It was not the worn-out Ly who had died, but a young and angelic Ly Pollack at the height of his beauty.

"Tony—" Ly said almost apologetically. "Don't come closer. And for God's sake don't try to touch me."

"I can hear you," Bulova breathed, incredulous.

Ly smiled. "Weren't we always able to talk? Ah, we wuz loverly then."

There was a distance and hollowness to the voice which chilled and saddened Bulova, his heart pounding like it hadn't in forty years.

"Tony," the ghost said wistfully, "you'll never guess who I've been with."

It was vintage Ly: even returning from the afterlife he couldn't resist sharing cocktail party chitchat.

"I've been with Jimmy Dean," Ly said. "He's caught over here. On the other side. They have him imprisoned in a way I can't even describe. He's with Natalie and Sal."

"It's really you . . . ?" Bulova heard himself ask.

"It's so sad beyond this world. He's held against his will, and there's nothing he can do about it. He can't rest because they have his body. It would break your heart— Don't come closer."

Bulova stopped. "Why not?"

"You can't trust me, because I'm weak."

"What happened to you?" Bulova asked sadly. "What's happening to you now?"

Ly sighed, but there was no breath to stir the room.

"I was loose-lipped, especially in my cups. And what wouldn't I give for a cup, now!"

His smile broke Bulova's heart.

"Tony, I want you to do something for me. You've got to warn Lou. He's going to die at the deathsite on the thirtieth."

Jealousy flamed up in Bulova, color returning to his face. "Wasn't it always this way?" he asked hoarsely. "Dutiful Tony, and you telling me about your latest conquest. You never cared how I hurt—"

"Tony, don't. I'm weak where you're concerned."

"You were weak where everyone was concerned," Bulova said.

Ly threw back his head, but the laughter was soundless.

Bulova's mouth was dry. "My God, Ly. Who did it to you?"

The words seemed to move what there was left of Lysander. Bulova saw the old sensuality there, before it had become lascivious.

The figure was impulsively approaching him, lips parted. Bulova was closing his own eyes, trembling at the flood of haunted tenderness.

Tony felt the lips and they were soft. He leaned into the kiss.

Then a slight sweet pain. Then a larger pain. There was a terrible fatal suction which was drawing all his insides up into his chest.

Bulova opened his eyes, but could not see for panic. Things were tearing loose inside him, drawn up into his throat. He realized he was strangling on his own guts.

Ah, we wuz beautiful, then. . . .

24

Thursday, September 29, 1955
Hollywood Hills, 9:53 P.M.

James Dean negotiated the Mulholland switchbacks
as the lights of Hollywood receded below. The essential
feel of the new 550 Spyder was making him uncomfortable, despite the fact he had been practicing power turns
throughout the day. There was something too responsive
and precipitate in the steering reflex. When it had come
back from the garage of Budd Kunstler—the car
customizer who had applied the red pinstriping and the
number "130"—he could not help but notice a new coat
of paint applied to the entire aluminum body.

He glanced in the mirror and saw himself cosmeti-
cally aged by the shaved hairline that helped transform
him into the 46-year-old Jett Rink. It was a constant reminder of morbidity and decrepitude, the inevitable suffering which was every organism's. Everything had
become symbolic to him.

He was living smack in the middle of the twentieth

century at the junction of an epoch. On Saturday Eisenhower had suffered a heart attack, and on Monday the
stock market had crashed 30 points. It was the grotesque era of Joe McCarthy and nuclear clouds threatening death and mutation. Kids were beginning to stake
out their own limbo of self-discovery which was merely
an inverted image of their parents' own rat race: a new
conformity exalting outward nonconformity. The time
was ripe for a messiah to them. *Rebel Without a Cause*
would premiere in one month. In one year when the
posthumous cult might be declining, there would be the
rejuvenating release of *Giant*.

The sight of the tennis courts and Olympic-size pool
through a cleft in the cypress recalled what Nick Ray
had said earlier in the week when he had first brought
Jimmy here.

"I hope you're flattered that, now that the Pontifex
investors feel it's the time for this type of picture, they
think of you first—the same people who originally saw
something special in Jimmy Dean way back in Indiana.
And hundreds of friends you never met. You've been
brought along like a fine racehorse. You were picked."

"Who are these investors?"

"They want to stay private. All you need to know is
they've sponsored you for years, and the artistic satisfaction was compensation enough—for a while. They're
those kind of people—big people. Pontifex is international. I can't even see the top! But Jimmy Dean will.
They got great things planned for you, beyond your
wildest. Tonight you're gonna meet our angel, the archi-
tect and guiding spirit of this particular project. Inside
the mansion he's 'the Goat.' Outside, you call him anything but that. Remember he's trustee of the preproduction money."

"I'm going to tell him I'm not going to make his film."

Nick blanched. "You don't dare. I've got news for you. The man you're going to meet has guided your career from the beginning. You create your roles and he created the phenomenon of Jimmy Dean. And it can all go away just this fast!" Nick snapped his fingers.

Now Jimmy drove past the colonnades and up a white gravel drive lined with cars. He knew that Cadillacs represented executives and guiding forces in the motion picture industry, Mercedes denoted men highly placed in the southern California business community. Small foreign jobs generally indicated the elite of the medical fraternity, especially plastic surgery.

He parked, thinking how if the southern California Pontifex fraternity chose to remain anonymous, it was a bad sign for him to meet them. It could only mean it was too late to make any difference.

A figure stepped from the shadows. Rolf smiled uneasily, indicating the Spyder. "It looks good on you."

"And that's what counts, isn't it?" Jimmy replied as he lifted himself from the seat.

"You haven't lost your sense of humor," Rolf said. "I'm glad."

The sudden fragility of Rolf's face encouraged Jimmy to ask a question. "How can you watch them do this to me?"

Rolf fumbled for a cigarette with trembling fingers. "Maybe I want to be there for you, make things a little easier for you."

"I'm somebody, now," Jimmy whispered urgently. "We could expose them. I have my own power."

Weutheric laughed sadly. "Not that much power, Jimmy. This started before we were born. What is my difference if they use me, or you use me? I don't make my life any more than you make yours."

Jimmy took the cigarette from his own lips, placed it in Rolf's. "Say I don't get in that car on Saturday. What happens to Jimmy Dean then?"

Rolf inhaled the smoke gratefully. "You mean, 'Does he live?' Maybe, for a while. Or maybe all this goes away. You don't know what they can do. Maybe your last sixteen months never happened. Maybe you wake up a nobody."

"You think they can turn time backwards? Maybe that goofy four-eyed kid 'Rack' Dean grows up to work in a tractor dealership in Indianapolis?"

Rolf half-smiled. "I don't know. Except they would start over. They've already waited twenty-four years. Sixty if you count when Valentino was born. There's nothing I can do."

"No?" Jimmy stepped closer and his voice was intimate. "You know, even Jesus got a kiss at the Last Supper."

Their faces were close. Rolf's frightened eyes faltered, his lips parting.

Then there was the crunch of gravel on the walk.

The Goat was approaching on sandaled feet, a large and powerful shadow, which nevertheless moved very quietly. There was chilling iciness to the serene blue eyes set in a bronze face. "Hi, Jimmy," he said smiling. "Ready for tomorrow?" He took the keys from Dean's hand and tossed them to Rolf, who slid behind the wheel. "I want him to look at the engine."

He draped his arm over Jimmy's shoulder and led him up the walk, through a large room in which pungent incense bubbled in brass thuribles, and into the paneled office where he closed the door. "Jim," he said gently. "I can tell something is troubling you. What's wrong?"

Dean let himself sag into the upholstered chair opposite the desk from which the Goat ran his foreign car empire. "I don't want Rolf along tomorrow. It's not fair to him, he's coming apart."

The other raised eyebrows almost white beneath platinum hair, a magnetic man with implacable hauteur. "Rudolph? We need him for the car. The Spyder isn't like anything you've driven before. It takes fifteen hours to tune it, and there'll have to be adjustments in the carb for the coastal weather."

"Hickman knows cars."

The man snorted. "He may know violins, but this is a Stradivarius! By all means invite him, the more the merrier. But Rudolph is a must. I have some prestige on the line here. You got the car from me. I would be embarrassed if the Spyder threw a piston through some oversight." He leaned suddenly forward. "Have you thought of this? Sandy Roth's shooting you for a photo essay that could wind up in *Cosmo*, or *Life*. The Spyder's temperamental—German, like me. You see what I'm getting at?"

"I don't want Roth, either," Jimmy said.

"Sandy? He's done a lot of beautiful work on you." He softened and lowered his voice. "It's more than the race, isn't it? It's the script. All along, we've insisted you be an equal partner in the artistic end of this. Your contribution is essential at all levels. New York feels the same way. There are important people in European capitals watching us with interest."

Jimmy managed an ironic smile. "I guess what bothers me, since you brought up the script, is that Jamie Starr goes more or less like a sheep to the slaughter. He's got himself involved with all these bizarre characters—"

"Bizarre? Their passion and sincerity is beautiful in an insincere age."

Jimmy hated this subtle game where the Goat pretended that what was going to happen was not going to happen. "He has to have some clue what they're gonna do to him . . . unless he's a moron."

The blond lashes fluttered. "He's not a moron. . . . He must never think that about himself. He must think he is special, the unique one of all other ones."

Jimmy's voice was ragged. "Why should he go to that race where he suspects he's being set up to die?"

The other man was thoughtful, pursing judicious lips. "You've got a point. I think the key word is 'suspects.' Perhaps this possibility exists only in his own mind. A delusion?" Then he had an inspiration. "How about this? Jamie has these farm people who raised him, back in Nebraska, or wherever—let's say he even has this little cousin who worships him."

Jimmy did not like the clammy sweat which broke on the back of his neck. "I'm listening."

"Let's say, Jamie knows that if he does not cooperate, these . . . demented people . . . will harm the boy and the old people? This would even further point up the impassioned, committed quality of these individuals— they will do whatever is necessary to accomplish their purpose."

The hairs at the base of Jimmy's head went erect. "Like, what might happen to them?"

The other man said thoughtfully, "Let's imagine an additional scene. Think of Jamie Starr's uncle and aunt—and his little cousin—asleep in the farmhouse in the Midwest where Jamie grew up. We see them asleep in their beds, see their faces as the doorbell wakes them—"

He stood to pantomime the action. "See the old uncle cursing under his breath, and glancing at the alarm clock. 'Why, it's midnight!' Then, pulling on his shirt to hobble muttering downstairs and answer the door—" He framed the scene through his hands. " 'Who the hell is it at this hour?' the old man says as he opens the door."

He leaned closer. "In the doorway, a moldering form with a festering face. It's dead Jack Drummond! Or at least, his doppelgänger. He grabs the old man by the neck and—"

"Stop," Jimmy said hoarsely.

The big man snapped his fingers. "That's why Jamie does it! Out of love! You're forgetting something. Jamie does not really die. He will be resurrected as a *god*."

He stood to massage Jimmy's tense shoulders and spoke soothingly. "You feel like everything's coming apart, but it's all coming *together*. You just need a rest. It can be exhausting having everything you want." There was camaraderie in his laughter. "I'm the one who should be nervous, coming out of retirement from racing! It will be an honor to compete with you on the track."

Rolf stuck his head in the door, face gray as his eyes met Jimmy's. "We're set."

The Goat nodded. He handed Jimmy a white surplice adorned with the figure of a bull and directed him to the shower in the bathroom off the office. "It's necessary that you purify yourself. Don't be long."

In the shower, Jimmy closed his eyes against hot needles of water. The threat of Jack Drummond took him back to that night at the Texas location after Rolf and Jeff had flown away. He had been walking through the

night with Hinkle, rifle in hand, when the older man
had stiffened in the darkness like a bird dog pointing to
a pheasant.

Hinkle had cleared his throat and spat in the dark.
"Holy shit," he coughed, his leg stuck in the ground up
to his boot top. "There's graves collapsed here. It's that
little Mexican boneyard. I thought it was over yonder."

Jimmy could see depressions in the ground around
him where cheap coffins had decomposed and sucked
down the earth. Hinkle was moving on cautiously, but
Jimmy found he couldn't unfreeze himself. It was the
idea that anywhere he might step the dry crust of earth
could give way and send his foot into the hollow sink-
hole of a dead Mexican.

Hinkle walked on with the flashlight, unaware.
Jimmy found himself all alone, a foul mist rising from
a mound. He saw a form standing there, a boy dressed
in racing togs and about his own build.

The impression was that his clothes were ripped by
violence, one arm hanging loose like a scarecrow's.
Jimmy could not see the face at first. There was a smell
of burnt flesh, flesh peeled like a banana skin by fire
until there were neither eyelids nor lips. Just staring
eyes and white teeth in black crisp. One hand was missing a racing glove.

Hinkle called from the dark, "Where are you? What's
wrong?"

A hysterical giggle rose in Jimmy's throat as he realized the racing glove Rolf had brought was the relic
used to raise the form. "It's a friend of mine," he said.

"Huh?"

Jimmy was laughing, tears in his eyes. He might
throw away the glove, for all the good that would do.
Hell, they might even have the body somewhere.

"A friend of mine," Jimmy repeated as Hinkle ap-

proached. "Bob, I'd like to introduce you to Jack
Drummond."

Hinkle had looked at him like he was nuts, because
suddenly the form of Jack Drummond was vanished.

Jimmy toweled off and slipped the surplice over his
head, then followed the Goat down steps to the garage.

The older man said over his shoulder, "I want you to
steel yourself, Jimmy. Do not be shocked. In the ceremony there are some words about death, but they are
merely figurative. Our old self must die for the new to
be born."

Jimmy saw the Porsche Spyder dead center of a large
pentagram permanently inscribed in the concrete. Two
dozen brown-robed men stood nervously, the people
who had helped to guide and build his career the last
sixteen months.

"Hey, Jimmy," Nick Ray said clapping him on the
back. Other voices added, "Jimbo." "Nice car." "A
beaut—"

The Goat spoke to all. "Our friends in New York,
London, and Munich extend their congratulations. We
welcome our young brother to the thirty-second degree
of Adepthood. It's a reward for his diligence and his
successful completion of the initiatory tasks. Let's give
him a hand."

Applause was enthusiastic.

"He has attained the Twenty-Fifth Path, the Intelli-
gence of Temptation, whereby the Secret Chiefs tryeth
all righteous persons. The Tarot attribution is Temper-
ance, and the astrological attribution Sagittarius—
because this path is the Flight of the Arrow up the
middle pillar of equilibrium. He has passed up the sphere
of manifestation and successfully through the sphere of

illusion, where the falsity of the images of this life have been revealed."

There was more applause, and the man's muscular arm was around Jimmy.

"Let me tell you something about our friend here. The other day I asked him, 'If you could have anything in this world, what would it be?' Do you know what he replied?"

There was respectful silence.

"He replied, 'To be remembered after I'm gone. That to me is greatness.' A very spiritual answer. I knew his selection was no mistake. He is special. Now, for his car."

The robed Greenspacht came forward bearing a chalice and intoning, "Overhead twinkles Uranus, the planet in ascendancy at the birth of James Dean." He raised the chalice. "I bear the Holy Grail, in the center of which is radiant blood, symbolizing the presence of Light in Darkness. Cain and Abel represent the refusal of God to hear the children of Eve until blood is shed. I embody the history of the Car."

Nick Ray stepped forward. "A room has been prepared. 'This is to me the saddest landscape on the Earth. For it was here that the Little Prince appeared and disappeared.' "

The Goat took the chalice from Greenspacht's hand, turning it slowly until a black thread of blood was strung down to the hood of the Spyder. It puddled darkly and began to run.

When the cup was empty he lifted it to his lips, licked the rim and said with a red mouth, "You see, Jimmy. Nothing ever dies. It merely translates to another plane of energy. Know you, too, will live forever. I promise you. We will never forget, and neither will the world."

Jimmy had an insight at that moment. In the last two days he'd found that when he was perfectly isolated by fear and hopelessness, he received insights. Now it came to him that everything was suffering—not just for him but everybody. At the core of all life was misery. That was why everybody tried to distract themselves. People wanted movies to forget for a while who they were, forget what in the depths they were.

The thought enabled him to smile with bravado mostly for Rolf's benefit, as he lighted a cigarette.

He even winked.

25

Thursday, September 29, 1995
Hollywood Hills, 9:02 P.M.

It was more than carsickness, the queasiness Lou felt as he negotiated the switchbacks climbing toward Cottlee's mansion in the Hollywood Hills, the mezuzah which Bulova had turned over to him dangling from the mirror.

Cherie saw his change in complexion. "What's wrong?"

"He's gone," Lou answered nervously. "Ernie Hockman. He's been with me every minute for five years, and suddenly he's gone." But he was feeling abandonment instead of relief; Ernie was letting him know that since he hadn't heeded the warnings, he was going out on this one naked and alone.

"Someone wanted me to have that script, and no one else," Lou said to distract himself. "That's why George was killed. Someone doesn't want me bringing anyone else in on this. And if it's worth killing someone over,

Pontifex was more than a figment of Jimmy's imagination."

"You think Liv was lying?"

It was all about blood sacrifice and mythic calculation to control the psychic forces of the collective unconscious, Lou thought; the god-form always draws life from its believers. "Maleficarum was all-male," he said. "What if Pontifex was, too? What if Liv had been on the outs in the fifties, embittered and rejected? It's the pattern of her lifetime. What if she's methodically re-creating that program after four decades with new generations of bright-eyed sycophants?"

Cherie snorted. "She couldn't organize a brunch."

"But Cottlee could."

Her expression was equal parts disgust and resignation. "Dean Day Minus One, and Lou's back in the ball game."

Lou did not like the distance between them. "Don't think I haven't been thinking about us. It's just that I have to find out who I am. There are things I have to confront before I can go on, that's why I have to come back here."

"You've been to Cottlee's before?"

Lou opened his mouth, then fell silent. The millionaire's mansion came into view through the pruned cypress. Iron security gates opened automatically and admitted them up the white gravel drive. He saw Devereux's bronze Oldsmobile and felt sharp sexual jealousy.

Cheri was attacked by last-minute misgivings. "Is this Dean thing more important than us? It always was with Cleve."

"We're not the same. He's a nut who goes on about cultists, while he's got his own bastardized psuedo-religion."

Her voice was icy. "You're saying he's a bush league Manson, and I'm a brainwashed sheep?"

He didn't want to fight, to go into that house distracted. He tried to be conciliatory. "I know you're right. I know that when I brought you to my place on Saturday there was a part of me that was egotistical and thought I was supposed to . . . deprogram you, or some damn thing."

"By fucking me?" she said.

His face reddened.

She continued, "When that cop showed up, you treated me like a little kid. At the cemetery you and Cleve sent me off so the men could talk. And people wonder what I see in Jimmy Dean. How about sensitivity?"

When they parked she was unwilling to get out of the car. Lou felt grimly as if they had exhausted the whole cycle of a relationship in six compressed days, discovery, excitement, confession—and now, sulking impasse. He had nothing to lose by asking the question which had been bothering him all afternoon. "What was Cleveland doing at Valentino's grave?"

"It's a crypt," she said irritably. "Are you gonna change the subject?"

"Why did he want to meet you there?"

She looked at him in amazement. "Does everything have to have significance?"

He urged her out of the car, head throbbing. "This time tomorrow it'll all be over."

Sheena met them at the door. Cottlee's beautiful wife Francoise was serving wine and cheese while her husband was out by the pool showing off the Silver Ghost motorcycle. The presence of the three well-mannered Cottlee children was reassuring; but Francoise was just sending them up to bed.

Terry was coming up the stairs from the pool deck followed by the lord of the manor in conversation with Devereux, who looked relieved to see Lou. There was no sign of Liv yet, apparently.

Cottlee greeted Cherie with a hug. "Well, is there life after Dean?"

She pressed closer to Lou as Childes hurried to refill Cottlee's glass.

Cottlee was relaxed and expansive. "How are you holding up, Lou? I was sorry to hear about your friend Bluestein."

"I'm okay," Lou replied as Francoise brought him an imported beer. "That painting on the wall looks like a Ly Pollack." The canvas showed Rudolph Valentino in a bullfighter's suit of lights.

"It is," Cottlee said. "Apparently from his pre-Dean period. Oddly, it came with the house."

Cherie's eyes darted uncomfortably as Cleveland crossed the room toward them. "Lou," he said, "I need to talk to you for a minute."

Lou felt Cherie's pleading eyes, but followed Cleveland onto the veranda.

"Well," Lou said as Devereux checked the sliding door after them, "have you seen any death car? Paraphernalia for a black mass?"

"He's got this massive garage and all kinds of crap under tarps—his 'collection' he calls it, classic motorbikes and things. If it's anywhere, it's there. But why'd you bring Cherie?"

"She insisted, if it's any of your business."

Cleveland looked pained. "Lou, they've got the car and they've got the body. Just one element remains: if the god gives life to man by dying, man must also die for the god to give him life—I'm talking about a sacrifice. Cherie's the one of 'royal blood,' and you've brought her right to him."

"How would Cottlee know anything about her blood?"

"Bulova guessed, didn't he?"

Lou flushed. "Is there anything she hasn't told you?"

Cleveland's jaw tightened. "If the superfans have their way, tomorrow at midnight there will be an invocation at the deathsite and the god-image of Dean will reenter this plane of existence to divert the course of culture and history. There'll be a demonstration of his power so awesome . . . I don't want to think about it. If you still don't believe me, submit it to the test. Let me regress you tonight. Hypnosis."

"So Jimmy Dean can talk through me?" His laugh was sarcastic, but there was the inkling of fear.

Cleveland stood face to face. "Liv's coming tonight. See her reaction when I start to put you under. I've sold Cottlee on the idea, he's expecting it. And you want to get to the bottom of this as much as I do. You want to know who killed James Dean."

It was true, but the idea of Devereux putting him under rubbed Lou wrong. "I think I prefer just looking in the garage."

"That's just it," Cleveland said tensely. "He's pointedly avoiding taking me down there. But he does want to see you regressed. I'll tell him the vibes are stronger in the garage—I'll make it a condition. What are you afraid of?"

You crumb chicken, Lou thought, recalling the detonator words from *Rebel*. "Cherie would freak," he said. *What the hell are you considering?*

"Then do it for the both of you. To put yourself back together."

I've got to know who I am. There's things I've got to confront before I can move on. Before we can move on.

"What's going on, guys?" Terry asked as he poked his head out the sliding door. "I think Jonathan's getting pissed."

When they stepped back into the front room the conversation stopped expectantly, the air crackling with tension. Lou realized he was supposed to be the entertainment this evening.

"Where's Liv?" Cleveland asked anxiously.

"I don't know," Cottlee said. "Apparently, the Hawk, her chauffeur, is out of town. So I sent a car around for her. What's wrong?"

Cleveland hesitated. "So did I."

"A sort of goodwill gesture?" Cottlee smiled. "Well, the odds are somebody will deliver her to our door. Another drink, anyone?"

Liv Ermaine wrapped a caftan around herself as a bevy of cats purred against her ankles. She checked her hair in the mirror, wondering where her ride was. She lay carefully on her bed with head propped on plumped satin pillows so as not to disarrange her hair. Basking in the reflected glow of the late Jimmy always wore on her this time of year.

But her nipples thrilled at anticipation of her plot against Cleveland, the execution of which was her only reason for attending the little get-together. She had baked the author a raisin cake, somewhat lumpy in consistency because she had larded the dough with minute paper shreds of Devereux's cursed book. She had vowed he would one day eat his words.

Other rough incantatory magic worked into her recipe included sprinkled roots and cat poopoo. One bite, and the bastard would be beset by terrors and visions. Two, and he would become a mere slavish extension of her will. *If it works.* It was an old recipe, but untried by her.

And Cottlee. There were things in store for him more delicious for the slow savoring. *He will know who is in real control—who is using whom.*

She crossed her arms and her eyes rolled shut like death, black ceremonial candles flickering at each corner of the bed. She would live forever.

There was a hesitant knock on the door. "Mother-fucker," she rumbled. *Finally.* She checked her hair again.

"Yeeaas?" she said sweetly, making the single word two melodic syllables.

"Miss Ermaine . . ." timorous voices squeaked through the plywood.

She opened the door to two girls reeking of "Deanfan." Had she had seen them at DeanCon? Perhaps with Polmquist? "Are you my ride?"

"Ride?" they asked, confused.

"Apparently, my mistake. What may I do for you, dears?" There was something of the infant about all of Jimmy's novitiates. These women-girls fairly gushed.

"We're visiting in town for the Dean weekend. Patsy said you might talk to us. Would you do a Tarot reading for us? Like you did for Jimmy?"

Something in her stomach wilted with the effort to be charming. "I'm so sorry, and you both seem so sweet, but I will be going out momentarily."

"We'll pay you of course, Miss Ermaine."

Liv paused. "Yeeass?"

"Would one hundred be . . . okay? For two? It really would mean that much to us."

"Well . . ." Liv reflected. A quick C-note? Two weeks' tips at the restaurant? "I suppose so. I don't re-

ally feel at my most psychic right now. But if you're
game, I am."

She beckoned them to enter and lighted sandalwood
incense. "Your faces are familiar. What are your
names?"

"Lisa Neeley," chirped the pie-faced, pudgy one with
Coke-bottle lenses.

". . . And Jerrell Morris," said the rougher-looking
girl with shaven scalp, her red Mohawk moussed into a
ridiculous coxcomb. She closed the door and Liv saw
the upper half of James Dean's tattooed face peering
over her halter top from the flesh of her back.

It startled Liv. The names rang bells, but she could
not place them. A ridiculous pair.

She removed the silk-wrapped cards from the sandalwood box. "You'll be at DeanCon this weekend, I suppose?"

Nods in unison. "We're going out to the intersection
where Jimmy died. The fans are going to have a memorial service. Cleveland Devereux's going to be there."

"Oh?" Liv said. *Don't count on it, you little ghouls.*

The girls giggled in the flickering candles. Liv sup-
pressed uneasiness.

The pie-faced one asked, "Can you do us both at the
same time?"

It would save time. *Morons.* "Very well. We'll use
the bed for a table. Pick a card to represent—"

"Death," the tattooed one interrupted. "Death will be
us."

Jerrell Morris? Wasn't that a boy's name?

Liv batted her lashes, placing Death as a significator
in the center of the coverlet on which they all sat side-
saddle. "Why, of course. You girls have done this before, haven't you?"

They beamed proudly, and the peculiar worm in Liv's

stomach tightened. She tried not to show her anxiety. Suddenly she recalled the names from a faded article she had run across just the evening before, while rummaging through her "Jimmy" scrapbook for anecdotes to appropriate for her talk at the convention.

Lisa Neeley and Jerrell Morris were the high school kids who had committed suicide by ramming speeding cars into trees in emulation of the violent death of their idol Jimmy Dean.

But these two were very much alive. Why were they using the names of two dead kids?

Suddenly their eyes seemed malevolent.

Liv knew she had to run to the bathroom and lock the door. She said breathlessly as she stood, "Young ladies, excuse me. I feel the need to obey a call of nature."

"Don't go," the girls begged.

Liv tried to smile. "Dears, I'll only be in the toilet, not Burbank."

Pudgy reached into her dopey tote bag and handed something heavy to Mohawk-head.

Liv saw a large hammer.

She did not make it to the bathroom door.

"Something tells me we're going to have to carry on without Liv," Cottlee mused sadly. "In a few minutes it'll be the witching hour, dawn of the forty-year anniversary of the death of James Dean."

Devereux said nervously, "I gave specific directions. Even if they couldn't find her, they should be back by now."

"Same here," Cottlee offered convivially. "Maybe they were ashamed. What say we continue with the very interesting activity you mentioned? Is Lou game?"

Lou was aware of alarm on Cherie's face as she sat

curled against the wall with arms protectively around her knees. "What activity?"

Lou's glance was placating. "Cleveland wants to regress me, despite the fact I'm leery about being hypnotized. Especially around strangers."

"Strangers?" Cottlee said. "Don't we all have something in common?"

"Jimmy," Cherie said softly.

Cottlee smiled approvingly. "That's right. It's Jimmy who's brought us all together, in his inscrutable and mysterious way. With Lou's help, we can make an attempt to contact him."

Francoise Cottlee was uncomfortable. "Couldn't that be dangerous?"

"Not in the least," Cottlee said. "He's among friends."

"I don't feel very suggestible," Lou said.

"Maybe you aren't. But maybe Jimmy *wants* this." Cottlee rested his drink on the mantel. "Perhaps you can help Jimmy tell the real story of that day. Liv told me she thinks his restless spirit is in some kind of agony—maybe even imprisoned in this very house."

There was a sheen of sweat on Devereux's lip. "Is that why you bought it?"

Cottlee ignored him, concentrating on Lou. "May I say something? My impression the first time we met was that you were someone unsure of who he is. Perhaps you can find out. I really don't think there's any need to be afraid."

"I'm not afraid," Lou said evenly.

"Well then?" Cottlee sipped his glass.

"All right," Lou said thickly as he tried to ignore Cherie's betrayed face. "Let's go for it."

Cleveland added, "How about we do it in the garage?

I have the feeling that vibrations are the strongest there."

Cottlee was distressed. "The garage? It's so cold and so uncomfortable, nowhere to sit."

Cleveland was insistent. "I just have a feeling, Jonathan. Is it a problem? Now that Lou's willing?"

"All right," Cottlee said reluctantly. "Let's bring some chairs."

The millionaire led the way to the stairs, down to the garage with its shrouded forms of his automotive collection. Cleveland had brought candles and began arranging them, Cottlee positioning two chairs facing each other in the center. He formed a spectators' circle with the remainder.

Cherie squeezed Lou's hand painfully. "Don't do this," she whispered tensely.

Her eyes told him what she was thinking: you're obsessed. He tried to relax her. "It probably won't even work."

"What if Jimmy *wants* it to happen?"

"The worst thing that could happen is I go under, and Cleveland tells me to act like a chicken, or something. And you won't let that happen, will you?" His own argument sounded unconvincing to himself.

When the lights were turned out, candles wavered in the shadows. Francoise Cottlee rubbed her arms against a chill.

"One more thing," Cleveland said as he took a cassette tape from his pocket, "to focus the vibrations. I always knew this would come in handy."

"Christ," Cottlee said irritably. "Is there anything else?" He had risen to whip the tarp off a vintage car.

"Is that a Stutz?" Terry asked.

Cottlee had taken the tape and was fiddling in the dash. "A classic Bearcat. Rumor has it once belonging

to Rudy Valentino. But I've installed a tape deck.
—Anything else, Cleveland?"

The garage and its shadows were filled with the
sound of wind howling over Dean's grave, the snapping
of tree branches and rustling of dead funeral tributes.

Lou found it unnerving, and had to suppress the
shiver between his spine and the hard back of the chair.

"Concentrate," Cleveland said in a quavering voice
as he rearranged Lou's hands palms up on his lap.
"You're going to relax."

"Relax, or concentrate?" Lou said.

Cleveland said, "I want you to concentrate on a point
in the center of my forehead, and I want you to feel all
the tiredness and weariness of this last year. Your chest
is relaxing," Devereux said soothingly. "The breath
from your chest is like the tide ... in and out."

Not going to work, Lou thought. The candles flickered. Cold came up from the concrete floor.

"I want you to envision a line on a highway,"
Devereux was saying. "The line is moving beneath you,
and this line is relaxing you. Then, it moves more
quickly ... and you are fascinated as it passes."

Lou's felt his eyes growing heavy despite himself.

Devereux's voice droned. "At the same time, I want
you to recall today, and then yesterday. And then I
want you to start recalling backward, through years. Back
to your childhood, and your very earliest memory."

Bullshit, Lou thought as he tried to slow and deepen
his breathing.

Devereux's voice was almost a whisper.

"When you have that very earliest memory, I want
you to go back, further still. To before you were born
... to the time before this incarnation, when you
waited. ... We are going back through the years. ...
You see the calendar pages turning. ... See them turn-

ing? 1960 ... '59 ... '57 ... until we stop at ... 1955."

Baloney, Lou thought dully.

But he could not move his lips. Over in that dark corner, Ernie Hockman was zipping up a windbreaker as if going for a drive. Lou did not even feel shock; it was somehow so natural to see him again that he might have smiled. If only his face wasn't so numb.

Don't do this, Ernie's eyes said.

"I want to take you to a specific place in time," Cleveland said. "It is Friday, September thirtieth, in the year 1955. Are you with me?"

Lou fought eyelid heaviness, enveloping darkness, and panic in which Ernie's face was the only real one in the garage. Swallowing darkness like a drowning man, he was assaulted by ugly images, but couldn't move. He saw Cherie naked atop Devereux.

She was biting her lower lip as Devereux kissed her breasts, the kisses turning into bites.

Pulling on her nipples with his teeth—

Then, something about a cat. The cat was a gift from Liz Taylor.

Suddenly Lou realized the date and time.

Friday, September 30, 1955. Hollywood. 8:38 A.M.

And he was sitting behind the wheel of a 550 Spyder in the garage of Racer's Edge Motors on Vine Street.

It was Lou who began to blur.

Jimmy Dean was thinking about his kitten named "Marcus," which Liz Taylor had given him. Last night he had left it at the house of an actress friend along with finely detailed written instructions about the cat's formula.

Sitting in the Porsche, Jimmy looked in the side mirror and saw his own shaved hairline and swollen purple bags beneath hollow eyes. Bill Hickman sucked reflectively and obliviously on a cigarette as he watched sport-shirted Sandy Roth jockey for a camera angle to catch the preparations for the race. Jimmy had spent most of the night in a rambling monologue to his Telefunken tape recorder, recalling the story of his life and meditating on his death.

He had achieved an insight in the last twelve hours: it was important to do very small things well and invest each moment with meaning. Even the littlest action could be an act of creation, a surrender to the infinite.

"Try her," Rolf was saying thickly from behind the hinged rear cowling after changing the plugs.

Jimmy ignited the engine and vibration ran up his legs with all the power of the 547 behind it. In the mirror he saw the reflection of Frank Saunders coming through the grimy bay doors. The somber Hickman was unaware of the tension around him, but Roth snapped to attention and busied himself inventorying the boxes of film in his battered travel bag.

Saunders wore a black flight jacket which accentuated his massive shoulders and offset the golden mane of hair above his broad forehead. He shouted testily to other mechanics before consulting quickly with Rolf. "Shut it off," he said imperiously to Jimmy. He unlocked his office door and strode inside.

Jimmy stepped out of the car and stretched his legs like a cat. Standing in the doorway, he saw Saunders studying a diagram.

"Turn on the radio," Saunders said distractedly, folding the diagram and stuffing it into a travel briefcase. "I want to hear the weather on the coast."

Jimmy complied, lighting a cigarette. "You seem nervous," he said as he played with the model of a Porsche Spyder on Saunders's desk.

"Do I?" Saunders looked up from shoving more papers in the case. "Well, it's been a while since I've been on a track. I'm coming from retirement to compete with some excellent drivers. Including you."

Jimmy looked through the glass door at Saunders's Spyder, a twin to his own except that it was shiny black. Across the cowling was stenciled its name: THE GOAT. He took a breath and sagged into a swivel chair. What did he have to lose? "I don't think I want to use the trailer today. I think I want to take the Spyder on the highway."

Saunders's glanced was disturbed. "And why is that?"

Jimmy spun the wheels of the toy. "She's only got 800 on the odometer. I want to get the feel of the engine."

Saunders said, "I don't think it's a good idea. Things could happen."

Jimmy smiled ingenuously. "What things?"

Saunders preoccupied himself locking papers into desk drawers. "Mechanical things we can't deal with on the road. We're on a schedule, and I don't want problems."

Jimmy said, "Well, I think I'll do it anyway."

Their eyes met. Saunders considered a long moment. "Sure, Jimmy. If that's what you want—but Rolf rides with you."

The little victory emboldened Jimmy. "I been having some other thoughts, too. About the script. I think it's a real drag that our hero dies. I was thinking that maybe he should pull out of the race at the last minute."

"An upbeat ending?" Saunders said cynically. "That's not life." He absorbed himself in the telephone memorandum he carried everywhere. "Don't spoil the point of the film."

"Well," Jimmy said as he set down the toy, "I've been talking to some people, and they agree with me."

Saunders's eyes were livid. "Who are we talking about?"

Jimmy shrugged. "Just some people."

Saunders controlled his facial muscles. "Maybe you have a point. It's certainly something we could discuss when we come back. For now let's try to avoid anything which diverts our attention from this weekend."

He brightened at something he saw out the glass partition. "By the way, I heard your uncle was in town, visiting from Indiana. Why didn't you tell me? I thought it might be nice if they saw you off. Look who's here."

Jimmy turned in the swivel chair. There were his uncles, Marcus Winslow and Charles Dean. And his father, Winton, standing uncomfortably to look over Rolf's shoulder into the Spyder's engine. Eleven-year-old Markie was dashing in from outside, eyes wide as he saw the racers.

Jimmy was stunned.

Saunders clapped him on the back. "Aren't you going to go talk to them? The little guy looks like a nice young man. Are you close?"

"Yeah," Jimmy said.

Saunders nodded approval. "Family is important. Look at his face—'A real race car!' Maybe I should take him on a little ride?"

"No," Jimmy said.

Saunders frowned. "Just around the block? You know, I have friends on the East Coast and sometimes I go back there myself. It would not be too much out of my way to stop in on them. I might even take Jack Drummond."

Jimmy confronted the bigger man, oblivious to the

stares from the other side of the glass partition. "I don't want you to have anything to do with him. He has no connection to any of this."

"Connection to what?" Saunders was petulant. "If he's close to you, I feel close to him. What's important to you is important to me. And Pontifex." He zipped the jacket and checked his hair in a mirror. "Go out and talk to them, I need to make preparations. Rolf's going to be a couple more hours on the engine. Why don't you take them to lunch?"

Jimmy looked out into the garage where young Markie waved.

And his father. Winton was a coldly taciturn man with a face an ice sculpture of his son's own. Jimmy wondered what he would think if he knew his son had made the Winslows and Markie beneficiary of his insurance. "Tell me about him," Jimmy said softly.

Saunders leafed through papers. "Your father? Don't torment yourself. You think he's the one who turned you over to DeWeerd so long ago? If he made a pact with the Devil, then Jimmy Dean renewed it a hundred times. You were taught death was the only thing to respect, but that's not true. It's to live without excuse." He chuckled. "I understand your stepmother makes his life a trial, if you insist on justice. Go get them a doughnut, or something. I have loose ends."

It's Autumn, Jimmy thought. *That's when nature dies. When dies the fertility god who will be resurrected in the spring.*

It was almost five o'clock and he was on Highway 466 west through the California desert. He had been stopped for speeding at two o'clock, and as the patrolman approached Jimmy had sudden hope of reprieve. But there was Rolf, and Roth pulling up in the Ford wagon right behind. The moment passed. Jimmy watched the cop walk back to his cruiser after the ticketing, recalling ironically the safety spot he had filmed for the Highway Patrol earlier in the week.

The sun was hot in his face, and the wheel in his hands gave him the illusion of control: he had been right to insist on taking the racer on the road.

Rolf broke the long silence. "How did you spend last night?"

Jimmy answered over the engine noise, eyes hidden behind clip-on lenses. "The condemned man? Seriously? I didn't sleep. I was up all night preparing myself like a ritual Samurai. I wound up cleaning my whole house. Top to bottom."

"You're kidding?"

What'd Hamlet say? "The readiness is all?" Jimmy knew the allusion would be lost on Rolf. He would not tell him about the tape recording, or that in the background his hi-fi had played not Charlie Parker, but Handel. "What came to me was that one learns by forgetting, stripping off all conscious ego from the self. All oppositions and distinctions—even between yourself and others—have to vanish. That's enlightenment."

"It sounds like acceptance," Rolf said, adding uncertainly, "I feel that way, working engines."

Dean glanced in the mirror. Roth had been snapping pictures from the station wagon. In the Pontifex script there was also a mercenary photojournalist who would take the famous pictures of the dying Jamie Starr in his smashed racer, the gruesome images that would help stimulate the death cult. It gave Jimmy pleasure to accelerate and leave the wagon behind.

Rolf stiffened suddenly, noticing a black convoy on the highway ahead. "Slow down," he said.

Jimmy saw the equipment trucks with the cameras

Saunders had contracted. He lurched out in the other lane to pass the phalanx. In the lead was a massive black diesel pulling a trailer emblazoned by the Racer's Edge logo. He knew the black Spyder was in that trailer.

The diesel growled as Jimmy pulled the "Little Bastard" even to see Saunders in the passenger's seat poring intently over some papers.

Rolf leaned over and pounded once on the horn, and Saunders' head snapped around. He smiled and gave the thumbs-up sign.

Already, Jimmy was gunning the engine and pulling ahead.

Two large cedars above a yellow Richfield sign marked the junction of highways 33 and 466. Blackwell's Corners was a couple of gas pumps and a small market, where other racers were parked. Jimmy was decelerating, pulling off.

Rolf mouthed, "What are you doing?"

Jimmy smiled enigmatically. "What's my hurry?"

Rolf nervously stationed himself on the shoulder of the highway to flag down Roth in the Ford wagon, Saunders in the diesel.

Jimmy bought a Coke and an apple, then stood in the shade of a tree looking out onto the heat waves of the highway. He had the feeling of coming full circle, starting out in the verdancy of Indiana and winding up in the California desert.

Say I don't get in that car tomorrow? What happens to Jimmy Dean?

He lives. For a while.

What else?

Maybe all this goes away. You don't know what they can do. Or, maybe it never happened. No Hollywood, no movie star. No Jimmy Dean with a face forty feet high.

He walked to the outhouse in back and locked the door behind him. *And maybe that goofy kid "Rack" Dean grows up to work in a tractor dealership in Indianapolis.*

His hands were shaking as he unzipped his pants, glancing into the broken mirror over the stained urinal. The god Narcissus had become enchanted with his own image in the nymph's reflecting pool, and lost his soul there.

Jimmy peed once more and splashed water on his face.

Emerging, he saw Rolf still by the highway. *I am going to die in the race. Probably at one of the curves. The clue will be where the cameras are stationed.*

"It's time, Jimmy," Rolf said guiltily.

The station wagon was slowing to pull alongside the Spyder, Sandy Roth dismounting to remove the lens cap from his Nikon.

Jimmy put his arm around Rolf, walking him to the car. He was almost calm as he got back into the Spyder, pressing the accelerator to swerve back onto Highway 466. All that was really bothering him was that *Giant* would be the last movie, that he would fade out as the blurry and dissolving Jett Rink. But maybe that was appropriate.

In the rear mirror Jimmy saw the black diesel growing larger. They climbed into brown hills, the road twisting and the diesel growling in low gear as it fell a quarter mile behind, disappearing and reappearing around the hairpin turns. At the top Jimmy saw the highway unfurl straight as a rifle shot across the plains below.

Rolf's face was pained. There was something on his

mind. "Jimmy," he said hesitantly over the motor, "I
brought something that's yours." He reached under the
seat for a paper sack. He carefully removed the teakwood box.

Jimmy's hand trembled as he hefted it. It brought
back all of his childhood in a rush and he winced beneath the sunglasses. But there was a pleasant emotional warmth when he placed it between his legs.
"Thanks," he said, focusing again on the highway.

Rolf was not through. "I wish it could be different. I
wish there was something I could do for you tomorrow."

Jimmy smiled. "Sit in my lap while I drive?"

Weutheric had to look away.

To Jimmy the light and the land were becoming
strange. He had never driven this highway yet it was familiar. There was an intersection a half mile away, the
Porsche equidistant between it and the trucks. He was
feeling serene because he had come to a decision.

At least it could be on his own terms. The big black
and white Ford coming around the curve from the west
was a sign. The Ford straddled the white line readying
for a left-hand turn across traffic.

The Spyder's needle quivered at eighty. The Ford
hesitated because of the racer's speed. Jimmy knew the
other car weighed about 2,000 pounds, its driver safely
ensconced in what amounted to a Panzer tank compared
to the fragile aluminum Spyder so low to the ground.

Jimmy calculated quickly. The quarter-mile to the intersection was evaporating in fractions of seconds.

Time slowed. Rolf's face was disturbed as he
shouted, "What are you doing?"

Jimmy taunted the Ford like a bullfighter with his
cape and provoked him to turn by tamping the brakes.
Do it, you bastard.

He glanced at Rolf and picked his last words, a smile on his lips. "You know, you just don't look like a Rudolph to me."

In that instant he thought he saw understanding and forgiveness in Weutheric's eyes. He tamped the brakes again, and the Ford made its committed charge across the bow of the Porsche.

Jimmy accelerated, imagining his mother behind the wheel of the other car. *Woman, behold thy son.* The Ford's rear tires were smoking, brakes locked. The sun glared directly into Jimmy's eyes with searing light, but it was different. His mind was flooded with a brightness.

Panic energized Rolf, who made a desperate movement to grab the steering wheel. Jimmy blocked his hands with a forearm.

Jimmy did not flinch or apply the brakes at the last microsecond. That was the way of the warrior.

The impact was to the left front of both cars, accompanied by the hammer of god sound of hurtling metal against metal. The Ford's left front tire exploded, severing the shriek of the Spyder's engine. Debris hovered in a fine mist of oil and gasoline that hung on the concussion of air. There was a grating noise as the Ford's rim scraped the highway while it slid past the muffled poundings of the Spyder as it whirled, scooping ugly clumps of earth.

Cars pulled over. Rolf was in the dirt, many bones crushed but alive. Jimmy Dean lay flung over the rear cowling, arms outstretched and head hanging. His feet were held in the clutch and brake.

In the field beyond the barbed wire was a teakwood box. Its open lid was split. Inside and tied with faded ribbon, clumsily as if by a child's hand, was the frayed lock of a woman's hair.

26

A hammer arced end-over-end gloriously high in the air, momentarily lost in the photosphere of the sun. A hand reached up to pluck it from the sky, at the end of that arm a smiling Ernie Hockman.

Hammer in hand he strode to the wrecked Spyder on the road's shoulder and began to break the trapped Lou out of the wreckage, aluminum skin breaking and falling away like eggshell. Like a baby bird, Lou felt himself birthed from the mangled ball of metal.

He woke with a squawk in his throat, blinking to find the sun high in the sky through the louvered blinds of his Westwood apartment.

He grimaced against a headache and realized he was in his own bed, Sheena sitting opposite in a wicker chair reading a magazine. His voice was rusty. "What happened?"

"He's awake?" Terry stood in the open bedroom door.

Sheena ignored Childes, pressed Lou back onto the bed from which he was trying to rise. "Don't get up."

"How did I get here?"

"Terry and I brought you early this morning after the . . . scene . . . in Cottlee's garage. I wanted to take you to a doctor. It was confusing."

Terry resumed what apparently was an interrupted monologue. "All I wanted was a little part in the picture—just a line so I can get a SAG card!"

Lou suddenly realized it was Dean Day, and he had lost how many hours? "Where's Cherie?" he asked. "Why isn't she here?"

Sheena took a breath. "Left with Cleve this morning."

"You think you got problems?" Terry spluttered. "All you're out is a chick—you can always get another. But Cleveland fucked me out of a deal! I got his book all locked up, I got a lock on him. So he does an end-run and signs on as technical consultant so they don't have to use the book. Cuts me out!"

"Shut up, Terry," Sheena said coldly. She turned back to Lou. "It gets worse. Cottlee's man called last night, the one Cottlee sent to get Liv. The door to her apartment was open, and when he walked in he found her. Dead. She was killed, Lou. Her head bashed in."

"What?"

"But when Amy and Sharon got back, they didn't say anything about it. Except that Liv's door had been locked when they got there to pick her up. I saw blood on Sharon's tennies. Their eyes were so bright and they had these eerie smiles."

"What are you saying?"

Sheena took a breath. "I just saw in my head pictures

of those Manson girls at their trials, those happy-glazed weird smiles."

"That's goofy," Terry said contemptuously. "Those girls are harmless, they can barely pack a lunch."

Sheena ignored him. "I thought Cleve was the only one who believed all that sacrifice shit, so there was really nothing to worry about. I think we should have been worrying *because* he believed it. And now Cherie's with him. I'm sorry, Lou."

"Get hold of that cop, Bulova," Lou told Sheena urgently. "Tell him what's happened and where everybody's going." His voice was ragged as he lurched from the bed. "I gotta get dressed."

27

said the race. And Devereux who had lured the crew north. Devereux who . . .

Friday, September 30, 1995
Coast Highway North, 4:53 P.M.

The sun was sinking by the time Lou came upon the sizzling flares of the highway patrol funneling traffic west of the intersection where the film crew was about to re-create the crash.

Jimmy Dean was supposed to die during the race on October 1, Lou thought, but cheated Pontifex by killing himself on the highway instead. The irony was that a durable Dean cult came about anyway. Pontifex underestimated the power of the cultural force they set in motion. Jimmy Dean had the last laugh. His image outlived its engineers. Forty years later, a megalomaniacal high school teacher was picking up where Pontifex had left off.

It was Devereux all the time. Devereux who had persuaded Terry to release that tape, probably Devereux who had put that strongbox out on the highway for Lou to find, probably doctoring the painting before assigning him the room. And Devereux who had killed George, and Liv—and how many others?

Lou parked on the shoulder opposite the monument. Vintage roadsters were arriving beneath Chinese lanterns strung from the monument to a bandstand where a pompadoured group of rockabilly Dean clones played electric guitars. The mood was bizarrely festive. Hawkers hawked souvenirs, and greased pork glistened in a portable deep-pit barbecue.

Lou continued on foot and saw the sound and equipment trucks massed at Ground Zero, the deathsite.

*Highway Closed Temporarily for shooting of
Dino Shackleford's
"The Last Days of Jimmy Dean"*

Around the curve were three 1950 Ford two-tones painted identically—if only on one side. Most of the cameras were camouflaged, Highway Patrol cars discreetly positioned out of range. Lights and signs had been removed to restore the intersection to its 1955 condition.

It was a lavish shoot. Lou counted five ground-based cameras. Overhead, two military-type Apache helicopters were chukking and swooping noisily.

Someone shouted for Lou to stop, but he ignored the voice. He had recognized director Shackleford from television. Shackleford was conferring with Devereux, who held transparencies of the original inquest photos against the hills to telemetrically confirm the point-of-impact chalk markings on the highway. Nearby was Sharon in a skimpy outfit, bare shoulders oiled with sunscreen as she eyed Lou suspiciously. He did not recognize her at first because she had shaved her head in a weird red Mohawk. When she turned, he saw the eyes

of James Dean peering over the label of her halter top.
Someone grabbed his arm.

"He's with me," the preoccupied Devereux said to
the security man who restrained Lou.

Lou shook the man off. "I want to talk to you," he
said to Devereux. "In fact, I'm going to talk to you—"

"Not now," Devereux said. "Don't press me, or I'll
have you removed." He indicated nearby policemen.

Lou simmered, then saw Cottlee pulling on racing
gloves and checking a Spyder. Lou approached incredulously.

The millionaire explained, "I told you I was rather
involved in my hobbies. This is sort of what James
Dean is all about, eh?" He winked.

"You're driving one of the cars?"

"I'm paying for all this, aren't I?" A technician was
applying mousse to Cottlee's dark ringlets. "Like the
song says, 'Thought he was James Dean, for a day'—
something like that."

"What have you and Devereux done with Cherie?"
Lou demanded.

Cottlee was bemused as he shouted above the igni-
tion of the engine. "Can't hear. Later, okay? I'm having
my little moment in the sun just now."

An assistant director was pushing Lou to the side-
lines, but he still would have a better vantage point than
the hundreds of fans behind the barricades.

Tension was mounting as the sun began to dip in the
west, overhead the thundering of the copters positioning
for an aerial view. A sweating Shackleford was swearing into a walkie-talkie, Budd Kunstler in last-minute
consultation with Cottlee, who drove the Spyder
replicar the quarter mile to the top of the hill to the east,
a Rolf lookalike in the seat next to him.

Lou knew from the television publicity what was

supposed to happen next: two professional stunt drivers carefully simulating Dean's fatal collision for a slower-speed camera with special film which would later be speeded up to give the impression of higher velocities. The Spyder would strike a glancing blow to the Ford's left front, and spin off into the ditch. The cars' occupants would emerge triumphant and unscathed. But despite his high opinion of his reflexes and driving skills, Cottlee was no professional stunt man. And it was too obvious that Devereux, rather than Kunstler, was the real choreographer.

Lou, wavering on ground radiating poisonously up to him, had to hand it to Devereux as far as ensuring authenticity. But then, Devereux had been planning this moment all his life.

Lou looked at a security man. "Can this be stopped? I mean, if there's reason to think something's going to happen?"

The man scowled, then walked off to confer with an assistant director.

Where's Bulova? Lou lost himself near the equipment trucks. *What would I say? "Your technical advisor Devereux may be planning more authenticity than you anticipate"?*

Shackleford was making a bullhorned announcement for the press. "The Porsche replicar will build momentum on the ten percent downgrade as the road drops one hundred feet in a quarter mile. The restored 1950 Ford has to follow a precisely calculated schedule of speed which will bring it to the intersection the same time as the Spyder. To minimize possibility of fire, both vehicles have been rationed mere ounces of gasoline—"

Lou knew Shackleford had to get it right the first time, or he'd lose the sun.

Cows swatted themselves lazily, and glanced over

their shoulders. Fire trucks and ambulances stood by. The sun's rays flashed, bent by reflectors. Sound men were impassive beneath baseball caps. An airplane passed overhead, Shackleford waiting until radio contact was established and the pilot waved off.

Then he raised the flare pistol.

The sun turned pink as it dipped just beneath the Cholame Hills. Light bathed the intersection in an aura. Everyone was quiet, a few consulting watches. Some of the fans beyond the barricade were holding one another.

Shackleford fired, the magnesium bullet sizzling high in the air as he shouted into his radio, "Go GO GO GOOO!"

Lou saw the Spyder glint in the sun as it sped downhill. He shivered at the reconstruction of those few seconds in time at this same spot exactly forty years ago.

The Ford drifted over the line. Corrected. The first application of squealing brakes—smoke spinning off from the rear tires.

The Spyder was almost to the intersection.

The Ford accelerated again. The point of impact would be almost on the shoulder of the westbound lane.

"Too fast," Kunstler mumbled in a dead voice. "Damnit, Cottlee." He removed his ball cap.

Time stopped for that moment—as Lou knew it had stopped exactly forty years earlier. Everything was frozen as the two cars compressed into a blur.

The concussion came a second later, a gut-wrenching grind and crunch with shattering glass at its edges. The ground seemed to buckle, the impact like a fist in the face as the Porsche floated in a haze of debris, shapelessly spinning toward the telephone pole.

Real-time was horribly restored as the cameras ground away.

"My God," someone said under breath.

The Ford was skidding sideways at the nearest camera, and there was the smell of gasoline and burnt rubber. Someone near a camera tore off his earphones and took tentative steps. "Jesus Christ," came over a loudspeaker before it squawked off the air.

The sirens of the two ambulances started. Lou noticed that several other assistants and technicians were running full-speed toward the smoking, crumpled Porsche on the side of the road. As if a wave had broken, everyone stampeded toward the cars, some carrying fire extinguishers. Lou ran with them.

They came on the dark-headed Rolf stuntman in the dirt on the left-hand side of the mangled replicar, and they saw he wasn't really dark-haired. His wig was lost.

Lou found himself muscling through the shoulders, to see what he didn't want to see through the dust that still hung. He hadn't gone over to look at Ernie Hockman five years ago, but his cracked and gushing head must have looked something like that of the dead millionaire entangled in the Spyder's splintered fiberglass. He had been thrown backward and his head hung over the passenger side door, rivulets of blood slipping like tentacles through his hair.

The irony, Lou thought, was that the on-camera death would only stir public morbidity and enhance box office receipts, not to mention the Dean mystique. Then he saw Devereux standing behind the car. Steam from the popping and ticking engine made his image shimmer. His eyes were bright, an excitement almost sexual.

Shackleford had locked himself inside a car and was talking on a cellular phone. No doubt to the studio. They would in turn call the attorneys. Someone had probably already fled with the negative, which would be studied closely over and over and over again as they girded for lawsuits.

When Lou turned, Devereux had disappeared.

It was dark by the time Lou arrived at the Paso Robles Inn, where he searched DeanCon for Cherie's face. Where could she be in the convention-clogged town thronged with Deanfans? He knew he could bank on the probability she'd be in the vicinity of the deathsite at midnight. He was exhausted and nauseated, adrenalized purple darts swarming his vision. Yet he had to think, if possible—get himself together, and he had to get access to a phone.

He drove twelve miles up 101 to San Miguel and got a single room at the lone motel. The calls in search of Bulova were an exercise in frustration, and night already was falling. He turned on the television before he showered, and came out toweling to find Cleveland interviewing in front of Dean's chromium monument.

"It's a real tragedy," Devereux was saying. "Here it is, all these years later and that intersection's claimed another life. It reminds me of Ulysses. Homer tells how the hero dug a trench in the earth, where he poured a libation of blood. The dust lapped it up, and it summoned the dead so Ulysses could speak with them. And here we are. . . ."

Fuck you, Lou thought as he punched off the TV.

He slipped on a T-shirt and walked out on the landing to have a cigarette with still trembling hands. He heard another door open, and soft steps en route to the ice machine. He waited for them to pass. But they didn't.

He turned reluctantly, and there was Devereux. It was a shock; Lou did not trust his voice.

"This is quite a coincidence," the freshly showered

smiling Devereux said, towel around his neck. "But I guess we've learned by now there are no accidents."

Lou's knuckles were white on the railing. "Where is she? In there?"

"No. You'll have to be at the intersection tonight if you want to see her."

Lou smashed him in the face.

Devereux reeled into the wall, crumpling and sagging to the concrete.

"Tell me where she is right now," Lou panted, "or I'll beat it out of you."

Devereux stanched a bloody lip with the heel of his hand, then smiled despite the pain.

"Cherie's going through some intense preparation for tonight's ceremony, which will include her symbolic marriage to Jimmy. She'll be a sort of 'Bride of Christ.' "

"You had better not be talking about a sacrifice."

Devereux managed a chuckle as he struggled warily to his feet. "Not involuntarily, Lou. She's always had a suicidal bent. She's almost serene as she embraces what she feels has always been her karma. We're blessed if we know who we really are. Let us ask for no other blessing."

Lou's own eyes were livid, and he felt himself on the verge of out of control as he spat, "You're crazy."

"Try repeating this story to the police and they'll tell you who's crazy."

"Whatever you've got planned tonight, it won't happen," Lou said huskily. "I've talked to Bulova and he believes me—he's on his way here right now."

Devereux fumbled for a cigarette, eyes amused. "You're lying. The snake Bulova was chasing bit him."

Lou felt the blood leaving his face and sinking into feet suddenly heavy. "You killed him, too?"

"He's dead as Bluestein."

Lou's voice was hoarse. "How deep is Cherie in all this?"

"You really want to know? Let's just say, a close examination of her palms might still reveal callus from cutting through that Indiana permafrost with a shovel. In fact, it was Cherie who painted the little cross on Ly's painting. Are you going to be sick?"

"Why did you want to pull me into this?"

Devereux's voice was conciliatory, but his eyes sadistic.

"Last night was traumatic for you, but I had to know what happened. We both did. No one meant to hurt you, Lou. If you'd let me explain it might help the pain. —You better not touch me again."

Lou barely restrained the violence that threatened to overwhelm him. "I'm not interested right now in your explanations. I just—"

"But you're going to listen, goddammit!" Devereux said furiously. Then he composed himself, trying to assume a dark confidence.

"I want you to know everything. You've got to be totally conscious and *aware* of everything that's happened. I talk—you listen. Because if you don't, no one'll ever see her again. The others would line up to take her place tonight—they're that jealous. Maybe that's why you were drawn into this, to witness to me—to make a record. You have the qualifications, many more than Schmallhorst. He was an exploitative hack."

Lou was incredulous. "You actually—"

"All I want you to do now is hear and remember. Can you handle that?"

Lou stood with his fists bunched at his side. "What have you got to say"

The other man circled him warily. "Cleveland Carroll Devereux began to put two and two together some years ago. He picked up where Saunders left off. With a difference: I've purified the original motive, which was all about power. Whatever you think of me, it's more than that to me."

"George," Lou said. "What did he ever do to you?"

"I could say that the script was for your eyes only, but it wouldn't be true. I'd been playing with the idea of a corpse at the monument as a sort of publicity coup on anniversary week. Just another little touch, like the Elvis tape. I set that afloat over a year ago, stocking the pond of public consciousness with red herrings in case any investigator got too close to my choreography. Liv and your friend were killed crudely, because with them I didn't have the luxury of setting traps and arranging for the astral forms as I did with Bulova and Ly."

"You killed Ly."

Devereux said sadly, "It was actually on account of you that he died. He was guilt-ridden from his involvement in 1955, and guilt-ridden again in the nineties because he had given me the script—and perhaps too much of the methodology of the original plotters. See, Ly went through a period of intense infatuation with me, which I encouraged—up to a point. It was probably the same way he himself got the stuff from Saunders, whom I wish I had met. But after the fiasco on the highway in 1955 there were recriminations and demotions within Pontifex. A stroke landed Saunders in a Woodland Hills convalescent home in the early sixties, where he died. Ly began to suspect how I was going to put all that information to use again. Fear kept him in check—until you. I saw how he felt about you, and it was just a matter of time before he confided everything. *The Last Supper* was just too close to home."

"Why'd you kill Liv?"

Devereux made a wry face at the interruption in his chronology. "What's this, 'Twenty Murder Questions'? I've been resentful of her since the eighties when my Dean book came out. She tried to sue, said I libeled her. It was all kinds of bother, and the publisher made a settlement against my account, and my objections. She will dispense no more autographs. Now, Cottlee I really liked. He even let me borrow his replicar the weekend I terminated Schmallhorst, though Jonathan had no way of knowing about that. But blood had to be spilled at a certain moment in a certain place today, and damn him, he just seemed to want to be in that car. It goes to show how we run to embrace our destinies." He laughed.

"What now?"

"That's all for now, Lou. You better get ready for Cherie and the deathsite. Me too." He went back into his room, clicking the door locked.

Lou stood there for with his bruised knuckles pulsing, trying to decide what to do.

28

Friday, September 30, 1995
Highways 41 and 46, 11:17 P.M.

Lou waited at the monument but there was no sign of
Cherie. He walked in the dark to the intersection wishing he wasn't alone and—for the first time in his life—
that he had a weapon. *Even a hammer?* The throng who
kept deathwatch at the deathsite at the deathtime had
long dispersed, but he discerned shadowy forms gathering in the field to the north of the fatal spot.

As in an eerie silent film, Dean Widows dressed as
bridesmaids were arranging themselves expectantly.
Sharon's shaved head looked purple with cold, and Ruiz
was no more than bright eyes mounted in the dark.
Magic made strange bedfellows: Bill Bario and the
Hawk toted a cardboard box of candles and occult paraphernalia. There were others Lou did not recognize.
Individually each seemed pathetic, but together in the
dark they were frightening, not least because of the
glinting linoleum knives in their belts, the blades cus-

tomized with "blood gutters" so they wouldn't clot with gore.

Sheena materialized out of the night. "You made it."

"I guess you made sure of that. Where's Terry? And Devereux?"

"Terry's actually not one of us." She shrugged as she receded to form a link in the gathering circle. Her laughter was crystalline. "But Cherie's here."

Then he saw Cherie shivering in a red coat beneath which a white gown trailed, looking very small and apart. In her hair was a chaplet of orange blossoms.

She started guiltily at his approach. "You shouldn't have come."

"I'm not leaving without you."

"Nice thought," she said, "but it's too late."

"Who are you supposed to be? Mary Magdalene?"

"The fans are the body, and Jimmy's the head. The body has to be married to the head."

"You think you're going to join him by dying for him?" His adrenaline fought the constrictions of fear. "Whatever you've done, it wasn't really you. We can get you help, and I'll be with you." He hesitated. "We owe each other that much."

Her laugh was harsh. "Because we fucked? You need a reason? Try this: I get scared when good things happen to me. I guess I just wasn't ready for the heaviness." She looked to the lonely people milling on the holy ground.

"This isn't heavy? They're all carrying linoleum knives, do you know that?" He pictured her splayed on the highway, staked at the extremities with flickering candles while Bario and the Widows removed her heart.

"You told me you had to find yourself," she said. "Maybe I've found myself. You want to take it all away from me? Please don't mess with my head anymore."

"Listen," he said "I did find something. About the real danger of getting obsessed with anything. You can't see the people around you, or know their feelings."

Her reply was to walk resolutely to the protective arm of the surly Sharon, who turned her back so the tattooed Jimmy glared at Lou.

He found himself standing outside the circle. "What's the program?" he demanded, words hanging on the air in puffs of cold.

Vonda smiled at him, but it was not a relaxing smile. Bario's face was contemptuous. Amy tried to light candles, but the wind blew them out. Several flashlights were positioned on the ground so they illuminated Cherie's face from below.

All were quietly expectant until Sheena said, " 'This is to me the saddest landscape on the Earth. For it was here that the Little Prince appeared and disappeared.' "

Others repeated it in antiphonal response.

Ruiz said in a strong voice, "James Dean is dead."

Lou was startled. He had imagined an entirely different voice for the Texan. Instead he sounded exactly like Elvis Presley. Lou remembered the Elvis tape Devereux claimed to have set afloat in the Hollywood underground.

The bizarre liturgy continued with Dean Widows chanting, "Where is the blood?"

Male voices made response: "There was no blood in the Body. He bled to death and His neck was broken."

Cherie's voice rose a cappella. " '. . . There are some noises, the Mexicans say—like the scream of a young girl dying, or a mother being torn from her young—that are so piercingly intense with emotional energy that they leave their imprint on every tree, rock and grain of sand around them. To echo back for a long time to come. . . .' "

Lou recognized the quote from *Whisper* magazine, 1957.

Pudgy little Amy began to cry out as if touched by flame. "Only in death shall we meet. Jimmy, you'll always be remembered; you were the greatest, the absolute greatest. Why did you leave us, Jimmy—why were you in such a hurry?"

The murderous Sharon spoke in a masculine voice as she dribbled a handful of dust on the ground. "He's hot. He's sexy. He's dead."

Vonda intoned with a thrill in her voice, "The One links all the opposites together in unity and it combines male and female. If man was made in God's image he must originally have been bisexual. The magician cannot become the One unless he becomes bisexual. That is the step on the karmic ladder Jimmy had attained."

Bario broke ranks to hold out a red windbreaker to Lou. "You look cold. Would you like to wear this red jacket? It's warm."

Lou recognized Sal Mineo's lines from *Rebel*, and looked at Bario like he was crazy.

The first part of the service apparently over, the disciples began to move to the fence, where the Hawk held strands of barbed wire apart so they could cross the new highway. A procession formed and began walking east up the shoulder behind the beams of three industrial flashlights in the direction from which James Dean had come the day he died.

Lou followed, briefly entertaining the idea of trying to signal passing cars. But any "normie" would find his plight ridiculous; they hadn't seen the demented eyes of the glazed fan, the DeanCons, and the private shrines.

The night was very black and cold as they trudged toward the knoll where new highway 46 joined the ghost of old 466. Ruiz held more barbed wire apart, and they climbed onto the last existing road surface on which James Dean had actually driven.

Cherie was last, and Lou took advantage. "Cherie—"

She shook her head as Sheena fell back to intervene. "Where's Devereux?" Lou asked angrily.

Sheena's beatific smile. "Can't you feel him? He's here."

He spoke to Cherie. "I want to talk to you!"

She walked more quickly, the others closing protectively around as the old highway began to climb to the hills. Lou felt the strain in his calves, and demanded of them all, "What happens when we all get to the crest of this sacred highway? Do you turn on her like animals?"

He saw that Bario now held his blade at his side against his Levi's. In lieu of inspiration, Lou decided to act. He smashed his fist into that simpering face, sending Bario flailing and the knife off into darkness.

Bario recovered, bewildered as he tasted blood on split lips. He spat thickly, then lunged. There were shouts as they pummeled across the road in the dark, Lou hardly feeling the blows or the rough hands which grabbed him.

For the moment all was confusion, until Sheena's voice pierced the dark. "Cherie?"

The gasping faces around Lou froze.

"She's gone," Amy said desolately.

The Hawk's hands weakened on Lou's shoulders; Sharon's lips were pale in the sweeping flashlight beams.

"Christ!" Bario spat bloodily.

"Something's wrong," said a disturbed Vonda. "She could've slipped down the side in the dark, and we didn't hear it."

Lou instinctively made his break, twisting away to plunge off the cracked roadway and tumble down the decline into darkness and clouds of dust. More angry shouts, flashlight beams. His own breath was loud in his ears as he huddled alone in the dark. He heard Vonda calling for Cherie, and began his own search below the roadway in a furtive crouch.

Someone clutched his arm, and he almost swung on them.

It was Cherie, and she was frightened. "Run now," she whispered urgently from white lips. "Far away from here, and don't stop."

"I won't do it," he said resolutely, "not without you. We can make it to the main highway."

Her eyes were feverish as she pressed her fingers to his lips. "Can't you see? Nothing's going to happen to *me*. It's you, Lou. This is all about *you*."

His lips relaxed at the touch of her fingers. Flashlight beams crisscrossed overhead.

"They just wanted to get you out here," she said. "From the beginning—Cleve believes you're the avatar who has to die. I was only the bait."

It took him a moment to comprehend. It was so hard to think around the pounding of his heart. When he spoke, his voice was a rough whisper. "You come with me. This isn't you, what you're doing now proves that."

Her face was amazed. "Nothing happened with us, can't you accept that?"

"I don't believe it. Whatever hold Cleveland has on you, I know it's not love."

"You think this is about Cleve?" There were tears in her eyes.

"Not without—"

But she was not looking at him, instead looking at something in the distance which made her gasp, "My God."

Lou turned and saw a splinter of light against the hill to the east. There was a distant shrill whine.

"It's happening," she breathed with fear and awe.

The light came again from the top of the old road.

Lou realized the light was following the zigzagging line of the old highway through the hills. Then it split into two lights. *Headlights.* But no earthly car could negotiate those eroded and collapsed curves untended since 1959.

The light again—they saw it through the vapor of their breaths.

"It's Jimmy," she said reverently.

The lights burst around a corner halfway down the pass. The scream of the engine seemed to be coming from nowhere and everywhere, from the rocks themselves. An unearthly noise like the howling on Cleveland's tape— "*. . . some noises, the Mexicans say—like the scream of a young girl dying, or a mother being torn from her young—*"

"Christ," Lou said as he realized the predicament of the Deanfans on the road above.

There were noises of confusion from them as they saw it—and Cherie was running and crashing up through the brush to join them. Lou grasped her ankle, but it slipped through his fingers. With breaths tearing his lungs he scrambled up the hill after her, but stumbled and slid back.

He heard Bario's laughter, heard Cherie screaming as the car roared around the corner overhead. Lou clambered up again, the swerving beams of light blinding his eyes as they cleared the road's shoulder. The rush of concussive air knocked him down and back again. There was no squeal of breaks, just the sickening impacts like ripe fruit slammed into a wall.

His pant cuffs flapped when he steadied himself on

the still-trembling road. Then nothing. The night was still, silent as the echo of a sound.

Wails started up weakly, each in its own pitch of isolated agony, which distant coyotes simultaneously mimicked. Lou unfroze and hardly began to walk on watery legs when he stumbled over Ruiz crumpled on the roadside, gasping through a face black with blood.

Sobs and cries rose around Lou. Amy whirled in panic, screaming for Vonda. Sheena rocked back and forth in the tall grass, cradling Sharon's shaved head.

Bario was sitting up in the center of the roadway, splintered bone protruding from the knee of his Levi's. "Did you see it?" he asked through a bloody, if rapturous smile. "She was beautiful. . . ." His smile was intact as he slumped forward.

Lou saw the back of his skull was missing.

29

Saturday, October 1, 1995
Cholame, California, 1:38 A.M.

Lou waved his hands, but was hardly surprised that oncoming cars swerved away at sight of a suspiciously Deanlike figure in torn clothes covered in dirt trying to flag down a ride at the deathsite. Giving up, he walked heavily against the wind a mile up Highway 46 toward Cholame, until he reached the tree of heaven and the chromium monument with its symbol of infinity.

Gold medallions of Jimmy's face were inset in the surrounding benches, Lucite scarred by fans trying to pry them loose with violence.

JAMES DEAN
1931–1955

There was the café with its sad red trim, the foundations of gas pumps from 1955 still visible as he walked to the Cholame Garage with its sliding corrugated doors. Overhead, frazzled severed wires dangled in disconnection where a light had once been; leaves shivered dryly as he saw a beam of light beneath the doors.

A light which went out.

He stood there in a remove from reality and present and future, a warp in the universe. A diesel passed on the highway and he felt that familiar flapping of pant cuffs.

"Lou," Ernie Hockman said entreatingly behind his ear. "Don't go in there. It's ugly."

The words were not aloud, just as Lou knew he did not have to answer aloud.

I've got to, Ernie.

He pushed the side door inward and it dragged on the concrete in darkness. There was just the impression of corrugated metal siding, and beams with rusted nails on which hung ancient cracked fan belts.

A flashlight blinded him.

"Cherie?" he called, shielding his eyes.

Cleveland held the flash at his chest so that its beam threw shadows on his face, then flicked the beam to the wall long enough for Lou to see Cherie paralyzed as a mouse before a snake. The light switched off, but Lou heard Devereux moving.

"Don't come closer," her voice quavered in the dark.

Devereux said, further away, "Did you see it?"

Lou groped along the wall, felt with his hand one of the sacks of the polished stones from Japan which were stored for replenishment of the monument against souvenir hunters. "I saw it," he said.

"Was it bad?" Devereux asked hopefully.

"Yeah," Lou said. "Real bad."

Devereux said with quiet satisfaction, "It was beyond all expectation, and at the exact moment I performed the ritual here in the garage. You didn't even have to die to bring it about, Lou—you ought to be one happy camper."

"Your friends are hurt. Some dead. How's that make you feel?"

"I don't feel anything," Cleveland said. "That's my problem. I'd like to give you more information."

"You think I'll compile a *gospel* for you?"

"Why not? It's an amazing story, maybe the most amazing of this century."

Lou had the impression Devereux was moving in a slow circle around something no one named. What ceremony had he performed?

"Turn on the light," Lou said.

The only response was a hydraulic thrum, which Lou recognized as the garage's hoist being raised.

"Are you sure you want to see?" Devereux said.

Lou wasn't sure; he had the intuition that something else was in the garage, another presence.

"Get out, Lou!" Cherie shouted.

Lou moved closer, but his shoes gave him away.

Devereux had started a monologue. "I think everyone wants to be obsessed—possessed—by something. It's a religious longing. You get the feeling you're approaching some revelation, the promise of resurrection. It's all right here, for people the world over."

"Don't show him," Cherie said suddenly.

Devereux turned on the flashlight, but held it down his leg so it made only a puddle of light on the floor. "This is it," Devereux said, "this is what it's all about."

He flashed to the big greasy cylinder, then followed it upward to the object balanced on the runner blades of the hoist.

Lou saw the mangled rubber of a racing tire, and dull reflection of twisted aluminum. The shredded number was visible in red across the grinning gash of a cowling.

Death Car.

Devereux directed the beam to the gnarled steering wheel, and something behind the wheel. "Do I need to make introductions?" he asked. "I suppose this makes me the ultimate *Dean* collector."

Chills rippled up Lou's legs, stopping only at his solar plexus.

It was shrunken and small, incongruously dressed in a suit covered by small radiating patches of mold. The blurred face was the color of parchment.

"You're a ghoul," Lou managed to say when the light blinked out. He felt like retching. "You're sick. That belongs in its grave."

"It's been in reverent hands," Cleveland said. "A magical link is needed. It isn't about earthly power for us, but union. At-one-ment with the godhead. An ultimate religious ecstasy of translation into light. And it's the witching hour!"

"They're going to lock you up," Lou said. "You won't be able to answer all the questions they'll put to you."

Devereux's voice was tolerant. "But you will."

There was a light outside, and Lou would have thought it was a descending helicopter, but there was no noise.

"That's Him," Devereux said softly. "He's here."

Finally there was the sound of the ghostly Spyder's engine, and through the cracks in the walls Lou saw eerie luminescence falling in, a glow from which he almost had to shield his eyes.

Cherie went to the sliding door and pulled it open. Light suffused the garage. Lou saw low-slung rapacious lines bathed in white light, a star fallen out of the Cholame night. It was a Spyder made of multicolored skeins of electricity, a skeleton networked by pulsing

red, green, and blue membranes. Like a cutaway sche-
matic, the drive train and transaxle were outlined by
tracers of light. The motor began to hum with ethereal
music which did not cover the sound of approaching sirens in the distance.

"They're coming for you, Cleveland," Lou said desperately. "Somebody must have made it to the highway
and flagged down a CHP. It's all over."

Devereux said, "I don't care. We won't be here.
You're the only one they'll find."

Cherie turned to glance at Lou with regret. Devereux
saw she was transfixed, and joined her. They formed
two cut-out forms against the radiance.

A wind rose, not out of the hills, but deep space.

"Let 'em go, Lou," Hockman's voice said gently in
his ear.

But Lou was thinking. The body and the car had been
finally united like battery cables, to jump-start the god.
He knew what he had to do.

He glanced quickly around for the lever of the hoist,
but could not find it. He ran across the concrete and
reached up to the cadaver positioned stiffly in the cockpit. He fought repulsion and fear as his hands closed on
its arm. He would have to pull it from the car and break
the connection— Lou yanked, felt something give as a
sleeve—if not an arm—came loose.

At the same instant a galvanized Devereux jumped
onto his back with a cry of rage.

Lou found himself pounded to the concrete, looking
up at the enraged man standing protectively before the
hoist on which the wreckage was balanced. Devereux
had a hammer upraised in his hand, poised to attack.

Lou was struggling to regain his feet when the temblor hit. He felt it through the concrete. It was small,

but enough to cause the hoist to sway slightly. There was a wrenching creak of metal as the wreckage shifted.

Devereux looked up startled at the wreckage tilting toward him, but could not move. It all came down with a resounding crash that raised a cloud of dust.

Lou saw Devereux's gasping mouth expelling thick blood in a final burst of air as the racer settled on his crushed chest. Only his agonized head was visible. The smashed lungs emptied with a guttural croak, and his lifeless face assumed a beatific expression.

The radiance of the ghostly Spyder outside the door vanished at the same instant, leaving Lou in darkness with only the memory of Cherie's stricken face until the police cars pulled up with howling sirens.

30

Tuesday, October 11, 1995
Fairmount, Indiana

The reburial was on October eleventh, exactly forty
years to the day after the original service in Dean's
hometown. Lou was not himself sure of his own reasons for taking the Tristar Whisperliner to Indianapolis
and renting a car to drive eighty miles to the second funeral at Back Creek Church.

Donna with her swollen eyes slept in the seat next to
him. Mutual grief had brought them somehow closer together. He had supported her through the days following
George's funeral, and she would not let him make this
haunted trip by himself. He knew she wanted to believe
he was still shaken from that week's trip to the psychi-
atric detention where Cherie was being held for obser-
vation and evaluation pending the investigation, but he
actually felt a calm.

As they sat in a pew at the far back of the church and
listened to the Quaker service, Lou wondered whether

he was not looking for some sense of closure or completion. Five thousand people stood out front in the rain to hear the service carried to them over loud speakers. The family occupied the front pews, along with representatives of the licensing agency that controlled the marketing of the icon. Celebrities in attendance included not only the governor and state senator of Jimmy's home state, but Bob Dylan, Bruce Springsteen, Don Henley, and all the Butthole Surfers. Martin Sheen, a lifelong Dean fan who had already made several pilgrimages, delivered the eulogy.

Four of Jimmy's old Fairmount High School basketball teammates were still around to act as pallbearers. In 1955 there had been six of them. The funeral cortege crawled slowly up Main Street, which was massed not only with fans, but with representatives of all three major television networks. In front of the hearse on a Harley-Davidson motorcycle rode an Indiana character who called himself Nicky Bazooka. He wore a black jacket and a motorcycle cap. It was rumored that he was a mechanic from Bloomington. Each year for the past decade he had led a foot parade to Park Cemetery on the anniversary of Dean's car wreck. His black jacket was shiny in the rain.

The sky was gray and the cypress trees trembled in the wind. Floral tributes spilled over each other, and tears mingled with raindrops on the faces of the faithful. A helicopter with a film crew was bullhorned out of the air space by state troopers who felt its proximity to the crowd too hazardous. Patsy Polmquist was the only person whom Lou recognized. If she saw him, she did not acknowledge it.

His own thoughts were preoccupied with the hope that now Jimmy Dean's uneasy spirit could find rest. It had been conjectured in the local newspaper that, this time, the family would have concrete mixed with scrap iron poured into the grave to protect the burial vault.

They spent the night at a motel in Marion, where Jimmy had been born. On their way out of town in the rental car, Lou stopped off at the Marion cemetery and inquired at the office for the location of the grave of a Mildred Dean who had died in 1940.

Donna stayed in the car with the engine idling. Lou stood silent for a moment at the rain-slicked stone and thought it was sad that Jimmy, who had lived most of his life without a mother, could not have been placed to rest beside her. And he thought of his own mother and father, and of a sportswriter with a cracked head.

Then they drove on to Indianapolis and caught the Whisperliner. He liked that name, and on the flight he repeated it like a mantra to once more lull himself to the first peaceful sleep he had had in years. Despite the fact that they were going to stop off in Ohio on the way back, where he would pay a long-overdue call on the aged parents of a sportswriter named Ernie Hockman.

Two weeks later he picked up the *LA Times* to read that James Dean's new headstone had been stolen.

It was the third time.

AUTHOR'S NOTE

Who Killed James Dean? is fiction, a creature of imagination born in the cracks and uncertainties of history. We know a lot about the life and final days of James Dean, but despite everything at our disposal, he remains one of the enigmas of this century. My intent was to take what is known and weave these facts in an alternative pattern, another fictional possibility.

In 1986 my nonfiction book *The Death of James Dean*, the culmination of fifteen years of research and interviews, appeared in the United States and the U.K. Replete with unpublished inquest diagrams, it was a detailed physical reconstruction of the crash that claimed Dean's life, and a picture of the bizarre posthumous adulation his death spawned. But it was only after publication that some intimates of Dean, impressed, hopefully, that I was a sincere student and had done a creditable job, approached me with a different interpretation of the events I had documented. I was skeptical, but intrigued.

Over the next eight years, and after following many fruitless leads both in Hollywood and Indiana, I succeeded in further identifying and interviewing a significant number of credible people involved in Dean's life and career who—though often strangers to one another—had something in common: the sincere belief that Dean's highway death was no accident. Many unknowingly possessed small but vital parts of a puzzle, the significance of which they did not appreciate. That puzzle came together in this story.

I continue to interview and research. But in the meantime, I think a reinterpretation of the life and death of James Dean is worthwhile—even in fiction.

Anyone not familiar with James Dean but who is inspired by this book to crack one of the numerous biographies will recognize some of the names and events portrayed here. I have not allowed speculation to distort the recorded history. No imagination could improve on the bizarre odyssey of Dean's missing death car, or the chain of unnatural deaths that befell so many of the people involved in the filming of *Rebel Without a Cause*. Fortunately, many of the occult aspects of the Dean saga were already entrenched in public consciousness.

The Maleficarum coven was real, and Dean attended meetings.

Rogers Brackett and *James DeWeerd* were *real people*, but for reasons and considerations that should be obvious, a number of characters are entirely fictional, or composites. Certain minor figures were actual fascinating and tragic individuals: Henry Willson was Rock Hudson's agent; Jack Drummond was the actual race driver killed on Turn Three of the Bakersfield sports car meet at which Dean competed.

With one exception, the magazines and news articles quoted throughout are genuine.

If anyone doubts the fanaticism of some Dean devotees and the extremes to which feelings run, I offer as evidence the personal threats I received after my first Dean book appeared. Many fans considered it an ungenerous survey of their world and attempted to halt publication with a signature campaign.

I would like to acknowledge the help and inspiration of several people, with the caveat that in no way are they responsible for the creative conclusions of the novel. I would like to thank Jimmy's close friends Joe Hyams and Lew Bracker, who visited me in my home when Joe was researching his own Dean biography. It was that enjoyable afternoon and lunch which motivated me to turn an avocation into this book.

I thank Corey Allen, and apologize again for bringing up his 1958 film *Juvenile Jungle*. Donald Dooley, an inquest witness and eyewitness to Dean's death, shared his unpublished Polaroids of the tragedy with me; I looked for him for fifteen years only to find he lived two blocks away!

Thanks to Dean friends Leonard Rosenmann, John Gilmore, and, especially, the late Bill Hickman.

But others who made invaluable contributions to this book did so only on condition of anonymity during their lifetimes. I hope this book pays my debt to them by providing a measure of the expiation many claimed frankly to be seeking by opening their hearts and memories for the first time to me.

If there is any explanation for my personal lifelong obsession with Dean, it will be found in the preceding pages.

My craven gratitude to Jane Jordan Browne and her
Multimedia Product Development, whose faith was
buoying when the diverse elements of this book seemed
overwhelming. Thanks also to Greg Cox of Tom
Doherty Associates for his enthusiasm and editorial
skills.

Warren Newton Beath
Bakersfield, California